IF I BELIEVE

A PROMISES OF GOD NOVEL

KIM CASH TATE

IF I BELIEVE

A Promises of God Novel

Kim Cash Tate

Cover Design: Jenny Zemanek at Seedlings Design Studio

Scripture quotations are taken from the NEW AMERICAN STANDARD BIBLE ®, Copyright © 1960, 1962, 1963,

1968, 1971, 1972, 1973, 1975, 1977, 1995 by The Lockman Foundation. Used by permission. (www.Lockman.org)

Tate, Kimberly Cash.

If I Believe / Kim Cash Tate.

ISBN 978-1-946336-01-9

1. African American women—Fiction. 2. Christian fiction.

ALSO BY KIM CASH TATE

For every brown girl who ever felt excluded from tales of "ever after".

∼

All things are possible to him who believes.

MARK 9:23

CHAPTER 1

I don't believe in fairy tales.

Cinda Ellis had reminded herself more than once on the six-hour drive to St. Louis and needed to tell herself again as the house came into view. *Could this be right?* She checked the address as she pulled to the front curb, eyes sweeping the mansion that wrapped around the corner. Partially hidden by stately trees. Flanked by quaint streets. Overlooked by a vast park across the way. It was more than she'd dreamed.

Back when she used to dream, when she'd had a thing for fairy tales. The distressed life of the heroines, that's what drew her. The longing for something more. The promise of ever-after.

She had to see every Disney adaptation. Begged for the princess gown. But when her mom could finally afford one—canary yellow with poofy sleeves—it mocked her and her Afro puffs. *I wasn't made for you*, it said. *Where's your fair skin and long flowing hair?*

She knew right then, deep down. She had no right to dream,

1

which meant no right to hope that one day her father would knock on the apartment door, and she'd answer—in her dream she had to be the one who answered—and say, "Yes, may I help you?" And he would say, "Cinda, it's me. It's your dad."

She got a spanking for taking scissors to the dress that night and trashing the DVDs. She wouldn't tell her mom why. The conversation never went well when she mentioned her dad. And she didn't have words to explain the hope she'd had, and how it was no more.

But now . . .

Her eyes floated again to the perfect house framed by the perfect scene, and her stomach clenched. What if he rejected her? What if he was upset that she'd just shown up like this? What if he didn't believe her?

Her eyes cut away, resting on the steering wheel. *I should've called first.*

Now that she was here, it made more sense. He could've processed the news before a face-to-face. Hearing he had a daughter would be jarring. Who could blame him for needing time to respond?

Then again . . . If he rejected her, she'd rather it be in person. At least she could see him. And not just his face, but his height and build. His gait. His expressions. The way he dressed. She could get a feel for his disposition and temperament. Maybe. Depending on how quickly he dismissed her.

But what if he wasn't even home? Or worse, out of town?

Lights illuminated the house inside and out, so *somebody* was home. And a BMW and Mercedes-Benz occupied the winding driveway. His law firm profile said he was married with two daughters. How long had he lived here in St. Louis, only a few hours—and yet, a world—away?

She checked her watch, the clock on the dashboard having died years ago. 7:22.

Just do it, Cinda. You have nothing to lose.

Maybe. Maybe a small part of her was hanging on still to the fairy tale. And now was when it would get shattered.

In the rearview mirror she adjusted her newsboy hat, then opened the door, stepped out, and took a big breath. Her eyes bounced window to window, wondering if anyone was watching. But with each step toward the house came added resolve. It had taken her twenty-five years to get to this moment. Come what may, she needed to see it through.

On the welcome mat Cinda pushed the doorbell and waited, taking in the arched wooden door that matched the trio of archways and windows, all of which made the house majestic.

She moved closer, ear to the door. Nothing stirred. No dogs. No voices. She pulled her jacket closer as the wind picked up, her heart growing more anxious.

This wouldn't go well. In minutes she'd be back on the road, devastated, kicking herself for hatching such a crazy scheme.

The Lord is your very present help, Cinda. Pray.

Grandma's words. If only they were a comfort. She'd done that. Prayed and believed and lost her grandmother, then her mother. What was the point?

Finally, footsteps. *Heels.* Cinda took a step back. She hadn't rehearsed first words. *What to say, what to say?*

The heavy door opened, and a woman dressed in dark denim and a black sleeveless sweater looked out. "Yes, may I help you?"

The setting was different, and the words weren't coming from Cinda's mouth. But they were the very ones she'd imagined.

"Um," Cinda said. "Hi. I'm wondering if . . . Randall Rogers might be home?"

The woman cocked her head a little, showing more of her pixie cut. "Can I tell him what it's about?"

Her tongue grew thick. "My name is Cinda. I'm . . . a family member."

"A family member?"

"Janice, who is it?"

3

A man's voice. Cinda's heart pounded.

"A young woman, says she's a family member of yours." She opened the door further. "He's actually on his way out, but come in. I'm his wife, Janice Rogers."

"Nice to meet you," Cinda said.

She crossed the threshold as the man came into view, casual in jeans and a navy blue cabled sweater. His hair, faded short, showed handsome flecks of gray. Complexion several shades darker than her mom's, landing her in the middle. And tallish height, which, with her mom's short stature, put Cinda at five seven.

He came closer. "Pardon me for staring, but there's definitely something about you that's familiar. You say you're a family member?"

"Yes, sir." Her fingers tingled. "And I'm sorry, I caught you at a bad time—"

"No, it's okay. Boys' night out at my pastor's house." He waved her along. "Come into the family room. Oh"—he turned as he led the way—"let's make it official. I'm Randall Rogers."

Cinda shook the hand he extended and couldn't help staring into his brown eyes. He had a handsomeness about him. What must he have looked like when her mom met him? "Cinda. It's good to meet you," she said.

They walked around a curved hallway with olive green walls, into an area with plush leather furniture, beautiful framed art, family photos, and, from what she could see, a kitchen that would swallow half the apartment Cinda had shared with her mom.

Randall led her to a sofa in the family room. "Have a seat, Cinda. Can I get you a glass of water? Iced tea?"

She swallowed, her throat like cotton. "Water would be great."

"I'll get it," Janice said, walking to the kitchen.

"I don't have much family left." Randall joined her on the sofa, his eyes warm. "So if I had to guess, you must be on Momma's side, one of Aunt Delores's grandkids."

"I don't know Aunt Delores, but . . ." The nerves made her stomach cramp. "Thank you," she said, taking the bottle of water from Janice. She took a sip, gathered her thoughts. "Do you remember studying abroad one semester in college?"

His focus went adrift. A few seconds later he gave a nod. "I do," he said.

Cinda glanced at Janice, suddenly wondering if she should be sharing this in private. "And you met a young woman. Stacy Ellis."

Randall exhaled. "Wow," he murmured.

A door opened and closed somewhere off the kitchen and two young women scurried in with shopping bags, looking in the direction of the flat screen on the wall.

"Mom, you're not watching the Academy Awards?" One of them picked up a remote and aimed it, bringing the television to life. "We need to know if we missed Alonzo Coles up for Best Supporting Actor."

"It's recording." Janice smiled slightly. "You know I didn't forget. That's my future son-in-law."

"As long as I'm the wife," the other one said. She glanced over. "Oh, we have company?"

"This is Cinda," Randall said, "a family member we're getting to know. Cinda, our daughters, Jade and Jordyn." He smiled. "Twins, as you can probably tell."

"Family?" one of them said. "Cool."

Cinda stood as they walked over to give her a quick hug. "Nice to meet you," they both said.

"You too," she said. Cinda had thought they were identical, both with full natural curls. But up close she could see the difference.

"Girl, there he is, in the audience," one of them said, focus back on the television screen. "Aww, Alonzo must've taken his mom as his date."

"I wondered if he'd take Simone," the other said, "since he's never acknowledged they're actually dating." She shook her head at his close-up. "I might be tongue-tied when we meet him at the premiere. He is ridiculously fine."

Randall stood, looking at Janice. "Why don't we move to my office," he said.

Cinda followed them down a hall and into a spacious office where they each took a seat at a round table across from his desk. She knew exactly where they'd left off, but was nervous about picking it back up.

"Cinda asked if you remembered Stacy," Janice said, eyes on her husband. "Who was she?"

Randall looked at her. "I met Stacy the semester I spent in Rome."

Janice turned to Cinda. "And I take it Stacy's your mother?"

"Yes," Cinda said, heart racing.

"It should've been obvious from the moment you walked in." Janice turned to her husband. "Her facial features and yours—the resemblance is uncanny."

"Cinda, is that why you're here?" Randall said. "Because you think I'm . . . your father?"

"Yes," she said. "That's . . . that's why I'm here."

"How old are you?" he said. "When were you born?"

"Summer 1991. I'm twenty-five."

Randall stood and walked across the room. "There's so much going through my head. So many questions. Why am I only now finding this out?"

"I only found out myself," Cinda said, "about a month ago, right before my mother died."

"Stacy's dead?" He moved back to his seat. "How?"

"Doctors said cirrhosis of the liver."

"Oh, dear God . . ." Randall stared into the distance.

"I'm so sorry for your loss," Janice said. "So your entire life you'd never heard anything about who your father was?"

"I would ask," Cinda said, "but my mom never wanted to talk about it. When her health was failing, she started opening up."

Janice looked at Randall. "I'm guessing you acknowledge the obvious—you got involved in a relationship with Stacy?"

"I did," Randall said, "but—"

"When you were supposed to be in a relationship with me."

"If you recall, that was a rocky time for us," he said. "But clearly I was out of order in several respects. You know I've asked God's forgiveness for so much of that time in my life. I was a different person."

"I certainly won't argue with that," Janice said. She turned to Cinda. "I have to ask—what exactly do you hope to gain with this visit? You must know Randall is a successful attorney. And his profile has increased with all the buzz from the upcoming movie."

"What movie?" Cinda said.

"*Bonds of Time*," Janice said. She gestured toward a framed picture on the wall. "That's the official movie poster with Alonzo Coles, who plays the lead. It comes out in June."

Cinda looked at Randall. "You're a filmmaker too?" Somehow she'd missed that when she Googled him.

"No," he said. "I wrote the book that inspired the movie."

"Honestly, I didn't hope to gain anything," Cinda said. "Other than seeing you in person and hopefully staying in touch."

"Where did you drive from, Cinda?" he said. "Where's home?"

"Madison, Wisconsin," she said. "That's where I grew up."

"Who's there for you now?"

Her eyes fell a little. "No one."

"But you've got other family, right?" Randall said. "Grandparents? Aunts and uncles?"

"I have a cousin in the Houston area," Cinda said. "That's where I'm headed. Hoping to get there by late morning."

"You're driving through the night?"

She nodded. "That's the plan."

He and Janice looked at one another.

"You should stay here and get some rest before you get back on the road," Janice said.

"Oh, thanks, but I'll be fine." The last thing she'd wanted was to be needy. "I can stop for a power nap now and then. I just, wanted to keep this short. I feel like I dropped a bomb on you all. I need to get out of the way so you can process it all."

"You did drop a bomb," Randall said. "Trust me, I'm stunned. But hearing more about you and your life will help me process it. Plus, I'd have a hard time letting anybody get back on the road after a six-hour trip—with no rest—to drive another twelve. If you leave tomorrow, that's still a quick visit." His eyes rested on her. "Stay."

Cinda had imagined rejection every which way and questions tantamount to cross-examination. But never actual interest.

Never *stay*.

She wasn't sure how to receive it. But a lifetime of emotion welling inside told her she wanted to.

"Okay," she said barely. "Okay."

CHAPTER 2

*T*reva Alexander poured a melted cheese sauce over a big batch of blue and yellow tortilla chips. Next she began topping it with sautéed beef and beans, hoping she'd made enough for the hungry souls downstairs. They'd eaten Sunday dinner earlier, but between the card game and the Oscars party, everyone wanted a hearty snack.

With a ladle, she scooped more of the beef mixture from the skillet—and felt arms enclosing her from behind.

"I'm wondering who's hugging on me like that," she said. "I need to tell my husband."

"Tell him I kissed you too," Lance said, planting one on her cheek.

Treva spread the beef mixture over the chips. "You call that a kiss?"

"Hmm, you've got a point." He took the spoon from her, set it back in the skillet, and turned her around. "Let me try again."

Lance put his arms around her waist and brought her close, then kissed her forehead, cheeks, and finally her lips, softly—and deeply.

Treva felt the patter in her heart. "Now you've overcorrected."

She let the kiss linger a little longer. "Your night with the guys might've just ended."

"You would kidnap me like that?" His hand teased the small of her back. "I need to tell my wife."

"I knew it." Tommy stood by the door to the lower level. "We can't even send you on a basic errand to see about this delicious food." He gave Lance a look. "Uh, Pastor, Loverboy, whatever you want to call yourself—you mind returning to this game?"

Treva chuckled. "The food is ready, Tommy. You want to take the platter for me?"

"Gladly," Tommy said, coming for it. "You outdid yourself. It's smelling too good."

Treva grabbed appetizer plates, and Lance got the cooler with assorted beverages as they headed back down.

"Yeah, nachos!" Hope, Treva's youngest, jumped up as Tommy set the platter on the coffee table.

"What took you so long, Mom?" Faith sat on the end of the sectional sofa, her baby next to her in the bassinet. "You missed the Best Supporting Actress award."

"You already know, Faith." Tommy put some nachos on a plate. "The newlyweds—in full effect." He chomped on a chip. "I refuse to be this sickening."

Lance settled at the card table they'd set up a few feet from the sofa. "That must be why you're forever talking about 'my fiancée' and texting *in the middle of a game*." He shot a glance at Tommy's phone on the table. "Dude, you're sickening now. Come May it'll only get worse."

Cedric surveyed his cards as the game continued. "I have no problem with him texting during the game. Tommy losing focus is a win for us."

"And that's about the only way you *would* win," Tommy said, "which ain't happen—*Reg, come on, man*." He looked at the card his younger brother laid down. "You think that's the right play?"

"Really?" Lance said. "You're gonna coach your partner across the table?"

"I'm just saying," Tommy said, "you've got to play smarter than that, Reggie. It's kill or be killed out here."

Treva chuckled, looking over from the sofa. "We've got a pastor, an elder, and a deacon from the church, and it's kill or be killed? What happened to kindness? Preferring others?"

"Uhh, right," Tommy said. "Anywhere but the card table."

"Ah, my pumpkin woke up," Treva said, lifting her one-month-old granddaughter from the bassinet. "Come here, you little sweetie."

"Mom," Faith said, "you do realize you don't have to hold Zoe every waking moment?"

"It dawned on me the other day why I like to hold her all the time." Treva smiled at the baby. "You know how I was when you girls were little. Too focused on making partner to enjoy the season. Your dad was the one holding you, feeding you, spending quality time. Zoe gives me a do-over." She leaned over and kissed the baby's forehead. "And it helps that she's the sweetest little thing ever."

Faith leaned over and snapped pictures of the baby with her phone. "Jesse just asked for a pic," she said.

Treva looked at her. "How's that going?"

"How's what going?" Faith said.

"Well," Treva said, her voice lowered, "it looked like something was stirring again between the two of you when he was here for Zoe's birth. But I haven't heard a whole lot since."

"We're in touch about the baby," Faith said. "Other than that . . ." She shrugged.

"Ohh!" rose up from the card table.

"I *told* you we weren't playing around tonight," Lance said. "I see you, partner, with the Boston." He stood and high-fived Cedric across the table.

"First of all," Tommy said, "I need to know where Randall is, because if my real partner had shown up, this wouldn't have happened."

"Wow," Reggie said. "You're blaming me?"

"Umm." Tommy paused. "Yeah, absolutely."

Treva looked over. "Reggie, don't let those old guys get to you."

"Old is right," Tommy said, chuckling. "Reggie and I have twenty years between us." He looked at his brother. "I don't know if I told you, Reg, but Treva, her sister Jillian, and I went to the University of Maryland together. Jillian was one of my best friends. It's crazy that we're in St. Louis now at the same church."

"Reggie, you've been here, what, a few months now?" Treva said.

Reggie nodded as he came for nachos. "I graduated from Morgan State last May and moved here over the summer."

"How do you like it"—she paused, hearing the doorbell. "That must be Stephanie and Lindell. Can one of you get that?"

"I'll get it." Hope got up and went upstairs.

"It's dope working at Living Word." Reggie paused, eating a chip. "I followed the ministry for years, listened to Pastor Lyles's teaching online. Being able to write and edit content for the website and glean from everybody is amazing." He held up another chip covered with toppings. "This is really good, Mrs. Alexander."

"Tell me it's Spades tonight," Lindell said, coming downstairs with Stephanie.

His brother smiled at him. "Bid Whist," Cedric said.

"Aw, you know I can't play Whist."

"You couldn't play pickleball either," Cedric said, "but that didn't stop you."

"Ah, pickleball," Treva said. "Where it all began." She looked at Stephanie. "Can you believe these guys? Two months since the wedding, and they're still at it with the games and competition."

"Every time I think about that island and that house," Stephanie said, plopping onto the sofa, "I imagine us going every year. Seriously. That house can be our annual retreat. The guys can play pickleball to their hearts' content. Just give me the ocean at my doorstep."

"Clearly you're forgetting," Lindell said. "Treva's mom paid for us all to go as a wedding gift. Ocean at the doorstep is not in our budget."

Stephanie got a plate and added nachos. "We can do a Go Fund Me."

Treva laughed. "I can see it now, some sob story about how the ocean is your doctor's prescription for mental stability and—"

"Mom, please, *shh*." Fifteen-year-old Joy, seated cross-legged on the floor by the bassinet, held up a hand. "It's Best Supporting Actor time." Her shoulders did a dance. "Which means it's Alonzo Coles time."

Treva looked at Lance. "Isn't Alonzo Coles the one playing the lead in Randall's upcoming movie?"

"Yeah, he's on there?" Lance got up from the table to see, along with the others.

They watched as the winner was announced.

Joy groaned. "I needed him to win so he could walk up there. And speak. And get a camera close-up." She got a dreamy look in her eyes. "You don't even understand how cute he is. My man crush *every* week."

"Man crush?" Treva said.

"Instagram thing," Stephanie said. "I see we need to keep an eye on you, Joy."

"What's the latest with the bed-and-breakfast, Steph?" Treva said.

Stephanie sighed. "Girl, soon as we take care of one problem, three more pop up. And we've only got a little over two months before the grand opening. I don't know how in the world we'll make it."

"I didn't realize you were getting down to the wire," Treva said. "I need to be upping my prayers on that."

"Definitely needed," Stephanie said. "I added it to the list on my weekly call with Jillian, even though it's not a 'marriage issue.' But then, we added you to the list too."

"Wait, what list?" Treva said.

"Prayer requests."

"Why am I on the list?"

"Jillian wanted us to pray about your new season," Stephanie said, "that you'd be open to whatever God has for you. You know your sister is your biggest cheerleader. She felt like this was a time when you could finally step into gifts God's given you."

"She did, huh?" Treva held the baby close, rubbing her back. "I could always use prayer, don't get me wrong. It's no joke making all these life changes, especially being a pastor's wife. But I know my sister—she's got her own ideas about what I should be doing." She kissed Zoe as she cooed softly. "I'm actually loving what God has for me. I like my season just fine."

CHAPTER 3

"*I*'m still trying to figure out what to do in mine." Faith listened as her mom and Stephanie spoke. "I know I just had Zoe and I'm adjusting to being a new mom. But I feel like I put my own life on the back burner."

"What do you mean, sweetheart?" Treva said.

"I had to sit out this semester of school," Faith said, "so I have several months ahead of doing, what?"

"Girl, you just said it." Stephanie had a nacho in hand. "Learning to be a mom. How is that the back burner?" She popped the chip into her mouth.

"But I'll be twenty-one this year," Faith said, "and my life is nothing like I thought it would be. I wanted to be used by God, impacting my generation, like when I was holding Bible studies in my dorm." She heaved a sigh. "I'm literally doing nothing because of poor decisions."

Stephanie gave her a look. "If you don't stop saying you're doing nothing . . ."

"And maybe it's not about *doing* right now," Treva said, "at least in the sense you're meaning it. Maybe it's a season to be still and go deeper with God. Let Him continue to build you back up."

Faith let her eyes rest on the television as they presented a technical award. *Go deeper with God.* Maybe that was her problem. She'd *had* a deep connection to God. But after grappling with her father's death, then getting involved with Jesse . . . Seemed so much of what she'd had with God was lost. He'd forgiven her, she knew that. But she couldn't shake the feeling that she'd somehow forfeited plans He'd had for her. She'd put herself on an alternate track, with less than "good and perfect" gifts. What did God's Plan B look like?

She opened Jesse's text and sent him the pictures she'd taken, along with a video she'd recorded of Zoe yesterday. That was her other problem—Jesse. She hadn't wanted to admit it to her mom, but she'd indeed felt something stirring again. He'd come down from Chicago for the labor and delivery, was caring and attentive, and his heart seemed to be softening toward God. She'd dared to think maybe they could embark on a relationship, a real one this time.

But once he went back to the University of Chicago and got embroiled again in his studies, whatever might've been developing disappeared. He'd kept up with Zoe, though. For that she was thankful.

She looked down as her phone buzzed with Jesse's reply.

Thx. She's really growing. Planning to come see her spring break. How r u?

Faith sighed inside. Why did he add that? Casual, nothing question, yet now she'd wonder if she was on his mind.

She typed a reply. **I'm good. You?**

Voices boomed from the card table, and Faith glanced over. Looked like Lance and Cedric had won again.

"Y'all hear that?" Tommy said, acknowledging the doorbell. "That's the sound of the tide turning, if it's who I think it is."

Tommy went to answer and came back smiling.

"Randall, this is what you need to know." Tommy had an arm around him as they faced the guys. "Your pastor and Cedric have

16

gotten beside themselves because they've won a couple of games—"

"Try *all*," Cedric said.

Tommy waved him off. "Whatever," he said. "Point is, they now think they've got skills, which makes this beatdown they're about to get even sweeter."

"It's for sure they've got a beatdown coming," Randall said, "but it'll have to wait. I'm here only briefly, to ask for prayer."

All eyes fixed on Randall.

He took a breath. "A young woman showed up on my doorstep this evening. She says I'm her father."

"Whoa," Tommy said. "Seriously? What did you say? I mean, I'm guessing it's plausible?"

"She actually looks a lot like me," Randall said, "and the time frame fits. Her mom and I did a study abroad program overseas. She's twenty-five."

"So you were in college like me?" Faith said.

Randall nodded. "Except, you're way ahead of where I was. I didn't know the Lord in college."

"Where is she now?" Lance said. "At your house?"

"Yes, she's staying overnight," Randall said. "When I left she was taking a shower, getting settled." He sighed. "She just recently lost her mother, and she's moving to Houston. But it's a lot to process. I just want to hear from God about how to handle all of this."

Faith looked at her phone as Jesse's reply came.

Same. School is a major grind. Miss u.

Her insides reacted before her mind could dismiss it. Another text followed—**Got a min?**

She wanted to say no, she didn't have a minute just because he had a minute, and some fleeting desire to talk to her. But she was way too curious.

She typed **Yes**, and seconds later her phone rang. She quietly moved up the stairs.

"Yeah?" she said.

"*Yeah?*"

"I figured you had something specific on your mind."

"I really just wanted to hear your voice," Jesse said. "It's been a while."

Faith settled on a chair in the living room, unable to find a response.

"So, you said things are good. What've you been up to?"

"Taking care of Zoe," Faith said.

"Right," he said. "I know you're carrying the load. I wish I could do more."

"I'm glad you're in Zoe's life, Jesse. It's no small thing. Neither is the financial support."

"It's not much on a student budget," he said, "but I'll be working this summer and able to do more."

"Hey, Faith, your mom's looking for her phone. She asked if you could check the kitchen."

Faith turned and saw Reggie. She went to the kitchen and found the phone on the counter. She handed it to him, and he went back downstairs.

"Is that your boyfriend?" Jesse said.

"Who?" Faith said.

"The guy in the background just then. Wondering if I've got competition."

"Jesse, stop."

"What?"

"You talk just to be talking, and it never means anything."

"I only asked a question."

"Well, I'm not answering."

"So motherhood's got you all mean and ornery, huh?"

Faith glared at the phone. "Maybe getting hurt by you made me mean and ornery."

Jesse fell quiet a moment. "In the hospital after Zoe was born, I told you I had messed things up, and I was sorry. You said it was a new year, with new beginnings. Now I feel like you're throwing it all in my face."

"When you start making comments like you're interested in me," Faith said, "it brings the old stuff back. I don't have time for games."

"I'm not playing games," Jesse said. "When I heard a guy's voice and thought you might have a boyfriend . . ."

"What?" Faith said.

He paused. "I can't help it, all right? I still have feelings for you."

"Which never actually meant a whole lot, did it?" Faith sighed. "I have to go, Jesse," she said, and clicked off.

CHAPTER 4

*A*lonzo Coles posed with two others from the Best Supporting Actor category at his third after-party. They hammed it up, draping arms around one another, champagne glasses raised, grinning big for the *Elle* magazine photographer. After several shots Alonzo whipped his phone from his pocket.

"Hey, let's get this for the Gram." He held his phone aloft as they leaned in for a selfie. Two nominated actresses rushed to join them, one in Converses, the other barefoot, stilettos in hand.

"Cheese!" they said, falling into one another.

Cameras clicked around them as others caught the shot.

Alonzo uploaded the picture and typed a quick caption: *And the celebration continues.*

Noelle LeGrande sidled up to him and whispered into his ear. "I've got a gift for you."

"For me?" Alonzo had never met the chart-topping artist. "What is it?"

She produced an In-N-Out burger from behind her back and handed it to him. "I heard you say you were starving. Hope you're not vegan."

Alonzo smiled. He hadn't had a chance to grab one from the platters floating around. "This is perfect." He eyed her deep V-neck gown. "Thank you."

"I was surprised to see you came alone," Noelle said.

He swallowed a bite. "My mom couldn't hang anymore after the Governors Ball, so she went home. The night was still young, so . . ."

"And congratulations. Pretty impressive for only your fourth movie."

"Well. I didn't win."

"Are you kidding? The nomination was the win. At your age, with your skills? You'll bring home several statues. I love your work."

"I appreciate that. I'm a fan of yours as well."

She moved closer. "I'd love to get to know you better. From what I can see, you're rather enigmatic."

A brow raised. "How so?"

"In movies you kill it as a bad boy," Noelle said. "I've heard rumors that you're a ladies' man in real life too, but I hardly ever see you with anyone." She gave him a curious look. "I just wonder how much of the on-screen Alonzo meshes with real-life Alonzo."

He finished the burger and followed it with a sip of champagne. "I'm known as a ladies' man, yet you still want to get to know me?"

"I didn't say it was a bad thing." She glanced across the room at her date, an actor with whom she'd been linked for more than a year. "Let's get together. I'll call you," she said, walking away.

"You don't have my number," he called after her.

She smiled back at him. "Actually, I do."

"This is officially ridiculous," Shane said. Alonzo's best buddy —and director on two of his films—had watched the whole thing. "Two offers tonight alone from the hottest actresses on the planet, now one from a pop star, and you won't pursue any of them."

"Nah, too messy." Alonzo gazed at the crowd. "Noelle especially. When do you *not* hear about her love life?"

"Hey, it's the Dynamic Duo." A photographer approached, her camera at the ready. "I'd love an after-party shot of you two for the *Essence* Instagram page. The one from the red carpet is still blowing up."

"We appreciate the love," Alonzo said. "We wouldn't be here without the support of our fans."

She took her shots. "Can I quote you on that in the caption?"

"Absolutely."

"Since I'm starving," Shane said, "and no one brought me a burger, I'm going to go find one. By the way, Simone walked in a few minutes ago."

Alonzo glanced toward the entrance where a cluster of people had gathered. He looked to see who stood at the center and grinned. The man who'd given him his first big break—Rufus Bledsoe. With three decades' worth of movies and two Academy Awards, he could still pack theaters opening weekend. He spotted Alonzo and pointed through the crowd. "Just the man I want to see."

Alonzo waited as Rufus made his way through the circle, hugging him when he got to him.

"My guy! Look at you"—Rufus stepped back—"all cleaned up and fancy looking."

"It's been way too long," Alonzo said. "I was hoping I'd see you tonight."

"You know I wouldn't miss it." Rufus had grown a slight beard, peppered with gray. "I know I've told you, but I have to say it again—congratulations, man. I'm so proud of you. How are you feeling?"

Alonzo took a breath. "You know. It's a lot. Surreal. Exciting. Overwhelming."

"Exactly," Rufus said. "The endless luncheons and parties and newfound attention that come with awards season. More 'friends' than you can count and more women than you need."

Alonzo gave a knowing smile. "That couldn't be more true." He shook his head. "It's crazy. Seems like yesterday I was praying for an opportunity. Now I've got more projects coming at me than I can take on, and a big film coming out yet this year."

"I'm hearing Oscar buzz already for that one. *Bonds of Time*, right?"

Alonzo nodded. "My first starring role. I'm hoping it's well received."

"Knowing you and the work you do, it'll be compelling," Rufus said. "You know I'm in your corner. You always struck me as special."

"What do you mean?"

"Those talks we used to have in my trailer." Rufus looked at him. "Remember those?"

"How could I forget? I was awestruck just to be working with you. The fact that you took time to talk at the end of a long day blew my mind."

"I was impressed that you had vision and purpose. Your faith was driving you. You wanted to shine a light in Hollywood."

Alonzo's brow furrowed a bit. "I was so naive, though. I didn't know *anything*."

"You didn't sound naive to me. You were dreaming, in all the right ways. And look at the platform you've got now."

"Hey Rufus, can I steal a minute of your time?" A producer put an arm around him, looking at Alonzo. "Sick, isn't it? Two in the morning, awards night, and we can't help but talk a little business."

"Alonzo, let's connect again tonight before you leave," Rufus said.

Alonzo stayed there a moment, pondering what Rufus had said, trying to recall his frame of mind back then. When was the last time he'd—

Simone entered his line of vision, near the dessert bar. He walked up behind her.

"I didn't think you were coming," he said.

She looked over her shoulder. "I couldn't waste this dress."

Alonzo let his gaze travel the length of it. "No. You sure couldn't."

"Would have looked better next to you on the red carpet, though." She took a bite of a pastry.

"We're going there again?"

Simone turned. "I totally understand taking your mom."

"But . . ."

"I just wonder if you would've taken me, had your mom not been able to go."

Alonzo grabbed one of the mini pastries himself.

"So you're just going to ignore me," Simone said.

"We've already been over this."

"And you never answered."

"Simone, why is this important? Can we just enjoy the party?"

"That's the thing," Simone said. "It was fine for me to meet you at the after-party, be one in the crowd. But being on Alonzo Coles's arm—well, that's another thing entirely, isn't it?"

"We both said we wanted our private lives to stay private."

"So that's your answer. You wouldn't have taken me."

"Since you want me to say it—yeah. I probably would've gone alone. But come on, Simone . . ." His face leaned closer to hers. "You showed up tonight wearing the sexiest dress in the place—to pick a fight?" He smiled slightly. "At least I didn't say I would've brought someone else."

She narrowed her eyes at him. "You couldn't be more insufferable."

"Oh, wait a minute now." The *Essence* photographer was back. "You two are looking real cozy. Are the rumors true?"

Alonzo gave a wry smile. "You already know that's a no comment."

"Can I get a picture then?" She smiled. "Hey, just two celebrities chatting at the after-party."

"I don't have a problem with it," Simone said.

Alonzo knew they'd be pouring fuel on those rumors. "It's awards night," he said. "Let's do it."

Simone slipped an arm around his waist, and he did the same, leaning in. Several flashes went off at the same time.

CHAPTER 5

inda awoke confused, glancing about. Her heart hammered when she realized anew—

I met my father.

And not only that. They'd talked until two in the morning. And she'd slept there, in the same house. She sat up and surveyed the room decorated in varying shades of blue and gold, everything perfectly appointed, down to the tissue holder and picture frames. The color scheme continued in the adjacent bathroom, which she was surprised to learn was dedicated to this room alone.

She sighed, thinking about the day ahead. She'd get back on the road and head to Houston to start a new life. It was what her mother had wanted, so Cinda wouldn't be alone. Though she'd have been fine staying in Madison had she actually *been* alone. But her mom's boyfriend wouldn't leave the apartment, and everything about him made her anxious. With no one else in the area— her closest high school friends had gone off to college and settled elsewhere—there was nothing keeping her there.

Still, she'd never even met this cousin in Texas. And what would she do with her life? The past few years had been all about her mom—working and taking care of her. Cinda hadn't had the luxury of thinking what she might *like* to do. She'd done what she needed to do. And as she thought about it now, nothing had changed. She was still in survival mode.

She showered, enjoying the perfumed body gel and plush towel, then threw on a shirt and a pair of jeans, and tucked her two-strand twists beneath a baseball cap. She left the guest room and took the back stairway, hoping to grab a bite before hitting the road.

As she moved down a short hallway, voices floated her way. Soon studio lights came into view. The twins sat on the sofa in the family room, looking into a camera set on a tripod.

"So you know we couldn't wait to come on here and talk about it, because we are on Alonzo-watch, counting down to June when we'll get to meet him at the LA premiere of *Bonds of Time.*" She looked at her sister. "But Jordyn, now the question is—will he show up with Simone on his arm?"

Jordyn focused on the camera. "I know everyone's speculating about that picture of the two of them late last night on Instagram, but I don't think they're dating."

"Why not?" Jade said. "It's been rumored for weeks."

"Because number one, it wasn't on *his* Instagram page. And Alonzo is famous for keeping his love life private. I think he posed for the pic because he knew there was nothing to it. He's playing with y'all."

"And I think he was celebrating, had too much champagne, and it threw him off his game. Simone had that look, like, 'Back up, ladies. This is my man.'"

"Oh, but we do need to back up—and talk about Mr. Coles looking scrumptious in that black tux."

The other twin fanned herself. "Girl, those brooding eyes, that pretty brown skin, and no he didn't rock the five o'clock shadow —" Her eyes caught Cinda. "Cut." She clicked a small remote, and the red light went out on the camera.

"Sorry," Cinda said. "I didn't mean to interrupt." She walked closer and looked at the setup. "What's all this?"

"We're filming for our YouTube channel," Jordyn said.

"You do entertainment-type videos?"

"Mostly hair and makeup," Jordyn said. "Some fashion too. But yeah, we've been adding entertainment stuff as well."

"Sounds like a full-time job," Cinda said.

"It is, actually," Jordyn said. "We started five years ago as a hobby and thought we'd have to get a 'real' job after college. But the channel's grown to half a million subscribers. We're brand ambassadors for a natural hair company, doing more travel and speaking . . . It's become a career."

"Wow, I'll have to check out your channel." The thought had hit Cinda last night—she'd not only gained a father, but sisters, and she'd always wanted siblings. Binge-watching their videos would be a great way to learn more about them. "Okay, I'll get out of your way." She smiled a little. "And make sure I stay real quiet."

She moved to the kitchen, which looked undisturbed. Had to be a box of cereal somewhere. And bread to toast. But she didn't feel comfortable rummaging through the refrigerator and cupboards.

"I have to admit," Jade was saying, "Alonzo and Simone are gorgeous as a couple. But I need him to be single when we meet. Or at least alone." She chuckled.

Cinda spied a Granny Smith apple in a fruit basket as the door from the garage opened. Randall walked in, clad in casual clothing.

He smiled when he saw her. "Good morning. How did you sleep?"

"Pretty well, actually."

"Good, good. I was hoping—"

"Dad! We're filming. Aren't you supposed to be at work?"

He walked out of the kitchen toward the twins. "I went in early to take care of some things and took the rest of the day off," he said. "I thought it'd be nice if we all went to breakfast."

"Mom left for an early-morning appointment," Jade said, "and we've got to get this video finished and uploaded."

Randall looked at Cinda. "Tell me I'm not the only one who's hungry."

"I'm kind of starving," she said.

"Now we're talking."

"Bring us some pancakes to go, though!" Jordyn called.

"Strawberries and whipped cream on the side?" Randall said. "And Jade, you want the pecan pancakes?"

"Perfect!" they choresed.

Cinda got her coat, and they hopped into Randall's Mercedes and backed down the driveway.

"I hope you like breakfast food," he said.

"I could eat pancakes for breakfast, lunch, and dinner." Cinda checked the surroundings as they drove. "So how'd you get to St. Louis from California?"

"Well, I told you I started out as a law professor." He glanced over at her. "That was here at Wash U."

"Is that when you started writing fiction?"

"Just dabbling at the time," he said. "I thought I must be crazy at first. I was writing scholarly articles for law reviews, then these ideas for crime dramas would come to me."

"And now you've got a movie coming out. How did that happen?"

"It was my fifth novel," Randall said, "and when it got optioned, I didn't think anything would come of it." He turned down a different street. "Next thing I knew they were working on the screenplay and producers had come on board. Then they signed Alonzo Coles for the lead, right when his star was rising. Everything fell into place."

He pulled into the restaurant's parking lot and they hopped out and went inside.

"Mr. Rogers, good morning," the hostess said.

"How are you this morning, Linda? Table for two, please."

They settled at their table, Cinda's head full of questions. Once they'd ordered, she asked the one that had edged to the forefront. "So, you and my mom—was it like, a fling in your mind? Did you even remember her?"

Randall sipped his coffee. "You shoot pretty straight, don't you?"

Cinda shrugged. "Sometimes."

"Those three months in Rome, we were practically inseparable," he said. "We weren't looking to get involved—I told her early on I had a girlfriend. We were friends—studying together, hanging out in a foreign city, seeing the sights. But over time, things deepened." His thoughts drifted a moment. "We both felt that whatever we had would stay there. Still, my heart was torn when I got back, and I reached out to her. But she was slow to return calls, and when we'd talk, she seemed distant. Things just faded."

"She was torn too," Cinda said. "She realized she'd fallen in love with you, but your heart belonged to someone else. Then she found out she was pregnant, and she decided not to keep me. She just wanted to move on."

"She decided not to keep you? Obviously that changed."

"My grandmother persuaded her, promised to help raise me."

He stared off for a moment. "Cinda, the way she died, cirrhosis of the liver . . ."

"Mom struggled with drinking," she said. "She felt like her life never amounted to what she'd hoped and dreamed."

"That's heartbreaking," he said. "What was life like for you growing up?"

"My grandmother was amazing. We didn't have a whole lot, but she was always cheerful and grateful for what we had, so it *seemed* like a lot." Cinda took a sip of water. "And Mom was always there, but she lived this parallel life, doing whatever. When Grandma died, and Mom had to be Mom . . ."

"How old were you?"

"Fourteen. Life was suddenly unpredictable and hard, even scary sometimes."

"Why scary?"

"Being left alone for long stretches of time. Or if some guy would stay over and start talking to me, and get a little too close. I learned to stay in my room and lock the door." She looked at Randall, surprised to see his eyes looking watery. "But there were happy times too," she said. "Mom had this infectious smile, and she loved to dance. And sometimes we'd go ice skating and fall on our butts and laugh so hard . . . Those are the times I like to remember."

He heaved a sigh. "I hardly slept last night," he said. "I kept asking God what to do. And asking, *why?* Why did I have to miss twenty-five years of your life? Now, hearing all of this, I'm just . . ." He stared off again, letting a few moments of silence lapse. "I keep hearing this Bible verse in my head, about making the most of the time that we have. So much time has already been lost. Cinda, what would you think about putting down roots here in St. Louis?"

❧

"I got your messages," Janice said. "You invited her to stay? Indefinitely? You haven't even done a paternity test yet."

Cinda's eyes widened as she stood in the kitchen, slicing an apple. Janice had come home through the front door, and Randall must have met her in the family room. Cinda paused the knife, debating whether to announce herself.

"You said yourself it's obvious she's my daughter," Randall said. "But we're going forward with the test tomorrow. Janice, I prayed about it. And it was so clear what God was moving me to do."

"Oh. Right," she said. "Once you've prayed about it and supposedly heard from God, that's that."

"I'm simply trying to explain how I got here," he said. "I know this impacts us all, and it's not easy—"

"Randall, you invited a veritable stranger to live with us, then told me after the fact. And say what you want, you know nothing about the girl or her motives."

Cinda glanced at the door to the garage. She could slip out. But wouldn't they hear her? And what would she do, roam the neighborhood in her shorts? It was freezing outside.

"You're right, I should've consulted you beforehand," he said. "All I can tell you is we were in the moment, and I felt moved. And actually, the fact that she's a stranger is the whole point. She's my daughter, Janice. I need to get to know her. I *want* to get to know her."

"You could invite her up for long weekends. Fly to Houston to spend time. We've known her for *twenty-four hours*. It's too much, too fast."

"I'm actually surprised it matters to you," Randall said, "given that you're gone much of the time. Maybe I should be encouraged that you still care what happens at home."

Cinda sighed to herself, more and more uncomfortable. She'd learned that Janice commuted weekly to Chicago for work, but she didn't know it was an issue.

"Oh, yes, of course—why pass up an opportunity to make this about me?" Janice said. "But guess what, Randall? You can't claim to be squeaky clean, not with this Stacy revelation."

"I never claimed to be squeaky clean," he said. "Our relationship was on-again, off-again for years before we married, and we both did things we shouldn't have. But are you really going to compare what I did in college with the affair you're having *right now*?"

This is not good. Cinda paced the floor. *I shouldn't be hearing this. Why can't they move upstairs?*

"You know I broke it off," she said.

"Oh, is that the latest?"

"And anyway, it would be nice if you'd at least acknowledge that you share part of the blame. If you hadn't put God and church before your family—"

"You know I never wanted my relationship with God to be a source of division between us," he said. "My prayer has always been that we'd worship together—"

"Well, here we are, Randall, what, eight years since you 'found the Lord'? And it's still not my thing. I'm sure you're praying, though."

"Janice, I love you," he said. "I've loved you since our study sessions in AP history in high school, through every up and down and twist and turn. And I want our marriage, still. So of course I'm praying. It's my relationship with God that strengthens me to fight for us."

She sighed. "I have to get ready for my flight." The sound of heels on the wood floor grew distant as she walked away.

"What about Cinda?" he said.

"What's there to say?" she said. "You've already decided."

Cinda blew out a sigh. The idea of staying there, of getting to know her father—all of them, really—had exceeded her wildest dreams. But had she kicked a hornet's nest?

CHAPTER 6

*T*reva was already sure she needed prayer in her new role as pastor's wife. Suddenly life had extra filters. And added scrutiny. And expectations, an abundance of those. But she was also sure—confirmed this moment—she needed special prayer for dealing with Johnelle Oliver.

"I was wondering why we hadn't seen Zoe's father," Johnelle was saying. She'd struck up a conversation with Treva after church, which always seemed like idle chitchat—until she got to her questions. "So Faith's a single mom . . . How is she doing with that? She's so young, it must be hard."

Treva glanced over at her daughter, holding Zoe a few feet away. "I'm sure she would say it's not easy," she said. "But God has been really faithful."

"Amen," Johnelle said. "I can attest to that as a single mother myself. My two are in their twenties now, and I could talk all day about God's faithfulness." She added quickly, "So, Zoe's father—is he in the area?"

"Actually, no, he isn't."

"I guess that was a silly question. He's probably back in Maryland where you all are from." She cast a glance over at Lance, near the front of the church. "How did you and Pastor Lance meet anyway? It's funny how many single women joined the church over the past couple years. I know they were hoping to snag him as a husband—let's face it, he's handsome and everybody loved the way he loved his first wife. But then he went and got somebody from the East Coast." She chuckled a little.

Treva took a silent breath, smiled. "We met at the Living Word women's conference last year. Were you there also?"

"I couldn't make it," Johnelle said, "but that must've been some weekend if you got the pastor's attention that fast."

Treva's eyes did a quick roam around the sanctuary, looking for a means of escape.

Johnelle leaned into the back of a chair. "I've only been to the pastor's house once," she said, "before Kendra passed, when they were having those Bible studies over there." She paused. "Is it eerie living there? Didn't Kendra actually die in the house?"

"Johnelle, are you holding Treva hostage over here?" Stephanie walked up and put an arm around the woman.

"You know I'm naturally curious." Johnelle chuckled again. "But I do need to get out of here. It was good talking to you, Treva," she said, walking away. "Y'all have a blessed week."

Treva looked at Stephanie. "How did you know?"

"I know Johnelle," Stephanie said, "and I know you. You had that I'm-trying-to-be-nice-but-I'm-drowning face." She spotted her sister and waved a hand.

Cyd came over, hugging them both. "Cedric said you all had a good time last Sunday night. I was sorry I missed it."

"We have to do better about getting the women together," Stephanie said. "The guys are on a roll. And they can do all the trash-talkin' they want. It's all about the male bonding, if you ask me."

"Lance basically said that." Treva saw a few of them gathered even now. "He said it's opened up conversations they haven't had before."

Faith walked their way. "I'm about to head home," she said. "Zoe's a little cranky, and I want to lay her down for a good nap."

"Ooh, not yet," Cyd said. "I need to hold that baby." She smiled at Zoe, taking her from Faith. "Look at you, pretty girl, getting so big."

"I wanted to talk to you about something, actually," Faith said.

"Okay, I'm listening," Cyd said.

"Too much of my world revolves around Jesse," she said. "If he sends a text, I get this thing inside, just seeing his name on the screen. I wonder what he's doing, who he's doing it with, whether I matter to him—even as I'm praying to get over him." She sighed. "Then just when I think I might be getting over him, he acts like he's still interested, which means *nothing*, but now *that's* on my mind. So I want to be proactive."

Cyd nodded. "What are you thinking?"

"Mom mentioned going deeper with God," Faith said. "But whenever I open my Bible or start praying, I'm so tired from being up at night with Zoe that I fall asleep."

"I remember those days well," Cyd said, bouncing with the baby as Zoe whimpered a little.

"So I thought about how Mom and Aunt Jillian had their group study for years," Faith said, "and they even did some of your studies. I wondered if we could do something like that, with you sort of leading a live version."

"I wish I could," Cyd said. "But with my university and ministry load, I know I can't add one more thing. But I'd attend—shoot, I need it myself." She nudged Faith with an elbow. "Did you ask your mom?"

"She would say something like, 'That's not my gift.'"

"You know your momma well, baby girl," Treva said. She turned and eyed Stephanie.

"Don't look at me," Stephanie said. "If it's not your gift, it sure ain't mine."

"Aww, what's wrong, cutie pie?" Cyd said, as Zoe's whimpers turned to a cry.

"She's sleepy," Faith said. "I'd better get her ready to go."

Treva's gaze drifted up front, where Lance stood talking with a woman in a tight dress with much cleavage. Seconds later, he was waving for Treva to come up there.

"See, that's why Lance is my boy." Stephanie had her gaze in the same place. "Mm-hm, I was peeping it too."

Treva walked up next to him, and he put an arm around her.

"Sinclair, I wanted to make sure you'd met my wife," Lance said. "I know I introduced her to the church when we got married, but personal introductions are always nice."

Sinclair gave Treva a nod. "Yes, I'm aware who she is."

Treva smiled slightly. Sinclair usually avoided eye contact with her, and only spoke when Treva spoke first.

"Okay, awesome," Lance said. "That personal issue you were about to get into? That's not appropriate for me to address, but I encourage you to get to know Treva—she's a strong woman of God with a lot of wisdom. And really, there are a number of women here who are willing to listen and offer biblical wisdom."

"I appreciate that," Sinclair said, "but I think I can work it out on my own."

She walked away, and Treva looked at her husband. "What do you consider inappropriate to talk to you about?"

"If someone wants to know how to deal with improper thoughts," Lance said, "and then hints that the thoughts are about me . . ."

"Whoa," Treva said.

Tommy walked up and joined them. "Deacons are about to meet downstairs," he said, focused on Lance. "I'll lock up. Also, electrician's coming tomorrow afternoon to fix the wiring with the sound system, so I'll meet him here. And somebody just told me there's a glitch on the website and your sermons for the past month aren't loading." He gave him a look. "You know that's the enemy, hard as those sermons were hitting. I'll look at that later today."

As they continued talking, Treva saw Faith coming back into the sanctuary, looking harried.

"The rain is starting to turn to ice," she said, "and it's already slick out there. You know how nervous I get driving on ice. I'll leave my car and ride with you all."

Tommy turned to her. "You don't have to leave your car, Faith." He looked a little ways over. "Hey, Reg, there's a damsel in distress who needs you."

CHAPTER 7

Faith held onto Reggie's arm as she slow-stepped across the church parking lot, glad she'd worn boots. "So much for the weather forecasters," she said. "They only called for rain."

Reggie carried Zoe in her car seat, snuggled under two blankets. "It could be worse. This is more like a drizzle."

"But it's an icy drizzle. Ice is so unpredictable, and inherently treacherous."

Faith clicked the remote and opened the back door wide so Reggie could move Zoe inside. He placed the car seat onto its base and tightened her safety belts.

"How did you know how it works?" Faith said.

"Babysitting my sister's kids back home when they were smaller."

Reggie headed for the driver's side, and Faith took the passenger seat, handing him her keys when he got in.

"Are you sure you know what you're doing?" she said.

Reggie looked at her. "You mean aside from the fact that ice is unpredictable and inherently treacherous? Yeah."

"That's not comforting."

"I'm curious how this Kia handles, though," he said. "It's front-wheel drive, right?"

"I think," Faith said. "Whatever that means."

"We'll be fine." He started the car. "I'll go ten miles an hour."

"Five."

Reggie backed out of the space, and the tires swerved to gain traction.

Faith gasped, looking out the back window. "This is a sheet of ice. Like, literally. It'll be a miracle if we make it home in one piece."

Reggie shifted to Drive and inched forward. "I can already tell you'll be a bigger problem than the ice. No gasping, fretting, or prophesying doom."

"What if my gasp is the one thing that alerts you to a coming collision?"

"Then it's probably too late."

He turned onto the main road and proceeded slowly in light traffic. "By the way," he said, extending a hand, "Reggie Porter. Nice to meet you."

Faith shook it warily. "What is that about? I see you all the time."

"And all the time, you're giving a brother that 'get lost' vibe."

"I do not."

"Oh, you do."

"You're just always with the guys," she said, "and I'm usually with the baby or doing something around the house."

"And *maybe* you'll say, 'Hey,'—quick, fast, and in a hurry, no eye contact." He shrugged. "Since I'm driving your car and your life is in my hands, thought I'd introduce myself."

She narrowed her eyes at him. "You're just used to girls falling all over you."

"What?" He took a look at her. "Now you're gonna snatch stuff out of thin air?"

"Didn't I hear you were captain of the football team?" She

almost added that he was good-looking, which would make the case. But she didn't want to flatter him.

"And?"

"Oh, cut it out. Like we don't know what that means."

"Girls falling all over me."

"Yep."

"That's loaded with assumption, but okay," Reggie said. "That's why you give me that, 'don't look at me, don't talk to me, just keep stepping' attitude?"

"If that's the vibe you got," she said, "it wasn't personal."

"Well, if it's an equal opportunity diss . . ." His eyes were smiling—until the cars ahead of them swerved in different directions. Reggie tightened his grip on the steering wheel and tapped the brake. He looked at her seconds later at a red light. "That was good. You stayed calm."

"Outwardly," Faith said.

"And I was just messing with you," he said. "I think it's cool that you're singularly focused. Jesse seems like a nice guy."

"Talk about loaded with assumption," Faith said. "If I'm singularly focused, the focus is on Jesse?"

Reggie glanced at her. "Okay, yeah, I assumed. He's Zoe's father, he was at the house when she was born . . . I met him briefly."

"What if I'm singularly focused on Jesus? Is that a foreign concept? What if I'm tired of guys and their game-playing and I want to put the past behind me and find out who I am all over again, at the core?" Her eyes fixed on him. "But see, guys like you —*with girls falling all over them*—can't understand that. It's all about whose mind you can play with, who you can get into bed, which one you can—oh, this is amusing to you?"

"You have no idea." He shook his head to himself as he made another turn, bringing them closer to home.

"Well? Care to elaborate?"

"Actually, no. I already know you won't believe me."

"I'm not that cynical."

Reggie took his time responding. "I had one girlfriend in college—end of sophomore year until fall of senior year—and I was faithful. I loved her, and was naive enough to think we'd get married one day." He focused on the road. "I was all-conference, offensive MVP, and everybody thought I was headed for the pros. But I had a career-ending injury senior year, and she broke up with me. Soon after she was dating one of my teammates, who got drafted."

"Wow. Okay, yeah, nothing like I assumed."

"And because of some other things I won't get into," Reggie said, "I've been taking some needed time"—he glanced at her—"to be singularly focused on God. So yeah, I found your rant amusing."

They fell into silence the rest of the drive. Reggie pulled into the right side of the driveway, and Faith opened the garage so they could walk through. He detached the car seat and brought Zoe inside.

Faith lifted her out gently as she slept, easing off her snow suit, then settled her back in the seat. She looked at Reggie. "Thank you for getting us home safely. I really appreciate it."

"No problem," he said. "And don't mind me. Do what you've got to do. I can wait downstairs for Tommy."

She hesitated. "Reggie, I'm sorry for—"

"No need," he said, shaking his head. "It's cool."

She moved further into the kitchen. "Well, it's inherently foolish to wait downstairs when I'm about to rustle up some brunch. I'm sure you're hungry."

"I don't know," Reggie said. "As long as there's no flirting. I'm a man who's singularly focused."

"And I'm about to snap back to 'get lost.'"

Reggie chuckled. "All right, what are we cooking?" He took off his coat. "Because I'm sure I can burn better than you."

CHAPTER 8

*A*lonzo wrapped up a call with his manager as the Range Rover neared the Paramount Theater in Austin, Texas for the South by Southwest Film Festival, where his buddy Shane's newest movie was premiering.

"I can't meet him for dinner tomorrow," Alonzo said. "I'm headed back to LA in the afternoon, remember?"

"I'll see if he can do breakfast then," Beverly said. "He can tell you more about the project and answer your questions, so we can move forward with this."

"Come on, Bev, you're killing me. Breakfast?"

"Get to bed at a decent hour like a normal adult. I'll send your itinerary in a few minutes for the entire day tomorrow."

Alonzo looked at the crowd as he hung up and turned to Shane, smiling. "You see this? Folk are *out here*. For *you*."

"For the movie," Shane said. "I'm loving it, though."

"They're here for the movie, because it's directed by you." Alonzo elbowed him. "Face it. You're the man."

The SUV came to a stop in front of the theater, and security walked up to escort them out.

"You go ahead," Alonzo said. "I'll use another entrance."

Shane looked back at him, one foot out the door. "Why?"

"I'm only here to support. It's your night. The focus should be on you and the actors in the film."

"When you show up on the red carpet," Shane said, "the movie gets ten times more publicity than it would have had otherwise. Get out the car."

Alonzo filed out behind Shane, feeling the brisk night air against his leather jacket. The crowd erupted when they saw them, moving down the rope line to get to where they were.

"Hey, it's Alonzo Coles!"

"Alonzo, can I get a picture?"

"I would marry you today, Alonzo!"

He chuckled at that one, glancing over. He'd never been to this film festival, which seemed a little more laid back than others. Still, a sea of camera phones and flashes filled the air, along with a throng of media.

"Alonzo, can my daughter get a selfie with you? She's your biggest fan!"

A woman stood next to a young girl about ten years old. He veered over to them in the rope line, and immediately realized it might have been a bad idea. People elbowed one another to get close to him, pushing the girl back, as security stepped in to maintain order.

Alonzo reached into the crowd and took the girl's hand, helping her under the rope.

"What's your name?" he said, bending a little.

She grinned. "Caitland."

"How old are you, Caitland?"

"Eleven. *When Hope Is True* is my favorite. I've watched it a million times."

"A million? That's crazy," Alonzo said, smiling.

"Well," she said, glancing down, "I get bullied sometimes because of my weight, so . . ."

He sobered a moment. In *When Hope Is True,* Alonzo played a teacher bonding with a student who had issues at home. Bullying had been a side issue, but the school bully had gotten his comeuppance. He looked at the girl. "We *have* to take a selfie then. Can I put it on Instagram?"

Her eyes widened. "I follow you on Instagram."

"What? Aren't you too young to be on there?"

"No," she giggled.

He took her phone and stooped to a knee, snapping a picture, then repeated with his own.

Her arms flung around his neck. "Thank you," she said, her voice breaking.

He walked her back, making sure she got reconnected with her mom.

"Alonzo, can I get a selfie too?" rang out in the crowd.

He paused a moment, thinking it might be fun to walk the rope line and take selfies. But the look on the faces of security said it wouldn't be fun for them. He held up his hands, apologizing to a collective groan.

He joined Shane and others from the movie, where they were talking to interviewers against a bright yellow festival backdrop. A local news reporter had Shane's attention.

"What made you take on an indie project given that your last two films had big studio backing?" the reporter asked him.

Shane leaned into the microphone. "This project has been in development for years, and I loved the story. Didn't want to give up on it."

The reporter nodded. "Any reason no big name actors were cast?"

As Shane answered, Alonzo felt a hand to his shoulder.

"Let's see if we can grab Alonzo Coles for a quick interview."

He turned, recognizing Dottie Griffin from the syndicated show *Entertainment Now*. "Hey, good to see you," he said.

"And a surprise to see you," she said. "You're here to support the premiere tonight?"

"Absolutely," Alonzo said. "I'm excited about this film and, of course, a fan of the director."

"And so sweet what happened a moment ago." Dottie smiled into the camera. "We've got footage—Alonzo taking a selfie with a young girl who said she's his biggest fan."

"And I believe her," Alonzo said, smiling. "She said she's seen *When Hope Is True* a million times."

"How does that strike you?" Dottie looked at him. "That's the last film of yours she would have been able to see, given the R rating of the ones that followed. Does that cause you to rethink your choices?"

"Not at all," Alonzo said. "I love that that movie appealed to a wide audience. The audience for the others is different but just as significant. Definitely proud of them all."

"Well, there's lots of excitement about your next release. We can't wait to talk to you about it."

"For sure. I'm looking forward to it."

"Alonzo, can we get a moment?" A guy came up beside him with a microphone and shook his hand. "I'm from *Premiere News* online . . ."

Alonzo listened to his questions and rattled off why he was there and how excited he was about his upcoming movie, bothered still by that last interview. Why would Dottie ask him that? His last two films had been critically acclaimed. He'd gotten an Oscar nomination. Regret it? Because an eleven-year-old couldn't watch? She couldn't watch PG-13 movies either.

"I'm guessing you didn't come all this way for me."

Alonzo looked to his left and smiled. "Amber, hey," he said, hugging her. "Congrats on the film. Shane is saying this is a breakout role for you."

"It was a journey, playing this part. And you know Shane has a way of bringing stuff out of you that you didn't know was there." She paused. "It's been a while, Alonzo. I'm not even sure what happened."

"Life. Work. But you're right," he said, nodding, "it has been a while. I think you were still on that television show, the medical drama."

"Wow, that was two years ago. So much has changed." Her eyes took him in. "But not everything. You're still gorgeous as ever."

"Likewise," he said. "You look amazing."

A reporter approached. "Amber, local CBS news—we'd love to talk to you about your new film."

She looked at Alonzo. "Promise we'll catch up after the screening."

$\sim$

"Shane, really? You're trying to tell me you weren't scared?" Alonzo spoke above the pulsating music in a private area of the club. "Come on, dude, no need to lie. We're all family here."

"You can clown me all you want," Shane said. "I wasn't afraid. I had a healthy preoccupation with preserving my life. Let's not forget it's one of the most extreme zip lines in the world."

Alonzo looked at the others in the circle. "Ladies and gents, I give you—fear." He sipped his cocktail.

"Well, don't leave us in suspense." Dale, one of the cast members of the film, looked at Shane. "Did you do it or not?"

"Not on your life," Shane said. "And still feeling good about my decision."

"Man, I'd love to do something like that." Dale looked at Alonzo. "Was it a blast?"

"*Crazy*. I want to work another one into my next vacation."

"Thanks for the heads-up," Shane said. "You can take that trip without me."

A server walked in, dispensing a fresh round of drinks. She handed Alonzo his.

Amber stood next to him. "So was Simone with you on that trip?"

He eyed her over his glass. "You should know—I'm not one to kiss and tell."

She shook the ice in her drink. "Just wondering if things are serious between the two of you."

"You have to wonder?"

"Same Alonzo, huh?"

Shane came up to him. "You told me to make sure you got out of here early."

He checked his watch. Going on one o'clock. "Yeah, I better act like I've got some sense."

Amber whispered in his ear. "You want company?"

Alonzo took a slow sip. It was early, for him. He could still salvage a few good hours of sleep—

The door opened again and the same server entered, walking up to Alonzo. "Excuse me, Mr. Coles, I have a message for you." She pulled him aside. "A VIP guest in another room would like to see you."

"Who is it?" he said.

"Noelle LeGrande, sir."

His curiosity heightened just enough. "Shane," he said, "I'll be right back."

He followed the woman to a different room. She opened the door and closed it after he'd gone in. Noelle sat at a candlelit table for two with a bottle of wine.

"You win the award for 'most full of surprises,'" Alonzo said. "What are you doing here?"

She got up and came toward him. "Seducing you."

Her lips touched his and lingered, and he was sure she'd meant exactly what she said.

He cleared his throat. "I actually meant, what are you doing in Austin?"

With a finger, she slowly wiped her gloss from his lips. "I'm performing on the main stage tomorrow night."

He should have known. South by Southwest was more music

than movie premieres.

"I couldn't believe it when I heard you were here." She took the glasses from the table and handed him one. "Let's toast."

"To what?"

"To us."

He quirked a brow. "There's an 'us'?"

"If you want to quibble, let's toast to possibilities."

He nodded slightly. "I can do that." He clinked his glass with hers and took a sip.

"You know what I'd love to do, Alonzo Coles?" She took his hand, played with his fingers. "Stay up all night with you, then watch the sunrise at the top of a mountain somewhere."

"I'm sure that would be amazing," he said, "except I was actually headed back to my room. I've got an early meeting."

"That's cute. What, you've got other plans?" She tipped his face toward hers and kissed him again. "I can't convince you to change them?"

"You know what?" He put his glass down. One more kiss, and he'd be a Noelle LeGrande tabloid story. "I'm gonna go, because my life is boring and I really do need to catch some z's."

She tore off a piece of napkin and wrote on it. "If for some reason you can't get to sleep—or your other plans change—this is where I'm staying."

She placed it in his hand, and he took a glance. They were on the same floor.

❧

Alonzo woke to a blaring phone. He reached for it on the nightstand and looked at it, then answered.

"I'm up."

"I knew you'd be asleep," Beverly said. "Why can't you set your alarm?"

"I slept through it."

49

"You sure you're up now?"

"Yes, Mom."

"Let me know how the meeting goes."

He clicked off, glancing at the body next to him. What a night. He'd come close to spending it with Noelle. But thankfully he'd been lucid enough to make the better choice. Amber had always been discreet.

"Hey," he said, rousing her, "I'm running late. About to hop in the shower and get ready to go."

"Okay," Amber said, "I'm about to head to my room." She was two floors down. "Alonzo," she said, "I enjoyed last night. I missed you."

His mind filled with the meeting ahead as he hopped up and got in the shower. He could remember dreaming about opportunities like this—being sought after for a coveted role. But something about this one wasn't sitting well with him. Hopefully his concerns would be laid to rest.

Forty minutes later a driver dropped him off at an omelet spot which, the driver said, was an Austin institution. He walked in, baseball cap shielding his eyes, and saw Gabe Donahue waving him over from a table in the distance.

The producer stood as Alonzo approached. "Alonzo, we've only met a couple of times briefly. Good to see you. Thanks for meeting with me."

"I appreciate your accommodating my schedule." Alonzo shook his hand and sat down.

"Unfortunately, my time is limited," Gabe said. "I've got to get to another appointment. But I wanted to hear any questions or concerns you have. We want to make this project happen."

"I'm humbled that you have me in mind for this," Alonzo said. "You have an A-team on board. It would be phenomenal to take part."

"Your career is already on the rise. This would take you to

another level." Gabe lifted his coffee cup. "You were our first choice. You'd be perfect for this."

"I've looked over the screenplay," Alonzo said, "and my first—"

"Sir, can I pour you a cup of—oh, you're Alonzo Coles. Right?" The server set down the coffeepot. "I just saw you last week, in the film you were nominated for. We made it a girls' night, and oh, *gosh*, you were incredible. Wait, can I get my phone and take a picture with you? They will *flip*."

"Ma'am, I wish I could," Alonzo said, "but I need to respect this gentleman's time and focus on our meeting."

"Oh, sure. Absolutely. Maybe when you're done? Okay, sorry." She picked up the pot. "I'll be back shortly for your order."

"I'll take some coffee, though, if that's okay." He smiled at her.

"Sorry. I just can't believe my luck." She poured the coffee and scurried away, missing the next table's attempt to get her attention.

"Here's my main issue," Alonzo said, leaning in. "The movie revolves around the female protagonist, a wealthy socialite who's leading a double life. So of course her character is well-rounded and complex. My character is a vehicle for her to play out her fantasies. Almost every scene they're in together is a love scene."

Gabe nodded, waiting for more.

"I don't see any other aspect to his life," Alonzo said. "After reading it through, I couldn't even tell you how he's employed. I prefer meatier roles."

"It's a psychological thriller," Gabe said, "so it has a different edge to it. I see your character as very dynamic. You're seeing a side of her that no one else sees. You're the one who forces her to examine her life and why she does the things she does."

"Right before or after they have sex."

"I'm not understanding," Gabe said. "The sex scenes are a problem? Because, Google yourself. You're the man who's known for 'sex scenes that sizzle.' That's why you're perfect for this."

"But in my other movies my character's got a lot more going on, more complexities. The sex is just part of it."

"So if we could develop your character more, show other aspects of his life . . ." Gabe was taking notes. He looked up now. "That would satisfy you?"

"That would be sweet."

"I'll take this back, see if it can be done." Gabe gave a wry smile. "I thought for a minute you were trying to downplay your sex symbol status. Which would have been odd, given the post I saw just before you walked in."

"What post?"

"On IG. Amber Holley." Gabe pulled it up on his phone and gave it to him.

Shout out to my old friend, Alonzo Coles, for supporting my premiere last night, the caption began. *Loved catching up.*

Alonzo stared at the picture—Amber sitting against the headboard in his hotel room, wearing the shirt he'd worn to the premiere the night before.

CHAPTER 9

*C*inda rounded the bend towards the kitchen as the twins set up their film equipment in the family room.

"Comments rolling in all morning," Jade said. "People can't wait for us to dish on this love triangle. I guess Alonzo Watch is officially a thing."

"Our subscribers have even made it a hashtag—why didn't we think of that?" Jordyn positioned one of the studio lights. "The funny thing is, we're not making this stuff up. If these celebrities want to put their lives out there, we're here for it." She chuckled. "I love the comment that said, 'I need both these women to leave my bae alone.'"

"I still can't believe Amber went there," Jade said. "She was like, he ain't your man, Simone. Not for real."

"Good morning," Cinda said, looking at the twins. "Hey, if you two aren't doing anything tonight, we should go to the movies or something."

"I'm down," Jordyn said. "Sounds like fun."

"Actually," Jade said, "my boyfriend invited us to a comedy show tonight."

"Oh, yeah," Jordyn said. "We should ask if we can bring Cinda."

"I'm pretty sure he said it's sold out," Jade said.

"Okay, no problem," Cinda said. "Maybe another time."

She continued to the kitchen, sighing inside. Every effort she'd made to get to know them, Jade rebuffed. But Cinda had to remind herself what a radical change this had been, some stranger showing up, suddenly part of the family. By blood, yes —test results had confirmed it—but the heart was another matter.

She came into the kitchen and found Randall buttering his toast. "The best I have are these faded jeans and plaid shirt. I'm telling you I should stay home."

He turned to look at her. "Oh, you'll be fine. You'll fit right in with most of the folk there, including Pastor Lance."

"Grandma would've had a fit if I tried to wear something like this to church."

He nodded with a knowing smile. "It took some getting used to, I admit. But I'm old school." He carried his food to the table, looking preppy in nice khakis and a button-down. "Help yourself to a plate. I made my famous chicken breakfast sausage."

Cinda surveyed the stove. "What do you mean, *made?* Bought it and browned it in the pan?"

"No, ma'am," he said. "Mixed ground chicken and other ingredients in a bowl, made several patties, *then* browned it."

"Ah, more hidden talents. You made these hash browns and cheesy eggs too?"

"With a little kick in the seasoning," Randall said.

Cinda got a plate, looking over as Janice walked in. "Good morning," she said.

Janice headed for the coffee mugs. "Good morning, Cinda."

"I was going to bring your coffee up in a few minutes," Randall said.

"I needed to get up and moving anyway." Janice poured a cup. "I've got a lot of work to get done before I head back to Chicago tomorrow morning."

"You better fuel up with some of this good food then," Randall said.

She peered over at it. "I was going with oatmeal, but looks like you did your thing." She looked at him. "What's the occasion? You don't usually cook like this before church."

"I'm usually the only one up," he said. "But the girls got up early and I knew Cinda was getting ready for church, so I decided to cook."

Janice leaned against the counter with her coffee. "You're going to church, Cinda? Is that your usual Sunday routine?"

"It's been years since I've been." Cinda moved to the table with her food and a glass of juice. "Randall was telling me about it last night and asked if I'd like to go."

"I bet he did." Janice sipped her coffee. "You two are certainly finding your groove," she said. "Late-night talks, weekdays at Randall's office, now church on Sunday morning."

"Well, no church groove yet," Cinda said. "I'm just visiting today, hoping it doesn't feel too weird."

"No pressure at all," Randall said.

Jade walked in and checked out the food.

"Wow." Janice faced her husband. "Why am I thinking all of us felt pressured to go at one time or another?"

"Well, granted," he said, "I've brought it up over the years, I admit. I kept thinking if you'd just visit, you'd like it."

"You must be talking about church." Jade fixed her plate. "I never felt pressured to go, Mom, because you said we didn't have to."

Janice nodded. "Good to know you listened."

"Jade, I just checked our analytics." Jordyn walked in, beaming. "Total confirmation of what we thought. Every time we feature Alonzo Coles—from that first video announcing the movie and showing pics Dad took during filming, to every Alonzo Watch since—there's a huge spike in new subscribers."

"I'm not surprised," Janice said. "The entertainment channels seem to feature him at every turn. Just wait till you cover the premiere."

"I meant to tell you, Cinda," Randall said, "I got you added to the VIP list for the premiere."

"Wow, I get to go to LA?" Cinda said. "That's so cool, thanks. I'm really looking forward to seeing the movie."

Jade took a seat next to Randall. "Dad, I just got the best idea— aren't you about to do a promo shoot with Alonzo? We could go and get footage for our channel."

"Ohh," Jordyn said, fixing her own plate, "an exclusive like that? The main news outlets might not even have access."

"Exactly," Randall said. "I highly doubt they'd allow for extra people, let alone outside cameras. And you have to remember this is actual work. We'll be on a tight schedule, and my part is limited." He held his toast. "But hey, how about helping your dear old dad shop for the shoot? Fashion is right up your alley, right?"

"Umm," Jordyn said, joining them at the table, "women's fashion. Shopping with you is kind of . . . boring."

"I think you've got this thing all wrong," he said. "You need to do 'Randall Watch.' Follow along as I get ready for the photo shoot and the premiere. Get a behind-the-scenes look at the author on his day job."

Jordyn gave him an amused look. "That's actually worse. Your job is *super* boring."

Cinda chuckled. "I kind of came to that conclusion myself this past week." She'd been curious what his job entailed and found out it was lots of client meetings and paperwork. "Randall said corporate law wasn't nearly as exciting as the criminal stuff he wrote about, so I ended up devouring all eight of his novels." She looked around the table. "What're your favorites? I loved *Bonds of Time,* but the latest one is a real page turner too."

Jordyn glanced at Jade. "I think with so much going on, we haven't actually had a chance yet to read the novels."

"Oh," Cinda said, nodding, "I can totally see that. Your production schedule is crazy, then you've got tons of other stuff. I'm the one who needs to get a life." She gave a sheepish smile. "Speaking of which, there's a Target near here, right? I need to start looking for a job tomorrow and thought I'd start there. I worked my way up to manager at the one in Madison."

"I thought you were thinking about community college." Randall checked his watch and took his plate to the sink.

"But I can't start classes till summer." She took a last bite, seeing the cue that it was time to go. "And even then, I want to be working as well."

He drank the last of his juice. "What are you interested in? What's your passion?"

Cinda took her plate to the sink and rinsed it, thinking. "If I'm honest—and this isn't a job-type thing in my mind—I've always loved clothes, fashion, all that."

Jade gave her a look. "Really?"

Cinda glanced down at herself. "I know, who could tell, right?"

"Well, hey," Randall said, "maybe I can corral you into shopping with me for this photo shoot."

Cinda shrugged. "I'd love to, actually."

"Okay, what else?" Randall said. "Do you have a flair for writing, numbers, art . . ."

"Well. Cleaning."

"A flair for cleaning?" Jade said.

"You haven't noticed?" Jordyn said. "She basically took over my chores in the kitchen, and I ain't mad about it." She chuckled. "She does stuff I never bothered to do."

Janice looked at Cinda. "Maybe we should talk," she said. "I've been asking around for recommendations for someone to clean our home, since the woman we loved moved away."

"You mean you'd pay me?" Cinda said.

"If you're good? Absolutely."

"I can clean the whole house this week, as an interview." She knew Janice wasn't thrilled to have her there, but there was something about a spotless house. It had always put her mother in a good mood. Maybe it would help with Janice also.

"I certainly can't refuse that," Janice said.

"We'd better go," Randall said. "We'll see you all when we get back."

The eyes of all three women followed them as they walked toward the door and left together.

～

Cinda had had no expectations of church. You simply went, endured the service, and got on with the day. But Randall had been right—something was different about this place, or at least, about the people.

She looked around as they moved out of their seats at a part of the service where the pastor invited them to greet one another. The way they hugged and chatted, you'd think they hadn't seen one another in forever. But presumably this happened every Sunday.

Randall had moved out of his seat also, but instead of greeting people, he worked his way to the pastor. A moment later he had the microphone.

"If I can interrupt the revelry for a quick minute." He smiled. "I want to introduce a special visitor to our church, someone I met only two weeks ago today." He gestured toward her. "My daughter, Cinda."

Applause rang out and people began making their way over. Before Cinda knew it, a slew of strangers had surrounded her, hugging and welcoming her.

The pastor took back the microphone and walked down the aisle, closer to where she was. "Cinda, I want to personally welcome you. I'm Lance Alexander, senior pastor here at Living Hope. You should know your dad is beloved here, and I'm grateful to be able to call him a personal friend. We look forward to getting to know you."

Randall walked back to where they were seated and enfolded her in a hug.

"That's the last thing I expected." Her head in his chest, Cinda felt a rise of emotion. "That you would introduce me to everyone."

"Why is that?" he said.

"I guess . . . I figured you'd be embarrassed for people to know, especially people at church."

He looked into her eyes. "Why would I be embarrassed?"

"You're this upstanding attorney with the nice intact family, and I basically ruin the picture," she said. "Plus, I'm from a time in your life that you said yourself you're not proud of."

They sat as everyone returned to their seats and the collection basket was passed.

"Cinda, listen," he said, leaning in, his voice low. "I've felt a lot of things since you've come into my life—stunned, confused, upset that I missed so much—but never embarrassed." He added, "And I left out the most important thing—thankful. God knew you were out there, and in His time He brought you to me. Cinda, you're a gift."

She felt her arms tremble a little. "You think *God* brought me to you?"

"I know He did," Randall said, "just as sure as He led you here today." He paused. "This is more about you and Him than you and me."

She frowned a little. "I don't understand."

"I'm your earthly father," he said. "But the One who created you and loves you—He wants to be your Father eternally. This may sound strange, but I have this picture in my head—like I'm placing your hand in His."

Cinda moved her gaze forward, unsure what to make of that. But something about that image—herself with two fathers—took her breath away.

CHAPTER 10

APRIL

*T*reva sat with her Bible open, phone propped in a tabletop tripod, the last bit of coffee in her favorite mug. "This worked so much better than I thought it would," she said, FaceTiming with her sister. "I might've even spoken up more than I usually do." She chuckled.

"It was awesome." Jillian paused, hugging the last woman good-bye, then looked back into her phone. "It's been so weird not having you here. Remember when I started the group? You were there from the very first meeting."

"I'd been feeling like a part of my world was missing," Treva said. "Thank God for technology. I'm just mad it took me this long to think of it. My Tuesday mornings are back on track."

"You don't plan to do this every week, do you?"

"Why wouldn't I?"

"I thought maybe you'd start a group yourself. Spread your wings a little."

"Spread my wings?" Treva said. "Like I'm a child in need of independence?"

"Umm. Sort of?"

"What in the world does that mean?"

Jillian seemed thoughtful as she looked at her sister. "I remember you as a little girl, vivacious, chatty. And then I remember you shutting down little by little, whenever you got ignored and pushed aside. Like the slow leaking of air from a balloon."

Treva could see that girl, could feel the pain she endured, from her own mother and grandmother, and from others in her parents' social circle. *She's so dark. Nowhere near as pretty as her sister.* She blinked back the threat of tears.

"To this day," Jillian said, "you suffer the effects of that. Self-conscious. Afraid of rejection. Can't see your worth—definitely can't see what God's put in you. That's why you'd rather FaceTime with us for Bible study than start another group."

Treva swallowed the emotion. "There's nothing wrong with valuing the relationships I have."

"All I'm saying," Jillian said, "is so much was stolen from you. God has already done an amazing work in you. But this is a new season, and healing comes in stages. He's not done yet. That's why I put you on that prayer list."

Treva heard the garage door rise. "That must be Lance. I'm gonna go."

"Hey," Jillian said. "You're my favorite sister in the whole world."

A thousand memories flooded. As a girl, Jillian would climb into Treva's double bed at night, knowing nighttime was when Treva's thoughts tormented her most. And Jillian would say, "I love you, Treva. You're my favorite sister in the whole world."

"Stop trying to be nice after you kicked me out of the Bible study," Treva said.

"I did no such thing."

"Then I'll see y'all next Tuesday morning."

"Girl, bye."

Treva clicked off, wondering why Lance hadn't yet come in. She walked to the door and opened it. A bouquet of red roses in a beautiful vase greeted her, a smiling Lance behind them.

"Babe, they're gorgeous." She reached beyond them and hugged him. "But what's the occasion? And I thought you had meetings all day today."

Lance walked in and set the roses down, then hoisted himself onto the counter. He brought her close and put his arms around her waist. "Do you know how much I love you?"

She looked into his eyes, unable to find words.

"Hey," he said softly, wiping a tear. "What's going on?"

She shook her head, looking downward a moment. "Just talking to Jillian about stuff from the past, and here you come. You have no idea how much I love you."

"That was my line, though."

"Can we share?"

Lance tightened his embrace and kissed her, his hands caressing her back. "This actually wasn't my plan right now," he said. "But it's your fault for looking so irresistible in the middle of the day."

"Note to self—tarry in sweaty workout clothes more often." She pulled back a little. "But now I'm even more curious. What plan? And what are the flowers for?"

He looked at her, eyes penetrating. "Kicking off your birthday celebration."

"My birthday's not till Friday."

"I know. And I still hate that I won't be here."

"Lance, I keep telling you it's fine. You had this on your calendar before you met me."

"I feel like you're having to adjust to so much that you probably didn't anticipate," he said. "My phone blowing up day and night—how many evenings have we had plans that got interrupted? Last week we'd just sat down to dinner on an overdue night out, and I had to leave because of an emergency. Now I'm speaking at this pastors conference and can't be with you on your special day."

Treva looked into his eyes. "You really don't get it, do you?"

"What?"

"Every day is special, because I'm married to you. It's surreal when I wake up beside you. When you hold me like this, I still get butterflies. I'm overwhelmed that I can look into those pretty brown eyes and say, 'This fine, sexy, gifted, godly man is *mine*.'"

He blew out a breath. "So the *initial* plan was to pack a picnic lunch on this nice spring day and enjoy the weather, because my early afternoon appointment got canceled. But since it's your birthday celebration, I'll let you choose whether you want to do that"—he drew her closer and kissed her—"or something else."

"Hmm, let's see . . ." Treva stared upward a moment before looking at him again. "Not even close."

She took her husband by the hand and led him upstairs.

CHAPTER 11

Faith climbed atop a bench, aimed her camera phone at the Tasmanian devil high up in the tree, and waited to get a clear shot.

"This is not a good look—in the Children's Zoo, pushing a stroller, with a diaper bag on my shoulder." Reggie gave her a look. "Come on, Faith."

"This is so cool, though. I've never seen a Tasmanian devil." She watched as it maneuvered to another part of the tree, closer in view, and then she snapped a few pictures. "And what's the problem anyway?" Faith looked back at him. "Afraid it'll scare off the ladies?"

"Right. That girl of my dreams who happens to be strolling by the billy goats on a Thursday afternoon."

"Hey, you never know, beautiful as today is." Faith jumped down and did a twirl. "It feels *so* good out here. Having Zoe in January, plus the cold of winter, felt like I was cooped up for months."

"The weather is definitely incredible," Reggie said. "And I could think of at least fifty other ways to enjoy it."

"You are such a zoo grinch." She took the diaper bag from his shoulder.

"I came, didn't I?"

"After I promised to go to that nasty Thai restaurant," Faith said, taking over the stroller, "which is ridiculous because who has to bribe someone to come see these amazing creatures? And if it weren't for me, you wouldn't be enjoying the weather at all. You were sitting at home."

"Working, actually. Until somebody called with a shameless pitch about how much 'Zoe' wanted to go to the zoo today."

Faith grinned. "You might not have a proper love for zoo creatures, but at least babies hold a special place."

Reggie looked aside, his expression changed.

"What?"

He shook his head. "Nothing."

"Oh. My. Gosh." Faith hit Reggie's arm. "Look at momma kangaroo eating next to her joey." She moved closer to them. "Tell me that's not the most adorable thing you've ever seen."

"Adorable?"

She looked back at him. "You must have been traumatized as a child. Sprayed by a skunk or something."

Reggie chuckled, moving closer to watch as the joey and its mom munched leaves. "All right, yeah, I guess it's cute."

She snatched his ball cap off and hit him with it. "Grinch."

"You see how your mom does me, Zoe?" He looked into the stroller as Zoe blew bubbles. "Like a pesky little sister." He took his hat back.

"That's funny," Faith said. "I told my Aunt Jillian we'd been hanging out, and she said we must be the next generation brother/sister duo."

Reggie looked confused.

"She's the one who was best friends with Tommy in college."

He nodded, remembering. "Two generations. That's pretty

dope. I always wanted a little sister." He gave her the eye. "At least I thought I did."

"And as the oldest of three girls, I always wanted a big brother. To pester." She smiled at him. "Seriously, I used to think if I had an older brother he could give me advice about guys and protect me. My dad definitely did that, but once he was gone . . ." She stared off. "A big brother might have been helpful to talk to when Jesse came along."

Reggie looked at her. "From comments you've made, sounds like you went through some things."

"Ha. That's fair. I'm still waiting to feel like it's all behind me." She looked at him. "Are you still dealing with the stuff you went through?"

He walked in silence a moment. "I hit a low point, Faith. Everything I thought was sure was gone in an instant. And when I thought it couldn't get any worse—it got worse." He focused on the pathway in front of them. "I was depressed, questioning God, questioning my faith, didn't want to talk to anybody . . ."

"So what happened?"

"Tommy flew out and sat me down," he said. "I ended up telling him everything I was dealing with. He shared things he's dealt with. Took our relationship to a whole new level."

"Wow," Faith said. "That's that big brother action I was talking about."

"He's actually the reason I got the job at Living Word," Reggie said. "He found out about it a few weeks later and told me to check it out. It was perfect—in my lane professionally and what I needed spiritually. Studying the Scriptures is in my job description."

"You have such a cool job. Big responsibility, though, working on content for the Living Word site. It must have millions of visitors." She gave him a puzzled look. "And you have time to be out here at the zoo?"

"If you had a hat on, I'd hit you with it." He chuckled a little. "The problem is, I should've never told you about my flex days."

"Why? I need to know when I can especially bug you—"

"Look at that," he said.

Faith watched him walk toward a man encircled by kids. When she got closer, she saw that everyone's focus was on the snake in the man's hands.

"Oh. I don't do snakes." Faith backed up with the stroller, shaking her head.

"It's not just any snake," Reggie said. "You see how big that thing is? It's a python."

"That's supposed to reassure me?"

"Come on. The two-year-olds are closer than you. Let's pet it."

She backed up more. "Look how that thing is slithering across his arm."

Reggie turned to her with a look of surprise. "You say that like it's not one of God's amazing creatures."

"Oh, be quiet."

"If you pet it," he said, "we'll go to that Mexican place you like instead of the Thai one."

"Why do you care if I pet it?" she said.

"Because this is irrational. They wouldn't let toddlers near it if there were any danger."

"Touching with the tip of a finger for half a second counts as a pet."

"Fine," Reggie said.

Faith sighed, inching forward with the stroller. Reggie took her by the arm to help her.

"I'll get there in my own sweet time," she said, shaking loose.

He took out his phone and aimed it at her.

"What are you doing?"

"Capturing a shot of this," Reggie said. "Send it to your Aunt Jillian and tell her, 'This is how the next-generation brother/sister rolls—we help each other conquer fears.'"

She turned, hiding a slight smile.

$\sim$

Faith opened the front door and held it for Reggie as he carried Zoe, nestled inside her car seat, into the house. Her mom came immediately from the kitchen with a funny look.

"Did you know Jesse was coming today?" Treva spoke in a low voice.

Faith's heart skipped a beat. "What do you mean? He's here?"

"Got here a few minutes ago. I tried to call you. He's downstairs."

"He gave me the dates he was coming for spring break," she said, "but it must've snuck up on me. I didn't see his car outside, though."

"The garage door was up, and Lance told him to pull inside so you'd have room in the driveway."

Footsteps bounded up the stairs. "Hey, that must be my—" He stopped short upon seeing them, his eyes traveling between Faith, the car seat, and Reggie.

"Hey, Jesse." Faith gave him a quick hug.

"Good to see you again," Reggie said. He moved forward, shaking Jesse's hand.

"You too," Jesse said. He glanced down at the car seat, where Zoe had fallen asleep.

"Oh, I'm sure you want to . . ." Reggie set the seat down, unhooked Zoe, and lifted her out, handing her to Jesse.

"Hey, my little princess." Jesse kissed her cheek. "She's grown so much, more than the pictures show."

"She really has," Treva said. "Why don't you all come into the kitchen. Dinner will be ready in about twenty minutes."

Jesse followed with Zoe.

Reggie leaned into Faith. "I'm gonna head home. You good?"

Faith glanced Jesse's way. "Yeah." It was actually a good thing she'd forgotten he was coming, rather than dealing with her feelings about it. "Thanks, Reg."

She went to the kitchen, where her mom had set out some lemonade and bottled water, then slipped downstairs. Jesse was at the table holding Zoe against his chest.

"Look how she's looking into your eyes." Faith stood beside them a moment. "Like she's mesmerized."

"I couldn't wait to get down here and just hold her." He kept his eyes on the baby. "I keep thinking, she's not going to know me. I don't want it to be like me and my dad."

Faith took the seat across the table. "You've never talked about your father."

"I don't like to think about all that," he said. "He and my mother never married. He came and went, and after my younger brother was born, we rarely saw him. I heard later he started another family."

"That had to hurt."

"I'm afraid I'll do that to Zoe." He stroked the baby's back. "I'm just like my father. I see that now. The way I treat women, selfish, no commitment." He looked at Faith. "How do I know it's not in me to do that, to start a life somewhere and never look back?"

"I see what's in you as you hold her," Faith said. "You love Zoe. I have no doubt about that."

"I appreciate your saying that," Jesse said. "I know I'm not your favorite person."

"All right, don't start feeling sorry for yourself."

"I'm just saying, last time we talked, I told you I still had feelings, and you basically hung up on me."

"I didn't simply hang up," Faith said. "I told you it didn't mean anything."

"How are you gonna tell me my feelings don't mean anything?"

"Because you claimed to have feelings before, while you were seeing me *and* Brandy."

"As if it's not possible to have feelings for two people at the same time."

Faith could feel her jaw set. "Can we move on to something else?"

He looked at her. "Let's talk about you and Reggie then. You wouldn't answer before when I asked if you had a boyfriend. I guess I got my answer."

"Not really," Faith said.

"Meaning?"

"We're friends. He's like a brother."

Jesse's eyes rested on her a moment. "While I'm here I want to take Zoe around to different places, enjoy the outdoors. Would you think about hanging with the two of us?"

"I don't have a choice," she said. "Zoe doesn't take a bottle yet."

Jesse nodded. "So you're stuck with me," he said. "I'll take it."

CHAPTER 12

*A*lonzo posed stone-faced, feet apart, staring down the camera in a midnight blue designer suit with matching vest. The photographer clicked away, orbiting him—until his stylist held up a finger to interrupt. Pins in her mouth, Bianca walked over and tucked a couple of places inside his jacket.

"I'll have a talk with the tailor later," she said. "Should have been tighter." She tugged on it. "Much better."

The photographer resumed, directing him to look in different directions as Alonzo got back into character. It had been several months since the filming of *Bonds of Time*. He'd forgotten how much this character resonated with him.

"Let's break for an early lunch," the photographer said. "I need Alonzo and Randall together right after, because Randall's got a flight to catch, then Alonzo with the cast."

His stylist lifted the suit jacket from him, then removed the vest. "In the shots with Randall, we've got a few choices for casual looks." Bianca flipped through the pieces hanging on the rack, pulling button-downs and sweaters and facing them outward.

"Excuse me, Bianca?"

Both Alonzo and Bianca turned as Randall Rogers approached.

71

"Am I supposed to change into something else? When we spoke briefly, you indicated you would bring a couple of options."

"And I did," Bianca said, "but . . ." She walked a circle around him. "I'm loving that creamy cashmere with denim and the brown suede oxfords."

"I'll tell my daughter," Randall said. "She picked it out."

Bianca nodded. "Simple. Strong. Conveys what we want to convey. I say let's go with that."

"Sounds good." Randall smiled. "Now if someone could point me to catering in this massive penthouse."

"I'm starving," Bianca said. "I'll walk with you. Alonzo, we can pick this back up after."

"Amber is giving me a headache." Beverly stood nearby looking at her phone. "More requests for comment. A month later, and she won't let it die. So I've got to deal with endless chatter about the so-called love triangle."

Alonzo gave her a weary look. "What's she saying now?"

"Same stuff," his manager said. "She's coy about whether she was in your hotel room. When they ask if it's your shirt she's wearing, she says, 'You'll have to ask Alonzo'—so they do, over and over."

"As they show a side-by-side pic of me wearing the shirt the same night."

"It's marketing genius," Beverly said. "She's gotten tons of movie promo from it. But that's not the coverage you want, not with everything you've got ahead of you." She looked at him. "We haven't gotten the revised script yet, but Gabe says they're working on it and want to accommodate you. So you'd better be ready to say yes."

"Depending on what the revisions look like," Alonzo said.

She gave him a hard look. "I honestly don't know what's going on with you. What more do you want? Top director, A-list actress, big studio backing, and more money than you've made on a film. Plus it'll introduce you to a wider audience."

Alonzo had been telling himself all of that, but other things gnawed at him. Like the brief convo he'd had with Rufus at the Oscar after-party. The comment by the reporter at South by Southwest. And he'd Googled himself as Gabe suggested, for the first time—and wished he hadn't.

"Your career is on an upward trajectory right now," Beverly said, "and we want to keep it that way. Everything you do has to be strategic."

Alonzo nodded as he stared into the distance, her words weighing heavily. He changed into sweats and made his way to catering, grabbing a turkey on wheat and adding fixings. He spied Randall at a table with his food and a laptop, and walked over to him.

"Mr. Rogers, I know you're probably working," Alonzo said, "but I wondered if we could eat together on the terrace."

Randall looked a little surprised. "Sure," he said. "But, 'Mr. Rogers'? Help me feel a little younger than my midforties."

Alonzo smiled. "Wasn't even thinking age. Just much respect."

They situated themselves on the terrace with a view of downtown LA.

Alonzo was suddenly unsure what he wanted to say. "I haven't had a chance to talk to you much since you got here," he said.

"Well," Randall said, "you're the star. You've been a little busy."

"I guess I just want to thank you," Alonzo said, "for creating this role. I know I told you that during the filming, but I appreciate this character even more now."

"Why so?" Randall ate from a bag of chips.

Alonzo thought a moment. "It's such a mixture of elements. You've got the 'hood in the way he grew up and started dealing drugs. It's a family business, so you explore those dynamics. There's sophistication in the way he takes the business international. And there's the coming-of-age aspect, when he's at a crossroads. Even though it's not spelled out, it's basically spiritual." He looked at Randall. "For some reason that's what's hitting me right now."

"The spiritual element is actually deeper in the book," Randall said. "We wrangled about it, but you know how it is. The studio can do what it wants." He drank some of his water. "I won one battle, though. They backed off of going more graphic with the love scenes."

Alonzo looked at him. "Why was that important to you?"

"Alonzo, I'm a Christian man. I know that label doesn't mean a whole lot these days, but it means everything to me. I wanted the work to reflect my heart, my faith."

Alonzo stood and walked a bit. "You have no idea," he said, staring into the skyline, "my mind is so blown right now. It feels like a rewind to four years ago."

"What happened four years ago," Randall said, "if I may ask?"

Alonzo turned to face him. "I had a small part on a soap opera and was really cool with the assistant director. First time I got to know someone who said he was a Christian and it actually impacted the way he lived. He would say stuff like you just said— that his faith informed his work." He hadn't thought about those conversations in a long while, but now it seemed like yesterday. "I started asking questions," he continued, "and one day I knew I wanted to give my life to Jesus. It was real. I know it was. I had this excitement. I started praying for God to use me in Hollywood."

Randall nodded. "You're saying all this as if there was a problem."

"I left that show a few weeks later and got my first big break." He took his time, piecing it together in his mind. "Seemed like my life went from zero to sixty overnight. I had been visiting this church but wasn't really learning. It was easy to stop going when life got hectic. Now . . ." He sighed. "Deep down I still feel like it was real, but I don't know . . . I feel so far from there now." He looked at Randall. "I just dropped a load on you, didn't I? You must think I'm crazy."

"It's making perfect sense actually," Randall said. "Your connection to the character. Feeling like this is a rewind. It's all God, trying to get your attention."

Alonzo frowned a little. "He would do that?"

"And more," Randall said. "He loves you, Alonzo. He wants you near."

"But how do I do that?" He felt like a kid in need of a million answers. "I don't know how to begin looking for a church, let alone find time to get there each week. And then I'd have to find a way to go incognito. Not that I'm a huge star, but I'd rather go unnoticed, you know?"

"When I said He wants you near," Randall said, "I wasn't thinking of a building. You could start with getting to know Him. Reading the Bible. Praying. He'll lead you to a church, and to people who can help you grow."

"What are you, a pastor on the side or something? An angel?" Alonzo smiled a little.

"Just an elder at my local church," Randall said.

"You're familiar with the Bible though?"

"I am," Randall said. "I love reading it, and I teach on occasion."

Alonzo hesitated, looking at him. "So, could you help me become familiar with it?"

"What are you thinking?" Randall said. "How would that work logistically?"

"I don't know," Alonzo said. "Maybe I could text to get your thoughts on something I'm reading, ask a few questions?"

Randall nodded. "I could do that."

Alonzo stared into the skyline again. This was probably one of those *Be careful what you ask for* things. He had no idea where it would lead, only that he felt he had to follow.

CHAPTER 13

Cinda stood on the uppermost rung of a stepladder, spraying vinegar onto the top of the kitchen cabinet. Next she sprinkled baking powder and watched it fizz.

"Girl, what are you doing?" Jordyn came into the kitchen. "You're gonna fall and break your neck."

"Ha. Thanks." She started scrubbing. "I'm used to it. I did it all the time at home."

"I never saw our last cleaning person do all that."

"Yeah, you should've seen all the grease and grime up here," she said. "It's actually been fun to tackle."

"You're weird, just so you know." Jordyn opened the refrigerator.

"Hey, how was your date last night?" Cinda said.

Jordan happy-sighed. "We went to dinner and a movie, and it was everything. And he *paid* for everything, unlike these boys who still live with their mommas and want you to front the bill." She popped a can of soda. "Were you seeing anyone back in Madison?"

Cinda used a clean wipe to gather remaining residue. "Nope, no one," she said.

"Hmm, I need to think who I can hook you up with."

"Thanks, but no thanks," Cinda said. "When it's meant to be, it'll be."

"How will you know if you're not out there meeting people?"

"I don't know," Cinda said. "But it's just not a priority for me."

"Have I told you you're weird?"

"What's this dinner Dad's talking about for tonight?"

Cinda glanced down as Jade walked in, looking at her phone. Like her sister, her hair was pulled back in a sleek bun.

"I texted him to see how the shoot went," Jade continued, "and he sent this when his plane landed back here, to remind us about a get-together at Lance and Treva's. I'd honestly forgotten he mentioned it. Who are they anyway?"

"I asked him about that," Jordyn said. "Lance is the pastor of his church, and Treva's his wife."

"Why are they inviting all of us, though?" Jade said. "We don't even know them."

Cinda backed down the ladder slowly with her bucket of supplies. "I think they want to *get* to know all of us," she said. "They're cool people. You should go."

"We've got other plans," Jade said. "But I should've known you were going. You love sharing all this church stuff with Dad."

"I'm not sure what you mean." Cinda rinsed out the scrub brush. "I do like the church and the people—"

"And those father/daughter Bible studies at night."

"I wouldn't call it a Bible study. We're mostly just talking, but —" She turned to Jade. "Did I offend you in some way? I get the feeling you really don't like me."

Jade's eyes widened a little. "Oh, you want to go there?" she said. "I'll tell you what I don't like—you trying to breeze in and become Daddy's little favorite." She fluttered her eyes. "'I love all your books, Randall. Oh, you're headed to church? Of course I'll come.' And surprise, surprise. You and Daddy are shopping for a brand-new car." She rolled her eyes. "Sorry, I see right through it. You're phony and desperate."

Jordyn looked at her sister. "Jade, why are you—"

"She asked, didn't she?"

"I'm sure I'm a lot of things," Cinda said, at the sink still, "but I don't think phony is one of them. And desperate for what? A car? I'm fine with my '96 Nissan. Randall was the one who had it inspected and said it had too many issues."

"How about desperate for love and attention?" Jade said.

"Meaning what?" Cinda said.

Jade moved closer to her. "I get that you didn't have a father growing up," she said. "But you can't make up for it overnight. Stop trying so hard. Every night there you are—camped out in Daddy's office."

Cinda wondered how she could even know. Most nights she was gone or preoccupied. She'd never seen either of the twins spend more than a few minutes with their father, though he'd suggest this thing or that. "You're right," she said. "I've never had a father's love or attention." She felt the onset of tears and willed them back. "I don't know if I'm desperate. Maybe so. Should I feel bad for enjoying his company?"

She felt Jade's eyes on her as she put her supplies in the bucket.

"Jordyn, FedEx dropped this off earlier." Janice walked in, handing her an envelope. "It got mixed up with a couple of my packages. Must be the deal memo. Pretty exciting."

"What deal memo?" Jade said.

"It's nothing official yet," Jordyn said.

"You haven't told your sister?" Janice said.

Jordyn hesitated. "It's a collab with JM Cosmetics to do liquid lipsticks."

"What? JM?" Jade's face lit up. "This is what we've been dreaming about, branding in makeup as well as hair. What, you wanted to surprise me?"

"Well . . . they only extended the offer to me, since I do the makeup vids," Jordyn said. "I didn't feel good about that, but I had Dad look at the deal memo and—"

"How could they not include us both?" Jade said. "We're a brand, as twins. Did you ask them?"

"I did, but they've got a different vision for it."

"Jordyn, if you really did ask, it was so tentative and passive that they probably didn't take you seriously." Jade sighed. "You have to tell them, 'It's both of us or neither of us. We're a package deal.' Or you should've let me—" She paused at the sound of the doorbell.

"Randall must've forgotten his house key," Janice said.

"I want to hear about his trip," Jade said, moving toward the front door.

The three of them left as Cinda tucked her supplies into the kitchen closet and headed for the back stairs to take a quick shower. She looked forward to hearing about the trip herself. Randall had texted before his flight to tell her they'd liked his outfit, which blew her away. She couldn't wait to—

"I'm Officer Samuels, and this is my partner, Officer Meyer."

The man's deep voice permeated through the lower level. Curious, Cinda moved toward the front door, listening.

"This is the residence of Randall Rogers?" Officer Samuels said.

"Yes," Janice said. "I'm his wife. These are his daughters."

Cinda tipped around the corner so she could see.

"Ma'am, I regret to inform you that there's been an incident."

"What kind of incident? Was Randall in a car accident?"

"No, ma'am," the officer said. "The incident took place at a local gas station. There was an altercation, and Mr. Rogers attempted to step in." He paused. "He was shot."

"What?" sounded in the foyer as the three of them reacted.

Cinda's hand went to her mouth. "Oh, God, no," she whispered.

"Let me get my shoes and purse," Janice said. She turned, then turned back toward them. "What hospital? How critical?"

"Ma'am, I'm sorry. He did not survive."

Cinda stared at the officer. His words were too calm. She couldn't grasp them. *He did not survive.* She felt herself shaking even as she struggled to understand.

"What are you saying?" Jordyn said. "Daddy's *dead*? You're here to tell us our father is *dead*?"

"This can't be real," Janice mumbled.

"Where is he right now?" Cinda moved from the shadows.

Janice looked at her, then to the officer, wanting to know herself.

"It's a crime scene," Officer Samuels said. "Our investigators are handling it. At present you wouldn't be able to see the body, but we'll let you know—"

"This is not acceptable," Janice said. "I don't care what you have to . . ."

Cinda moved back down the hallway as the police officer's words sank in. The way he said *the body*. That's all he was now?

She got her keys, went out the garage door, jumped in her old Nissan, and drove. Same as she did when her mother died. She had known it was coming, but it was heavy nonetheless. She'd helped take care of her and gotten to know her in ways she never had before. There'd been times in her life when she'd wanted nothing to do with her; suddenly she'd wanted more time. And her mother was gone.

With Randall, every day she looked forward to what they had —time. Eating together. Talking—late nights especially. Time seemed to stretch forever before them.

Two months.

And he was gone?

Cinda kept her foot on the gas, no idea where she was going. Just a stretch of highway. And his words. Right now, his words from last week rang loudest.

He'd been working in his home office one night, and Cinda was on a laptop at the office table. He'd bought the laptop for her soon after she arrived, and she'd been enamored with discovering all that she could do with it. That night she'd made a casual comment—"Randall, check out this cool app I downloaded."

And he'd looked at her. "I just want you to know, whenever you're ready . . . You can stop calling me Randall. And call me Dad."

Cinda had wanted to, but for some reason hadn't been able to bring herself to say it out loud.

She gripped the steering wheel, tears gathering from deep within. *How did this make sense? Shot and killed?*

All her life she'd wanted to hear his voice, look into his eyes. As much as she hated to admit it, she'd wanted her very own fairy-tale moment, her father as her Prince Charming. And her dream had come true.

But it wasn't supposed to end like this.

"Why?" Her fist pounded the steering wheel as tears began to cloud her vision. "Daddy, it wasn't supposed to end like this."

CHAPTER 14

*T*reva lined the kitchen counter with entrees prepared the day before and warmed minutes ago—baked chicken, mashed potatoes, green beans, cabbage, potato salad, corn bread, desserts, and, in Randall's memory, red beans and rice.

She looked at Stephanie, who was helping her. "I feel like I'm moving in slow motion. None of this seems real. The entire day— funeral home, cemetery—my mind can't grasp that he's gone."

"The fact that we were *at* a funeral home made it surreal to me." Stephanie took a pitcher of sweet tea from the fridge. "We just assumed it would be at Living Hope. The whole vibe would have been different. It *felt* like a funeral rather than a home-going."

"I wonder if the guy who gave the eulogy even knew Randall," Treva said. "Everything he said was superficial. And no mention of Jesus or the hope and faith Randall had. Lance would've talked about his heart. And he would've shared the Gospel." She sighed. "I felt so heavy leaving there. It made me sadder."

"Sad is a good word." Lance came into the kitchen, changed out of his suit. "Just all around. Sad."

"I kept watching his daughter," Treva said, "the one he just met. Such a vacant look on her face. I can't imagine finding your dad after all these years and losing him that fast." She dipped serving spoons into the entrees.

Stephanie got glasses from the cabinet. "And did you notice she wasn't included in the obituary?"

Treva looked at her. "Are you serious? I missed that."

"I only got to know Randall in the last few months, since moving back." Lindell sat at the kitchen table. "But it felt like I'd known him for years. He was that kind of guy."

Heads nodded soberly in the room.

"His heart was so big," Lance said. "As tragic as this whole thing is, I'm not surprised he did what he did. He saw that woman being forced into that car, crying for help, and he reacted."

Treva's own heart reacted whenever she heard the story. "He's being hailed as a hero," she said.

"That's when I broke down," Stephanie said, "seeing that woman walk into the funeral home. She's been talking about it on the news all week, how Randall saved her life."

The doorbell sounded, and Cyd and Cedric walked in with their son.

"Sorry we're late," Cyd said. "We picked up Chase from my parents' house on the way."

"You're right on time," Treva said. "We're ready to eat."

"Let's circle up," Lance said. "Tommy, can you pray?"

Tommy nodded from the table, quieter than usual. He stood, along with his fiancée, Allison.

Treva went partway downstairs, calling for Reggie and Faith, who'd also gone to the funeral. Joy and Hope were at school.

They all grabbed hands in a circle and bowed heads. Silence hung in the air for several seconds.

"Lord, I'm struggling with this, You know I am." Tommy took his time. "I always called Randall my big brother. And it didn't register until today that we're only a year apart. His wisdom and kindness, his calmness, made him seem beyond his years. Lord, I just . . . I really loved that guy."

Tommy's voice broke, and Treva could feel Lance's hand tremble. She gripped it tighter.

Tommy exhaled. "Thank You, Lord, for the gift that he was. Thank You that we got to experience Your love and grace through him. Comfort our hearts, Lord. Be glorified through this senseless act. And thank You that the perpetrator's been caught." He sighed. "Somehow, Lord, in the wake of his death, bring many to life through Christ Jesus. And we thank You that death has no sting for brother Randall. He's with Jesus this very moment."

"Yes," Lance murmured. "Thank You, Jesus."

"We ask that you bless the food," Tommy said, "and the hands that prepared it. Bless our fellowship also, Lord. We're hurting. We miss our brother . . ."

Seconds passed before the circle broke amid quiet sniffles and murmurs of "Amen."

"I'm not replacing him in the wedding." Tommy took a plate. "It'll just have to be out of sync, which seems appropriate."

Allison put her hand on his shoulder. "You couldn't have replaced him if you tried. I think we should acknowledge him in some way in the service."

Tommy nodded. "It's only two weeks away. I'm supposed to be in a celebratory mood in two weeks?"

"Randall would say you'd better be." Lance stood by the counter as people got their food. "You know his favorite line."

"'Again I say . . .'" rang out among the men.

"He meant it, too," Cedric said. "He didn't hide the fact that he had stuff he was dealing with. He said he *had* to live by that verse —'Rejoice in the Lord always, and *again I say*, rejoice.'"

Lance looked at Tommy and Allison. "Plus, he introduced you two. You have to celebrate in his honor."

Stephanie looked at Allison. "How did you know Randall? Was he your attorney?"

Allison nodded. "He helped me set up my boutique and was there every step of the way as it grew. I told him I was looking for a church home, and he told me about Living Hope." She looked at Tommy. "Then he started playing matchmaker."

"And brazen about it," Tommy said. "Telling me all the reasons why she's the bomb—my word—and how I wouldn't find a woman better suited. I said, *Congratulations. You've built her up so much I'll be nothing but disappointed.*" He smiled slightly. "That doggone Randall was right."

"We were supposed to be neighbors," Stephanie said. "We've got the grand opening of the bed-and-breakfast next week, and it's right around the corner from Randall's house."

"Well, we'll still be neighbors," Lindell said, "with his wife and daughters."

"Which could be interesting," Stephanie said. "His wife wasn't feeling us at all today."

"We've been praying for his family for a long while," Lance said. "We need to be praying especially now."

Treva slipped away and moved upstairs with that very thought on her mind. She couldn't stop thinking about Cinda. Though she knew little about the young woman, she felt a burden that had her on the verge of tears.

Treva knelt by the side of the bed and let them fall as she prayed.

CHAPTER 15

"*L*ife is so messed up. Why do the nicest people, the people actually making a difference on this earth, and the innocent people—why do *they* have to suffer?"

Faith's heart was heavy as she listened to Reggie. They'd settled back downstairs with their plates but hadn't touched their food. Ever since they'd returned from the funeral, he'd been on edge.

"Think about Randall's daughter." Reggie was back up, pacing. "She goes her entire life not knowing her father, then finally meets him—and he's gone. And on the flip side, Randall goes twenty-five years not knowing she exists. *Think about that.* All those years he could've been a part of her life, if only he'd known. Life is so *messed up.*"

"I know," Faith said. "Times like this it's hard to make sense of anything. Some things we'll never understand."

"But you know what I kept thinking at the funeral?" Reggie looked at Faith but seemed to stare through her. "At least he had two months. He got two months with his daughter, days upon days of talking to her and finding out who she is and what she's about. I got *nothing.*"

"What do you mean, you got nothing? What are you talking about?"

"Mia was pregnant," Reggie said. "My old girlfriend."

Faith struggled to understand. "When she broke up with you?"

"I didn't know. Her best friend had to tell me." He sat back down. "And here's something to blow your mind—I didn't even want to have sex. I mean I *wanted* to, but we were supposed to be committed to celibacy. And I couldn't understand why she was turning up the pressure . . ." He stared aside a moment. "She wanted to get pregnant and have my baby, as if she needed assurance that I would be there. She didn't even *know* me."

"Reggie, what happened?"

"When I got injured, she no longer wanted me or the baby," he said. "I pleaded with her, 'Just let me keep . . .'" He looked away as emotion filled his voice.

Faith could feel the pain in her own chest—for Reggie, for Randall, for her own dad. She moved closer to him and nudged his arm. He wiped his face, sitting back, nestling her against him. And they wept silent tears together.

～

Faith woke to Zoe's cries. She slid from under Reggie's arm and checked her watch. About an hour had passed. Lifting Zoe from the bassinet, she could hear voices upstairs still. She brought the baby to the sofa and began nursing her, her heart turning over and over. *Why, God? So much of life doesn't make sense.*

Reggie sat forward with a sigh. "Did I have an emotional meltdown? Tell me I was dreaming."

"It wasn't a meltdown." Faith looked over at him. "And if it was, that's not a bad thing. You can't manage grief. Trust me, I've tried."

Reggie looked at her. "I haven't asked how you've been affected by all this. Your dad was killed suddenly also."

"Three years ago this month," Faith said. "It brings it all back. I can't see it ever getting easier. My dad meant the world to me."

"I almost feel like I have two dads," Reggie said, "since Tommy is twenty years older. My parents divorced when I was a teen, and things were rocky for a while." He shrugged. "My dad and I aren't close, but we're cool. I'm looking forward to seeing him at the wedding."

"That's right," Faith said. "Your family will be in town in two weeks."

"You're going to the wedding, right?" Reggie said.

"I hadn't planned to," she said. "I was included on the invitation but in my mind, this was their thing—my mom and Lance, Aunt Jillian and Uncle Cecil, who are coming to town."

Reggie gave her a look. "Hello? I don't count?"

"You're *in* the wedding. You'll be busy. And I'll just be sitting there—"

"Uh-uh." Reggie was shaking his head. "I've gone too many places with you, including the Butterfly Garden—I mean, really? —because you've now latched onto, 'But you're my brother, and I can't help that it's fun hanging with you.' So now," he said, "you're my sister. And that reception will be too boring—all my cousins are either a lot older or a lot younger. You're going."

"Well, there's also a conflict." Faith lifted Zoe and patted her back. "Jesse's driving down that Saturday because Zoe's dedication is the next day. We're supposed to be doing something."

Reggie looked at her. "You sure about this, Faith?"

"What do you mean?"

"You said you were praying to be over him," Reggie said. "But the two of you were hanging strong when he was here spring break, and now you've got more plans."

"We sort of had to hang strong when he was here. I'm Zoe's food source."

"I'm just asking," Reggie said. "If I'm your brother when it comes to watching butterflies, then I'm gonna be your brother when it comes to your heart. I know you don't want a repeat of last year."

"I'm in a good space," Faith said. "I feel like he and I are redis-covering the friendship we had at first. But my goal still is to stay focused on Jesus."

"Okay." Reggie looked at her. "But you owe me. I'm waiting for the thing I *know* you'll find least enjoyable—and you'd better go."

"You would do that to me?"

"Easily."

"I don't think so. I saw your softer side today."

"I only let him out once a year." He picked up his plate, then got hers. "I'll go warm these up."

She watched him head for the stairs, thinking about life's twists and turns. Suddenly, in the face of tragedy, getting to know Jesse all over again didn't seem so bad. Maybe a good thing even, when she thought of Zoe. Reggie never got to know his baby. Randall had a short time with Cinda. But Zoe had a chance for more. Maybe a lot more.

CHAPTER 16

MAY

*A*lonzo sat on a cushioned sofa in the backyard of his Hollywood Hills estate, fire roaring in the pit, gazing into the heated pool, his thoughts a jumble. Everything right now seemed a jumble. Just as he was beginning to get some clarity, at least an idea of how to *get* clarity, just when he could see a path that had answers—it was gone.

But it was more than that. More than clarity and answers. *Randall* was gone. Strange that it had hit him so hard. Alonzo hadn't known him, not really. But after that photo shoot, he'd *wanted* to know him. Had even sent a text early that evening to let Randall know how serious he was about staying in touch. And Randall had replied, apparently minutes before his death.

Alonzo had asked himself the same question over and over. Why hadn't he gotten to know Randall earlier? He could have gotten his number during the filming, spent months going back and forth. And why hadn't he read the book on which the movie was based? Yesterday, finally, he'd done so. And he was even more sick that he didn't have Randall to—

"Alonzo, what are you doing out here?" Simone's heels clicked across the limestone until she was standing before him, stunning in a strapless floral dress. "You do realize there's a party happening inside, in your honor?"

"I told you I didn't want a party, Simone." He looked at her. "You knew I wasn't in the mood."

"It's your birthday." She stared down at him. "Your mom and I planned this party hoping it would put you in a better mood."

"You and my mom." Alonzo nodded. "But throwing a surprise party was your idea, wasn't it? And you created the guest list, contacted everyone, *including* Amber's housemate, who I'm not even close to." He eyed her. "That was your goal, to put me in a better mood? Or was it more strategic than that?"

"What are you talking about, Alonzo?" She folded her arms. "I took time out of my busy schedule to do something for you because I care about you, and you're trying to find an ulterior motive?"

"You've been upset ever since that thing with Amber in Texas—"

"Oh, she knew exactly what she was doing, telling the world—me especially—that the two of you were together that night." Simone cut her eyes away. "She's been jealous of me ever since I got that part she desperately wanted. Of all people for you to hook up with—"

"Simone, do you know how trivial this is?"

"Is it really? Sleeping with Amber was trivial? I guess sleeping with me is trivial too. Who else are you sleeping with, Alonzo? Doesn't matter, does it? Because it's all trivial—*meaningless*—to you."

"That's not what I meant."

"It's exactly what you meant."

He stood, walking closer to the pool, feeling suffocated by his own life. Maybe relationships *were* trivial in his mind. What did that say about him?

"You're just going to stay out here and ignore your guests?"

Alonzo turned, walked toward her. "Listen, I'm sorry. I appreciate your throwing this party for me. I do. And I do care about you. I don't want you to think you're trivial to me."

Simone stared at him a moment. "I know it's been a rough week for you." She wrapped her arms around him. "Apology accepted." She kissed him. "But it's your special day. You should enjoy it."

He nodded. "You're right. Let's go."

They walked back inside through the patio doors, where music was pumping through the sound system and servers passed hot hors d'oeuvres.

"A.C.!"

Alonzo looked, smiling when he saw one of the first guys he'd met in Hollywood. "I know that's not Corey. Mr. Can't-Return-a-Phone-Call."

"I'm here when it counts, though." Corey hugged him. "For free food and drinks."

Alonzo caught up with him and other new faces that had arrived, glad he'd come inside.

"You still upset with me?" His mom pulled him aside.

"Momma, no, I wasn't upset with you." He put an arm around her. Several inches shorter with a closely-cropped Afro, his mom was his favorite girl. "I was trying to figure out how all this came together. You have to be careful, giving people access to the house."

"But it was Simone," she said. "How many times has she been here?"

"Always with me, though," Alonzo said. "Not alone. You know I'm not comfortable with people trying to get close to you, asking favors."

"I think you're being paranoid," she said. "She needed to set up. It was all for you."

A server handed him a flute of champagne, and Alonzo glanced around, seeing hands filled with them around the room. Someone muted the music, and Shane walked to the center of the gathering.

"A toast," Shane said, holding up his glass, "to one of my closest friends, a man I admire greatly. We have yet to see all that's inside of you. You have a gift, my brother, and it's deep and wide. Here's to many more years on this earth and many more films—that hopefully I'll get to direct you in."

Glasses went high, clinking with others to the sound of "Cheers!"

Shane joined him following the toast. "Nice to see a genuine smile on your face," he said. "Not the one you had when you walked through the door."

"I should've known you'd be able to read that," Alonzo said. "Simone convinced me to get in here and have a good time."

"I'm impressed," Shane said. "You didn't even let her post bother you."

Alonzo's jaw tightened. "I don't even want to know."

Shane gave him a look. "Yeah, you probably do."

Alonzo pulled his phone from his pocket and pulled up Simone's Instagram profile. She sat propped against the headboard in Alonzo's bed, similar to Amber's pose, with the caption, "Sending birthday love to my favorite actor and friend. Happy 28th."

Alonzo walked over to Simone and showed her the picture.

"What?" Simone said. "Nobody will know where I am—unless they've been to your bedroom."

"I don't get it," he said. "You could've taken the picture at your house. Why would you take it here in my bedroom and post it?"

"Because she needs to know—being with you on your birthday in your house is greater than a random night at a Texas hotel."

Alonzo stared at her a moment, then looked vaguely into the faces of his guests. "I take full responsibility for how ridiculous this has gotten," he said. "Lets me know how out of control my life is." He lifted his hands. "I'm done."

He walked away, frustration, grief, and sadness mixing into a fiery ball within. He wanted to head back outside but saw his space overtaken by guests. He took the steps instead, moving upstairs to the second level, where his manager was coming out of an office bedroom.

"I was just coming to find you." Beverly looked into his eyes. "What's wrong?"

He shook his head. "What's up?"

"I've been on a conference call with the studio for the past hour," she said. "The Randall Rogers story is gaining in coverage, due to its heroic nature and being so close to the release of the movie. They've decided to hold the very first premiere of the movie in St. Louis, in his honor." She glanced at the papers in her hands. "You won't be able to attend, so what we'll need from you is a special video tribute to be played before the start of the movie."

"Why won't I be able to attend?"

"You'll be in Italy presenting at that charity ball."

Alonzo shook his head. "I don't care what we have to do. I'm not missing a special premiere of this movie in honor of Randall. I'm going to St. Louis."

CHAPTER 17

The vacuum droned beautifully on a Saturday night. Cinda ran it every night room to room, content to shut out the world. It's what she'd always loved about cleaning—the escape. And an escape was what she needed more and more.

In the morning she'd see her mother's face, watch her take her last breath. In the quiet of night she'd hear Randall's voice. And in the hours in between she fought to sidestep them both, certain grief would swallow her whole.

She had no one. With each passing day that reality stalked her, especially in this house. Her presence was unwanted, that was certain. And she couldn't blame Janice or the twins. She wondered herself what she was still doing there. Then again, she knew. Holding on—to everything new that she'd lost so soon. New memories. New good feelings. New habits.

Her heart dipped as she slowed the vacuum near Randall's office, the one room she hadn't touched since his death. Taking a deep breath, she ventured in. She could do this. She had to do this.

She moved the vacuum back and forth, focusing on the grooves in the carpet, under the table, to the far side of the room. Then finally, his desk, her eyes resting on his chair. She could see his smile, the way he threw his head back when he laughed. Her eyes closed as she gripped the vacuum handle, thinking about what his last moments must have—

Don't go there, Cinda.

She shut off the vacuum and lowered herself into his chair. "I miss you, Daddy," she whispered.

A faint smile appeared as her eyes fell on his desk. He hadn't been the neatest person. Cinda had spent a full Saturday helping him organize it all, and days later it had fallen into disarray again.

"Really?" She picked up a pile of legal magazines a decade old from the edge of his desk. They'd gone back and forth about them, Cinda insisting he was hoarding useless clutter. Randall had muttered some excuse as to why he'd held onto them, ultimately agreeing to toss them into the recycling bin—and had somehow sneaked them back onto his desk.

She set them back down and spied a single sheet of notebook paper with a name written across it—*Lucinda*. She lifted it, her heart in her throat. She'd never liked her given name. The subject came up one night and Randall Googled it, curious what it meant. Seconds later he'd looked at her with a glimmer in his eye. "It means light," he'd said, and proceeded to write it by hand on that piece of paper.

Cinda's eyes filled. She folded it and looked for a pen to jot the date on which he'd written it. With all this clutter, how could there be nothing to write with? She opened the drawer, sifting— and her heart stopped.

She blinked, wondering if she was seeing things. Was that Janice, with another man? She lifted a group of photos paper-clipped together. The one on top showed Janice standing on a doorstep in his arms. Cinda looked at the others, all some version of Janice and this man. The date stamp on the photos indicated they'd been taken two weeks before Randall's death.

She put them back and rose from the desk, tucking the *Lucinda* note in her pocket. *What must Janice be going through?* She resumed vacuuming, thinking how Janice's attitude had grown worse toward her. It wasn't shocking. She'd only tolerated Cinda before. But if her affair had continued right up to Randall's death—what kind of turmoil would that bring? In an odd way Cinda felt sorry for her.

Finished with the office, she worked her way toward the family room. She shut off the vacuum to find a closer outlet and heard voices.

"Momma, this can't be real," Jordyn was saying. "The movie will premiere right here in St. Louis?"

"In honor of your dad," Janice said. "They'll still have the Hollywood premiere as scheduled, but this one will be a full red carpet affair too. And afterward, a special tribute from the cast and members of the community, plus food, dancing, everything."

"I hate that it's all because Daddy's gone," Jade said. "But it's incredible that they'd do this. And you know I have to know—did they say whether Alonzo Coles is coming? Please tell me he's coming."

"Alonzo Coles will be right here in St. Louis."

"This is crazy," Jordyn said. "And since Dad is being honored, that means *we'll* have a place of honor, which means we'll surely get some face time with Alonzo Coles."

"But that's not all," Janice said. *"Entertainment Now* wants to come into our home the day of the premiere and interview Randall's family."

"You're saying we're going to be featured on *Entertainment Now?"* Jade said. "I can't even process all this."

"Wait, when is all this happening?" Jordyn said. "What's the date of the premiere?"

"Three weeks," Janice said.

Cinda moved toward them. "This sounds amazing," she said. "I know the tributes will be uplifting. I'll be able to go, right?"

Janice looked at her. "We were only allotted three tickets for our household."

"But . . . I'm sure if you simply told them—"

"Told them what?" Janice said. "That a daughter of Randall's recently surfaced?" She shook her head. "He would go from being a hero to a guy who fathers children around the globe."

"That's not true at all," Cinda said.

"Bottom line, the focus would shift," Janice said. "I plan to honor his memory by keeping it quiet."

Cinda fought to keep tears from her eyes.

"Also," Janice said, "we should talk about your plans. I'm sure you don't see yourself staying here long term. Are you moving on to Houston?"

"I'm not sure what I'll do," Cinda said. "But no, I wasn't planning to stay here."

"I'd been thinking another month would work," Janice said, "so you could save up and plan your transition. But with *Entertainment Now* filming here in three weeks, it makes sense to let that be our date."

Cinda nodded, turning quickly as the first tear fell. She left the vacuum where it stood and went up to her bedroom, closing the door. Why did it feel like she'd been severed from Randall? No premiere, no tangible reminders, once she was gone from the house. She should have taken more pictures with him, and video. How long before his voice faded from memory?

She swiped her face, catching a glimpse of a postcard on the nightstand—*Grand Opening & Open House ~ Promises Bed-and-Breakfast*. She'd seen it in the mail pile and saved it since it was just around the corner, thinking it could be a possible second job. But that was before, when she was putting down roots in St. Louis. Still, she needed a job, and if she could find one right here . . . She snatched it up and checked the date. *Today.*

Without thinking she jumped up, threw a baseball cap over her twists and tennis shoes on her feet, and headed out. The sun had set, so she walked with quick steps, hoping the open house hadn't ended. In less than ten minutes she was walking up to the B and B.

The house was gorgeous, like the Rogers home, directly across from Lafayette Park. Taking a breath, Cinda rang the doorbell and waited.

A woman answered. "Hi, you're here for the open house?"

"I actually . . . Well, I wondered if I could apply for a job."

"Oh," she said. "Okay. Come on in."

The woman led her to a dining area filled with people. Cinda stood just outside, waiting.

Another woman came and ushered her into the kitchen, extending her hand. "Hi, I'm Stephanie London, caretaker of Promises Bed-and-Breakfast."

Cinda was suddenly nervous. Had she thought this through? What did she even look like, since she'd been cleaning all day? "Cinda," she said, lightly shaking her hand.

"And you're looking for a job here?"

"I heard you just opened, and you probably have all the help you need." Cinda felt discouraged already. Of course they had the help they needed. "But it's a big house, and if you need help cleaning it . . ."

"Are you with a cleaning service?"

"No," Cinda said. "It's just me."

Stephanie focused on her a moment. "Do you have references?"

Cinda hesitated. "How would I have references?"

"From the owners of the houses you've cleaned."

"Oh." Great. She didn't even have real experience. "No. I mainly just cleaned my own house. And the house where I live now. But I clean well. Everybody says so."

The woman looked less than convinced. "Everybody."

Cinda shrugged. It was all she had. "I'm just saying."

"Okay, first of all," the caretaker said, "you should've called and made an appointment instead of just showing up. At night. Who does that?" Her eyes swept Cinda from head to toe. "And you show up looking like you don't care one whit about your appearance and acting like you don't care too much whether you get the job. So—"

"No, I do care," Cinda said. "I need this job. Desperately. That's why I showed up like this." She had to think fast. "How about this? I'll clean this house for one week. If you like it, you pay me. If you don't, you got a week of the best cleaning job you'll ever see, for free." It had worked with Janice. Why not here too?

"You really want my expectations that high?"

"Yes, ma'am."

The woman paused, looking at her. "Deal. But we're not doing the ma'am thing. Just call me Stephanie. We need to talk about all the details, though. Can you be here tomorrow morning at nine?"

Cinda nodded. "I can be here at eight or eight thirty, if you want."

"Girl, nine is already pushing it for me."

"Yes, ma'am. I mean . . . nine it is." Cinda smiled. "Thank you."

She exhaled as she walked out the front door. She got the job. *She got the job.* Which meant she'd be staying in St. Louis, whatever *that* meant. She was just glad to—

"Hey! Cinda?"

She turned at the end of the walkway and looked back. "Miss Treva?"

Stephanie and the woman who had answered the door appeared behind Treva.

"Girl, we didn't recognize you with that hat pulled low," Stephanie said, "but Treva remembered your name. Randall's daughter, right? We're all from Living Hope Church. Come on back in here."

Cinda walked back toward them. "I'm sorry, I didn't recognize you either." Her heart beat a little faster. "So all of you knew Randall? It's amazing I happened to come here."

Treva hugged her and held tight. "Precious girl, I don't know you well, but I can tell you that you didn't just 'happen' to come here. I know deep in my heart—God sent you."

Cinda felt her grip tighten around Treva in a rush of emotion. That's the second time she'd heard that, the first from Randall. Could it be true? Did He see her? Did He care what she'd been going through? The sobs overrode her attempt at restraint. "I'm sorry," she said, her words choked. "I don't . . . mean to . . ."

"It's okay," Treva said. "Let it out." After a few moments, she put an arm around Cinda and led her further inside. "We'd love to spend some time getting to know you. Randall was family. That means you're family too."

CHAPTER 18

"I need you and Cecil to sell your house, move to St. Louis, and buy something within a mile of us." Treva poured her sister a cup of coffee and handed it to her. "I didn't think I'd miss your behind this much."

"It's terrible." Jillian sat on the bar stool, adding cream. "Sometimes I'll think *Let me run by Treva's real quick*, then I'm like *Ugh*." She tasted and added more. "Tommy's wedding couldn't have come at a better time. I couldn't wait for this weekend to get here. And who knew all of you would be so close?"

"Crazy, right?" Treva said. "I hardly knew Tommy in college—he was *your* friend. Now I see why. He's good people; his brother, too."

"Yesterday was my first time meeting Reggie," Jillian said. "And you know I had to ask Faith what the deal was. She was out with Reggie last night, and said she and Jesse had plans for today."

"She and Reggie are like siblings," Treva said. "They squabble and get on each other's nerves, but they've got this bond." She leaned against the counter. "Faith and Jesse—you know the deal. Complicated. But looks like they're working on a friendship." She looked over as Cecil came into the kitchen. "Hey, Cecil, I'm about to fix breakfast. Can I get you some coffee?"

"Good morning," Cecil said. He gave Jillian a kiss. "No time for breakfast," he said. "Lance and I are getting some work done at the church."

"Really?" Treva said.

"Oh, yeah," Lance said, coming in to the kitchen. "When you've got a brother-in-law who's a handyman, and he offers to help? You move quickly."

"But how are you doing that, babe?" Treva said. "They're setting up over there for a two o'clock wedding, and you're in it."

"We'll work every place but the sanctuary," Lance said, "and if we're running late, at least I'm there. I'll go stand up front."

Treva shook her head at him. "Not at all, sir. I need you to keep an eye on the time so you can get back here and get changed. You wearing that black suit is everything."

He came and put his arms around her waist. "I remember what happened when I tried on the suit," he said in a whisper, then kissed her lobe. "Maybe I need to build in more time."

She whispered back. "Two words—yes and amen."

"All right, Cecil, let's get it moving." Lance winked at her over his shoulder. "We'll hurry back."

Jillian was smiling at her once they'd left.

"What?" Treva said.

"You two are like youngsters in love. I love it."

"Girl, I've never felt farther from 'youngster.'" Treva poured herself another cup. "I'm inching closer to menopause. I was reading up on the symptoms and nodding my head—fatigue, breast soreness, lack of a cycle."

Jillian sipped her coffee. "Which happen also to be signs of pregnancy."

"That's hilarious." Treva took out a skillet. "If I thought it remotely possible that I could be forty-six and pregnant, I'd faint."

"Couple years ago," Jillian said, "a neighbor of mine had a baby at forty-seven. Total surprise."

"Still, it's statistically improbable, right?" She nodded, convincing herself. "I never had to think about it before because Hezekiah got a vasectomy after Hope. And with Lance, it never entered my mind that I could . . ." Her heart pounded suddenly. "It can't be."

"There's an easy way to find out."

Treva sighed as the doorbell rang. "Can you get that, Jill?" She got out eggs, spinach, and other ingredients to make omelets.

"Hey!" Jillian said as she opened the door. "So good to see you two!"

Treva turned toward the chatter as they hugged and greeted one another. "Cyd and Stephanie stopping by early morning? Steph, I thought you had a B and B to run."

"Girl, hush," Stephanie said, walking toward her. "I'm depressed I don't have any guests yet."

"It's the first full weekend," Treva said. "Watch. Soon people'll be complaining because you're always booked."

"I'm looking forward to seeing it tonight." Jillian moved to the kitchen table with Stephanie. "We're still having our girls' night, aren't we?"

"Right after the wedding," Stephanie said. "Get changed and head on over."

Cyd took a seat at the table. "I haven't seen you since Hawaii, Jillian. What have you been up to?"

"Same ol' same ol'," Jillian said. "Four kids—three teens—keep me hopping 24/7."

"Um, ma'am?" Stephanie said. "Same ol' same ol'? You better get to testifying in here about that date night life."

"Ooh, tell us," Cyd said.

"Stephanie, Dana, and I are still doing the 'praying wives call' we started after the conference last year," Jillian said. "You know Cecil and I had issues. One thing was date nights had been a fail.

We prayed on the call for us to be able to make it a priority and stick to it." She lifted her hands and did a little dance. "Going on three months straight, every week."

"Woo!" sounded in the kitchen.

"I need to be taking notes," Treva said. "Lance and I haven't been proactive about making that happen every week."

"Girl, what?" Stephanie said. "You two stay on a date. Room can be crowded and you'll find a way to make a private moment."

"That's what I told her," Jillian said. "They're like youngsters."

Treva felt her stomach cramp, thinking about the conversation with Jillian minutes before. *Lord, I'm almost fifty. I'm just saying. Please let there be nothing to this.*

"Can I get you two some coffee?" Treva said. "Juice?"

"We just had breakfast," Stephanie said. "Cyd let me try one of my recipes on her for the B and B."

"It was good too," Cyd said, smiling. "And I got her to come with me, since Jillian's here. But here's what's on my mind. You see it's May, and we didn't have another women's conference."

"I was bummed about that," Jillian said. "I hoped it would be an annual thing."

"We were overwhelmed by the response," Cyd said, "even from women who couldn't attend but heard about it or watched video clips online. But instead of diving into planning another conference, we started planning an entire ministry under the umbrella of Living Word. Books and Bible studies written by and for women. A blog with content created by women. And yes, annual conferences down the road."

"That's exciting," Jillian said. "When do you plan to kick off all of this?"

"We have lots to do yet," Cyd said, "but right now we're approaching people to write the books and Bible studies that we'll launch with." She looked at Treva. "That's where you come in."

"Me?" Treva said. "How?"

"We'd love for you to prayerfully consider writing a Bible study. We talked about you in our meeting yesterday."

Treva's brow bunched. "Why would my name come up?"

Cyd pulled a notebook from her bag. "Because of this." She handed it to her.

Her eyes widened. "I was looking for that."

"Lance brought it to the meeting," Cyd said. "He wanted us to see what a serious student of the Word you are. Girl, reading through that notebook was a study all by itself."

"These are just notes I take," Treva said. "It's nothing special."

"Lance knew you'd say that," Cyd said. "He also knew you wouldn't take it seriously if he suggested it. That's why he wanted us to see it." She pointed at the notebook. "You have a gift. I can tell from the insights you've written. Trust me, it's special."

Jillian looked at her sister. "Mm-hm. I told you God had something new for you in this season."

Treva thought to herself a moment. "I don't know," she said. "I'll definitely have to pray about it. 'Student' is more my speed."

"And I hope you stay a student," Cyd said, "while you add this other role."

Treva squeezed toothpaste onto her brush, thinking about the day. She'd never had more fun at a wedding, even with tears as Tommy and Allison spoke at the reception about Randall. And girls' night at the B and B had been perfect, especially since they'd picked up Cinda to join them. But now, in the late-night quiet of her bathroom, she was feeling unsettled.

She began brushing, her mind in a million directions. What would she say to Lance? When would she say it? And how would he respond? Whenever she thought about what this all could mean—

She glanced in the mirror, and there he was.

He hugged her from behind. "We couldn't follow through with our plan earlier."

She spit into the sink. "Somebody lost track of time at church."

"I knew exactly what time it was," Lance said. "Every time I tried to tiptoe out, another fire erupted." He kissed her cheek. "But the day's not over."

She set the toothbrush on the sink, staring down at it.

He turned her around, looked into her eyes. "What's wrong, babe?"

She heaved a sigh. "I um . . . bought a pregnancy test today."

Lance looked dazed for a moment. "I had no idea you thought you might be . . . What are you saying?"

"I told Jillian about symptoms I was having of *menopause,* and she tossed in pregnancy as a possibility, which seemed *so* farfetched, but then I was gripped with *What if?* and drove to the drugstore—"

"Treva, did you take the test?"

She shook her head, buried inside his chest. "I'm afraid. What if it's positive? Lance, I'm too old to have a baby. And the chances of complications are exponentially—"

He tipped her chin up and quieted her with a kiss. "Let's not deal with speculation. One step at a time. Let's find out, right now."

Treva took the test from the cabinet and read the back. "This thing boasts results in one minute. Like I want to know that fast." She looked at Lance. "I want you to be the one to read it when I'm done."

Lance stepped out, and Treva's heartbeat went erratic as she read and followed the directions. By the time she'd flushed the toilet and washed her hands, she was certain the result showed on the stick, but she couldn't bring herself to look at it. She opened the door, handed it to Lance, and held her breath.

Lance looked at it, staring, his head moving in a vague sort of nod.

"What does *that* mean?" Treva said.

He looked up. "Babe. We're having a baby."

Treva's eyes fell, and she walked around him a little ways. "I don't even know what to say. My child just had a child. I'm enjoying being a grandmother. Now *I'm* pregnant? This can't be real." She imagined months of getting bigger, doctor appointments, labor and delivery, sleepless nights, while knocking on the door of fifty—and thought she might hyperventilate. She turned finally. "Why are you so quiet? What's going through your mind?"

"I don't think you want to know."

"You're happy."

"Ecstatic."

"That's because you're young," Treva said, walking toward him. "Remember I told you you should marry someone younger so you could have a family? Remember I said we're in two different seasons of life? *Of course* you're happy . . . while I'm wondering if I can even survive this."

Lance took her hand and pulled her close. "Did you just tell me I should've married someone else?"

Treva looked away. "You know that's not what I was saying."

"I'm glad you cleared that up. I thought you were suggesting that the woman I gave my entire self to, the one I love more than life itself, who's now pregnant with my child—is not the woman for me." He kissed her. "I love you, baby. We're not on separate sides. We're in this together."

"I know," Treva said. "My mind is just . . . overwhelmed right now."

Lance wrapped his arms tighter. "Then I say we go to bed and put our minds on other things."

"That's how we got into this." She sighed. "Honestly, I just want to go to sleep."

She turned down the covers, got in the bed, and closed her eyes, knowing sleep was probably the last thing she'd be able to do.

CHAPTER 19

$\mathcal{F}$aith licked ice cream from the side of her waffle cone to keep it from dripping. "Why am I having so many issues," she said, catching it between her fingers now, "and your cone is just fine?"

"Because I got real ice cream." Jesse sat on a bench outside the ice cream shop. "You got that frozen yogurt stuff."

"I'm pretty sure 'real ice cream' melts just the same." Faith sat beside him, taking in the balmy night. "You think Zoe woke up yet?"

"I doubt it," Jesse said. "It's only been twenty minutes. You worried?"

"Not really," Faith said. "I fed her again just before we left, and we won't be gone long. Plus Joy and Hope are both on bottle duty."

She thought about that. Twice today, she and Jesse had been out together, without Zoe. Before, feeding the baby was Faith's reason for spending time with him. She didn't know what reason she'd give, now that Zoe was learning to take a bottle.

Jesse chuckled. "I couldn't believe she was screaming her head off when we came in from the movies, giving Joy the blues. She said, 'I'll starve to death before I take that bottle.'"

Faith laughed. "Got the nerve to be picky. That little girl better eat."

"She gets it from her momma." Jesse held his cone in front of her. "Taste it."

She wrinkled her nose. "You know I don't like food in my ice cream."

"It's only pistachios." He crunched into his cone.

"All ground up and mixed in. Yuck." She finished her cone and wiped her hands, tossing the napkin into the trash can. "So you're driving back right after Zoe's dedication tomorrow?"

"Yeah," Jesse said. "I've got end-of-semester papers and projects due. Also," he said, looking at her, "I got word last week that I got a summer position—in DC."

"So you're going back home," Faith said. "Makes sense."

"It's a great opportunity with an engineering firm, but I hate that I'll be so far from Zoe."

"It's only for the summer. It'll pass quickly."

"But I'm already wondering about next year when I graduate. What if I get a job that's far from here?"

"Anything can happen," Faith said. "*I* might get a job that's far from here. Zoe and I could be anywhere. We'll just have to work to make sure she spends time with you, wherever we happen to be."

Jesse looked at her. "Sometimes I think, what if you get married and another man is Zoe's primary influence."

Faith was quiet a moment. "That's just reality. Just like you'll get married and have kids who'll see you every day, while Zoe only has a handful of weeks a year."

Jesse stared into the distance before looking back at her. "But sometimes I also think—what if Zoe's able to grow up with her family, with her mom and her dad."

Faith let her gaze follow a passerby.

"You don't have a comment?" Jesse said.

"What's there to say?"

"The thought of us being together *never* crosses your mind?"

"I didn't say that," Faith said. "But the three of us as a family? Say it out loud, Jesse—you're talking *marriage*. And you're nowhere near ready for marriage. Or any form of commitment."

He gave her a look.

"Am I wrong?"

He sighed. "True, I'm not ready for marriage. And I admit, commitment isn't my strong suit either. It's just . . . When I'm down here around you two, it's hard to hold back what I'm feeling. My heart takes over."

"Well, you'll have an entire summer away from us to rein it back in." She got up. "Ready to head back?"

She walked toward Jesse's car and waited for him to open the passenger door. He paused by it instead, inches from her face.

"You think a summer away from you is going to rein my heart back in?" He tugged her fingers, pulling her closer. "Like it or not, Faith, I still love you."

His lips touched hers for the first time in a year. Her heart hammered as they kissed again, more deeply.

"I've been wanting to do that for a long time," he said, holding her. "You mad at me?"

"How can I be mad? I kissed you back, didn't I?"

He kissed her once more, then opened her door, holding it for her. Faith tried to catch her breath as she got in.

Jesse climbed into the driver's seat and headed the car toward the house.

Faith looked at him. "Did I ever tell you you were my first kiss?"

Jesse glanced at her, then back to the road. "I never knew that."

"The first time you kissed me," she said, "I didn't know if I was doing it right, and I felt awkward and had all these butterflies."

She turned her gaze to the window. "For some reason it all came back. The awkward and the butterflies."

Jesse grew quiet for the rest of the short drive. In front of the house, he turned off the engine but didn't move. He looked at her. "I always knew you were special. And I hate that I didn't know what to do with that. I didn't know how to treat *special*."

Faith listened, trying to rein her own heart in.

"But I want to get there," he said. "I don't know anyone like you, Faith. The way I feel about you—it's different from anyone else. I just hope you don't say *never* when it comes to us."

Faith stood beside Jesse at the front of the church, Zoe in his arms, as Lance prayed a final prayer over the baby.

"And Lord, we pray that Your thoughts would be Zoe's thoughts, and Your ways would be her ways. We pray she loves You with her whole heart and that she knows Jesus as her Lord and Savior from an early age." Lance paused. "And I pray, Lord, that her parents, Faith and Jesse, live lives that are devoted to You, setting the example of what it means to follow after You. May Zoe see in them a strong love for Jesus that's reflected in all that they do. In Jesus' name."

"Amen" rang throughout the church.

Lance said the final benediction and dismissed the church, with people coming to hug them and the baby.

A woman Faith didn't know approached. "She looks absolutely adorable in her frilly white dress." She played with Zoe's fingers, smiling at her. "What a sweetheart."

Faith smiled. "Thank you so much."

"Beautiful family," one guy said, shaking Jesse's hand. "I'm a visitor today and had to tell you how nice it is to see a dad embracing his role and taking care of the main thing—raising your child to know the Lord. God bless you."

Faith watched Jesse give a sober nod as the man walked away.

The area was somewhat crowded now with people—many also coming to talk to Lance—but Faith caught Reggie's eye a little ways away. She waved him over.

"Hey, stranger," she said.

"Didn't I just see you Friday night?" Reggie said.

"But you usually find a way to bug me daily, by text if nothing else."

"I think you're confused about who's bugging who," he said. "But I had the wedding yesterday, and you were busy with other things." He glanced at Jesse, who was talking to someone. "How did it go?"

"It was um . . . interesting," she said. "I'll tell you about it after—"

"It's good to see you again, Faith."

She looked, unable to believe her eyes—the woman she'd caught Jesse with a year ago. "Brandy?"

Jesse spied her at the same time and moved to where they were. "What are you doing here, B? You drove down from Chicago?"

Brandy's green eyes took in the baby in Jesse's arms. "Wow, she looks just like you, Jess. You aren't going to introduce me?"

Jesse looked perplexed. "Brandy, I don't know what this is about or how you knew where to find me—"

"What this is about," Brandy said, "is a little update." She stood between Faith and Jesse, shorter than both. "Last year I was in the dark about the fact that Faith was expecting your baby, and she was kind enough to let me know. I figured this time around she might be in the dark about *our* situation."

"We're in a church," Jesse said, stepping closer to Brandy, "celebrating my baby's dedication—"

"No, let her finish," Faith said.

Brandy trained her eyes on Faith. "Did you know Jesse and I are living together? I know you think because you had his baby, the three of you can be one big happy family—I saw pictures of you all out and about over spring break. But you need to recognize that *I'm* the woman in Jesse's life."

"Brandy, stop." Jesse spoke in a low voice. "This is not the time or the place—"

"Tell me what the right time and place is then, Jess . . ."

Faith glanced around as they went back and forth. Brandy's tone had drawn a couple of curious looks, but there were so many pockets of conversation, most didn't notice.

Reggie leaned in, whispered in her ear. "Just tell me what you need me to do. I'm not going anywhere."

"You should know," Brandy said, looking at Faith, "Jesse and I are looking for a place in DC because I just graduated and have a position there. He got a summer position out there as well—to be near me. That's what couples do, plan their lives together. I need you to plan yours accordingly." She looked at Jesse. "I'll be waiting outside."

She walked off, moving through the crowd in high heels and skinny jeans.

"Faith, please," Jesse said, "don't take her words to heart. She's upset, jealous about Zoe—"

Faith reached for the baby, taking her from Jesse. "I need to leave."

"Nothing I've said to you was untrue," Jesse said. "It's just that Brandy—"

Faith held up a hand. "I don't want to hear it. I don't care."

She turned to walk away, and Jesse turned her back around.

"I need you to hear me out," he said. "Just a few minutes."

Faith looked at Reggie, and he stepped in, putting an arm around her and ushering her and Zoe away. She picked up her things, including the diaper bag, and made her way out.

Stephanie came toward her up the aisle. "Was that that girl Brandy?" she said. Stephanie had been the one to discover last year that Brandy and Jesse were seeing one another. "What is she doing here?"

"I'll tell you later," Faith said. She sighed, realizing the direction they were going. "I don't feel like seeing her outside."

"Take the back exit," Stephanie said.

Reggie led her out of a back door and walked her to her car.

She secured Zoe in the back seat and turned to him. "Did you have plans for after church?"

"Almost everybody flew back this morning, so no real plans."

Emotion from the confrontation caught up with her. "Can we do something? Go somewhere?"

"You're getting good at this damsel in distress thing." He wiped a tear from her face. "You're my sis. I'm here for whatever you need."

CHAPTER 20

*A*lonzo walked onto the set of the late-night show as the audience applauded. He shook host Brandon Kiel's hand, laughing as he added extra hand and arm motions. "Ah, I see you remembered," Alonzo said. He'd taught him the shake on his last visit. Alonzo turned, acknowledging the audience, and took his seat as female voices extended the welcome.

Brandon leaned back, letting it go on. "You know, Alonzo," he said, "I've been meaning to tell you—you really need to work on your rapport with the ladies."

The shouts got louder, and Alonzo lowered his head a little, motioning for quiet. "Okay, this is awkward."

"Is it really?" Brandon said, having fun with it. "So what was it like for, let's say, sixteen-year-old Alonzo? Were all the girls chasing after you?"

The audience quieted now, listening for his response.

"Are you kidding?" Alonzo sat back, casual in jeans and a black tee. "I was the kid who was in all the school plays, loved Shakespeare and whatnot—which was *not* cool. The cool guys in my school played sports. *And* I wore glasses and had crooked teeth. The girls ran the *other* way when they saw me."

Brandon came forward in his chair. *"Really?* I can't quite picture that—oh, wait"—he looked around—"maybe we *do* have a picture."

Alonzo shook his head, already chuckling. "You're gonna do me like that, Brandon?"

The picture came on the screen, young Alonzo with a semi-Afro, glasses, and a closed-mouth smile, which he always wore to hide his teeth.

The audience gasped, laughing as Alonzo stared at the screen in disbelief.

"Just wait, Mom," he said, laughing with the audience. "Just wait."

"But because we're nice people," Brandon said, "we'll also preview *People* magazine's next issue. You're in it, as one of the hottest men in Hollywood."

The magazine spread came on screen, Alonzo in a short-sleeved shirt that showcased his muscles, igniting renewed shouts and applause.

"Just goes to show you," Alonzo said, "what braces, Lasik, and some weightlifting can do."

"In all seriousness, though," Brandon said, "we wanted to touch on your growing-up years because that's what your latest movie is about—the evolution of a young man's life. And it's a pretty complicated evolution."

Alonzo nodded. "Absolutely."

"You're starring in *Bonds of Time*—his first leading role, by the way." Brandon waited for applause to die down. "The movie already had a good deal of buzz, but now even more so because of the tragic shooting of the man who wrote the book on which the movie is based."

Alonzo nodded soberly. "Randall Rogers," he said. "It was devastating, what happened. I had just seen him that day."

Brandon's eyes widened. "That very day?"

"He came out to LA, and we did a photo shoot for the movie."

Alonzo stared once more as pictures of himself and Randall came on-screen.

"He's a hero," Alonzo said. "That man is a hero."

The audience gave a standing ovation for Randall, clearly familiar with the story.

Brandon continued, "So four days from now—this Friday—there will be a special premiere of the movie in St. Louis, Randall's home. You were scheduled to be out of the country, but changed your plans to be there. Why?"

"To honor him," Alonzo said. "Even apart from his heroic deed, Randall Rogers was just one of those people who makes your life tilt a different way because of the way he impacted it. At least, that's how it was for me. I have to be there." He added, "And I look forward to meeting the people who impacted him—his family, of course, but I also want to meet people like his pastor."

Brandon had a curious look. "His pastor?"

"I know," Alonzo said. "Sounds crazy, doesn't it?" He nodded to himself. "Yeah. Definitely."

"Well, there you have it, St. Louis," Brandon said. "Alonzo Coles on a mission in your city, this Friday." He looked into the camera. "Be back after the break with more."

Alonzo lay in bed late that night, unable to sleep. What had gotten into him, putting out a call on national television to meet Randall's pastor? And say what? *I'm generally confused about everything these days and was hoping Randall could help me. Now I'm wondering—can you?* He groaned inside. Lame.

Besides, things had unfolded so naturally with Randall. Those dynamics were rare. And the nice thing about Randall was that he *wasn't* a pastor. He was normal. Relatable.

Still . . . He stared at the ceiling. He couldn't deny the void he felt. Something in him was reaching out, even if he didn't know exactly what he was reaching for.

He got up and walked out onto the balcony in his bedroom, looking into the night sky. *It's been a long time, God.* He exhaled, those few words enough to transport him. *I don't really know what to say. I feel like I just . . . I need You, Lord. I need You.*

My dreams are all coming true. Those prayers I prayed for a big break? You answered them. And then some. But why do I feel so empty?

He paused at that. It was the first time the thought had come to him, but it was true.

Randall said I need to get to know You. I don't know what that looks like. Could you help me, God? He sighed at his own prayer. God was supposed to help Alonzo get to know Him? It didn't even make sense. But he didn't know what else to do.

He stood on the balcony a little longer, then walked back inside and glanced at his phone. He picked it up and opened to the single text convo he'd had with Randall.

Shooting u a text already...no clue where to start in my Bible... Thoughts? really appreciate u...

Alonzo, I recommend the Gospel of John. Read Psalms with it. And pray for understanding. Here for you, son.

Alonzo read the exchange three times until his eyes glazed over. He turned on the bedside lamp and opened one drawer then another, looking for his Bible. No telling where it was. Picking up his phone again, he downloaded a Bible app and clicked *John* from the books listed.

A text popped in overtop it. Simone. Alonzo read it: **Still up? Still upset with me? I miss you. Let's talk. I can come over.**

Alonzo edited different responses in his head. He wasn't upset, but if he opened up conversation, she could wind up at his door. And life was complicated enough.

Switching back to the app, he stretched across his bed and started reading. *In the beginning was the Word . . .*

CHAPTER 21

*C*inda combined baking soda with vinegar and poured it down the sink drain in one of the B and B's guest bathrooms, flushing several minutes with hot water. She sprayed the basin with a cleanser and wiped it down, then leaned in on the faucets, wiping carefully. Next she used dental floss to get the grime at the base of the faucet, then started on the marble countertops.

"Cinda!" Stephanie called. "Where are you? Girl, it worked!"

She moved out of the bathroom. "I'm in here," she said, moving into the second-floor hallway.

Stephanie was almost to the top of the stairs. "Two rooms got booked for this weekend," she said, beaming. "People coming into town for the premiere. And guess what? They found us from Google."

Cinda grinned. "I told you people would be searching for places to stay. And since downtown hotels got booked up . . ."

"You were so right." Stephanie looked stylish in an asymmetric tunic over jeans. "I still don't understand all that search engine stuff, but whatever you did put us near the top for places to stay in St. Louis."

Cinda shrugged. "I only Googled to find out what to do. It was easy."

"All the work you're doing to keep this place spotless. We'll finally have bodies to appreciate it."

"It'll be so different around here with actual guests," Cinda said.

"Oh, man, actual guests." Stephanie started back down. "That just hit me a different way. I better go grocery shopping."

"Um, Stephanie, can I ask a favor?"

She turned back. "What's up?"

"Is it possible to get paid this week instead of next?"

"Mrs. Cartwright writes the checks, but I'm sure it won't be a problem," Stephanie said. "You do a week's worth of cleaning in a day anyway."

Cinda exhaled. She'd been hesitant to ask. "Thanks. I need to put a rent deposit down."

"You're moving?"

Cinda nodded. "I found a room to rent in Tower Grove."

"Okay, I'm confused." Stephanie came closer. "You have two jobs, here and at your house. You can walk here from your house. But you're moving miles away, from both jobs. How does that make sense?"

"I had sort of a deadline to move out—this Friday," Cinda said. "After Friday, this will be my only job."

"They said you had to leave, and gave you a deadline? And the deadline is the day of the premiere?"

"It was time to go anyway. And Friday because *Entertainment Now* is coming to the house to do a special segment on Randall, interviewing his family and all that."

"And you won't be part of that?"

"Janice thought it would make Randall look bad, if people knew he had a daughter that showed up out of the blue."

Stephanie's brow went up. "O-kay . . . But you're going to the premiere, right?"

Cinda looked away. That part hurt. "No," she said. "I can't go."

"Wow," Stephanie said. "Well. Here's the deal. We've got three bedrooms in the owner's quarters upstairs. You can take the lavender one."

"That room is huge, with a private bath. There's no way I can afford that."

Stephanie looked at her. "Dear, you're not paying."

"Why would you do that?"

"We weren't playing when we told you that you're family," Stephanie said. "Stay as long as you want. And don't be cleaning up 24/7 either—live, rest, *be*. This is your home now."

"I don't know what to say," Cinda said. "Thank you so much." She paused. "Would you mind if I went ahead and moved in today?" She'd been growing more uncomfortable at the Rogers house by the day.

"Of course not," Stephanie said. "I'll help you. Let's go take care of it right now."

~

Cinda came through the front door with Stephanie, glad there were no cars in the driveway. Someone could have parked in the garage, but if she had to guess, the J's were out shopping for the big event. They'd hit the stores every day for the past week, vowing to find the perfect dress, perfect shoes, and perfect piece of jewelry. This morning they'd declared their mission more urgent, after Alonzo Coles confirmed their dream on late-night television—they'd get a special meet and greet with him.

"I don't have much," Cinda said, leading the way up the stairs. "It won't take long to pack up and get out of here." She started down the hall toward her room as the master bedroom door came open.

"What time tonight?" a male voice said.

"About ten," Janice said.

"Wear that sexy red lingerie."

"As if I'll have it on for any length—" Janice spotted her. "I thought you were at work."

Cinda paused, staring at the two of them. She recognized the man from the pictures in Randall's office. "I, um, came to get my things. I'm moving into the B and B."

The man whispered into her ear and moved to the stairs.

Cinda turned toward her bedroom.

"I know what you're thinking," Janice said.

Cinda glanced back as she opened the door. "It's none of my business."

"Life is complicated," Janice said. "And there's always more to a story. Your father wasn't perfect."

Cinda looked at her. "I'm not sure why you feel the need to explain—"

"I see it in your eyes—you're judging me."

Cinda frowned. "Are you sure it's not your own conscience bothering you?"

"My conscience is just fine."

Cinda shrugged. "Okay." She walked into the bedroom, Stephanie behind her.

"And how dare you even ask me that," Janice said, following, "as if I should feel guilty. You're just like Randall—start going to church, become holier than thou—"

"Janice, I can sort of tell you've been drinking," Cinda said. "And no, I'm not judging. I just think it's better if I don't engage right now."

"You know what?" Janice came closer. "Your Little Miss Perfect routine is wearing on me. You might've fooled Randall, but I think there's much more lurking beneath—"

"Okay, excuse me. I'm Stephanie London, we met at Randall's funeral."

Janice eyed her.

"This just keeps spiraling downward," Stephanie said. "Cinda only wants to get her things and get out of here. Can she do that? In peace?"

Janice glared at them both, then walked out, closing the door behind her.

Cinda sat on the bed with a sigh. "I was planning to thank her for letting me stay here and work here and . . . I still can't believe we saw what we saw, right here in the house."

"Randall was going through way more than I realized," Stephanie said.

Cinda nodded. "And I think Janice is going through way more than she realizes." She got up and started packing. "I was upset I couldn't go Friday night, but after what just happened . . . Who wants to see Randall being honored while Janice is acting like the devoted wife?" She thought a moment. "Maybe we can have our own tribute," she said. "When the movie comes out in theaters, will you go with me? Maybe a group of us can go and have dinner beforehand and share stories about him."

"That would be amazing," Stephanie said. "We'll do our own thing. Who needs *Entertainment Now?*"

"Or Alonzo Coles," Cinda said. "I'm so sick of hearing his name around here." She jumped up and started pulling clothes out of the drawer. "I feel better. I get to honor Randall after all."

CHAPTER 22

JUNE

*T*reva walked into the house, dropped her purse on the counter, and headed toward the stairs, thankful for Wednesday afternoon quiet. With Joy and Hope at school—their final week before summer break—and Faith over at the B and B, Treva was free to curl up in a ball and nap all afternoon.

"Treva," Lance called from behind, "you didn't say anything the whole ride home."

"I don't have words." She slowed her pace but kept moving. "Not the right ones anyway."

"So you're just gonna shut me out?"

She paused by the stairs, turning to him. "I'm not shutting you out, Lance. It was a lot. I just need . . . time." She started up.

"You've been saying that for days." He moved with her. "I thought seeing the doctor today would help. We were able to sit down with her, ask questions. And she said you're in excellent health." He paused at the top of the stairs. "Treva, we even got to hear our baby's heartbeat."

"You heard 'excellent health' and a heartbeat," Treva said. "I heard *fourteen weeks* pregnant. Here I am, thinking I'm going through the change, and an entire trimester has blown by. I'm trying to catch up with my own *life*." She started toward the bedroom. "Did you hear all the risks that kick in at my age—for me *and* the baby? I'm not only dealing with the shock of being pregnant and the shake-up of the season I *thought* I was in—let's throw in some serious health complications too."

She slipped out of her unbuttoned jeans and into sweat pants. "And nothing fits. So, yay."

"Babe, I agree it's a lot," Lance said, "and it came out of left field. But we don't have to live in fear about what could happen."

"Don't do that, Lance," she said. "Don't you dare try to get spiritual on me. I told you I didn't have the right words, that I needed time. But you wanted me to talk. So that's what you got—raw, unfiltered *me*. I'll get to spiritual eventually." She lay down, overcome in every way with fatigue.

Lance's phone buzzed and he glanced at it. "This is the studio rep. We need to RSVP about the premiere and the dinner."

"Of course you're going. You have to go."

"You're coming with me, right?"

"I want to, for Randall," Treva said. "I've just had zero energy to do anything."

Lance stood near the bed. "I have a meeting over at Living Word, but I don't want to leave you like this."

"I'll be fine," Treva said. "But you just reminded me." She turned over, looking at him. "Cyd said you recommended me to write a Bible study. Even if I would've considered it, this is clearly not the time. You can tell them I declined."

Lance sat next to her on the bed and rubbed her back, his eyes closed. He was praying for her, and she knew without a doubt she needed it.

He kissed her cheek. "I love you, babe."

Treva closed her eyes, willing herself to sleep. But once Lance had left, too much was stirring. Her mind, her heart, her body—everything seemed on edge.

Come to Me, all who are weary and heavy-laden, and I will give you rest.

Treva sat up a little, her pulse quickened. Those words threaded their way through her mind a second time, and she got up, getting her Bible from the nightstand. Sitting back on the bed, she tried to remember where that verse was, then glanced around for her phone so she could search—but it was downstairs in her purse. Then she spotted her notebook.

She grabbed it from the nightstand and flipped to the "promises" section she'd made. Skimming, skimming . . . There it was—*Come to Me, all who are weary and heavy-laden, and I will give you rest (Matthew 11:28).*

Treva opened her Bible to the passage and read it again. And again. And her heart was pricked. *Lord, I haven't come to You. I not only shut Lance out, I shut You out.* The realization saddened her.

I guess I'm resentful, Lord. You blessed me with an amazing husband, and I was enjoying my life. Enjoying him. Enjoying this season. My girls are growing toward independence, and I have freedom to do so many things. But now . . . She sighed, reality descending. *I want control, Lord. There. I said it. I want control over my life. This is huge—and I feel like You just dumped it on me without warning. And why, Lord? Why at this age? What are You doing?*

Treva read the words again, then got a pen and sat back on the bed, opening her notebook to a new page. She wrote the words *If I come . . .* and under it, *I will receive rest.*

Sighing, she stared into the distance. *Lord, I've been nothing but tired these past few days—mostly emotionally and mentally—and here You are, promising rest, if I will only come. Forgive me, Lord, for my attitude toward You and my husband. Forgive me for not wanting You to be sovereign over this season of my life. And help me, Lord, because I'm still not where I need to be—You know how I am.*

She slid to the floor, on her knees beside the bed. *I come, Lord, asking for Your grace and strength—and for joy, Lord. There's a* baby inside *of me. Life. And I have not celebrated, because I'm focused on* myself. Tears fell from her eyes. *Deliver me from myself, Lord. Help me to surrender to You and Your will. Thank You for the rest that You've promised . . .*

~

Treva waited in the kitchen for the door to open, dressed still in workout clothes, holding a series of hand-lettered signs—black Sharpie on poster board. As Lance inserted his key and walked in from the garage, she lifted the first one: I HAVE BETTER WORDS.

She peeked around the sign to catch his reaction. He had a wry smile that said he was waiting for the rest.

Treva flipped to the next one: I'M SORRY.

And the next: I LOVE YOU MORE.

She peeked again. The smile had reached his eyes.

She showed the last one: WE'RE HAVING A BABY!

Treva dropped the signs to the floor and went to him, wrapping her arms around his waist. Without a word she kissed him, and felt the warmth of his whole being enfolding her.

She stepped back, cutting short the kiss, and took his hand, leading him to their room, and proceeded to light candles all around.

Lance took it all in. "Definitely not what I was expecting when I walked through the door. Where is everybody?"

She returned to his arms. "Banished," she said. "Sent them out for pizza so I could focus."

He kissed her neck. "On what?"

"On the husband I haven't been showing proper attention. And the baby that's made up of the two of us." She looked at him. "I assumed I couldn't give you any children. This is a gift from God, and I wouldn't let you celebrate."

Lance's forehead fell softly into hers. "It's so overwhelming, for me too. The last thing I would've expected. A *baby*. No one even knows yet. Well, except Jillian."

"Yeah, the one who called it," she said. "We do need to announce it. We need prayer."

"This is all new to me," Lance said, "but I've been reading up on what to expect. I know this is hard, but I'm here for you, babe. I'm here to serve you, every step of the way."

He kissed her, letting it deepen slowly. Treva wondered how she could still get so lost in him. Her hands caressed the back of his head as his hands massaged her back.

"Lance," she said, pulling back suddenly, "did you tell them I wasn't doing the Bible study?"

He gave her a look. "Really? Right now?"

"It just came to me."

"You said you didn't have the right words, so I basically ignored what you said."

She narrowed her eyes with a slight smile. "I feel like God just told me what to do the study on, which means I guess I'm doing it. But can we talk it through?"

"*Right now?*"

She chuckled. "No, silly."

Treva put her lips to his, transporting them once again.

CHAPTER 23

Faith escorted the first guests to the lower level of the house, wearing Zoe in a baby sling.

"So what's the occasion?" Reggie said, following with Tommy and Allison. "Something related to the movie premiere tomorrow night? That's all people are talking about in St. Louis."

"I don't know what's going on. Mom said dinner will be ready shortly but for everyone to wait downstairs." She looked at Reggie. "People are definitely going crazy over this premiere. Local news said some are planning to line up at dawn to get a good spot to see Alonzo Coles and the rest of the cast."

"Everybody and their momma are hitting me up for tickets." Tommy took a spot on the sectional. "I love that they think I'm that important"—he chuckled—"but I'm not the one."

Allison sat beside him. "Yeah, but sweetie, you do have four tickets. I don't know how many others could say that."

"How did you get four?" Faith took a spot next to Reggie, shifting Zoe a bit.

"As an entertainment reporter I got two," Tommy said. "Then yesterday Lance said I've got two allotted from the studio."

"That was really something," Allison said, "that they would

invite the guys from church that Randall got together with, plus their wives."

"I guess Randall said something to Alonzo about it," Tommy said, "and since they want to honor him . . ."

"So you're sitting on two extra tickets," Reggie said, "and I'm just now hearing about it?"

"I got so busy I wasn't thinking about it," Tommy said, "but I told Lance I'd find someone to pass them along to."

"You'd find someone." Reggie deadpanned him.

"I didn't think you'd want to get all dressed up," Tommy said. "Do you even own a suit?"

"Reggie, pay him no mind," Allison said. "You know he's got you. He already told me those tickets were yours."

"But I did honestly forget to tell you," Tommy said.

Reggie nodded as it sank in. "I get to walk the red carpet and go to the tribute afterward too?"

"Tribute, yes. Red carpet, no. You get to walk through a side entrance to the theater while the celebrities do their thing."

Faith elbowed Reggie. "You're taking me, right?"

"Taking you where?"

"Don't play. You know I love movies, and I've been looking forward to Randall's especially."

"I'm remembering a conversation," Reggie said, "back when you said you weren't going to the wedding with me because Jesse was coming to town—"

"Don't remind me."

"And I said I was waiting for the thing you would *least* enjoy, and I'd take you. This ain't that."

Faith shook her head. "You have way too much leverage."

"And will squeeze the life out of it."

Footsteps descended the stairs, and Cyd, Cedric, and little Chase appeared, followed by Stephanie, Lindell, and Cinda.

"I see we've got a Thursday night party going on," Stephanie said.

"Cinda, I didn't know you were coming." Faith got up with the baby and hugged her.

"Your mom invited me." Cinda's eyes were lively under her gray ball cap. "So we get to hang out two days in a row."

"That was so much fun at the B and B yesterday," Faith said. "Didn't even feel like work."

"Y'all were a lifesaver," Stephanie said. "I didn't know how I'd get everything ready for these guests. I'm just now realizing what I've gotten myself into."

Lindell put his arm around Stephanie. "Can we celebrate something real quick, everybody?" he said. "My wife is amazing. You already know how she oversaw all the renovations for months to get the B and B up and running. Then she worked hard to furnish and decorate each room with her impeccable style. Now she's got her first set of guests coming tomorrow night. She's stressed, so can we just acknowledge this moment. I think it's awesome."

He kissed her as everyone whooped.

Faith smiled, knowing what they'd been through the past couple of years. Stephanie's heart had to be full.

"I'm so proud of you," Cyd said, hugging her sister. "You were passionate about this from the beginning and have worked your heart out. What are you stressing over, girl? The hard work is done. Serve them a good meal in the morning and watch them rave over how beautiful everything is."

"Hey, everybody." Lance called from upstairs. "Come on up. Dinner's ready."

They filed up the stairs and looked at one another as they gathered around the island counter. Baby food jars had been positioned on a platter, representing a full meal—chicken, lamb, rice, peas, even dessert. And blue and pink carnations were displayed, with pacifiers attached to the stems.

"Um," Joy said, "is this for Zoe?"

Treva came down the stairs and walked into the kitchen.

"Oh. My. Goodness." Stephanie pointed at her shirt. "Girl, are you *pregnant?*"

Faith moved to get a good look, along with everyone else. A Bible verse was emblazoned across Treva's tee: BEHOLD, CHILDREN ARE A GIFT OF THE LORD, THE FRUIT OF THE WOMB IS A REWARD. Faith's eyes widened as she looked at her mom. "Mom! Are you? Really?"

Treva took Lance's hand. "It's true. We just found out, and I'm fourteen weeks along."

Shock gave way to cheers as she and Lance were overrun with hugs and congratulations.

"Cyd," Treva said, "I'll need you to hold my hand, since you went through this yourself in your forties."

"Oh, I already know the thoughts in your head," Cyd said, hugging her, "because they were in mine. You know I'm with you. This is amazing news."

Faith rocked with Zoe as the baby whimpered. "Mom, this is so wild," she said. "Your baby will be Zoe's aunt or uncle."

"They'll probably be best friends," Allison said. "That'll be so cute."

Hope put her arms around Treva. "Mom, I'm really, really glad."

Treva hugged her back. "Why, sweetheart?"

"Number one, I won't be the baby anymore. And remember you said you wished you enjoyed us more as babies? Now you get your chance."

Faith looked at her baby sister. "Wow, Hope. You really are almost a teenager. That was deep."

Treva had tears in her eyes. "I hadn't thought about that." She looked at Lance. "That's a gift in itself." She wiped them quickly. "All right, eat, everybody, eat. There's real food in the oven." She laughed.

Faith got her plate and joined Reggie in line, eyeing him.

"What?" he said.

"You're gonna make me beg?"

"For all you know I've got someone else in mind to take."

"She'll have to catch the next one."

"You think you've got it like that?" Reggie said.

"How many little sisters do you have?"

"About to be minus one." He sighed at her. "You really owe me big time now."

"Yes!" She looked across the room. "Cinda, we get to hang out again tomorrow, at the premiere. I'm going now."

Cinda hesitated. "Um . . . I'm actually . . . not."

"What?" sounded around the kitchen.

"Why not?" Treva said.

"Janice didn't get her a ticket," Stephanie said.

"That's easily fixed," Lance said. "We'll get you there."

"But it's okay," Cinda said. "I really don't have, you know, clothes or anything. And Stephanie and I talked about getting people together to see it when it's released in the theaters."

"Did you want to go?" Treva said.

Cinda's eyes couldn't hide it. She looked downward with a slight nod. "But seriously, it's fine. I'll be at the B and B helping with anything the guests need."

"Cinda, we need to go with a different plan," Stephanie said. She walked to the center of the gathering. "Okay, y'all, this is the way I see it. The big ball is tomorrow night, and if anybody needs to be there, it's Cinda. I say we not only get her there, but we get her there in grand style. Randall would want no less."

"Whoop, whoop!" Faith said.

Treva nodded. "Total amen to that."

"All right, women," Cyd said, "after dinner, let's put our heads together for Operation: Get Cinda to the Premiere."

Cinda had tears in her eyes. "You all don't understand. All my life I never liked my given name—Lucinda—and I grew to hate my nickname. It reminds me too much of the fairy tale, which never fit me or my life . . ." She covered her mouth for a moment. "So for you all to do this . . ."

Stephanie hugged her. "Treva said it before, and I'll say it again: God led you to us. And I fully believe He's gonna get you there tomorrow night—with the help of a room full of fairy godmothers."

CHAPTER 24

*A*lonzo stepped out of the limo at the theater in downtown St. Louis, stunned by the crowd. He didn't know what he'd thought—maybe that the Midwest would be subdued—but people were everywhere. And they were energetic, shouting his name and waving wildly from bleachers set up to view the action outside the theater.

He waved back, walking with police escort onto the red carpet, Shane alongside. His friend had adjusted his schedule as well to support the premiere and Alonzo.

"Welcome to St. Louis, Mr. Coles," a woman said, shaking Alonzo's hand. "I manage this theater, and we're thrilled to have you here."

"Thank you, it's good to be here," Alonzo said. "And you didn't tell me your name."

The woman blushed. "Oh. Sorry. Adrian."

He smiled. "Pleasure to meet you, Adrian."

"Pleasure's all mine, Mr. Coles. Let me know if there's anything I can do."

"Hey, Alonzo, local news KMOV, can we get a moment?"

Shane moved to talk to a couple of studio executives as Alonzo approached the news station.

"Alonzo," the reporter said, "I imagine there's a mix of emotion as you celebrate the premiere of this movie while also mourning the tragic circumstances with Randall Rogers."

"True," Alonzo said, standing before a backdrop of a picture of him and Randall. "I'm proud of the work everyone did on this movie and excited that others will finally get to see it. But I can't think about the movie without thinking about Randall. This is special for me, being here."

"This city has experienced that same duality," the reporter said. "Grief over the tragic loss of one of its citizens in such a senseless manner and, well, as you can see"—he gestured at the crowd —"fever pitch enthusiasm over the premiere being held here in his honor." He paused. "What do you think people will take away from the movie itself?"

Alonzo thought a moment. "There's a powerful redemptive theme in the movie. I hope people feel that, especially in light of everything that's happened."

"Thanks so much, Alonzo."

He spotted the actress who played his mother in the film and bear-hugged her as she talked to a reporter.

"Hey, this is my sweetheart," she said, turning to hug him back.

"Tell him about the sweet potato pie you baked and brought to the set for me," Alonzo said. "Best pie ever. And you were supposed to bake me another one!" He chuckled and turned as someone else approached.

"Alonzo, hey, Tommy Porter with the *St. Louis Post-Dispatch*." He shook Alonzo's hand. "My question might be a little different from the ones you're getting, because Randall told me something about you."

Alonzo smiled. "You knew Randall?"

"He was actually supposed to be the best man in my wedding

two weeks ago," Tommy said. "He was like a brother. We attended the same church."

"So you were one of the guys he mentioned," Alonzo said. "Okay, what secret did he reveal?"

"He said one night after filming, he got a group together to play cards—Randall loved some cards—and he invited you to join him. But you said you didn't know how to play—*Spades*." Tommy gave him a look. "Man, I had to see if you confirm or deny. That was scandalous."

"Aw, man, you can't print that." Alonzo was laughing. "See, I was so dedicated to the arts that I missed out on some of the games."

"We're talking *Spades*, bruh—that's out-the-womb type stuff." He chuckled. "I know your time is limited, and I wanted to ask you this also . . . You were one of the last people to see Randall and, from comments you've made, your time with him was impactful. What did the two of you talk about?"

Alonzo thought a moment. "I thanked him for the character he created and told him how much the story resonated with me personally." He paused. "Off the record, it got more personal. Spiritual. Maybe we can talk later."

"I hear you," Tommy said. "Absolutely."

"*Entertainment Now* is here live with Alonzo Coles at the red carpet premiere of *Bonds of Time*." Dottie Griffin held her microphone before him. "Alonzo, this is a special day for you, is it not?"

"In so many ways," he said, and couldn't help but notice the trio of women standing behind her, smiling at him. "Both because of the film itself and because we're premiering it here in St. Louis to honor Randall Rogers."

"Well, it's about to be more special," Dottie said, smiling. "I have here with me the family of Randall Rogers." She ushered them forward. "We spent the day with them, and I'll tell you, they could not be more excited for the chance to meet you." She put a hand on the shoulder of one of them. "This is Randall's wife, Janice Rogers, and his twin daughters, Jade and Jordyn."

"Very nice to meet you, Mrs. Rogers," Alonzo said, shaking her hand. "I want to extend personally my condolences. I'm so sorry for your loss. Your husband was a special man."

"Thank you, Alonzo," she said. "We appreciate the kind words you've spoken about Randall, and your being here means more to us than you know."

"We are *so* thrilled to finally meet you," one of the twins said, hugging him. "You have no idea—we devote an entire segment of our YouTube show to you. We've been fans forever."

"Can I be honest?" the other twin said, hugging him. "You are even more fine in person." She stepped back, looking at him. "Seriously." She took his hand. "Can we get some pictures and video footage together? We can stand by the backdrop."

Alonzo had been about to extend condolences to them as well, but somehow it seemed misplaced now. He watched as the twins handed their phones and their video camera to two guys with *Entertainment Now*, instructing them what to do. They stood in front of a picture from the film and struck a pose, waving him over. He stood in between them, and they hugged him tight as the guys took several shots and some video footage. Next he posed one on one with each twin, then with Mrs. Rogers, then with all three.

"It was nice to meet you all," Alonzo said, moving away as they checked the results.

"Oh, wait," one twin said. "My eyes are closed in this one. Do you mind taking it over?"

"No problem," he said, moving back into place. He smiled for the picture.

"Thank you," she said, hugging him. "You're staying in town tonight, right?" She spoke inches from his face. "We should get together and hang out later. I can show you around St. Louis."

"I really appreciate that," Alonzo said. "I'm sorry, though. I have other plans."

The other twin moved in, hugging him once more.

Alonzo smiled. "Again," he said, "so nice to meet you."

He backed away, making his way to Shane who was mingling a few feet over.

"I know you saw me giving you the eye," Alonzo said.

"What was I supposed to do?" Shane said. "Who was that anyway?"

"Randall Rogers's family."

"I thought you wanted time with them."

"I did," Alonzo said. "And that was plenty."

Shane chuckled as he glanced over. "Twins, huh?"

"Yeah," Alonzo said. "Randall mentioned a daughter once, but didn't say she was a twin." He shrugged, turning as a cast member called him over for a group picture.

"Want me to be your personal bodyguard the rest of the night?" Shane said, clearly amused.

"Is that April Winters?" Alonzo focused on someone in the crowd. "What is she doing here?"

"More people flew in than I would've thought," Shane said. "But hey, national coverage, opportunity to be seen . . . And a red carpet premiere isn't complete until you bump into one of your old flames."

"That's not funny."

"Who's kidding?"

Alonzo glanced back at her. "She just had to be looking good too." He sighed. "Yeah, let's do the bodyguard thing," he said, moving to the group picture. "Guard me from me. I told you what mode I'm in—I don't need women anywhere on the radar, definitely not on this trip."

CHAPTER 25

"There's no way I'll be ready in time." Cinda scurried into the dressing room with three more possibilities. "Doesn't the movie start in less than an hour? This is crazy."

"Girl, what is the problem?" Stephanie stood outside the dressing room. "I've checked the guests in, and they've left for the theater. I came over here thinking I'd barely catch you walking out the door."

"I thought it'd be easy to find something after work," Cinda said. "Allison has so many amazing dresses in this boutique, but they don't look amazing on me. Either the color isn't right or the length or the cut . . ." She sighed.

"Okay," Allison said, coming into the dressing area, "Faith is in the makeup chair and almost done. She looks *gorgeous*. Reggie's picking her up in ten or fifteen minutes. Cinda, the limo will be here for you—"

"What?" Cinda worked to figure out the dress. "What limo?"

"Didn't we tell you?" Allison said. "Tommy's got a friend who runs a limo service. We told you you're going in grand style."

"Between Tommy and Allison," Stephanie said, "they've got

connects all over town. You see it was nothing for Allison to get hair and makeup people on board in less than twenty-four hours."

"I'm not riding in the limo by myself, am I?" Cinda said.

"Well," Allison said. "Tommy's already there with his reporter hat on. Lance and Treva are on their way with Cyd and Cedric."

"And you know I'm not going," Stephanie said.

"I know," Cinda said, checking herself in the mirror. "I still feel bad about taking your ticket."

"I don't know how I ever thought I could go," Stephanie said. "It's the first night with guests. Anything can happen. I need to be there to make sure everything flows smoothly."

"So, Cinda, it's you and me," Allison said, "but we need to kick this thing into overdrive. Let's see what you picked."

Cinda stepped out and did a turn. "You think it works?"

"It's perfect," Stephanie said. "For a business meeting." She stepped back as if trying to grasp it better. "A navy wrap dress? If I had known that's what you had, I would've taken it from you."

"The style is cute, though," Cinda said, looking down at it. "It's not like I'm dressing for the red carpet. It doesn't have to be fancy."

"Red carpet or not," Allison said, "you held a special place in Randall's life, and it doesn't matter who knows it. *You* know it. You're going to show up looking like the special person you are. We want heads to turn."

"That's what I'm talking about," Stephanie said, walking into the dressing room. "Let's see what else you got in here." She took one off the hook. "I need an explanation. You thought this tiered lace, high neckline thing was cute?"

"Not exactly." Cinda chuckled a little. "I was pulling dresses in a certain price range, and for a split second thought maybe it could work. Till I tried it on."

Stephanie looked at another. "This rosette on the bodice is a nonstarter." Another. "Basic black, no personality."

"Cinda," Allison said, "walk out here with me and look at

dresses without regard to cost. Humor me. I want to see what you *really* like and don't like."

The three of them walked onto the floor of the boutique, which had already closed to customers.

"Tell me what you think as I pull certain looks," Allison said. She took the first one and faced it outward. "What about this one? I admire it whenever I walk past it."

"Um," Cinda said, "it's cute, except A-line skirts don't look great on me."

"Okay," Allison said, pulling a sleeveless cocktail dress. "Now this would make a statement. You'd definitely stand out with this multicolor hue. Yet it's tastefully done."

"Ooh," Cinda said, running her hand across it. "Is this guipure lace?"

Allison looked at her. "How do you know it's guipure lace?"

"I used to ask my mom to drop me off at the mall," she said. "And I'd go to the bookstore and look at fashion magazines. Then I'd browse around the mall to see how certain styles looked in person—even try things on as if I could afford it. For a while there was this bridal store, and I loved looking at the pretty dresses. I thought the guipure lace stitching was so pretty."

"So do you want to try this one on?" Allison said.

"Well, the lace is pretty," Cinda said, "but I don't think the floral pattern is me."

"Here's a black dress that *does* have personality," Stephanie said, showing them.

"You had me," Cinda said, "until I saw the lower part. Something about the mermaid look . . ." She sighed. "You know what? This is too much. Look at me," she said, tugging her hat. "I have no idea what to do with this hair, even if I'm able to settle on a dress. Just yesterday, I was fine not going." She shook her head. "I'm hanging out at the B and B. We'll bake cookies and—"

They all turned as a knock sounded on the glass door to the boutique. Reggie stood on the other side in a dark-colored suit.

Allison unlocked the door and held it as he walked in. "Look at my brother-in-law," she said, locking the door again, "looking *too* handsome."

"I see you, Reggie," Stephanie said. "*Know* he looking fine. Stop acting like you're embarrassed."

"I'm just taking it for what it is," Reggie said, "like those obligatory compliments you get from mom." He looked at Allison. "Did I do this tie right?"

"Let me see that," Allison said, adjusting it for him.

Cinda gasped, seeing Faith coming from another area of the dressing room. She went to her. "Ohhh, wow, look at you."

Stephanie caught a glimpse as well and moved toward her.

Faith looked tentative. "How do I look? I feel so overdone. Like I have on way too much makeup."

"That's because you never wear any." Stephanie stared at her. "I hardly recognize you with your hair straight, face beat. You're pretty on an ordinary day. Right now it's just . . . *wow*."

Cinda felt the iridescent light chiffon of the dress. "I *knew* this would be amazing on you. Everything about it is perfect—the sheath silhouette is perfect for your height, elegant double straps, and this bronzy color against your ebony skin . . ." She shook her head. "You should be a model."

"You had to make me try it on," Faith said. "I have to admit, I love it."

"Faith, are you planning to gab back there all night," Reggie called, "or did you actually want to see the movie?"

"I'm coming, I'm coming," Faith said, moving further into the boutique.

Cinda followed to catch his reaction.

Reggie had taken a seat on an ornate chair. He stood when he saw her, his eyes wide as he took her in.

Cinda shifted, looking at Faith, who was taking in Reggie.

"Wow," Reggie said. "So, you're welcome."

Faith frowned at him. "What am I supposed to be thanking you for?"

"Taking you to work out at the gym. Your arm and shoulder muscles . . ." He nodded. "On point."

"Reggie," Allison said. "Just tell her she's beautiful."

"She doesn't need me to tell her, with the rest of you going on about it."

"Faith, I want to see how this bracelet looks with that," Allison said.

"Hey Cinda," Stephanie called. "I think I found something."

Cinda worked her way through the boutique to get to Stephanie.

"Before I show you," Stephanie said, "it's more formal than the ones we've been looking at in terms of length but, man, does it make a statement. *Please* try this on. I can totally see you in it."

Stephanie turned and took it off the rack, and Cinda took a breath, staring.

"That's one of the first ones I gravitated to," Cinda said, "but look at that price tag."

"I know what the price tag says. You like it?"

Cinda stretched out her hand, felt the crystal beading at the neckline. "I love it."

"We've all banded together to bless you with your dress," Stephanie said. "It's yours."

Tears formed in Cinda's eyes. "I can't. It's too much."

"Girl, if you don't get your behind in there and try this on, so we can move to hair and makeup. Ain't nobody got time for tears."

Cinda exhaled as she took the dress into her hands. Stephanie was right—she had to hurry. At this rate she might miss the start of the movie, but she wanted to catch what she could. She headed back to the dressing room, wondering what the night held in store. It would be perfect—as long as she didn't have to deal with the J's.

CHAPTER 26

"*D*id you know we had red carpet access?" Treva looked at the tickets she and Lance had picked up from will call.

"No," Lance said, walking with his hand in hers, "and weird no one else does, except Tommy, of course."

"Must be because you were Randall's pastor." Treva took in the energetic crowd as they showed their tickets and entered the roped-off pathway. "This is wild. I had no idea so many people would show up."

"What are we supposed to do?" Lance looked around at the media, the bevy of photographers, the glitzy celebrities. "Just walk through?"

"Don't forget to stop once or twice and strike a pose in that black suit."

"It's the same suit I wore in Tommy's wedding."

"And the same irresistible."

Lance put his arm around her waist. "You're the one who's killing tonight. This red dress is all kinds of fire." He kissed her.

"There y'all go. Red carpet newlywed action."

Lance turned at Tommy's voice. "Aren't you supposed to be working?"

"That's what I'm trying to do," Tommy said. "Interview you."

"Me?" Lance said. "That's funny."

"Alonzo Coles said he wanted to meet you, on national television," Tommy said. "That makes you a news item. So here's what I want to know—pretend you don't know me. You'll be saying a few words about Randall Rogers at the tribute afterward. What's one thing about Randall that you would share, that most people probably didn't know?"

Treva looked at him, thinking about Cinda. But he would never take it upon himself to break that news publicly.

"Good question." Lance thought a moment. "People know Randall was successful, both as an attorney and, of course, as a writer. But most probably don't know what a giver he was. He did it quietly, for all kinds of things. I remember once I half mentioned having car trouble. Randall asked a couple of follow-up questions, found out I was waiting till I could save up for repairs. Next thing I know, the service department was calling to schedule repairs, because Randall had set up payment." He seemed lost in the memory for a moment. "Just a really generous soul."

"Randall was an elder at the church you pastor," Tommy said, "so clearly the two of you worked closely together. But your relationship seemed to go deeper—"

News cameras and microphones surrounded them suddenly as *Entertainment Now* approached. A woman looked anxious to interrupt but stood aside, waiting.

"If you're here to interview Lance," Tommy said, "please, go right ahead."

The woman stepped in, motioning for her cameraman to start rolling.

"I am here with Randall Rogers's pastor," she said, "who, we just discovered, is Pastor Lance Alexander." She looked into the camera.

KIM CASH TATE

"If you recall, he's the pastor whose wedding drew much coverage because he married a woman with Stage 4 cancer—whose fiancé had dumped her one month before *their* wedding." She turned to Lance. "Pastor Alexander, just curious, was Randall Rogers at that wedding?"

"He sure was," Lance said. "I've known him for years."

"Clearly, you were a key figure in his life," the woman said, "so much so that Alonzo Coles mentioned you. Have you met him yet?"

"No, I haven't," Lance said.

"We're only minutes from the start of the movie," she said, "so we'd love to make that happen."

Treva and Lance followed her and her crew as they traveled the red carpet. It was easy to spot where Alonzo was—in the middle of the cluster of cameras. The woman walked through them and got his attention.

"Alonzo," she said, "I would love to introduce you to Randall Rogers's pastor. He's here with me."

Alonzo turned, looking beyond Treva and Lance.

Lance stepped forward. "Alonzo, Lance Alexander. And this is my wife, Treva."

"Very nice to meet you," Alonzo said, shaking her hand first. With Lance he paused. "You're the pastor?" he said. "Man, I pictured you about sixty or seventy years old." He chuckled as he clasped hands with him.

Lance smiled. "I wish I could claim that much wisdom. It's great to meet you," he said. "And you should know you made quite an impression that last time Randall saw you."

Alonzo looked at him. "What makes you say that?"

"He called from the airport in LA to confirm plans for dinner that night." Lance glanced at the cameras, which were still rolling. "I'll just say he felt that—"

"I'm sorry, excuse me," a woman said. "Alonzo, they need you inside for a press interview before the film starts."

Alonzo turned to Lance. "Will you walk with me? And your wife, of course. I'd like to hear the rest."

Lance shrugged. "Sure."

The woman walked at a rapid clip in front of Alonzo, along with two security guys, presumably to get him where he needed to go without interruption.

Treva looked around, glad the cameras were gone. Lance could say whatever he felt led to say.

"So here's the deal," Lance said. "A group of us have been praying from the time the book first got optioned for a movie. And when we found out you got the lead, you became a focus of our prayers. Not because it was you; we would have been praying whoever it was." He spoke faster than normal, keeping with the pace of their feet. "Randall really wanted God to use this movie, not only in the lives of moviegoers, but in everyone who worked on it as well."

Alonzo stared almost downward as they walked, as if focused.

"When he called after the photo shoot," Lance said, "he was in awe. He said he could see God doing so much in you. He would have never shared whatever you told him personally. But he wanted me to know that God was answering prayer."

They moved inside a secure area of the theater with a smattering of what appeared to be press people and others working the event. Their attention shifted when Alonzo walked in. They quietly stared as the woman and two guards led the procession down the hall, around a corner, and to a room with studio lights and a backdrop.

The woman turned to Alonzo. "I'll tell them you're ready. You have a couple minutes."

"Thanks, Bev." Alonzo walked a few feet away, exhaling. "I can't believe y'all were praying for me." He turned to look at them. "It's weird. I don't know what you were praying, but I feel like you know what I need more than I do."

"I wouldn't say that," Lance said. "I honestly don't know much about you. I'm not up on all the entertainment type news."

"So, can I ask what you were praying?"

"You sure you want to know?"

"Now you got me nervous," Alonzo said. He paused. "Yeah, I want to know."

"I know time is short," Lance said, "so briefly, I prayed you would know Jesus as Lord and Savior if you didn't already, for God to disrupt your life if need be to cause you to turn to Him, for grace and strength to obey God and live boldly for Him. I don't know a whole lot about Hollywood, but if it's hard out here in St. Louis, I figure it's a challenge there as well. I even prayed that you not be able to find satisfaction in anything else, including women, just God alone." He shrugged lightly. "Those are a few things."

The door opened before Alonzo could respond, a handful of people coming in.

"I know we need to go," Lance said. "We'll make our way to the theater."

Treva started toward the door, but saw Alonzo heading for Lance, hand extended. The handclasp became a hug.

"You got me at a loss for words," Alonzo said. "I don't even know you, but . . . I appreciate you, man."

Treva and Lance walked out, their first few steps in silence.

"I thought this night was about Randall," she said finally.

"So did I," Lance said. "God just did a full tilt."

CHAPTER 27

"This is such an incredible night." Faith let her eyes travel the beautifully decorated room—white lights, fanciful floral arrangements, creative touches—awed to be around so many whose work she'd admired. "I didn't realize the director would be here. *Dave Goodwin* is here. Do you know how many great films he's done?"

"We should do a Dave Goodwin movie marathon." Reggie glanced across the room where the director sat with others from the film. "Loved what he had to say about Randall too, how he was an encouraging presence on set."

"I know," Faith said, "and I love that more than one person referred to that scene where Alonzo's character almost died, and how Randall got teary-eyed when they filmed it." She looked up front, where Randall's wife was receiving a plaque in his honor.

"Not gonna lie, that scene got me too," Reggie said.

"That movie was so good," Faith said. "Alonzo better win some kind of award."

"I have to give him his props." Reggie focused up front as well, where the entire cast had gathered. "Alonzo killed that."

Janice Rogers moved to the microphone with the plaque in

hand. "I'm overwhelmed with gratitude," she said, taking a moment to collect herself. "Thank you, all of you, for this show of love in my husband's behalf. Not a day goes by that I don't think of him. He put his heart and soul into everything he did, and I know he was especially proud of this work and the way you've brought it to life. My family will never forget this day." She paused, overcome. "Thank you so much again."

The audience erupted in applause as she returned to her seat.

"Mom," Faith said, turning to her other side, "did you hear anything more from Allison? I'm really worried about Cinda. She's missed everything. And she's not responding to texts."

"Not since Allison let me know she wasn't coming because she didn't have time to get herself ready. But that was an hour ago, when she put Cinda in the limo."

"That concludes the formal part of our program," the mistress of ceremonies said, "but the night is far from over. Continue to enjoy the food and refreshments, mix and mingle, and of course, we've got some good music for you."

The lights dimmed and music kicked in from a deejay positioned to the side of the room.

Faith's phone lit up with a notification and she grabbed it from the table, seeing Cinda's name.

Come out here. I'm outside the ballroom.

Faith got up and walked as fast as her heels could carry her. She glanced around the ballroom lobby as people headed for the restrooms.

"Faith," a hushed voice said.

Faith walked in that direction, narrowing her focus. "Oh, my gosh, your hair! I didn't even recognize you." She turned Cinda around. "I had no idea you had this much hair or that it was so beautiful. You've got a serious curly mane happening. Who did this?"

"The hair stylist was going to take my twists out and give me an updo," Cinda said. "But she started pulling apart the twists and picking at the roots. I didn't know what she was doing. Next thing you know, I had *this*. It's so big, I'm kind of self-conscious."

"No, it's amazing. So full and curly. And this *dress*. Turn around again, because I was focusing on your hair the first time." Faith chuckled as Cinda obliged. "You look like you came straight out of a Greek myth—what did they call those outfits?"

"Togas," Cinda said. "That's the design. I fell in love with it when I saw it."

"Seriously, the white gown, the halter neckline with these encrusted jewels"—Faith ran her hand over them—"and those shoes. You look like a queen. And what took you so long to get here? I hate that you missed the movie and the tributes to Randall."

"I did miss the movie—I'll catch it in the theater," Cinda said. "I got here when the program was starting and didn't want to walk in with everyone seated. I watched from back here."

"You totally should've walked in," Faith said. "We had a seat for you."

"I didn't want to draw attention to myself," Cinda said. "And it worked well because I really didn't want Janice to know I was here." She got her phone. "Actually I'm about to text Allison to see if the limo can pick me up now that I've seen what I came to see."

"No way," Faith said. "All the time it took you to get ready? You better enjoy that dress, that hair, and that face. Who cares if they see you? And they won't recognize you anyway." Faith took her hand. "You're coming in and having a good time."

"Okay," Cinda said, "but let me run to the restroom first."

Faith gave her a look.

"I'll come in," Cinda said. "Promise."

Faith went back to the table as the music switched up.

"Oh!" Tommy started dancing in his seat. "I can't believe they took it back to Cameo." He got up and walked around the table. "I need a dance partner. Come on, Treva."

"Let's go, Tommy," Treva said, rising. "'Candy' was my song too."

Reggie pulled Faith up and started toward the floor along with many in the room.

"Umm," Faith said, pulling back, "not exactly my thing."

"What, you don't dance?"

"Not in any way that looks decent."

Treva waved her over from the dance floor. "Come on, Faith. It won't kill you."

Reggie kept her hand in his, moving to the beat. "If you don't come on out here. Can't be that bad."

She gave him a look as she followed. They grabbed a spot near Tommy and Treva, the three of them in their own groove. Faith focused on her mom and tried her best to mimic.

Reggie paused. "Wow, you weren't lying."

Faith glared at him.

"Okay, look, there's an actual beat. Come here." He took her hands and rocked side to side. "Don't concentrate so hard. Let yourself feel it."

Faith swayed with him, sure he'd broken it down to the simplest move possible.

"There you go," he said, smiling at her. "Now we're gonna step a little bit. Just follow me."

He added a step to one side, then the other.

Faith smiled to herself, feeling like she was getting it, this little bit anyway. "Wait, we're supposed to do that now?"

She looked around as the entire floor reconfigured. Tommy, her mom, Cyd and Cedric—everyone was joining in a line dance.

"Nah, we can stay right here," Reggie said. "I got you. But we're about to step it up again. This time back and forth."

Faith followed his movements, noticing he had much more swag in his, and noticing too—he hadn't let go of her hands.

The song changed up a few minutes later, a slow one taking its place. Many left the floor, others came on, including Lance, who switched with Tommy.

"You want to go back to the table?" Reggie said. He'd let her hands fall when the song ended.

Faith shrugged. "I don't know. It's up to you."

"If it's up to me, we're staying," he said. "I'm old school. And this is Luther."

He brought her closer, bringing his arms around her back, the faintness of his cologne taking her breath.

"You cold?" he whispered. "You're shaking a little."

Faith exhaled softly. "No, I'm okay," she said, her arms wrapping around him.

She closed her eyes, swaying with him once more, this time slowly.

"Faith."

"Yeah?"

"I don't know why I couldn't say it earlier. You really are beautiful."

"Well, Allison went out of her way to pamper us for tonight."

"Not tonight only." Reggie's voice held a different tone. "You're just . . . beautiful."

She looked at him, their eyes locking as his arms tightened around her. He could feel her heart beating. She was sure of it. And unless she was imagining, like a slow magnetic pull, his face was moving closer to hers, and hers to his, as if synchronized with the music.

A moment later he looked away, his arms holding her close as he sighed. She wondered if he knew—she would have followed his lead there too.

CHAPTER 28

"*Y*ou're just gonna show me up like that, Shirley?" Alonzo danced with his movie mom. "You know that's not right."

Shirley had an arm in the air, sashaying her hips to the beat as people around them cheered, more than a few recording on their phones.

"Come on, Alonzo," Shirley said, switching up. "Keep up now."

Alonzo laughed as she bumped her hip into his, launching into the dance.

"Oh, we're going there?" Alonzo raised his hands partway, getting into it.

"Y'all young folk don't know nothin' about this old school," she said.

The cheers got louder as they got lower and lower to the ground, bumping to the beat. Shirley suddenly grabbed for Alonzo's hand, almost toppling over. He pulled her to a hug as people roared all the more.

"That's all I've got for tonight," Shirley said, giving a bow. "These bones are telling me to rest."

Alonzo escorted her to the table, where the twins had apparently been waiting for him.

"We were fighting over who would dance with you," one of them said, "then we figured you could handle both of us at the same time."

From the corner of his eye, he could see Shane smiling. He'd gotten all kinds of joy watching Alonzo navigate the twins and their mom at the table.

"Actually," Alonzo said, "I was about to head across the room to talk to a few people." Which was true. And timely.

He'd wanted to connect with Randall's pastor again before the night ended. He started across the room, and as he approached, his attention was drawn to a woman who stood around the table with them. Had he seen her earlier tonight? He would've surely remembered. The white dress, the hair, everything—she was striking.

"Alonzo, can we get a minute?"

He paused, looking at two women who'd gotten up from a table as he passed.

"We had to meet you personally," one said. "We're big fans, work for a St. Louis radio station."

"Great to meet you," Alonzo said, shaking their hands.

"And we *loved* the movie," the other one said. "Definitely your best work yet."

"I appreciate that," Alonzo said. "Thank you."

"Do you mind if we get a picture?"

"Not at all."

They took turns snapping a picture of each other with Alonzo, then hugged him before he continued on.

Lance smiled when he saw him and came toward him.

"That movie, man," Lance said, hugging him. "We can't stop talking about it. Your performance was powerful."

"That means a lot," Alonzo said, surprised by how much he felt it. "Seeing it tonight . . . I really felt like Randall would be proud."

"No doubt," Lance said. "Been through all the emotions tonight thinking about him, but nothing but love for you on that screen." He gestured toward the table. "Mind if I introduce you around?"

"I'd love it," Alonzo said.

Lance brought him over, interrupting as they all stood chatting.

"Hey," Lance said, "I have a really good friend I'd love for you all to meet."

"Ha. Right," one of the women said.

Lance smiled. "Clearly he needs no introduction," he said. "Alonzo, you've met my wife and Tommy over there. This is Cyd and Cedric"—he pointed to each—"Faith, Reggie, and Cinda."

Alonzo moved to greet each one, shaking hands and chatting. He smiled when he got to Tommy, clasping hands. "You didn't tell my secret, did you?"

"Not yet," Tommy said, "but you know it's too good to keep to myself. Great movie, man. Can't wait to write up my review."

Alonzo had kept an eye on the one in the white dress, though she'd barely looked his way. Even now she was partially turned as he approached.

"Hey, Cinda, right?" he said. "Nice to meet you."

She turned, their eyes meeting. She was even more beautiful up close.

Cinda nodded, shaking his hand. "You as well," she said.

She turned back to her conversation with the other young woman, who paused to speak to Alonzo.

"I'm Faith," she said, "and I'd love to ask you a question about the movie. Reggie and I have a bet."

Alonzo shook hands with Reggie. "Good to meet you, man. So what's the bet?"

"That scene where they've got you singing?" Faith said. "Is that really your voice?"

Alonzo smiled. "Which one said it's me?"

Faith pointed at Reggie, and Alonzo fist-bumped him.

158

"But the runs and the falsetto—it sounded like a real singer," Faith said. "I mean, you know, a professional singer."

"For a while I wanted to do both," Alonzo said, "and there were times I did do both, in theater. But acting was always my main love." He glanced at Cinda, who seemed preoccupied with watching the dance floor. "So how do you all know each other? Same church?"

"Right," Reggie said. "Same church, plus a couple of us are related."

"And obviously you all knew Randall," Alonzo said.

"We did," Faith said, "and I was really moved by your tribute to him tonight."

"I can't explain it," Alonzo said, "but he impacted my life in a short period of time."

Cinda looked over at him, but only for a moment.

The energy in the room rose as the deejay took it back to the nineties again. Tables started emptying. Reggie grabbed Faith's hand and disappeared along with everyone else in their group except Tommy, who was talking to someone at the next table— and Cinda.

Alonzo cleared his throat. "So I'm guessing you're quiet or maybe shy?"

She glanced at him. "No, not really."

"I'm curious," he said. "You weren't here earlier, were you?"

She focused on him a little more. "No, I wasn't," she said. "Why do you ask?"

"I wondered how I could have missed you," he said. "I'll be honest, when I first saw you, I couldn't take my eyes off of you."

"So, let me guess. You've used that line about a hundred times?"

"Man, that's brutal," Alonzo said. "If you want to know the truth, I don't need pickup lines. I've never said that to anyone before." He paused. "Did I miss something? Why do I feel like you'd blow me away if you had a shotgun?"

She turned more toward him. "I just think you think that every woman you meet is an Alonzo Coles groupie, ready and willing to give you whatever you want."

"So you're ready to blast me because you think you know what I'm thinking?"

Cinda looked away. "I definitely know what you're thinking."

"That's incredible confidence—with no basis in reality."

"Really?" Cinda said. "Everywhere you go, there's more talk about your exploits with women than your craft as an actor."

"Huh. So you keep up with my whereabouts?"

"Don't flatter yourself," Cinda said. "I had housemates who were obsessed with you. Personally, not a fan."

"Let me modify my former statement," he said. "It's not a shotgun. It's a knife. I'm dying a slow death." He angled his head a bit. "Wait, was that a hint of half of a partial smile?"

"I see now," Cinda said. "It's not pickup lines. It's that you try to be charming."

"I'll take that as an admission that you think I'm charming."

"You don't know what I think."

"But somehow you can know *exactly* what I'm thinking."

Cinda couldn't hide her amusement. "Still," she said, "I'm right. You thought we'd wind up in your room simply because you claimed you couldn't take your eyes off of me."

"Wrong," he said. "I told my buddy Shane earlier that women were not on my radar tonight. Not what I was looking for at all."

"Then why'd you say it?"

Alonzo looked at her, wondering how he'd gotten pulled into a conversation with a woman he'd never seen in his life—yet seemed so familiar.

"I don't know what to tell you," he said. "I didn't have a motive. I said it because it was true."

The music changed up again, practically clearing the dance floor.

Alonzo chuckled as they all returned. "I guess y'all weren't feeling that."

Reggie looked perplexed. "How you gonna go from Mary J. to . . . what even is that?"

"It's definitely weird," Alonzo said, "switching to big band in the middle of an R&B set."

Cinda looked at him. "You've got something against big band music?"

"Not at all," Alonzo said. "I had to learn how to swing for a play once. It was fun." He pointed to the floor, smiling. "Dave Goodwin must've requested it. First time he and his wife have been on the floor all night."

"Look at them go," Faith said. "That's so cool."

"Brings back memories," Cinda said, watching. "My mom loved to dance. Sometimes she'd put on a big band song and we'd dance around the living room. Felt so carefree."

Reggie turned, looking at them. "Why don't you two get out there? Show us what you got."

"I'm not going out there," Cinda said. "Do you know how long it's been?"

"Same," Alonzo said. "I'm not even sure I remember the basics."

"I bet it's like riding a bike," Reggie said.

"The way they're moving," Faith said, "has celebration written all over it." She looked at them. "Can't you imagine Randall getting a kick out of watching the two of you dancing in his honor?"

"You just had to put it like that," Cinda said.

Alonzo shrugged. "I'm willing to look rusty and maybe a little foolish in Randall's honor." He glanced at Cinda. "As long as she leaves the knives back at the table."

Faith and Reggie frowned.

Alonzo held out his hand to Cinda. She stared at it for a couple of seconds, finally taking it, and he started for the dance floor.

"Are we really doing this?" she said. "Keep it simple. Nothing fancy."

"You don't have to worry about that," he said.

Alonzo and Cinda joined two other couples on the floor, drawing immediate attention. People came to watch, likely wondering if he knew what he was doing. He put his right arm around Cinda's back, grasped her hand with his left—and his mind drew a blank as to how to start.

With a hand to Alonzo's shoulder, Cinda led it off, taking a step behind, then a triple step to each side. Alonzo nodded, smiling as it clicked. They began to glide, first in the same space, then in wider swaths, coming in closer and going back out.

If Alonzo couldn't keep his eyes off her before, he was entranced now. She moved fluidly, as if immersed, legs nimble with the fast-paced rhythm. He lifted her arm, turning her, and she fell back in step, so he turned her again and again as the crowd cheered.

They glided around the room again as the song wound down. When it ended, he lifted her and swung her around as people whistled and cheered. He looked around, realizing the two other couples were applauding as well.

"What in the world was *that?*" he said, looking at Cinda.

"I don't know." She was beaming. "I just"—her eyes went to the crowd around the dance floor—"um, I'm gonna go."

"What?"

She headed off the floor toward the ballroom doors.

Alonzo followed. "Where are you going?"

"Not sure," she said.

He walked with her, seeing that she was headed outside the hotel. It was dark, and she surely didn't need to be roaming alone.

"Mr. Coles," a security guy said, following, "we weren't aware that you were leaving. Please wait while I—"

"No need," Alonzo said. "Thanks."

He pulled her aside when they got to the sidewalk. "Are you okay? What's going on?"

Cinda was catching her breath still. "It's a long story," she said. "But for the first time in a good while, I had an absolute blast. And I wanted to hold on to it."

"Hey, is that Alonzo Coles?" someone called out.

"Oh, my gosh, it *is* him," another voice said.

Alonzo glanced over and saw that a crowd was gathered still outside the hotel, including photographers. He turned to Cinda. "If you don't want to go back, I hope you're ready for more fun."

"What are you about to do?"

"Run."

"Where to?"

"No idea."

"Wait."

Cinda slipped off her heels and held them as Alonzo took off his suit jacket.

"Ready?" he said, taking her hand.

She nodded. "Ready."

CHAPTER 29

Cinda couldn't stop laughing. "This is insane," she said. "Running city sidewalks in bare feet and a long gown? And who knows where we even are." She bent over, winded. "You live a crazy life, you know that?"

"Me?" Alonzo said. "You're the one who ran out of the ballroom." He laughed a little himself. "I didn't even look to see if anyone was following. I just knew we'd be bombarded if we stayed there."

And Cinda knew she'd be bombarded if she'd stayed in that ballroom—by the J's. All three had stood at the edge of the dance floor watching them. She wondered if they knew it was her. "Ugh, my hair," she said, patting it with both hands. "I don't even want to see what I look like."

"I can tell you what you look like."

She narrowed her eyes at him.

"Seriously," he said. "Like you're straight from a graphic novel, warrior princess type thing, hair full and fierce, and we already know—attitude to match."

"Well, I don't really have 'attitude.' That was just with you."

"Ah, appreciate the distinction." He walked a few feet,

surveying the surroundings. "There's a bench over there, down towards the river. If you have nothing against, you know, sitting. With me of all people."

The moment descended at once. "I cannot believe I'm on some random street in downtown St. Louis at night with Alonzo Coles." She shook her head. "And I don't say that like, *ooh, awe.*"

"Trust me, I'm sure of that," he said.

"This is *crazy.*" She headed for the bench. "Sitting sounds good. My feet are killing me."

The lone bench stood off the beaten path with a partial view of the river. Cinda sat, massaging her feet as car horns sounded in the distance.

Alonzo sat back, legs stretched out. "I need a playback of the entire past hour," he said. "One minute I'm getting cut up, the next we're fleeing together."

"You forgot the *Dancing With the Stars* gig."

"Could never forget that." Alonzo looked over at her. "What happened to 'It's been so long'?"

"I don't know." Cinda thought about it. "Memories came flooding back, good ones. It was like I was floating on them. And thinking about Randall watching . . ." She nodded. "It felt good."

"So you'll be nice to me now?"

"That depends on you," Cinda said.

"I don't know what that means," Alonzo said, "since a compliment almost got me killed."

"I would apologize," she said, "except I think a reality check is good for you."

"Here we go."

"Seriously, you live in a bubble. And I don't care what you say, there are plenty of women out there ready to swoon at your every word and give you whatever you want. You need to run into a buzz saw now and again."

Cinda waited for a comeback, but Alonzo was staring into the distance, smiling slightly.

"Randall told me God will do things to get your attention," he said. "Since then I try to pay more attention to what's happening around me." He shook a finger at her. "This whole thing with you has been so completely wild—it has to mean *something*."

She looked at him. "You and Randall talked about God?"

"That's the next thing you'll get on me about," he said. "You can add 'prodigal son' to 'exploits with women' and the rest of the list."

"Randall talked to me about God too. He's the reason I went back to church." Her mind went to the late-night chats in the home office. "Guess we're both prodigals."

"This is a recent thing for you? Getting your relationship with God back on track?"

"So recent I can't even say I'm there yet." She stared into the darkness. "But for the first time I feel like I need to be. I want to be."

He eyed her. "Tell me about you, Cinda. Starting with that name. It's unusual."

"Not really."

"What's your full name?"

"I don't typically share my full name."

"Because?"

"I don't like it," she said.

He nodded. "Tell me yours, and I'll tell you mine—which I don't like or share either."

"You first."

He paused, looking at her. "Alonzo Zachariah Coles."

"What's wrong with that?"

"A and Z? Mom did that intentionally, thinking it was cute."

"I like it better than mine." She glanced at him. "Lucinda Marigold Ellis."

"Wow."

"Right? My grandmother picked it, after two of her favorite great aunts."

"Your grandmother raised you?" he said. "Here in St. Louis?"

"I grew up in Madison, Wisconsin," she said. "Grandma mostly raised me, until she died when I was fourteen." She paused, unsure how much she would share. "Mom had issues with alcohol, among other things, so life was always interesting. She died earlier this year."

"Just this year?" he said. "I'm sorry to hear that."

"What about you? Where are you from?"

"South side Chicago," he said. "Only child. We didn't have a whole lot, but Mom worked hard and made it her mission to keep me out of trouble. I'll always appreciate everything she did to keep me plugged into the arts."

Cinda looked at him. "I do want to apologize for one thing," she said. "I might've lied when I said I wasn't a fan."

He leaned in. "Might've?"

"I've only seen one movie of yours," Cinda said. "But your intensity, the way you lose yourself—that's a gift."

He looked at her. "I know that killed you to say. Thank you. So what do you do? What dreams do you dream?"

"Nothing big," Cinda said. "I work for a new bed-and-breakfast in town. Can't say I'm a dreamer."

"Come on, everybody has dreams."

"Not everybody."

He turned more toward her. "What's *one* thing you could see yourself doing and loving, if there were no barriers? Even if you don't have the talent. There's got to be something."

Cinda looked away.

"I see it in your eyes," Alonzo said. "What is it?"

"It's like you said," Cinda began, "it's not that I have the talent or skill for it. I don't even have training or education or access to it. This is purely *one thing* I always thought would be the coolest job, though I've never actually *dreamed* of doing—"

"*Okay.* Say it."

"Stylist."

"Like, wardrobe stylist? Really?"

"I can't believe I said it. I've never told anyone that."

Alonzo stood, put on his suit jacket, and faced her. "So. Tell me what you think of what I'm wearing tonight."

"No. That's silly."

"How is it silly? Someone gets paid to dress me for the red carpet, press interviews, photo shoots. I'm curious what you think."

She studied him for a few seconds. "Conservative black three-piece suit. You could've gone less formal in the Midwest, but it shows respect, given the purpose."

"We actually had a conversation along those lines," Alonzo said.

"But there's no color anywhere," Cinda said. "White shirt. Even your print tie is gray, black, and white. It's a good look, obviously. But you could be any other actor on the red carpet."

"Meaning?"

"It's cookie-cutter. Seems to me whenever you step on the red carpet, you should make some sort of statement. I'm not talking flashy. Could be a small thing, a different tie, a pocket square." Cinda shrugged. "Let them talk about your style instead of your exploits."

"Can we stay on topic?"

"That was on topic."

"I do lean conservative," Alonzo said. "Classic suits, neutral shades."

"And that's fine," Cinda said. "But test the waters here and there. Granted, you look good in anything, but try playing with color. Butterscotch suede bomber jacket over brown leather, merlot sweater over navy. See how it feels."

"That's some serious feedback," he said, nodding. "I'm impressed. But wait, did you say I look good in anything?"

"Stylist hat. Purely professional."

"Of course." He looked at her. "For the record, I have no problem telling you *you* look good."

Her eyes cut away. "Stop."

"What's up with you not being able to take a compliment?"

"If I feel like I'm the nine-hundredth person to hear it, it's not a compliment. It's an assembly line."

"You know what I think?" Alonzo sat back down. "I think you have issues."

She kept her gaze away from him.

"You're beautiful, but you don't know you're beautiful—I could tell when I first saw you, the way you carry yourself." He kept his focus on her. "And you've got natural talent, but you don't know you're talented. How can I see it in one night, but you're blind to it?" He shrugged. "One reality check deserves another."

Cinda turned his words over in her mind. She hadn't expected them to land so deeply, valid or not.

She jumped up suddenly. "I don't know what I'm thinking. I need to get back. I bet the event is over, and no one can reach me. I left my phone on the table."

She took a step and winced in pain. "Between the dancing and the running, my feet are aching something terrible." She lowered herself back onto the bench. "I don't know how I can walk back."

Alonzo took his phone from his suit pocket. "They've been looking for us," he said, checking notifications. He made a call. "We're good. Just need a ride back. I'm sending my location to your phone. All right, cool." He looked at her. "The driver's on his way."

"Thanks," Cinda said.

"No problem."

He aimed his phone at her, and Cinda threw her hands up.

"What are you doing?" she said.

"Taking your picture."

"No, my hair's all over my head—I look horrible."

"Let me be the judge of that."

"I'm not gonna sit here and pose for—I know that flash didn't just go off."

He showed it to her.

"Delete it."

"Only if I've got another to take its place."

She put a hand to her hip and glared at the camera.

"Come on, Warrior Princess, let me see that smile."

"You should know that right this moment, I like you less than when I first met you."

"Pretend you've got your buzz saw and you're coming for me."

The smile betrayed her—and the flash went off. Twice.

"Happy?" she said.

"Not yet."

He scooted closer to her on the bench and leaned in, holding out his phone.

"A selfie?" she said. "Really?"

"Two prodigals, impacted by Randall Rogers."

Cinda's breath caught. She could only nod.

Leaning her head next to his, they smiled and he snapped a few, then showed her.

"The driver's here," he said, looking at the notification.

They hopped up and saw the black SUV a few yards away.

Alonzo put his arm around her back, and she leaned on him, limping her way to the car. The driver opened the back door, and they got in for the short ride back to the hotel.

He looked across the back seat at her. "We're staying in touch, right?"

Cinda stared out of the tinted window. "I don't see why we would."

"You didn't feel tonight was special?" he said.

"It's one of a thousand special nights in the life of Alonzo Coles," she said. "I'm not being cynical, it's just true. When you get back to LA, you'll move on to the next thing."

"You're telling me you won't give me your number."

"For what?"

"I'd like to know more about you."

"And we'd exchange one text, maybe two. I don't need to be one more contact in your phone."

"You didn't answer my question," Alonzo said. "Did you feel tonight was special?"

"It was fun. It was . . ." She sighed. "Yes, special, I guess. And I'd rather leave it just the way it is."

The SUV pulled up to the hotel, and Cinda could see the limo waiting nearby, Faith and Reggie standing beside.

The driver opened the back door, and Cinda stepped out first, then Alonzo. Cameras flashed, taking her aback, and security stepped forward to escort Alonzo inside. He paused, taking her hand and looking into her eyes, even as onlookers called his name and began moving in his direction.

"We need to go," one of the security guys said, ushering him inside.

Cinda limped toward the limo, and Reggie came to help her.

"You were seen leaving the hotel with Alonzo Coles," a reporter said, coming up beside her. "Are the two of you romantically linked?"

"No," Cinda said, wishing she could quicken her pace. She held up a hand, and Reggie shielded her as a photographer ran in front, taking her picture.

Reggie opened the limo door and helped her get in, closing it behind her.

Faith was sitting inside. "I'm riding with you," she said. "I've got your bag and your phone."

Cinda tried to catch her breath. "Thanks," she said.

"What a night," Faith said.

"Yeah." Cinda exhaled. "What a night."

CHAPTER 30

*T*reva spread her Bible and notes on the coffee table in the B and B's main sitting room Monday night. "I don't know why I'm so nervous." She could feel it in her hands. "What am I saying? I do know why. You all could tell me I'm way off with this thing."

"Girl, if you don't stop worrying." Stephanie set a tray with a pitcher of water and snacks on the table. "I know it'll be good because Lance said he loves it."

"Lance is biased."

"Not when it comes to the Word," Stephanie said. "He would've told you if it was whack."

Treva couldn't deny that. "I'll just be glad when Cyd and Allison get here so we can get started. I want to know if I'm on the right track."

"Mom, Steph, look—they posted a video about the premiere." Faith walked into the room with Cinda, eyes on her phone.

"Who, the twins?" Stephanie said.

"I'm surprised it took them so long." Cinda was holding Zoe in her arms. "I thought they'd have their special edition of Alonzo

Watch up the next day. This was what they'd been building to—the moment they'd finally meet him."

"Except," Treva said, "that moment was eclipsed by the 'beautiful and mysterious woman who appeared late in the evening'." She smiled. "I loved that quote on the link you sent, Faith."

"Cinda got everybody wanting to know who she is," Stephanie said. "One site said they left the hotel and 'disappeared' together." She looked at Faith. "What did the twins say?"

"You've got to see for yourself." Faith walked closer to her mom and Stephanie, and held her phone in front of them.

Treva watched as their intro played, then the young women came on-screen, looking far from happy.

"Y'all know we've been hyping the premiere of our dad's movie, and we've had Alonzo Watch, counting down the days till our dream came true—meeting him in person." She sighed. "And first, we have to say, for most of the night, it *was* a dream."

"We met him on the red carpet," the other said, "got great pics and video, even sat at the same table for dinner. And y'all—he is *even more fine* up close." She clapped out the last words for emphasis.

"But then," the first one said, "you've seen it—this chick shows up."

Stephanie looked over at Cinda. "Do they know it was you?"

Faith elbowed her. "Keep watching."

The first one continued, "Talk about poor taste. Dancing and showing off with Alonzo when the whole occasion was built around sorrow and grief over our dad. All this talk about her being beautiful and mysterious. Whoever she was, I've got my own word for her—rude."

"And Alonzo basically forgot his purpose in being there," the second said. "He was supposed to be honoring our dad, which meant being with his family. Once she showed up, everything changed. We hardly saw him. Didn't even say good-bye."

"But y'all know the love is still real for Alonzo," the first one said. "Check out some of the footage."

Faith clicked off. "They were right about one thing—everything did change when Cinda showed up, for Alonzo at least. Even when he was talking to the rest of us, he had an eye on her."

"Only because I wasn't paying him any attention." Cinda rubbed Zoe's back. "I think it was all a game to him."

"Maybe," Treva said. "But in the little time that Lance and I spent with him, he seemed more thoughtful than that. He wanted to know how Lance had been praying for him. If anything, I felt he was on a journey, one he was serious about."

Stephanie looked at Cinda. "I still can't believe you refused to stay in touch with him."

"Let's see, three days later," Cinda said, giving a playful look at her watch, "had I stayed in touch? That part of his journey would be over by now. He's not thinking about me, just like I'm not thinking about him."

"Ha," Stephanie said. "Even Zoe gave you the side-eye when you said that."

"Okay, maybe a little," Cinda said. "But we can all agree it's pointless. I'm ready to move on from all talk of Alonzo Coles."

The front door to the B and B opened, and Stephanie called out, "We're in here."

"Hey," Allison said, walking in with Cyd. She hugged each of them. "And here's the belle of the ball," she said, hugging Cinda. "I can't tell you how many people have come into the shop speculating about Alonzo's secret St. Louis romance."

Cinda groaned.

"You missed it, Allison," Treva said. "This is now a no-Alonzo zone."

Cyd chuckled. "You know how it is, Cinda. People stay on stuff like that for a few days, then it's on to something else."

"Just like we're 'bout to be on to this new Bible study." Stephanie smiled. "Y'all like how I did that?"

"I'm ready," Allison said, taking her Bible from her bag and sinking into one of the sofas. "Been looking forward to this all day."

"I've been looking forward for weeks," Cyd said.

Treva took a breath as everyone got settled and looked to her. "So." She smiled. "You're the guinea pigs."

"What are we doing, Mom?" Faith said. "How will it work?"

"Every week when we meet," Treva said, "I'll have a new lesson prepared, and I want us to dig into it. Nothing formal. Just talk it out. I want to hear how it strikes you, where it takes you. Real and raw."

"And then you can use the feedback?" Stephanie said.

"Yes," Treva said. "I can make changes to the lesson as needed. And it'll help when I craft questions to go with the lesson. I know I'll gain insight from you all."

"And we'll gain a lot too," Cyd said. "I'm praying for God to move powerfully among us every week."

"Amen," Treva said.

Cinda raised a hand partway. "Am I supposed to be here? Randall and I would do a little Bible study sometime, but I don't know much at all. I don't see how I can help."

"You'll be invaluable," Treva said. "I especially want to know how it's hitting you, whether I'm breaking it down enough, using language you can understand, that sort of thing." She paused. "But only if it's something you want to do."

"What's the study about?" Cinda said.

"Great question," Treva said. "Wait a second—I'm feeling really pregnant right now." She shifted in her seat and stretched out her legs. "This is actually how I got the idea for the study." Her hands rested for a moment on her stomach. "I had a hard time accepting that I was pregnant at my age, and acted pretty ugly toward Lance."

"Mom, for real?" Faith said.

"For real," she said. "And as I was sulking, the Lord checked me. But He did it using a promise. And I kept thinking about that and took notes on it." She looked at Stephanie. "Then it hit me that this is the *Promises* B and B. And I thought about how you chose the name because of what you and Lindell had been through, and how you were standing on God's promises."

"So this study is about the promises of God?" Allison said.

Treva nodded. "Yes. Promises of God."

"You're telling me I'm about to do a study on the very thing that's been on my heart all year?" Stephanie said. "I'm about to run around this room."

"Treva told me about it last week," Cyd said, "and I loved it. I need this in my life."

"Are y'all ready to jump in?" Treva waved her notes. "The first lesson is the one God used to get my attention. Here's the title—If I Come."

"Ooh," Cyd said, "that's enough to make you think right there. The title of each lesson is the condition?"

"Right," Treva said. "The tendency, at least for me, is to jump to God's part. What is He promising to do? But in the study, I want to also focus on what's *our* part? What's the condition to the promise?"

"I need you to break that down," Cinda said. "I'm not sure I understand."

"Okay," Treva said, "let's look at Matthew 11:28. Cinda, can you read it for us?"

Faith scooted closer to her so she could look off of her Bible while Zoe slept in her lap.

Cinda looked at the page. "'Come to Me, all who are weary and heavy-laden, and I will give you rest.'"

"So Jesus is talking to the people of Israel," Treva said. "Before we get into the background of what's going on, what is the promise?"

Cinda looked at it again. "It says, 'I will give you rest.' The promise is rest."

"Awesome," Treva said. "A condition is something that needs to be done or satisfied before you can get to the promise. Is there a condition to this promise?"

Cinda nodded. "You have to come."

"Come to whom?" Treva said.

"You have to come to Jesus, if you want rest."

"Excellent." Treva leaned in. "The people of Israel thought that in order to be right with God, they needed to follow rules and regulations, and follow them exactly. But here was Jesus, who had come down from heaven, God Himself, basically saying, 'Following all the rules won't do anything but make you weary, because it's not even in you to do right all the time.' You can have *rest* from all of that. But you have to do what?"

"Come to Me," everyone said.

"And what's crazy is most didn't want to come to Him," Allison said. "He was offering the ultimate. They didn't have to sell their firstborn, didn't have to jump through twenty hoops, didn't have to clean themselves up. Just. Come." She sighed. "And I'm thinking about all the times I'm going my own stubborn way, totally weary, but don't want to come because I'll have to surrender something."

"Now that you went there," Stephanie said. "I'm the queen of *not coming*. I'll be broke, busted, and disgusted in spirit, hanging onto attitude for days, *know* I'm wrong. But I don't want to surrender my stubborn ways." She sighed. "And when I finally do, I *always* feel better. I get that rest."

"This reminds me of another verse," Faith said. "I just looked it up—John 7:37— where Jesus said, 'If anyone is thirsty, let him come to Me and drink.'"

"You're reading my mind, Faith," Treva said. "That was next in my notes. One thing we'll also be doing is looking at similar passages and talking about different applications. Clearly, the main message in both of these verses is salvation. Jesus is promising eternal life—rest, living water—to those who come to Him."

"And yet," Cyd said, "once we have eternal life, we forget to *keep* coming to Him when we're weary or thirsty day to day." She sighed. "Like me today when that little Chase was pushing every one of my buttons and I was about to lose it."

"I didn't even realize how weary I was."

Everyone turned, looking at Cinda. Her voice was bare.

"Losing my grandmother, then my mother, both times I was in survival mode. I was sad, I cried, but then I had to figure out what was next. I had to keep moving." She focused on no one in particular. "Then I found my dad and I lost him, and I was sad. I cried. But I knew I couldn't continue staying where I was, so I had to figure out what was next. I had to keep moving. I had to survive. And even now, as thankful as I am for all of you, I don't know what's next. At some point I'll have to keep moving. I'll have to survive. I don't belong *anywhere,* not really. And I'm *tired.*" She clutched sleeping Zoe as tears fell from her eyes.

Treva went to her along with the rest, and draped an arm around her. She'd prayed for Cinda daily, and her prayer now came straight from her heart.

"Lord, we thank You for Cinda. We thank You for putting her in our lives. She's such a gift." She squeezed her as Cinda's tears continued. "She's endured so much, Lord. Incredible loss. Incredible pain. And she's been bearing it all alone. It's no wonder she's tired, Lord. I know I couldn't make it through all that in my own strength."

Stephanie slipped Cinda some tissues.

"Lord, thank You for Your promise of rest if we would simply come to You. And You're so gracious, Lord, that You even help us to come. I see Your hand extended to Cinda. Give her the grace to grab hold and come. We thank You right now for the rest that she will receive. We praise You, Lord, for moving in such a powerful way already among us. In Jesus' name."

"Amen," rang out in the room.

Cinda's shoulders trembled a little as she looked up at them. "Is it really as simple as that? Just come?"

Allison nodded, her hand on her shoulder. "Just. Come."

CHAPTER 31

"*I*t's so weird I've never been over here." Faith walked into the house with a covered dish, her eyes roaming the decor. "I love the color scheme."

Reggie closed the door behind her. "Allison's been slowly transforming things," he said, sounding congested, "which hasn't been easy. Tommy was a bachelor for so long he wasn't used to anybody second-guessing his choices. She said, 'You've got black everything, no accent color.'"

Faith smiled. "She must have incorporated the red and tan." She stepped into the living room. "Were these her African pieces?"

Reggie nodded. "She actually bought them on a trip over there. So what's in the dish?"

"Oh." She looked down at it. "Lasagna."

"You made that for me?"

"You sounded awful—look even worse, by the way. And you were whining about how Allison and Tommy had a banquet tonight, and you were starving." She shrugged. "It was no big deal."

"Except, it's my favorite."

"I'm guessing that's the kitchen through there," Faith said, moving that way. She set the lasagna on the counter.

Reggie followed, coughing a bit. "This actually blows me away," he said. "Thank you."

"You're welcome. I'm gonna head back, though, since I left Zoe at home."

He leaned against the counter opposite her, in long athletic shorts and a tee. "She's by herself?"

"Of course not," Faith said. "Mom's got her."

"And she told you to hurry back."

"Well, no, but . . ."

"You're uncomfortable."

"Around you? Why would I be uncomfortable?"

Reggie looked at her. "We're going to pretend Friday night didn't happen?"

"What about Friday night?"

"The dance."

"Which one?"

He eyed her.

"That was just . . . Music has a way of stirring things, in the moment."

"Okay."

"You don't agree?" she said.

"I agree," he said. "Just wondering if that's all it was. A moment."

Faith looked away, distracted by the beat of her heart. "What else could it have been?"

"That's what I've been asking myself," he said, "because it's been four days, and I can't let it go."

She blew out a silent breath, staring at the floor. It didn't help that his cold had his voice sounding huskier than normal.

"I kept thinking," he said, "when I saw you back to normal—Afro puff, no makeup, jeans—everything else would return to normal. And here you are, and . . . no." He paused. "But one thing we have is we're straight with one another, so I wanted to know what you were thinking, whether it was even on your mind."

She brought her eyes to him, trying to see him like before—not the strong build, rich dark skin, and dreamy eyes that currently filled her vision. "Were you about to kiss me that night?"

This time Reggie looked away a moment. "I can definitely count on you to be straight." He met her gaze. "I wanted to."

"Why didn't you?"

"Because at the same time, I didn't want to. I didn't want to cross the line and potentially ruin what we had."

"That's what I figured." Faith sighed. "So, okay. I did feel uncomfortable. I hadn't seen you because you've been sick. And when I walked through the door, I wasn't expecting to feel what I felt during that dance."

"Which dance?"

She smiled a little.

"So what did you feel?" Reggie said.

"Like I was attracted to you. And I don't want that. I like the brother/sister vibe."

"So we're thinking the same thoughts. And feeling the same feeling."

"Like you said, though," Faith said, "things will return to normal."

"Okay, radical question," Reggie said. "We're protecting the brother/sister vibe as if that's the ultimate. What if our best is something else?"

"As in, a relationship?"

"Just what if? Are we afraid to take that path and see?"

"Yes. What we've got now works really well." She could focus on him now, strengthened by her position. "We know what it feels like to be hurt, and relationships breed chaos. Why take that chance? We could wind up hating one another."

He nodded. "You're right. That's good. I'll tell myself that next time I get a vision of you in that dress. *Man.*" He shook his head. "This is all your fault. I shouldn't have let you talk me into taking you."

She looked at him. "Was that the very first time you felt an attraction toward me, when you saw me in that dress?"

He stared at her. "Why are you asking that?"

"I want to know."

"You really think you can rummage around in my heart and soul, don't you?"

"It's that vibe we have."

He looked away for a moment before meeting her gaze again. "No. It wasn't the first time." He moved to the casserole dish. "Now can we swim back to the surface so I can get some grub?"

"Yeah," Faith said, "and I'm gonna go."

"You're not eating with me?"

"We're waiting for normal," she said. "Not there yet."

Reggie walked her to the door and paused before opening it, taking her into his arms.

She recoiled slightly. "Aren't you sick?"

"I'm no longer contagious," he said. "And anyway, if you can rummage in my soul, I'm thinking you can share some germs."

She wrapped her arms around him, her head against his shoulder, hyper aware of everything appealing about him, including the strength of his embrace.

"What was that again?" he said. "Something about relationships and chaos?"

"And we'd hate one another."

"Right." He sighed, holding her still. "Okay."

He took a step back and took her hands in his. "Lord, I just want to give this whole thing to You. You know what we're feeling. You know our fears. But I hope we're not ruled by either. Let us honor You and follow You, wherever that might lead. In Jesus' name."

Faith looked at him. "Really? You took it there? Do you know what that means?"

"It means we're giving up control," Reggie said. "I didn't hear your amen, though."

She opened the front door and stepped out, looking back at him. "My heart already said it, before you finished the prayer."

CHAPTER 32

*A*lonzo shouted across the table above the noise in the swanky LA nightclub. Noelle LeGrande's album release party had brought everybody out—music industry icons, athletes, models, and Hollywood celebs.

"So what's up?" he said. "You optimistic? You're coming up on a new season, new coach. 'Cause honestly, man, last season wasn't pretty."

"Absolutely optimistic," Dante said. The Rams running back smiled with confidence. "I know for sure the offensive line is focused on coming back strong and on the same page."

They looked up as the private event crowd went wild, but Alonzo had missed the deejay's announcement of the latest arrival.

"I won't lie," Shane said. "I'm Raiders Nation all the way. But Alonzo and I are talking about checking out some of the Rams games." He took a swig of beer. "How's the transition to LA been for you personally?"

Dante sighed. "If I can just get my wife on the same page." He chuckled. "Her family is in the Midwest, so she wasn't thrilled about leaving St. Louis."

Alonzo's thoughts floated—until he saw Simone heading for their section. In a body-hugging mini dress, hair flowing past her shoulders, she had every eye turning. Security let her through, and she stopped at the first table, hugging people she knew.

"Simone O'Dell." A music producer at Alonzo's table was looking at her. "I caught a film she was in a few weeks ago, and I couldn't even tell you what it was about. She had me too spellbound."

"She's beautiful," Dante said. "No doubt about that."

Simone made her way over. "Evening, gentlemen," she said.

Shane got up and hugged her, introducing her to the other guys.

"I don't think we've met." Simone hugged the music producer. "But I love your music."

He smiled, checking her out. "So we've got a mutual fan thing going. Was just talking about how mesmerizing you are."

"Nice to hear someone thinks so." She flashed a quick glance at Alonzo.

The producer took a card from his jacket and wrote on it. "I hope we can get together," he said.

Simone smiled and said thanks and greeted the others.

Alonzo stood as she approached, and hugged her. "It's good to see you," he said.

"Mind if we talk a minute?" Her words grazed his ear. She led him a few feet away. "I don't get why you haven't returned my calls."

"You've only called maybe twice," he said, "both times at night. I knew if we talked we might be right back to where we were before."

"And what would be wrong with that?"

"I told you," Alonzo said. "I needed time alone."

"Really? That's why you were caught up in some romantic escapade in St. Louis?"

"Now you're into headlines?"

"There's often a ring of truth to it." Simone moved closer. "I haven't seen you in weeks." She took his hand. "We should spend some time after this."

Alonzo looked away a moment. Part of him wanted to, but . . . "I can't, Simone," he said. "It's just not where I'm at right now."

"You can't tell me we weren't good together."

He could only look at her. Seconds later she walked away, and the guys at the table eyed him when he sat back down.

"I used to think you had it all together," the producer said. "But if you let *that* get away?" He shook his head. "That ain't normal."

"You have no idea," Alonzo said. "Nothing feels normal about my life right now."

The crowd cheered as Noelle took the stage, dancing playfully to one of her new songs as it boomed throughout the club. She hadn't reached out since he'd turned her down in Austin. But when she texted Alonzo a personal invitation for tonight, he was glad to support. With her longtime boyfriend in tow, she'd played the devoted girlfriend all night.

She took the mic from its stand as the music died down. "You all are completely amazing," she said, beaming. "Just look at this crowd."

More cheers and whistles sounded.

"*Thank you*, all of you, for coming out tonight." She added quickly, "It's not over. We're partying till they kick us out. Just had to say how much I appreciate the love and support . . ."

Alonzo got up and made his way to the restroom as Noelle continued. As he moved through the crowd, a woman stepped in front of him, smiling.

"Alonzo Coles," she said.

He looked at the woman, immediately familiar, trying to place her.

"*Once and Again*," they said at the same time. They'd each had a small part on the cable show.

"Wow," he said. "That was forever ago. Makenzie, right?"

"I can't believe you remember," she said.

He hugged her, also remembering the first time he laid eyes on her. He'd thought she was the prettiest young woman he'd ever seen.

"How've you been?" he said.

"Real good," she said. "I've been in New York for a few years. I'm only in town for a couple days." She looked at him, her smile warm. "I'm glad I ran into you. I think about you from time to time."

"I'm surprised to hear that," he said.

"Why?"

"Because you wouldn't give me the time of day back then, not that I blame you." He chuckled. "I was a lock for that nerdy guy role I played."

"It's no telling where my head was," she said. "But so many times I've thought about reaching out. I just didn't think you'd remember me."

"Definitely remembered," he said. "I don't mind telling you—I had the biggest crush on you."

"Okay, I might be blushing," she said, smiling. "But what if I'm crushing on you right now?"

Alonzo hesitated. "You actually got me with that. I don't even know what to say."

"Let me put my information in your phone," she said.

He unlocked it and passed it to her. She typed it in.

"I'm here tonight and tomorrow," she said, passing it back. "Between now and then, whenever you want to get together . . ."

"It was good seeing you, Makenzie," he said, continuing to the restroom.

*. . . Plenty of women out there ready to give you whatever you want .
. .*

Why was Cinda's voice in his head? Five days later, and he hadn't been able to shake it. The voice. The face. The attitude. Her words. So many of her words.

Guess we're both prodigals.

Both returning to God. That's what stuck with him most. Both traveling that same path.

At the table he let the guys know he was calling it a night. But back home he couldn't sleep, his mind cycling again through Friday night, from the moment he saw Cinda to the moment they parted. Maybe she'd been right. The idea of keeping in touch was unrealistic. Still, all he wanted to do was pick up the phone and talk to her.

He took it up now, scrolling through pictures he'd taken that night, reliving the scene. He paused, staring at their selfie. How was it he hardly knew her, yet everything about her seemed special?

If I feel like I'm the nine-hundredth person to hear it, it's not a compliment. It's an assembly line.

I don't need to be one more contact in your phone.

Alonzo paused a moment, then opened Instagram and uploaded their selfie. The caption came quickly, but he hesitated again at the last step. Was he really about to click Share?

He set the phone down. It was late. He was tired. If he waited till morning, he'd tell himself he'd been crazy to even consider it. But something inside of him . . .

He stared at the picture again, captivated. Would she even see it? He had to let her know.

His thumb took the leap for him. *Share.*

CHAPTER 33

*C*inda grabbed at her phone, eyes closed, wondering why it would be ringing so early. She didn't know what time it was—only that it wasn't time to get up.

"Hello?" she mumbled.

"Cinda, he posted it."

"Faith?" she said, eyes still shut. "Who posted what?"

"I was up feeding Zoe," she said, "Googling reviews of the movie to see what people were saying. And these headlines popped up about Alonzo and the mysterious woman. I thought it was the same story until I saw Instagram. Girl, he posted the selfie you two took."

Cinda's eyes came open. "What?"

"About two hours ago," she said. "Middle of the night and over a thousand comments already."

"Why would he do that?" Cinda sat up, looking at the time—5:26 a.m. "The twins used to say he never posts pictures of himself with a woman."

"People are even dishing about the mysterious caption," Faith said. "It says—#minus899."

Cinda's heart pounded as she stared into the darkness.

"You wouldn't give him your number," Faith said, "so I guess he found another way to reach you."

"But he doesn't know who I am," she said. "He saw someone in a pretty gown with done-up hair. That's not me."

"What are you going to do?"

"There's nothing *to* do," Cinda said.

"I guess that's true," Faith said. "Still. Wow, girl. Okay, gotta get Zoe back to sleep. I'll call you later."

It wouldn't be real until she saw it herself. Cinda downloaded the Instagram app to her phone and searched for Alonzo Coles. There it was. *He really posted it.*

She read the caption and a few comments, but mostly stared at the picture. At the two of them. Cinda Ellis and Alonzo Coles.

Was she actually on his mind?

She'd tried not to think about him, but he'd show up anyway—while she was dusting the base of a lamp, wiping a bathroom mirror, mopping a tiled floor. She'd see his eyes, the way he'd looked at her that night. And she'd wonder if there was anything to it. Then she'd wonder why she cared.

But as much of a hard time as she'd given him, he'd left an impression. A different impression than she might have imagined. Never would she have thought he'd talked to Randall about his relationship with God. As wildly different as her life was from Alonzo's, they seemed to be on a similar path.

Still, she'd told herself to put him out of her mind. Similar or not, those paths would never intersect again.

She looked at the picture once more, their heads together. So what was this?

"What are you doing, Alonzo?" she whispered.

Cinda walked into the kitchen, where Stephanie was stocking the pantry. "I found a hand towel in a bedroom drawer with makeup all over it," she said.

"What?" Stephanie walked out of the pantry. "Who does that?"

"Maybe they felt bad and tried to hide it," Cinda said.

She shook her head. "Do we not have a little sign that says please do not use face towels or washcloths to remove makeup? And do we not provide packets of wipes for just that purpose?" She sighed. "Looks like we need a bigger budget for replacing towels and such."

"I think we can salvage this one, at least," Cinda said. "I've got it soaking."

"You and your DIY solutions," Stephanie said. "How did you learn to clean so well anyway?"

Cinda leaned over the counter. "It started out as a way to escape. Mom would get drunk, and I would squirrel away in the bathroom or a closet—anyplace—and busy myself with cleaning or organizing."

"Oh, Cinda, I didn't know." Stephanie came closer. "That had to be really rough."

"Then I discovered," Cinda said, "that if mom's bedroom was clean or the kitchen was sparkling, it put her in a better mood. She'd even praise me for it—'It's the one thing you do well.' So I learned to do it really well."

"That praise was a little backhanded, though," Stephanie said. "I hope you didn't take it to heart, that that's all you did well."

Cinda shrugged. "Better than doing nothing well," she said. "I figure I'll always be able to get work, since the job of cleaning is never done for long. By the way, any bookings yet for the weekend?"

"Not yet," Stephanie said. "I know June is a slower month for a lot of B and Bs, but I had my hopes up after last weekend."

"We got some good practice," Cinda said, smiling. "Watching you handle breakfast was worth its weight in gold."

"Girl, wasn't that something else? I'm cooking my little heart out, serving folk, and somebody's got the nerve to complain about no almond milk?"

"The funny part," Cinda said, "was watching you force that smile as you opened the fridge and pointed out all the milks and juices you'd made available."

"Pray my strength," Stephanie said. "That's all I keep saying."

Cinda chuckled. "I better get back to work." She grabbed a broom and headed for the stairs as the front door swung open.

Cinda stared as if frozen as a camera was aimed her way and a flash went off.

"Got it," Jade said, Jordyn beside her.

"What is going on?" Cinda said. "You can't just walk in here."

"It's a B and B, isn't it?" Jade snapped another one. "I figured the door would be open."

"To guests," Cinda said.

"What is all this about?" Stephanie came into the entryway, eyeing the twins.

"I don't know," Cinda said. "They walked in and took pictures of me."

Jade walked toward her. "I was stunned that *you* were the 'mysterious woman' with Alonzo. I don't know how you pulled off that miracle makeover, but all those people wondering who you are?" She held up her camera. "We've already told *Entertainment Now* we've got a scoop for them. The glamour girl is a maid."

"You have nothing better to do?" Cinda looked at Jordyn. "And you're on board with this? I thought we were cool."

"It's the hot entertainment news of the day," Jordyn said. "And it helps our channel if we can be the ones to shed light. I mean, people were going to find out eventually anyway. Why not be the ones to break the news?"

"I have a question," Stephanie said. "How do you think Randall would feel about all this?"

Jordyn's gaze fell.

"It's nothing personal," Jade said. "We simply couldn't pass up the opportunity."

"Nothing personal?" Cinda looked at Jade. "You've never liked me. You jumped at this opportunity."

"Maybe some jealousy mixed in too," Stephanie said, "since Alonzo preferred you over them."

"It wasn't even real," Jade said. "She had to become someone else entirely to get his attention." She opened the door. "Let's go, Jordyn."

Stephanie exhaled hard as the door closed. "Lord, help me, because I really don't like them or their momma."

Cinda stared vaguely. "By nightfall people will see that picture and mock me and my broom."

"You know what?" Stephanie said. "So what. Who cares what they or anyone else thinks?" She paced a little. "But *man*, I wish I had snatched that camera and thrown it to the ground, just to see their faces. I can't believe they have no qualms about hurting you, just so they can grab some spotlight for themselves."

"It reminds me of the lesson this week," Cinda said. "Maybe it's not about me. Maybe they're thirsty and don't know where to drink."

Stephanie looked at her. "You just had to hijack every thought I was having about them." She sighed hard. "We should stop and pray for them. And I've got no problem praying at the same time for those pictures, that *they* somehow get hijacked."

Cinda lay across her bed reading one of Randall's novels—her way of hearing his voice—jarred suddenly by the doorbell. She'd been bracing for it all evening, the moment a camera crew would show up to catch her live—a photo wouldn't be good enough—in all her domestic glory. Stephanie had said she'd handle the door, but Cinda decided she didn't care. If some news outlet had nothing better to do than "scoop" her mundane life, they could go for it.

The bell rang again as she headed down, now telling herself she had an overactive imagination. It was probably someone from the neighborhood. They got that from time to time, people wanting to check out the renovations on the historic mansion. Who really cared about the stupid pictures the twins—

Cinda stood with the door ajar, unable to breathe. She stared into his eyes long enough to know she wasn't dreaming—and slammed the door.

Her heart raced as she dashed back up to the third floor. "This can't be happening," she muttered.

Stephanie came out of her room. "Who is it, some news person?" she said. "I'll get it."

"No." Cinda took a breath. "It's Alonzo."

"Alonzo Coles? How do you know?"

"I answered it."

"Then why is the doorbell still ringing?"

"Because!" Cinda said. "I don't want him to see me." She tried to shake the anxiety from her hands. "Do you think the twins somehow got him to come? That this is part of their sick joke?"

"I've never met him a day in my life," Stephanie said, "and could tell you with all confidence that he has not linked up with them."

"Then why is he here?"

"Girl, the way that doorbell is ringing, he's trying to tell you." Stephanie grabbed her by the shoulders. "Cinda. Get a grip and let that man in."

Cinda sighed and walked back down, adjusting her ball cap, smoothing her jeans, frowning at the big toe peeking through her sock.

She pulled the door open and stood aside.

"I knew I was in the right place when you slammed the door in my face." He walked in wearing a Dodgers hat, jeans, and a simple gray tee, shaking his head with a slight smile. "Still got that buzz saw."

She leveled a gaze at him. "What are you doing here?"

"I found out it was easier to get a last-minute ticket cross country than it was to get your number."

She led him to the kitchen. "What's going on, Alonzo? First you post that picture. Now this?"

"So you saw it?"

"Not because I follow you. Somebody called and told me."

"Of course you would clarify that. I just wanted to know if you saw the picture, and the caption."

She opened the fridge wide enough for him to see what they had. "What can I get you?"

"Perrier would be perfect. Thanks."

"I saw the picture," she said, passing him the bottle. "But I don't get why you did it. Or why you're here." She moved out of the kitchen and to the sitting room.

"This house is dope," he said, taking it in. "This is the B and B you work at?"

She nodded, taking a spot on the sofa.

He sat next to her, downing some of the water, then looked at her. "Remember I wanted to keep in touch, and you said it wouldn't work? Turns out, what didn't work was *not* keeping in touch. I couldn't stop thinking about you."

She focused on nothing in particular as she waited for him to continue.

"I went to an album release party last night," he said. "And back home at the end of the night, after all the people I'd seen and talked to, it was your face I saw. Your voice I heard. All I could think was how different you are." He tipped the bottle and took another drink. "I posted the picture to let you know I was serious when I said I wanted to get to know you."

She looked at him. "What made you get on a plane?"

He took a moment to respond, focusing on the bottle. "I've

been praying for a while for direction and clarity about a few things, and prayed again last night. When I woke up, I couldn't shake the thought of going back to St. Louis." He looked at her. "I had another motivation as well. I wanted to spend some time with Pastor Lance."

"With Lance?" Cinda said. "That's how you found me?"

"First I had to find him," Alonzo said. "But it wasn't hard. The studio had his contact info. I told him what was on my mind and asked if I could meet with him. Then I asked about you." He set his water on a coaster on the coffee table. "I knew you'd be shocked to see me, but did you have to slam the door in my face?"

She looked away. "I was embarrassed."

"About what?"

"Look at me," she said. "I'm not the person you saw Friday night. But this is me, every day. Nothing special." She hesitated. "And you might as well know—I clean this B and B. That's what I do. I'd be the maid cleaning *your* house. I knew once you knew that, you'd wish you hadn't wasted your time coming here."

"You thought it was your dress, hair, and all that that made you memorable? Or what you did or didn't do for a living?" His eyes penetrated. "Can I be really real with you?"

She could only focus on that big toe poking from that hole.

"I'm around gorgeous women all the time. I'm around women with glamorous careers all the time. I've never lain awake at night thinking about any of them." He dipped his head to catch her eye. "The only way I wasted my time is if you tell me I'm wasting my time. Matter of fact"—he took out his phone—"let me see right now." He opened to a new contact screen and handed it to her.

Cinda input her information and gave it back. "To be honest," she said, "I'm stunned by what you did today. I've never had a guy do anything special for me."

"As pretty as you are? You must've had some scrubs for boyfriends."

"I've never had a boyfriend," Cinda said. "I've never even kissed a guy."

Alonzo stared at her a moment, then stood, walking a few feet away. "I don't even know what to do with that. It's like, you're this beautiful porcelain doll on a glass shelf, and I'm the bull in the china shop. Maybe I need to back away. I don't want to make any wrong moves."

"When you thought about us getting to know one another, what did you envision? Was sex in the mix?"

He turned and looked at her. "No. That was something God was already dealing with me about." He came back and sat down. "I saw us talking, about any and everything. Doing fun stuff—sky's the limit after that swing dance. And studying the Bible together—that would be dope. And—what?"

Cinda had gotten a text from Faith and rolled her eyes at the story she linked. She showed him the picture, and he did a double take.

"How did they get this picture of you? Was this today? You've got the same clothes on."

"Randall's daughters, the twins, showed up and took my picture. They said they were giving it to *Entertainment Now.*"

"Why would they do that? How do you even know them?"

Cinda was quiet a moment. "I guess this is where you learn a little more about me. Randall Rogers was my father."

CHAPTER 34

"Ooh, which one was that, the chocolate lava sensation?" Treva eyed Alonzo's dessert across the booth and elbowed Lance. "Babe, we should've gotten that. I don't know what I was thinking. You know I'm all about chocolate these days."

"But when you ordered," Lance said, "you were all about caramel."

"I was, wasn't I?" Treva chuckled, looking at her own dessert. "I can't deal with these multiple cravings."

Cinda looked at Alonzo. "I'm confused," she said. "When you ordered your appetizer and main entree, you were so particular about fat intake." She pointed to the chocolate lava. "I'm pretty sure that blows all of that out of the water."

"That's why I was particular." Alonzo dipped his spoon into the mass of ice cream, fudge, and cake. "I look at the dessert menu and work backward from there." He picked up an extra spoon and gave it to her, sliding his dessert between them. "Plus I figured you'd join me."

Cinda didn't hesitate, her spoon colliding with his as she helped herself to a taste. "Mmm. It's as good as it looks."

Treva tasted hers, smiling to herself. Alonzo had invited her and Lance on the double date, and simply watching the two of them had been a joy.

"You two mentioned that you're newlyweds," Alonzo said. "How did you meet?"

"I came to St. Louis for a women's conference last May," Treva said. "Lance and I ended up doing a workshop together, so between preparing for the workshop and everything else—it sounds strange, but by the end of the weekend, this man had rocked my world."

"That's wild," Alonzo said. "Not saying it's the same, but after last Friday night, I get it. I'd never experienced anything like that." He looked at Lance. "Would you call it a God thing?"

"It was definitely a God thing with me and Treva," Lance said. "I know how I am. I tended to put up a wall where women were concerned, for various reasons. So I knew something was going on when she was breaking through the wall and knocking on my heart." He paused. "I think when God starts stirring something new and different, you recognize it, especially if you're seeking Him. God is so good He makes sure you recognize it."

Alonzo shook his head. "I know this is why I'm here," he said. "To hear things I never hear. You've been dropping stuff all night, and this is just light dinner convo. Real talk, Lance—thank you for taking time for me. I'm looking forward to tomorrow already."

"I could already see God stirring something in you," Lance said, "from the time we met. And it blows me away that Randall played such a part in all of this. If it weren't for him, we wouldn't be sitting here with either of you."

"I'm still blown away that Cinda is his daughter." Alonzo looked at her. "I wish you weren't dealing with all the drama today, though."

"I love how both of you turned off your phones at dinner," Treva said, "and let the chaos swirl without you."

"I'd appreciate prayers about what to say and do," Alonzo said.

"What they did to Cinda—I want to rise up and defend her. But if I say something, it blows up all the more."

"If the worst that people have to say about me is that I'm a maid," Cinda said, "I'll take it. I just feel bad because Alonzo has to bear the brunt of it. A couple of blogs were like, 'Poor Alonzo didn't know his mysterious woman cleaned toilets for a living.'"

"And you know what I say to that?" Alonzo said. "My mom used to clean toilets for a living, and I'm nothing but proud of her. That's how she raised me and kept me out of trouble."

"Hey, that would shut down a whole lot of talk," Treva said. "People forget where they came from. How many celebrities did so-called 'menial' jobs while they were struggling to make it?"

"Absolutely," Alonzo said. "I had a gig busing tables and washing dishes for a while, and was happy to get that paycheck."

Cinda quirked a brow at him. "I'm trying to picture you busing tables."

"See, you wanted to blast me, but I'm just a guy with humble roots." He scarfed down the last bit of cake.

"Whatever." Cinda beat him to the last of the ice cream.

"So, Lance, did you always know you'd be a pastor growing up?" Alonzo said.

Lance smiled a little. "I wasn't thinking about God until I was nineteen and locked up. A local pastor ministered at the jail. That's how God got hold of me."

"Okay, wow," Alonzo said, "that just triggered twenty more questions, at least." He chuckled. "Don't worry, ladies. I'll save some for tomorrow."

"Alonzo," Treva said, "I know you booked a hotel room and value your privacy and all that. But you're more than welcome to stay at our house. Lance is a night owl. You can max out your trip by talking into the night."

A smile alighted on Alonzo's face. "I thought that would be dope, but I was already imposing on you guys enough, showing up like this."

"Well, before you take us up on it . . ." Lance looked at Treva. "Should we warn him?"

~

Treva put fresh towels and toiletries in the lower level bathroom, cleaning as she went. Next she got the sheets from the dryer and carried them to the guest bedroom, passing Cinda and the guys as they talked on the sofa.

Cinda hopped up and followed her. "Are you sure you don't need any help?" she said.

Treva smiled. "You have the hardest time sitting and relaxing. You should be out there enjoying Alonzo's company." She looked at her. "How are you feeling, though? You've had quite a day."

"I don't think anything about this day has really hit me yet," she said. "Like, were Alonzo and I just on a *date*? I know it was a double date, but still."

Treva shook out the bottom sheet. "He's smitten with you, Cinda."

Cinda grabbed one end and fitted it to the mattress. "How long till that wears off?"

"Are you always so pessimistic?" Treva said.

"Pretty much."

"I can identify, actually," Treva said, moving to secure another corner. She stopped and looked at her. "Do you like him?"

"I didn't want to," Cinda said. "I was borderline mean when we first met. But the more I get to know him . . ." She nodded. "I do like him, and that's scary."

"What's scary about it?"

"The bubble will burst at some point." Cinda worked the top sheet. "He's Mr. Hollywood. Literally. The fact that he wants to get to know me—I can't make it add up."

"Do you believe he's sincere?"

Cinda thought about it. "After he posted that picture and flew out here—it's hard not to."

Treva added the comforter and they adjusted it at each end. "Give him a chance to be Alonzo. Give yourself a chance to know the real Alonzo."

"What do you mean?"

"You had your own notions about who he was and what he was like. And just now you said, 'He's Mr. Hollywood. Literally.' Really? Is that who he is at his core?" Treva looked at her. "I think God has him here so he can get away from all that and tap into who he is in Christ. That's the Alonzo who's drawn to you."

"Mom, are you downstairs?"

Treva gave Cinda an amused look. "Joy's been at a friend's house all day," she said. "I've been waiting for this." She moved out of the bedroom. "Yes, down here, Joy," she called.

"Can I go back to Lindsey's and spend the night?" Joy said, hustling downstairs. "Her mom said it's okay, and I did my chores and—" Her eyes hit Alonzo and she stared a good ten seconds before turning to Treva. "Why does that look exactly like Alonzo Coles?"

He stood, offering his hand. "Joy, it's good to meet you. I'm Alonzo."

"This can't be real," Joy said. "Why would you be in my house?" She glanced around. "Okay, who's playing games?"

"Shake his hand, Joy," Treva said.

Joy stared at him again and let it sink in, then bypassed the hand and hugged him. "Oh, man, this is so totally lit." She backed up. "Wait till I tell Lindsey and Barb and—"

"No, ma'am," Treva said. "You're not telling anyone. We want Alonzo to be able to enjoy his privacy."

Joy lifted her phone. "Can I post a picture?"

"Nope," Treva said. "And yes, you can stay at Lindsey's tonight."

"Why in the world would I go over there?" Joy plopped onto the sofa.

Lance chuckled. "This was what we warned you about, my man."

"Come on up with me, Joy," Treva said, heading for the stairs.

"I can't hang out?" Joy sighed, hopping up.

"Hey," Alonzo said, walking over to her. "Nobody said we couldn't *take* a picture."

Joy's eyes widened. She held out her phone for a selfie and made a super-surprised face. Alonzo matched it, and she snapped.

Treva continued upstairs with Joy following behind.

"But what is he doing here?" Joy said. "I need details. How did it—"

Treva's phone dinged across the counter.

"Joy, can you see who that is?" Treva said.

Joy went to look. "Faith," she said. "**Outdoor concert's over. Chilling in the park.**" Joy looked up. "Let me guess who she's with. Ummm . . ." Her eyes went upward.

"They're just friends," Treva said.

"Mom, sometimes you need to get a clue," Joy said. "First of all, if I were old enough, *I'd* date Reggie. He's a cutie." She grabbed a banana. "*And* unlike Jesse, he meets the requirements."

"What requirements would those be, Joy?"

"Christian. For-real, for-real." She started peeling. "If you ask me, the dating thing should have jumped off a long time ago." She shrugged. "It's only a matter of time." She tossed the peel and took a seat. "Now, back to Alonzo."

Treva leaned against the counter. Had she missed it? Were Faith and Reggie headed for a relationship? She loved Reggie, and he did have so much in his favor. So why was her main thought that it wouldn't be a good idea?

CHAPTER 35

"Fall semester is a little over two months away." Faith walked with Reggie along a quiet stretch in Forest Park as he pushed Zoe in the stroller. "And I'm trying to figure out how I'll be able to finish my degree this coming school year."

"Why, what's up?" Reggie said.

"Mom was going to take care of Zoe during class time," Faith said, "but now she'll be having a baby herself toward the end of the year. Since it's all unexpected, she's kind of stressing." The subtle breeze felt good across her face. "It'll be a lot for Mom to get back in the swing of life with a newborn. I'd feel bad adding Zoe to the mix. She'll be a walking handful by then."

"You need two semesters' worth of credits to graduate?"

Faith nodded. "I guess I could extend that to three semesters and graduate fall of next year. That way I won't have to take as many classes each time. Childcare will be cheaper if it's only two days a week or so."

"First, you're assuming your mom can't handle the two of them," Reggie said. "Second, you're assuming there'd be nobody else to help. If you needed me to watch Zoe for a few hours a week one semester, no big deal."

"You would do that? Maybe the question is—*could* you do that?"

"She might have the same diaper on when you got back, but . . ." He chuckled. "I told you I got skills, thanks to my sister and her kids." He looked at her. "You should think about knocking out some credits this summer too. Maybe you could graduate on time."

"I did that last summer," Faith said, "knowing I'd have to take off spring semester when Zoe was born." She nodded. "I think that's my answer, if they're offering courses I need." She looked at him. "You're actually helpful sometimes."

Reggie paused, taking his phone from his pocket and replying to a text.

"You're kind of a mystery," Faith said.

Reggie kept his focus on the path. "How's that?"

"I don't really know what you do when we're not hanging out."

"No mystery there. Work."

"What do you do when you're not working?"

"Answer questions from you."

She made a face at him. "When you're not working, and you're not with me, what do you like to do?"

He shrugged. "Depends. Those get-togethers with the guys, which we haven't done lately—come to think of it, not since Randall's been gone. Tommy and I watch sports. I like to get to the gym—but I guess that doesn't count since you've squeezed your way into my workout routine."

"Oh, is that how it went?" Faith said. "Like when Joy watched Zoe for me a couple Saturday mornings so I could go to the coffee shop to do Bible study and have quiet time *by myself*, and you worked your way into that?"

He paused, looking at her. "How about you wanting to know when I'm grocery shopping so you can tag along?"

She put a hand to her hip. "I can't run to the mall without you hopping in the car."

He fixed her with his gaze and wouldn't let go. She could feel it, the intensity coursing through her veins. His hand went to her back, her arm around his side, and she closed her eyes as his lips touched hers. Slowly their arms found a tighter embrace as the kiss deepened.

And suddenly Reggie pulled away.

He pushed the stroller to a park bench a few feet away and sat on it. Faith sat beside him.

He stared into the distance. "I was telling myself things were back to normal."

"Me too," Faith said. "Did you want them to be?"

He glanced at her. "Yes and no. I keep thinking about what you said. Neither of us wants chaos."

Faith let silence reign a few moments. Then, "I wish you were the first guy to come into my life."

He looked at her, waiting.

"I wouldn't be thinking chaos. I'd be thinking about talks I used to have with my dad about 'the right guy.' And I'd be thanking God because you're that guy." She gave him a glance, then looked away. "I don't deserve a guy like you. And I'm so jaded and skeptical now. Every ideal I used to have about relationships is out the window. For one thing, *I'm* not the ideal I envisioned. A single mom at twenty?"

"Nobody's ideal, Faith. I know I'm not—you know it too, much as you like to point out my flaws. And there is no ideal relationship." He turned toward her. "But two people who love Jesus and *know* they need mad grace? I'm thinking we can build on that."

"What are you saying?" Faith wasn't sure she wanted to know.

"We tried to pretend the dance didn't happen," he said. "Now we can try to pretend the kiss didn't happen. But I don't know if we can find our way back to normal, because of what's happening between us." He looked at her. "We can pull back and stop spending so much time. Or we can build a new normal."

Her insides flipped. "You're really talking about a relationship?"

"I don't know what word to put on it, Faith. I'm in the moment just like you." His eyes held an intensity. "I just feel like there's something here. Am I wrong?'

"No," Faith said, looking at him. "There's a lot here. That's what scares me."

"Then let's pull back," Reggie said. "I don't want you to do anything that doesn't feel right."

"I didn't say it doesn't feel right," Faith said. "We might fuss and get on each other's nerves—but being around you always feels right."

Reggie moved closer, put her head on his shoulder. "Instead of chaos, it just might be beautiful."

"Is this a new side of you, Reggie Porter? Are you a romantic at heart?"

He took his time answering. "You know I've been hurt, Faith. There's a whole lot in my heart that's been locked up. Believe me, this scares me too."

"So whatever we call this—what will it look like?"

"A lot like it's been," he said. "Strong friendship. Strong faith in Christ. You bugging the mess out of me. Except I get to do this." He took her hand in his.

"You have to admit it's weird, though."

"What?"

"Holding hands. *Kissing*. We weren't just friends. You were my big brother."

"Did the kiss feel weird while we were kissing?"

She looked at him, sure she was blushing. "I'm not sure. Can we run another test?"

He shifted a little and leaned in, kissing her again.

Faith exhaled. "Umm . . . Can't say it felt weird at all. I think we're safe there."

Reggie looked into her eyes. "Have I told you you're beautiful?"

"You have. Question is—have I told you you're handsome?"

"You've never said that, no."

"Everything about you is kind of dreamy." She let her gaze linger on him. "I can tell you that in the new normal."

Reggie smiled a little. "I'm liking whatever this is already."

CHAPTER 36

*A*lonzo watched the terminal come into view as Cinda's Nissan pulled into the airport drop-off spot.

She shifted the car to Park. "Seems like you just got here, and you're taking off already."

"I was thinking the same thing." Alonzo faced her. "I knew it would be a quick trip, though. That twenty-four hours was packed." He waved his phone at her. "And this time I've got what I need."

"You're really keeping in touch?"

"You're asking me that after I flew all the way out here?"

"You were coming to see Lance too."

"It wasn't Lance's face I saw when I got on that plane." Alonzo focused on her. "I have no choice but to keep in touch. Still too much about you that's intriguing."

"So when I'm no longer intriguing, you'll move on."

"Yes," Alonzo said, "to the next Cinda chapter."

Her sigh said she was highly skeptical. She glanced at travelers walking inside. "Won't you be mobbed walking through the airport? That ball cap only shields so much."

"The setup varies depending on the airport," he said. "But I'll have an escort to get me checked in away from the main areas."

"Did you dream about all this?" Cinda said. "'I'll be such a star that I'll be whisked through airports to avoid paparazzi and adoring fans.'"

"I'm not a big star, Cinda," Alonzo said. "I just love what I do, and I want to do it well. All the other stuff comes with it."

"Yeah, I got a small taste today when that photographer showed up," she said. "I can't imagine living like you do. No privacy at all. And whatever happened to basic manners?"

Alonzo smiled. "You played it well, though, Warrior Princess."

"He acted like he was catching me in the act or something." Cinda was getting riled again. "So what it got 'leaked' where I work. We can make it work to our benefit."

He was laughing now. "When you said, 'Come on in and take pictures so people can see how nice this place is—and make sure you print the full name so we can get customers'—I was dead."

"He should've taken me up on it," Cinda said. "The real story was you were right in the sitting room." She glanced at her watch. "Don't you need to get going?"

He stared out of the window, wondering whether to go with what was pressing on his heart. He looked back at her. "I'm not leaving just yet."

～

Alonzo followed as Cinda browsed polo shirts in a menswear department at Frontenac Plaza, plucking certain colors.

She turned suddenly and smacked his hand. "I saw you pick up that blue one. It's on the banned list."

"Why? It goes with everything."

"You said I could dress you."

"But if I'm staying an extra few days, we need *something* to mix and match and recycle."

"Mr. Coles," she said, "put it back."

"All right, but if I'm looking like a clown . . ."

Cinda looked amused. "You're not willing to look like a clown for me, Alonzo?"

"Nah. Not at all."

She handed a pile of shirts to the sales associate, who left to add them to the items in the dressing room. "Okay, last thing we need—couple pairs of pants." She eyed him. "You've got faded jeans. Maybe some dark wash and a pair of chinos."

"I'm guessing they won't be navy, beige, or black."

"You've got all that at home, I'm sure," Cinda said. "We're expanding your horizons."

She got what suited her in Alonzo's size and they walked back to the dressing area.

The sales associate approached them. "You won't be disturbed," she said. "Thankfully the floor is quiet this evening. I'll be sure to steer clientele to the other section of the dressing area."

Cinda went into his dressing room and paired the outfits she wanted him to try on, together with the footwear they'd gotten. "I'll be out here waiting to see," she said, smiling.

Alonzo watched her leave, certain he could watch her all day.

He turned to see which he'd try first as his phone rang in his pocket. He already knew who it was.

"Hey, Bev," he said.

"What's going on with you, Alonzo? First you take off with little notice, but, okay, it's just overnight. Now you're gone another five days?" She paused only a second. "You've got appointments, press interviews, and a fitting for the LA premiere, *which is next week*. Is this because of that woman whose picture you posted?"

"I've already thought about all that," Alonzo said, his voice low. "The appointments aren't time sensitive; they can be rescheduled. One of the press interviews is by phone, the other I can fly in for, if need be. And I'll be back in time for the fitting. We're good."

"You didn't answer my last question."

"It's personal, Bev."

She sighed. "This is not the time to go off the rails, Alonzo. There's too much at stake."

"I know," he said. "I'm good."

"I'll get with the publicist and see what we can reschedule. Call you tomorrow."

Alonzo put the phone down and changed into the first outfit.

"What is taking you so long?" Cinda said.

He opened the door and she walked in, beaming.

"Oh, man, look at you." She did a full walk around him. "Casual with the right amount of edgy. Those cuffed jeans with the suede chelsea boots? Bomb." She gestured toward the three-way. "Do you see yourself? Check the mirror."

"Never in a million years would I have worn cuffed jeans," he said. "But seeing it now . . ." He had to nod. "It's kind of tight."

"And olive looks really good on you," Cinda said. "Still subdued but different." She clapped her hands together. "Yay! On to the next one."

A half hour later, she stood in the dressing room doorway as he gathered the things that worked—three of four outfits had been a hit.

"Deep purple is your color," she said. "Makes the tone of your skin pop. Really pretty on you."

He looked at her. "Didn't you say that's one of your colors?"

"Makes sense." She moved closer and held her arm next to his. "Both sort of a medium brownish hue."

The sales associate showed up, her arms filled with clothes— women's clothes. She looked at Cinda. "I'll put these in the room next door."

"I don't understand," Cinda said. "This is the men's area. And anyway, I didn't pick anything out."

"Oh, but you did," Alonzo said, "when I asked you to show me what you'd pick for yourself."

"You said you wanted to see what kind of style sense I had

before you let me loose in the men's"—her eyes got big—"Alonzo, you can't do this."

"Ma'am, thank you," Alonzo said over Cinda's shoulder. "She'll be right over to try those on."

"No, I won't," Cinda said.

"I saw your eyes light up when you were looking at those pieces," he said.

"Where would I even wear that stuff?" she said. "Certainly not to work. I don't go anywhere. That's why I don't need nice clothes."

"Weren't you the one talking about expanding horizons when it comes to clothing?" he said. "We'll go someplace every night I'm here, just so you can wear it all."

"No," she said. "I don't need you to spend money on me like that."

"Just try on the purple one."

It took her a few seconds to move, but she walked over to the next room. A few moments later, he was outside her door.

"What's taking you so long?" he said.

She opened the door and looked at him. "You didn't."

He came into the doorway, with the purple shirt back on. "You're breathtaking," he said. "Do you see yourself? Check the mirror."

She turned toward it, her full length in view, ball cap to bare feet, wearing a purple shirtdress.

He moved closer, surveying the mirror as the sales associate returned.

"Oh," she said, looking from the doorway, "such a striking pair, the two of you. And that dress hangs perfectly on you." She nodded a moment more before moving on.

Alonzo moved to the other pieces. "How about trying this—"

"We'll get the purple dress," Cinda said, looking at him. "Thank you."

"And shoes."

She narrowed her eyes at him.

"Hey, you pushed the suede boots my way. They were the bomb. Just doing the same, looking out." He tugged the rim of her cap. "And thank you," he said, "for expanding my horizons. Friday night date in the menswear department. Who knew?"

CHAPTER 37

"Breakfast is my favorite time of day now." Cinda searched a kitchen utility drawer. "It always smells so good in here."

Stephanie pulled a sausage-and-egg casserole from the oven. "I didn't think I could do a B and B for a lot of reasons," she said. "One was I've never been a big cook, and people are serious about the *breakfast* part of bed-and-breakfast." She removed the oven mitts from her hands. "But I'm glad I decided to get up and test recipes whether we have guests or not. I'm actually liking this."

"And you might not have regular guests, but you do have an appreciative husband." Lindell rose from the kitchen table, his plate empty. "Those pancakes were delicious."

He kissed her as he passed by, putting his plate in the sink. "I'm off to work for a few hours," he said.

"You really have to work today?" Stephanie said.

"I know," Lindell said. "I thought the administrative side of medicine would be less intense, but it's just a different kind of intense."

"I can tell you love it, though," Stephanie said. "And that's a blessing." She added more batter to the griddle as Lindell walked out, then hurried after him. "Dinner date tonight, right?"

"Six o'clock reservation," Lindell called back. "Love you, babe."

"Love you too," Stephanie said.

Cinda smiled. "You two are cute."

"Girl, nothing but God," Stephanie said. "One day I'll tell you how I thought our marriage was over last year. I had left him and everything."

Cinda's eyes widened. "Are you serious?"

She flipped the pancakes, nodding. "Had to do a lot of praying and a lot of standing on the Word. The names we chose for the B and B and the guest rooms came out of that."

"Treva mentioned that at the Bible study," Cinda said. "I've been meaning to ask more about the names of those rooms."

"Good morning."

Cinda turned, her stomach doing the slightest flip. Yep, he was still here, under the same roof. "Hey, sleepyhead," she said.

Alonzo walked into the kitchen in his faded jeans and gray shirt. He looked at his watch. "It's not even eight thirty, which means it's six thirty my time, which means I could go back to sleep."

"Not if you're trying to get some of these pancakes hot off the griddle." Stephanie smiled at him. "How'd you sleep?"

"Really good," he said. "It's my first time at a B and B, and it's like a private retreat up there—flat-screen, whirlpool tub, all kinds of books. I was ready to get the fireplace going just for effect."

"So," Cinda said, "multigrain pancakes. You want yours plain or something mixed in? Blueberries, bananas, nuts, chocolate chips . . ."

"No-brainer," Alonzo said. "Chocolate chips."

Stephanie handed him his plate.

Alonzo looked at it, then at Cinda. "How'd you know?"

"After chocolate lava?"

Stephanie chuckled. "There's also some egg casserole over here, fresh fruit, coffee, juice . . ." She pointed to each. "Cinda's got the dining room table set."

He turned to her. "I'm not eating by myself, am I?"

She gave a slight smile. "I set it for two."

They piled their plates and carried them along with glasses of juice to the dining room. Cinda saw his head bowed after he sat, and she did the same, uttering a silent prayer over the food.

"So how you doing?" Alonzo said. "Last night was a lot."

Cinda sighed. They'd talked about her years growing up, finally meeting her dad, and more. "It was the first time I've ever laid everything out to this point, my entire life basically. Putting it all together, it's just . . . I don't know. Sad."

"I know," Alonzo said. "I prayed for you this morning."

Cinda looked at him as he started eating.

He turned a moment later. "But it's not sad *only*." He sipped some of his juice. "Losing your grandmother was sad, but the way she raised you and protected you was amazing. Your mom obviously had issues, but you also have good memories with her, like swing dancing." He paused. "And Randall . . . Sad. Tragic. All of that. But the time you had with him—even thinking about how God gave him that verse about making the most of the time—wow. You'll have that forever."

Cinda tasted her eggs, pondering that. "Staying up last night talking in the library—it reminded me of late nights with Randall." She looked at him. "That was nice."

"I'm always measuring what to say and how much to say," Alonzo said. "Being around you and Lance these past couple of days, I've unloaded more than I have in years."

She cut into her stack of pancakes. "Can I ask you a question? You don't have to answer if you don't want."

"Cinda, you can ask me anything."

"Just curious," she said. "How many women are you seeing, or 'getting to know'?"

He wiped his mouth and set the napkin down. "Don't ask if you're not going to believe my answer."

She gave him a look as she waited.

"One. You."

Her stomach dipped. "What about all the talk about the love triangle? The twins had a field day with that."

Alonzo turned toward her. "I was seeing Simone for several months. I liked her a lot. I'd even say I cared about her in my own way. But mostly our relationship was physical. In two days I've told you more than she ever knew about me." He took a sip of his juice. "Amber was someone I dated a while back. Ran into her in Austin, one thing led to another. The picture she posted was accurate—she stayed in my room that night."

"And you're not seeing either of them now?"

"No, I'm not." He looked at her. "Can I ask you a question?"

She gave a shrug. "Anything."

"Why haven't you had a boyfriend?"

Cinda looked at her food a moment, needing to figure it out herself. "I had a huge crush on a guy senior year of high school," she said. "He asked me out, and I got so excited. Mom did my hair and helped me pick out something to wear. And then . . ." The memory filled her. "By the time he showed up, she'd been drinking. A lot. She started coming on to him." She paused. She'd never shared this with anyone. "I could see how embarrassed he was for me. I couldn't blame him for getting out of there."

Alonzo kept his focus on her.

"After that, I did what I normally did—stayed to myself. Went to work, came home, buried myself in books and magazines from the library. And as time went on, caring for Mom as her health declined." She shrugged. "It just never happened."

"Cinda, girl, this is crazy." Stephanie walked into the dining room holding the phone. "Two calls in the last half hour from people wanting to stay here tonight because some article just posted that mentioned you—and Alonzo, of course—and where you work. I had to put this last woman on hold because she's telling me the four o'clock check-in won't work."

"What time does she want to come?" Cinda said.

"Around noon," Stephanie said. "They're on the road and were planning to find a hotel when they got to St. Louis. Says she likes how you've handled things and wants to support us—which is cool, but um, ma'am, this is a mom and pop shop. You can't even check in at a hotel at noon." Stephanie sighed. "You know better than I do all that it takes to get things ready. Think I can do it by three?"

"Go ahead and tell her noon," Cinda said. "I can do it."

"But it's your day off," Stephanie said.

Cinda gave her a sheepish look. "I'm the one who got you into this, so . . ."

"You're a sweetheart," Stephanie said. "I'll let her know." She walked back into the kitchen.

"Sorry," Cinda said, rising. "I thought we could explore some of the area today, but duty calls. I can run you to Lance's real quick if you want, though."

"I'm ready to go to work," Alonzo said, rising as well.

"Go to work where?"

"Helping you get the place ready. Just tell me what to do. Dust. Mop. Vacuum. Whatever."

Cinda gave him a look. "You're funny."

"See, you don't know about Miss Coles. Mom didn't play. *Every* Saturday morning I had chores around the house, and if I didn't come correct, I had to do it all over." He gave her the eye. "You don't have anything against teamwork, do you?"

"Well, for one thing, I can probably do a more thorough job—faster—by myself."

"Oh, a little bit cocky about it, huh?" He grinned at her. "All right, Miss Ellis. Challenge accepted. Show me to the cleaning supplies."

~

Cinda turned off the water in the sink and peeked out of the bathroom. She stifled a chuckle. "What exactly are you doing?"

Alonzo lay flat on his back on the floor of the guest room. "I don't care what you say. I know good and well this room is clean enough."

"You vacuumed?"

"Check."

"Dusted?"

"Check."

"I'm talking dresser, top to bottom, nightstands, lamps, picture frames, headboard, bedposts . . ."

He lifted his head a little and looked at her. "I didn't even see any dust on the parts I dusted. The room, bathroom, everything was clean when we walked in." He let his head fall back down. "You're an overachiever."

Cinda walked over and stood above him, gloves on her hands. "Aww, is poor Alonzo tired?"

"I didn't think we'd be all over the house," he said. "I thought we'd clean one or two rooms, tops."

"Guests might relax in their rooms, they might go into one of the sitting rooms, they might read in the library . . . Everything needs to be cleaned."

"I don't know what you do, but it isn't cleaning," Alonzo said. "It's some ultra, extra type stuff. I see why you were like, 'Teamwork? Nah, bruh.'"

"I'll give it to you," she said, "you did your thing, for as long as it lasted."

"Wake me up when you're done."

She shook her head at him, walking back into the bathroom to finish up.

"Hey," Alonzo called a few minutes later. "What's the name of this room?"

"Ever After," Cinda said. "Why?"

"This is dope."

She took her gloves off and went to see what he was talking about.

"I started dusting these picture frames"—he cut his eyes over at her—"and I realized these are Bible verses. Have you read these?"

"I don't think I've actually stopped to read them, no."

"Too busy being extra."

She bumped her shoulder into him.

"Look at this one," he said, lifting the frame in his hand—"'I am with you always, even to the end of the age. Matthew 28:20.' Here's another one." He got it and read the verse aloud—"'Even from everlasting to everlasting, You are God—Psalm 90:2.'"

"Wow," Cinda said, "Stephanie was telling me this morning the backstory to these room names. I didn't realize so much went into the themes." She walked around the room. "Look at this—a little plaque that says John 3:16."

"I should know it by heart, but . . ." Alonzo took out his phone and looked it up. "Ah . . . 'For God so loved the world, that He gave His only begotten Son, that whoever believes in Him shall not perish, but have eternal life.'"

"The real ever after." Cinda almost whispered it. "That's the part I always loved and hated about fairy tales," she said. "I loved the idea of living 'happily ever after'—but knew from my own life it could never be true for me."

"Except it *is* true now," Alonzo said, "in the real sense."

Cinda let that turn over in her mind. "When I prayed that prayer Monday night, it felt like I'd come to the end of a road. My grandmother had talked so much about Jesus, and finally I'd given my life to Him." She and Alonzo had talked about that too last night, their "prodigal" journeys. "But actually, a whole new road has opened up. I feel like so much has shifted—and I don't even know it's shifted."

"My life the past couple of years," Alonzo said, picking up another frame. "I'm finally getting a clue."

He stared at the verse.

"What does that one say?" Cinda said.

She went to read over his shoulder as he glanced back at her.

I will betroth you to Me forever.—Hosea 2:19

CHAPTER 38

"Oh, wow, you're starting this fall?" Treva stood in the aisle before church talking to one of the young women who attended Living Hope. "I didn't know you were going to law school."

Paula smiled. "I'm excited but nervous because I don't know what to expect, and I don't know any attorneys personally," she said. "But someone mentioned the other day that you're one. I had no idea."

Treva nodded. "I practiced for several years in Chicago. You want to get together? We can talk about what it's like, and I can share my experiences." She spotted Johnelle Oliver making her way toward her. "My dad was an attorney, and it was helpful having his insights as I started law school."

"I would love that," Paula said. She took out her phone, and Treva input her number. "I'll text you later this week to arrange a date and time, if that's okay—hey, Miss Oliver."

Johnelle smiled, waiting for them to finish.

"Sounds good," Treva said as Paula went to her seat. She turned to Johnelle and hugged her. "Good morning, Johnelle."

"Good morning," Johnelle said. "So glad I got here early

enough to talk to you. I didn't feel like waiting after church last week, with everybody telling you congrats."

"What's on your mind?" Treva said.

"That pregnancy announcement."

"Okay . . ."

"Not trying to get too personal, but I figure you're at least forty, aren't you?"

"Forty-six."

Johnelle's eyes widened. "You're about my age. You look good for forty-six. But now I'm even more concerned. You know there's a lot of risk with pregnancies at this age. I'm just wondering how you and the pastor are handling that."

Treva could feel herself tense. She'd worked too hard *not* to focus on the risks. "We believe in the power of prayer," she said. "So we're hoping that our friends and family, including church family, will be lifting us up."

"I had a coworker who was pregnant at forty-three and had more than a few complications," Johnelle said. "You can't ignore the little things like you might've been able to do when you were pregnant in your twenties and thirties. First sign of anything—you'd better get to the doctor."

"I appreciate that, Johnelle. I sure will."

"And the other thing I wanted to say—" She looked to her right, and her entire expression changed. "Either my eyes are going bad or that's Alonzo Coles walking into Living Hope Church."

Treva turned, seeing people's reactions.

Johnelle hadn't taken her eyes off of him. "Goodness gracious, that man *knows* he's fine as he want to be. And did he walk up in here with Randall's daughter Cinda? I've been seeing her name all over the place."

"I actually need to go talk to them," Treva said.

Heads were turning all over the sanctuary as Treva made her

way down the aisle. Faith, Zoe, and Reggie had come with them as well.

"Alonzo," Treva said, "Lance said you might want to sit in the front row near him. People might be less inclined to approach you, although that's debatable."

"I'm cool," Alonzo said. "I'll sit wherever they're sitting."

The four of them took seats a few rows back on the right. And in no time, the seats around them began to fill in. A few people introduced themselves and shook his hand, then more got brave enough to follow suit. Soon camera flashes started going off. By the time service would've normally started, a swarm of people had Alonzo surrounded.

Lance took the mic instead of the praise and worship team.

"Hey, Living Hope Church," he said, "in case you weren't aware, Alonzo Coles is visiting with us today."

Cheers sounded in the sanctuary.

"Okay, but"—Lance smiled—"wrong answer."

Chuckles sounded this time.

"Here's the thing," Lance said. "Alonzo is our brother in Christ"—he paused again for more cheers. "Absolutely, give God the praise," he said. "And all he wants to do is worship with us. He's not on display here. Jesus is."

Heads nodded throughout. "Amen."

"Can we be a refuge for him today," Lance said, "a place where he can get away from the things of this world and simply be another worshiper?"

The people around Alonzo began quietly dispersing.

Lance passed the mic to the worship leader as the band started up.

"Let everything that has breath praise the Lord," she said, energy on high. "Come on and stand to your feet!"

Lance came and stood near Treva, leaning to a whisper. "Now, if only we can get through the part of service where they're actually encouraged to greet visitors."

～

"Mom," Faith said, connecting with her in the aisle after church, "the four of us are going someplace for brunch. And Zoe of course." She smiled at the baby, who was smiling up at her. "I'll be home a little later."

"Sounds good," Treva said. "Alonzo doesn't look like he's in a hurry to leave. I'm glad he's feeling comfortable."

Faith glanced over at him. "That's so cool," she said. "Joshua was hanging back, nervous about approaching him—"

"Oh, he's a theater major, right?"

"Right. So I called him over and introduced him, and Alonzo's still talking to him."

"So, hey," Treva said, putting an arm around her daughter and walking a few steps away, "am I seeing something a little different between you and Reggie today?"

Faith's face flushed. "Umm. Possibly?"

"When did that happen?"

"Well," Faith said, "there was a little something the night of the premiere. But mostly, the past couple of days. I was planning to talk to you about it."

"I definitely think we should talk," Treva said.

"Why do you sound like that? I thought you liked Reggie."

"I love Reggie," Treva said. "I just wonder if you're sure about this. It wasn't long ago that you were fighting feelings for Jesse."

Faith rolled her eyes. "Why would you even bring him up?"

"My point exactly," Treva said. "You're still upset about what happened and won't deal with him. I'm the one who's sending him pictures and video of Zoe. But you can't avoid him forever." She looked at her daughter. "I just don't think you need to be rushing into anything. Even if you're over Jesse, you said you needed a long while before you got into another relationship."

"It's not like I could predict the future," Faith said. "I didn't know Reggie and I would become friends and that it might lead to more. You know better than I do how quickly things can change when the right person steps into your life."

Treva nodded slightly. "I can't argue with that," she said. "I just don't want either of you to get hurt."

"Mom, we haven't jumped into the deep." She pulled Zoe's fingers from her earring. "We're seeing what the 'more' looks like. But we're still very much—mainly—friends."

Reggie walked up, Zoe's diaper bag in hand. "You ready?" he asked Faith.

"Yeah," she said.

"I'll see you guys later," Treva said.

She watched as they headed out, Reggie's arm lightly around Faith's shoulder.

CHAPTER 39

"Don't think I didn't see you and Reggie all boo'd up at church yesterday."

Faith looked at Stephanie across the B and B kitchen table as she nursed Zoe. "I'd sure like to know why this is such a hot topic."

"Sounds like I wasn't the only one surprised," Stephanie said.

"I don't see how anybody could be surprised." Cinda glanced over from washing the breakfast dishes. "Faith and Reggie were already a couple in my mind."

"That's because you weren't around for all the Jesse drama." Stephanie paused, taking care of something on her laptop. "No matter what, Faith would be like, 'But I love him,'" Stephanie said, her voice up an octave.

"Oh my gosh, that is so not true," Faith said. "And I haven't been involved with him in over a year."

"Really?" Stephanie said. "I seem to remember a kiss just last month." She gave an exaggerated shrug. "I'm just sayin'."

Faith looked as Alonzo walked in and headed for Cinda at the sink.

"Hey," he said, "Lance and Tommy just pulled up, so I'm about

229

to go. I still feel bad that it's your day off. I should've rescheduled with them."

"I didn't know I'd be swapping Saturday and Monday," Cinda said. "Plus you're working with their schedules. Have fun. I'll be hanging with Faith."

"You good? You need anything?"

"I'm good," Cinda said.

"Okay. Probably won't be back till this evening."

"Okay," she said. "Hey," she called after him.

Alonzo turned.

"Loving that blood orange polo and those chinos on you."

"One of my CC's," he said.

"What's that?"

"Cinda creations."

Their eyes locked a couple seconds before he turned to leave.

"That's the hot topic we need to be talking about." Faith lifted Zoe and patted her back. "I could feel the fire way over here."

"Fire?" Cinda said. "Honestly, we've never so much as hugged."

"I just want to know what you're gonna do when he leaves in two days," Stephanie said. "No way you can spend this much time around him and not be affected."

"He says we'll keep in touch, whatever that means." Cinda rinsed a plate and put it in the dishwasher. "I'm not one to get my hopes up."

Their heads turned at the sound of the doorbell.

"Faith, can you answer that?" Stephanie said, her phone ringing. "I need to get this call."

Faith took Zoe with her to open the door. One of the twins stood on the doorstep.

"Hi," she said, distracted by the car moving down the street. "Is Cinda home?"

"I'll get her," she said. "I'm Faith, by the way." She shook her hand.

"Jordyn," she said. "Nice to meet you."

Faith left the young woman in the entryway and walked back to the kitchen. "Cinda, Jordyn's here."

"What now," Cinda said. "I'm so not in the mood." She looked at Faith. "Will you come with me?"

They walked back out as Jordyn approached.

"Was that Alonzo Coles I just saw leaving?" Jordyn said. "He's *here*?"

"Jordyn, why are you here?" Cinda said. "And where's your camera? Should I go get a toilet plunger for a different effect?"

Jordyn sighed. "I came to apologize." She looked weary, her hair pulled into a loose bun.

Cinda stared at her, waiting.

"What went down last week wasn't cool," she said. "I didn't like the idea from the beginning."

"You seemed pretty excited about it to me," Cinda said. "All the talk about breaking the 'hot entertainment news' of the day. How many new subscribers did you get?"

"I'm not gonna lie," Jordyn said. "This channel is our livelihood, and I'm all about increasing our profile." She paused. "But actually, it really wasn't about our channel. Jade said it wasn't personal, but that's exactly what it was."

"Why does she hate me so much?" Cinda said.

"I wouldn't say she *hates* you. It's just . . ." Jordyn hesitated. "A few years ago we tried to find our own father."

Cinda frowned. "I don't know what you mean."

"Dad—Randall—adopted us," Jordyn said. "Long story, but Mom started seeing someone else during one of their rocky periods. Randall married her knowing she was pregnant, with twins. Anyway, we went on a quest to find our biological father, just like you did. But our story ended differently. He wanted nothing to do with us."

Faith clutched Zoe a little tighter. Throughout most of her pregnancy she'd been anxious that Jesse would do the same—have nothing to do with his daughter. For all of Faith's issues with him, thank God that wasn't one.

"I know how heartbreaking that had to be," Cinda said. "That was my greatest fear."

"But you got open arms instead," Jordyn said. "Dad took you in, showed you love and attention, took you to work, to church . . . That's what we wanted, that kind of acceptance. And watching it up close every day—I think Jade felt she might lose him too, now that Dad had his 'real' daughter."

"You know that's not how Randall felt," Cinda said. "He thought of you as his own. You *were* his own daughters."

"I know," Jordyn said. "But to be honest I felt a little jealous myself, like I almost wished things had been more awkward between you two. Then you get Alonzo Coles's attention?" She shook her head. "Trust me, that added insult to injury for Jade. If she knew he was actually here with you . . .'"

"Does she know you're here?"

"No," Jordyn said. "And I won't hear the end of it when she finds out." She moved to the door. "I'd better go. I'm sorry, Cinda, for everything."

"Jordyn," Cinda said, "do you really have to go? You should hang out with Faith and me today."

She turned. "Why would you want to hang out with me after what I did?"

Cinda gave a slight shrug. "We're sisters."

Faith glanced down the sofa at Jordyn, hoping she didn't feel too out of place. The three of them had spent the day together, running to the mall, playing with makeup, trying on clothes. After grabbing a bite, Jordyn was set to drop them off, and they'd invited her to the Monday night study. She'd wondered if she'd be welcome, and they'd assured her yes. But what if that had been a polite way of saying she didn't really want to come?

"Full disclosure," Treva said. "Lesson two came straight from my own struggles this past week—again. One minute I'm absolutely awed by this pregnancy, the next I'm fighting all kinds of selfish feelings. I know that sounds awful."

"Listen," Cyd said, "if we can't be real then what's the point? We *need* a safe place to vent. We know the right things to think and feel, but we don't always think and feel them. We're human."

"But I'm 'the pastor's wife,'" Treva said. "I think that means I'm supposed to have my act together."

"Girl, whatever," Allison said. "Nobody handed you a cape when you said I do. If you can't be real anywhere else, you know we've got you." She crossed her legs. "Shoot, I was struggling this week too. I'm a *new* newlywed and already seeing that marriage ain't all cute and pretty. Tommy and I are older and both used to operating in our own worlds. I love him, but he is working my last nerve. And can we talk about sex, or is that over the top?"

Faith chuckled. "Jordyn is looking like, 'Who are these people?' and 'What have I gotten myself into?'"

"No," Jordyn said. "I thought it would be all, you know, super churchy and fake. You know? I can't deal with that at all."

"All right, Jordyn," Stephanie said. "We didn't start off on the right foot the other day, but we're tracking now." She got up and high-fived her. "Ain't nobody got time for fake." She turned to Allison. "As for you, Mrs. Porter, speak on. I might need to co-sign."

Allison moved forward. "Okay, so Tommy and I were both single for a long time. Then we dated for over a year and were committed to waiting." She glanced at each of them as she spoke. "So I get that we can now legit enjoy the marital institution. I just don't need to enjoy it every day."

"Oh," Stephanie said. "No, can't co-sign that. I have the opposite problem."

"Wait, you said you were 'committed to waiting,'" Jordyn said. "Are you saying you didn't have sex?"

"We had moments where I wondered if we could hold to it," Allison said. "But no, we didn't."

"What made you do that?" Jordyn said. "I know it's a Christian thing, but I didn't know there were people who took it seriously."

"I'm thirty-seven," Allison said, "and for most of my twenties I didn't take it seriously. But when I got serious about my relationship with God, I had to get my life in order when it came to relationships with men. Sex couldn't be part of it."

"So that's the case for all of you?" Jordyn said. "If you're married, you waited, and if you're single, you're in a holding pattern? Waiting to have sex until who knows when—whenever your future husband comes along? That's kind of crazy to me."

"Well," Faith said, glancing down at Zoe, "it was always my goal to stay a virgin until I got married, but you see how that turned out. I got sidetracked, but I'm recommitted to waiting. It's like Allison said, just comes out of my love for God."

"Waiting sounded crazy to me too, Jordyn," Stephanie said. "Lindell and I were basically living together before we got married, and I grew up in the church and knew better. *But* I also wasn't serious about my relationship with God."

"I was a virgin when I married my first husband," Treva said, "but not for any reasons that had to do with God. I had a lot of issues that kept me away from relationships in general, until Hezekiah came along. Then Lance and I waited—but thank God that was a short engagement."

"Okay, Mom," Faith said.

"Baby girl—real talk."

"That's like me, Treva," Cinda said. "Twenty-five and still a virgin, but only because of circumstances, not any commitment to God." She paused. "Except that's changing, even as I sit here listening. I want to make that my heart commitment to Him."

"I wasn't a virgin when I got married," Cyd said, "and although

Cedric and I waited, I was fighting temptation with him the very first weekend we met."

Faith gasped a little. "No way. I just *knew* you were a virgin when you got married, even at forty. And tempted the first weekend? Okay, sorry, I've still got you on my 'Bible teacher' pedestal. I guess you're human too." She chuckled.

Cyd smiled. "The struggle is real." She looked at Jordyn. "I don't want you to think that anything we're talking about is easy. It literally takes the supernatural power of God."

"Perfect transition to this week's promise." Treva opened her Bible. "Everything we've talked about so far—from my pregnancy to Allison's newlywed struggles to 'how on earth do I pursue sexual purity'—points to this—If I Call." She looked at her notes. "It's in many places in the Bible, but a favorite of mine is Jeremiah 33:3. Can somebody read that?"

A few seconds later, Cinda cleared her throat. "'Call to Me and I will answer you, and I will tell you great and mighty things, which you do not know.'"

"And can someone read Psalm 50:15?" Treva said.

Stephanie turned to the verse and began, "'Call upon Me in the day of trouble; I shall rescue you, and you will honor Me.'"

Treva nodded. "Psalm 91:14-15."

"'Because he has loved Me,'" Allison said, "'therefore I will deliver him; I will set him securely on high, because he has known My name. He will call upon Me, and I will answer him; I will be with him in trouble; I will rescue him and honor him.'"

"Psalm 86:5," Treva said.

"'For You, Lord, are good, and ready to forgive,'" Cyd said, "'and abundant in lovingkindness to all who call upon You.'"

"Let's do one more," Treva said. "Psalm 145:18."

Jordyn looked at Faith's Bible. "'The Lord is near to all who call upon Him,'" she read, "'To all who call upon Him in truth.'"

"And that's just a sample," Treva said. "Did you hear how God responds when we simply call? What would happen if we made this a habit throughout the day—calling on Him in any and every situation?"

"Huh," Allison said. "I already see how powerful that would be, if I actually invited God into all my frustrated moments."

"I was thinking about how He's 'abundant in lovingkindness' if I call," Treva said. "What if I took Him up on that every time I'm feeling this way or that? I would be overflowing with His goodness."

"I would have trouble believing God would really answer when I call," Cinda said. "You're talking about throughout the day? Why would He care about that kind of stuff?"

"He cares how many hairs are on your head, Cinda," Treva said. "So much so that He knows the number. He knows when you sit down and when you rise up. So if He concerns Himself with *those* things, do you think He doesn't care what's affecting you throughout the day?" She thought a moment. "Think about it this way. Do you think Randall cared about what was happening with you?"

Cinda nodded.

"And that was only after knowing you for a short time," Treva said. "God knew you before you were in your mother's womb. Think—Randall times a million. That's how God feels about you. He *wants* you to call on Him. He's waiting on you to call."

"I feel like I took everything for granted with my dad," Jordyn said. "He did so much my whole life. I didn't appreciate it like I should've. I didn't appreciate *him* like I should've." She shook her head. "So you can imagine where I'm at with God."

Cinda looked at her. "But there's one big difference."

"What's that?" Jordyn said.

"With God you've still got time to change things."

CHAPTER 40

"That's the problem, isn't it?" Lindell said. "Why does sex seem more interesting when you're single than when you're married?"

Alonzo leaned back at the card table, enjoying the back and forth as a game of Spades got interrupted with spontaneous talk.

"More interesting when you're single?" Lance looked unconvinced. "I guess that depends how you're living as a single."

"Nah," Tommy said. "Interesting wouldn't be my word for it. At all." He laid down his cards. "Unless you want to talk about how many times God had to deal with me and my thoughts. Now that was interesting."

"But when you know deep down you shouldn't be doing something," Lindell said, "I think it automatically becomes more interesting."

"The forbidden fruit syndrome," Cedric said. "But I never had that *Deep down I shouldn't be doing this* feeling. I was just out there. I'll never forget when I kissed Cyd and thought it would go further, and she said she couldn't go there—I thought she must have a husband somewhere. What other reason could there be?"

Lance laughed. "Cyd said, 'Oh, you gon' learn today.'"

"I only recently got that *I shouldn't be doing this* feeling," Alonzo said. "And I knew it was God trying to steer me a different way." He glanced over at Lindell. "But I get what Lindell is saying. It's like as soon as you tell a toddler not to touch a hot stove, he wants to touch it. How do you reprogram your thoughts?"

"I wanted to be able to pray hard enough for the thoughts to disappear altogether," Tommy said. "And I realized that wasn't happening, as long as I'm in this flesh. What helped was when I said, okay, let me dive into this word. Let me focus on who God is and the *best* that He has for me. And when those thoughts came, I could pray knowing He had the power to keep me, no matter what it felt like in that moment."

"I felt like I was doing those things in college," Reggie said, "but I found out how weak I was."

"Yeah, but she had a whole game plan going," Tommy said. "Let's hope you don't run into anything like that again." He added, "And hopefully you learned some lessons about taking things slow in general."

"What's that supposed to mean?" Reggie said.

"When you fall for someone, you fall hard," Tommy said. "I love that that's your bent. You're not out here trying to run game on these women. But at the same time, you set yourself up to get hurt." He looked at him. "I was there, Reg. I don't want to see you hurt like that again."

"Go ahead and say it," Reggie said. "You're talking about me and Faith."

"I'm talking about you. All I'm saying—take it slow."

Alonzo leaned in. "This is interesting," he said. "I've been trying to think about relationships differently, from a godly perspective. It's not about the physical—I got that. But what is it supposed to look like? Tommy's telling Reggie to take it slow. Lance and Treva had a whirlwind romance. And Tommy, how long were you with Allison before you got married?"

"About a year and a half," Tommy said.

"But there's no one-size-fits-all," Lance said. "Age is clearly a factor, the season of life you're in, all that. But what it should look like is you loving God first and foremost. That leads to you honoring the woman in your life. You're getting to know her—not her body, but soul and spirit. You're pursuing Christ together, instead of one hindering the other's pursuit." Lance paused. "And then what it looks like, is beautiful."

"So whenever you begin to see those things," Alonzo said, "then what?"

"I can tell you what I did," Lance said. "I held on tight and wouldn't let go."

∽

Alonzo was surprised by the butterflies he felt. Across the candlelit table, Cinda browsed the dinner menu, her face framed by ringlets of hair. It was the first time she'd worn makeup and her hair down since his visit. And she looked captivating in that purple shirtdress. But done up or not, she took his breath away.

She laid down the menu. "So your flight is at six in the morning?"

"Yeah," he said. "That way I still have a good chunk of the day to get things done."

She nodded. "Time went by pretty fast."

"It did," he said, "but it also felt like time stood still, at least for a little while."

"I'm sure you're excited about the Thursday premiere," she said. "That's been the main event all along."

He lifted his water glass, took a sip. "Actually, I was wondering . . . if you would dress me for it."

Cinda leaned in as if she hadn't heard right. "For the premiere? That's not even possible. Or necessary. You have a stylist. Won't you be picking up your suit from her tomorrow?"

"Not if you tell me you'll do it."

"Okay, so now we're back to—not possible." Her brow knit. "You don't wear suits off the rack. Your stylist has access to private showrooms and the clout to take what she needs and return it after. But you know all this." She lifted her hands a little. "What are you even talking about?"

"Cinda," Alonzo said, "assume you *could* do all of that. I'm asking would you be *willing* to do it?"

"Alonzo, this is not making sense. For one thing, I'd have to be in LA—tomorrow."

"That was my other question." He looked at her. "Would you be my date to the premiere?"

The server stopped by their table and refilled their glasses. "Have we decided? Are you two ready to order?"

"Sorry," Alonzo said. "Could we have a few more minutes?"

"Certainly, sir."

He couldn't read the look in Cinda's eyes.

"I feel like this is not a small thing," she said, "for you to ask me that."

"I've never taken a date to a premiere," Alonzo said. "Or to any industry event."

"So why are you asking me?"

He took a moment to respond. "I could tell you I really want you to be able to see Randall's movie, and it would be true. I could tell you I think it's important that you be there as his daughter, and it would be true. But what's also true is . . ." His gaze floated to the distance before returning to her. "I just . . . want you with me."

Cinda stared at the space between them. "I don't know, Alonzo." Her eyes lifted slowly to him. "It's one thing for us to hang out here in St. Louis, but Hollywood? That's your world. I wouldn't fit in."

"From the time we've spent in St. Louis, what are you thinking? How are you feeling?"

"About what?" Cinda said.

"About us."

240

"Can we really talk in terms of an *us?*"

"Okay," Alonzo said. "What are you thinking and feeling about me?"

She exhaled softly. "I'm surprised how easily we fell into a rhythm of sharing and acting silly and just *being* with each other. I was surprised by our Bible study late last night, how it opened up even more sharing. I'm surprised how . . . special it all feels."

"I think you were just talking about *us.*"

"But that's here," Cinda said. "Your real life is there. And why do I feel like we're suddenly talking about more than a movie premiere?"

Alonzo looked at her. "My mind is way beyond the premiere, Cinda. I've never . . ." He tried again. "You're the only woman . . ."

Cinda held his gaze.

"I don't know how to put this," he said. "I've never been around a woman I could see myself with, long term. I've never had a desire to give of myself in a deep way. Cinda, I've never been in love." He sighed. "But you make me wonder if all of that is possible, with *us.*"

She took so long to respond Alonzo began to wonder if he'd said too much.

"To tell you the truth," Cinda said finally, "I want to run. From you, from any notion of us." Her eyes held a softness. "I don't see how this works."

"How about one step at a time?" Alonzo said. "Fly to LA with me in the morning."

"I do have a job."

"I've already talked to Stephanie," he said. "She said she'd fire you if you tried to stay and work. And I was hopeful, so I bought your ticket this afternoon—fully refundable in case you said no."

"I've never been on a plane before."

"You expanded my horizons at the department store," he said. "Now we can work on yours, literally. You should apply for a passport too."

"Why?"

"You never know where *us* might take you."

"Where would I stay in LA?" she said.

"My house," Alonzo said. "You know my mom is there also. And in case the thought makes you uneasy, you'd be in a guest room on a different floor, kind of like the B and B."

"I'm not worried about that," Cinda said. "You've never done anything to make me feel uneasy."

"Also," he said, "we have an appointment at my favorite designer's showroom in the afternoon."

"Seriously, what's the deal with wanting me to dress you for this?" she said. "The shopping trip the other day was fun, but this is real. People will actually be looking to see what you're wearing."

He smiled. "Yup."

"That's a lot of pressure."

"How about one step at a time?"

"Combined, it feels like I'm taking several steps."

Alonzo reached his hand across the table and took hold of hers. "But not alone."

CHAPTER 41

The day of the premiere, Cinda woke up in Los Angeles in a beautiful guest room she was sure Alonzo had had a hand in decorating—neutral black and brown everything— feeling things she didn't want to feel. She'd never had a day like yesterday. Flying into LAX was experience enough, seeing first-hand the star treatment as they bypassed main corridors in the terminal. And then there was the showroom, browsing collections by a top designer with an actual purpose—to dress her "client" for the red carpet. Every second was surreal.

Then he'd taken her to a second showroom, where he'd arranged for Cinda to pick an outfit for herself. Two women catered to her like handmaidens, chattering about the need to find the perfect dress, since "everyone" would want to capture her and Alonzo Coles on an official outing together.

But it wasn't the experience in the showrooms that had her in her feelings. It was Alonzo. The way he tended to her, even stopping to get her favorite tea. She and Alonzo had enjoyed some of it last night as they talked outdoors by the fire. Now she stared at the morning text that greeted her:

Text me when u wake up. Will meet u in the kitchen. Got something for u.

Cinda typed a reply, then got out of bed, the beat of her heart disjointed, and not because he had something for her. She'd felt it every morning this past week—the anticipation of being near him.

She showered and threw on her usual—jeans and a top—and pulled her twists into a ponytail. Jordyn had done her hair for her date with Alonzo the other night, but today she was on her own. Hopefully it wouldn't look a curly mess.

She walked the winding halls of the modern mansion with its maple floors, high ceilings, and striking artwork, making her way to the kitchen.

She smiled, seeing Alonzo's mom cooking at the stove. "Good morning, Miss Coles."

The woman turned with a warm smile. "Morning, Cinda, did you sleep okay? I told Lonzo that mattress in there isn't firm enough for my liking."

"It must've been fine, Miss Coles, because I fell right to sleep and didn't wake up once in the night." Cinda moved closer to see what she was whisking in a pot. "Are you making cheese grits?"

"I sure am," she said, then paused. "You like grits, I hope."

Cinda nodded. "Reminds me of my grandmother. It's been a long time since I've had any. Thanks for cooking." She glanced around. "Can I help with anything? Or I can start on the dishes."

Miss Coles reached for some pepper. "You know what else I told Lonzo? I said it's about time you got a woman who's not just pretty but got manners and willing to pitch in and work."

"She sure did tell me that." Alonzo had snuck in, watching them as he leaned against a counter.

Miss Coles glanced back at him. "'Course I did. Cinda helped clean the kitchen last night. That's never happened."

"Miss Coles, I meant to ask you," Cinda said. "Did Alonzo really do weekly chores growing up?"

She let out a chuckle. "Let's put it this way," she said. "We had a weekly battle. That boy would tell me he'd done all his chores. I'd come behind him and find everything *half* done."

"Oh, really?" Cinda said, looking at him.

"Whether it's half done is subjective," Alonzo said. "I see why you two work well together. You're both extra."

"Boy, get out of here," his mom said. "You had no problem being extra when it came to the arts. I wanted to see some extra in those chores."

Alonzo laughed. "You got me there, Momma." He walked over to Cinda, looking at his mother. "Can I steal your helper away for a few minutes?"

Miss Coles removed the pot from the heat. "You're not going far, are you?" she said. "Breakfast will be ready before long."

He kissed his mom's cheek. "Won't be long. Thanks, Momma."

He took Cinda's hand, leading her out of the kitchen.

"Where are we going?" she said.

"I want you to see something."

He led her partway through the house and down an open stairway to a theater with cushy recliners and a giant screen. They sat next to one another, and Alonzo dimmed the lights and fiddled with a remote until the screen came alive.

"What are we watching?" she said.

"This was sent to me early this morning."

Seconds later, she saw him—and her heart leapt. "Randall," she whispered. "Where is this?"

"On set while we were filming," Alonzo said. "You said you didn't have any video of him, so I asked them to send whatever footage they had."

Cinda felt herself trembling a little. She took Alonzo's hand as she watched random scenes of Randall talking, laughing, walking, or simply sitting on set watching the action. But whenever he was talking, she inched forward in her seat. It'd been too long since she'd heard his voice.

"Wait, is this—" Cinda took a breath as the setting changed.

"They took video at the photo shoot as well." He looked at her. "Do you want me to turn it off?"

Cinda shook her head as she swiped tears. "Ohh, wow," she said.

Randall and Alonzo came on screen, posing together, and in between takes, talking and laughing together.

Randall looked into the camera as he locked his arm around Alonzo. "This guy is the real deal," Randall said. He eyed Alonzo. "Is it too late to adopt you? I don't have any sons."

"I'll talk to my mom, but I think we could work something out," Alonzo said. He smiled into the camera, pointing at Randall. "This is my man right here."

The camera guy called them back to attention, and they posed some more before the footage ended and the screen went black.

Cinda couldn't stop crying.

"Maybe I shouldn't have done this," Alonzo said, his arm around her.

"No." Cinda wiped her face. "Seeing Randall, then seeing you and Randall together. It's beautiful." She looked at him. "Can I have a copy of that?"

"It's already on a flash drive for you. Also the pictures he and I took."

"I hate that he's gone." Her head lay on Alonzo's shoulder. "How did he get so deep in my heart in such a short period of time?" She thought about it. "I guess in a way I'd carried him in my heart my whole life."

Silence engulfed them for a few moments.

"Alonzo," she said, "thank you, for everything. You've gone so far beyond—"

"No," he said softly. "I haven't gone beyond anything. I haven't come close to what's in my heart. I'm just trying to do that one-step-at-a-time thing."

"So when the premiere is over and I leave tomorrow, what happens then?"

"Every day for a week now," he said, "I've heard your voice. I've seen your face. I'm spoiled now." He looked at her. "I need my daily dose of Cinda—texts, calls, FaceTime." He paused. "But in a month and a half I start filming my next movie in London. So it'll be a little challenging, with the time difference and the production schedule."

"How long will you be over there?" she said.

"About two months."

She stared downward. "I honestly still don't see how this will work," she said.

"Do you want it to work?"

"What would that even mean?"

"Us."

"I'm not even sure what *that* means." Her insides swirled nonetheless. "It's hard for me to say it, but yes. I do like the thought of us."

Cinda could feel her heart pounding as she and Alonzo stepped onto the red carpet. She'd never seen so many cameras. So many people. So much focused attention. He'd prepped her about what to expect, but experiencing it was something altogether different. She looked about as fans crowded the rope line, reaching for Alonzo, screaming his name. Within seconds, microphones and video cameras had hemmed them in.

He held her hand, leaning to her ear. "You ready?"

She nodded. "I'm ready."

"Alonzo, you've taken everyone by surprise, showing up at the LA premiere with a woman on your arm." The reporter hailed from a major cable news network. "And not just any woman, but the one people have been buzzing about. You're infamously protective of your private life, but do you care to finally comment? She must be special to you."

"Not just to me," Alonzo said, "but to the man behind this movie. I'm happy to comment, and to introduce you to Cinda Ellis —daughter of Randall Rogers."

A flurry of flashes went off.

"Daughter of Randall Rogers?" the reporter said. "We saw the interviews of his family at the St. Louis premiere. Cinda, where were you?"

Microphones shifted her way.

"For reasons beyond my control, I couldn't be part of that." She focused on the woman. "It's complicated. I only discovered Randall was my father recently, and he hadn't known about me until recently either. That's all I will say about that, except that I loved and respected him very much."

"Well, mystery solved as to how the two of you connected," the reporter said. "Randall Rogers obviously introduced you."

"No," Alonzo said, "he didn't. We connected because Cinda is an amazing woman." He gripped her hand tighter. "Now I'm sure we're all here to talk about this amazing movie, right?"

Alonzo fielded questions about the movie—and more about the two of them, which he ignored—before they moved down the carpet, never getting more than a few feet before the next round of questions.

"So this is the woman that's got Alonzo hard to find these days."

A guy had an arm around Alonzo, and was looking at Cinda.

Alonzo was smiling. "Cinda, this is my boy Shane—excuse me, Shane Humphrey, director extraordinaire."

"Whatever, man." Shane extended his hand. "Nice to meet you," he said, "and looking forward to getting to know you, because you must be one special sister."

"Nice to meet you too," Cinda said.

Shane looked as another interviewer approached. "I'll catch up with you two a little later," he said, moving along.

"Alonzo, Barbara Sterling, *InFashion*, always good to see you." She kissed both his cheeks. "And I'd love to meet your beautiful date."

"Absolutely," Alonzo said. "This is Cinda Ellis."

Cinda shook the woman's hand. "Glad to meet you."

"Everyone is fascinated by you two as a couple," she said, "but what struck me most was what you're wearing." She stepped back, eyeing Alonzo. "Your suit, sir. What happened?"

Cinda's stomach dipped.

"What do you mean?" Alonzo said.

"Hello?" Barbara said. "You finally stepped up your game."

"Wow," Alonzo said. "How did I look before?"

"Always handsome. Debonair." She looked down the nose of her glasses. "And boring. But this light gray suit with the muted powder blue shirt? You're giving me classic *and* youthful, and the patterned pocket square gives it an edge. Darling, you're a star. Now you look like one."

Cinda eyed her "client" with a slight smile. She had to agree he looked especially handsome. Last-minute tailoring had given him just the right fit.

"Are you and your stylist working to change up your look?" Barbara said.

"Cinda actually styled me for this event," Alonzo said.

"You put this look together?" Barbara said. "Why was there no mention that you're a stylist? I read that you're a . . . That you work in . . ."

"That I'm a maid," Cinda said, smiling. "That's true, and I enjoy what I do. I only chipped in for this one event."

Barbara leaned in with a fake whisper. "May I suggest you chip in more often?" She took a step back. "And this look on you, Cinda—I'm going bananas. Who are you wearing?"

"It's an Armani," Cinda said. She'd loved the beaded silver cocktail-length dress the moment she saw it.

"She might be showing you up, Alonzo." Barbara motioned to her camera guy. "Are you getting oodles of pictures of these two? To. Die. For."

Alonzo moved to the next interviewer, and Cinda looked around, for the first time taking in all the celebrities who'd shown up.

She felt a hand on her shoulder. "Girl, how you gon' look better than you did at the St. Louis premiere?"

Cinda smiled and turned, hugging Jordyn. "Heyy," she said, beaming, "you're wearing that dress from Allison's store. Who could pull off lime green but you? You look stunning."

"And look what you pulled off." Jordyn fluffed Cinda's hair. "The curls, the shine, so full and pretty."

"Umm," Cinda said, "why is Jade looking over here like that?"

Jordyn followed her gaze. "She's got an attitude about a million things," she said. "She doesn't like the fact that you and I are cool. I didn't choose a dress that complements hers, so we don't look right on camera, according to her. The fact that Mom didn't come—"

"Why not?" Cinda said.

"Now that we know about her affair, she says she doesn't have to pretend." Jordyn had confided in her that they'd discovered Janice's boyfriend at the house—and Cinda had acknowledged the same. "Oh, and seeing you and Alonzo? Jade will forever be unhappy about that."

Alonzo turned at the mention of his name.

"You remember Jordyn," Cinda said. The twins weren't his favorite people, especially after the photo stunt. But he knew she and Jordyn were forging a relationship.

"Hey," Alonzo said, "good to see you again."

"You too," Jordyn said.

Someone called Alonzo and he moved in that direction, taking Cinda's hand.

"Jordyn, we'll catch up later," Cinda said.

Cinda listened to his next interview, a fun one by two film students from Pepperdine. As they moved on, a woman walked up and hugged Alonzo, one long enough to cause his hand to slip from Cinda's.

The woman remained next to him, her arm brushing his, as she extended a hand to Cinda. "Simone O'Dell," the woman said.

"Cinda Ellis," she said, shaking it.

"You two are the hot couple tonight," Simone said. "You must be the one who lives in the Midwest."

"I do," Cinda said.

Simone tossed her head to Alonzo. "Nice," she said. "You're so relationship phobic you're thinking long distance is perfect." She turned back to Cinda. "Be careful." Simone looped her arm in his. "With Alonzo you never know when one of his old flames might end up in his bed."

Alonzo shook his head and pulled away from her, taking Cinda's hand and leading her off.

"That's the one you told me about?" Cinda said.

"One and the same."

"She was telling the truth."

"The old truth."

"I'm just saying."

"You upset?" Alonzo said.

"Why would I be upset?" Cinda said. "You told me your story. I wouldn't hold your past against you."

He squeezed her hand. "I just hope you won't be worried that I'm with someone else."

"What are you saying?" Cinda looked at him. "Are we calling this a committed relationship?"

"Oh," he said. "We didn't establish that?"

Photographers came near, calling for them to pose in front of the movie backdrop.

"You're the only woman I want in my life, Cinda." Alonzo spoke under his breath as cameras flashed. "That's what I want, a committed relationship."

"Isn't it too soon to know that?" Cinda looked out at them, smiling.

"You need more time?"

"I'm not the one who *has* relationships, such that it'd be hard to commit to *one*. I'm making sure you know."

"I said that's what I want."

"But how do you know for sure?"

Alonzo gave her a look.

"You're supposed to be smiling," she said, turning toward the camera.

"After you tell me." His fingers entwined hers. "Can I be your first boyfriend, Cinda?"

Cameras flashed, photographers beckoning them to look here and there.

She stared into his eyes, her insides fluttering as everything around them faded. She knew her answer. It's what she'd been dreaming about all week.

CHAPTER 42

JULY

*T*reva clutched Lance's hand as she took a closer look at the monitor. "Lance, it's a real live baby boy. A *boy.* Look at him."

Lance stared at the screen, blinking back tears. "It's so real right now. Seeing him in there moving around . . . I've never experienced anything like this in my life."

Treva noted the technician taking measurements and pictures, but mostly her eyes remained on the baby.

"I thought this part of my story was written," she said. "Mom of three girls. It's amazing to think God knew one day I'd have a son." She looked up at her husband. "He'll be here before we know it, end of November."

Lance's eyes fell a bit. "Two major life events within a year—marrying you, now having a baby—and my mother can't be part of any of it."

"Not physically present," Treva said, "but I wouldn't say she's not part of it."

She paused and thanked the technician as he finished up, telling her she could get dressed.

"Babe," Treva said. She moved herself to sitting, her stomach nice and round at twenty weeks. "We got to visit your mom right after we returned from our honeymoon. We e-mail back and forth, keeping her updated. She thinks of Zoe as her own great-grandbaby, with all the pictures we send. So you know how it'll be with this baby."

"Sometimes it seems like she'll never be out of prison," he said. "It's been *ten years*. That's how much of my life she's missed. And think about it—our son will be old enough to play Little League baseball before she gets out."

"I know, babe." She brought him close and held him. "It's really hard."

"God knows I'm grateful," Lance said. "She could have over-dosed and died, given the road she was on. She says herself that God saved her and freed her from behind bars. Still, knowing her son is having a son, and she can't be a regular part of his life . . ." He sighed.

"We'll make sure we get him down to Tallahassee as often as we can," Treva said, "for both their sakes. Our son needs to know what an amazing grandmother he has in your mom."

Lance nodded, looking away a moment. "I do thank God for the best news today," he said, "that you and baby boy are both in excellent health."

"One good thing about finding out so late that I'm pregnant is that time is moving pretty fast," she said. "I'm halfway there."

Lance helped her up so she could get dressed.

"I have to say," Treva said, slipping out of the gown and into her pants, "I could go a little crazy buying boy stuff for once. And it'll be too cute seeing a little Lance running around."

"A little Lance?"

"Not saying that'll be his name." She pulled her blouse over her head. "Just picturing a miniature version of you, rugged good looks and all."

"Oh, really."

She moved closer and kissed him. "Really."

He caught her before she could walk away, wrapping his arms around her. "You shouldn't be starting stuff you can't finish."

"Who said I can't finish it?" She gave him a coy smile. "Remember I told you to keep your calendar clear the rest of today?"

"I thought you might have another baby-related appointment."

"Something like that." She kissed him again. "First stop—home, so you can pack your bag."

"In the last six hours," Lance said, "I hopped a plane to New York, took a taxi to mid-Manhattan, and checked into a hotel—and I still don't know what's going on." He looked at his wife. "You said you'd explain it when we got to the room."

"I know," Treva said, "but I was starving." Her gaze flitted from one person to the next on a bench in Times Square. "This has to be the best pepperoni pizza I've had in my life." She held the slice before him so he could take another bite. "Right?"

Lance wiped the corner of his mouth with a napkin. "You do realize whatever you're craving is 'the best' at that moment."

"No, but this really is." She took another bite and savored it. "Okay, so," she said, pausing to sip fresh lemonade, "you know how my emotions have been all over the place with this pregnancy. I was praying to really understand what was going on with me, besides basic hormones."

"Okay," Lance said.

"And even though there's a mix of things," she said, "I realized something. My main problem was you."

He frowned. "What do you mean?"

She turned more toward him. "I didn't know I could love someone the way I love you," she said. "I didn't know I could want to be around someone as much as I want to be with you. Even when I'm mad at you, deep down I can't wait to kiss and make up."

"And this is a problem?"

"Our lives will be so different when the baby comes. It's just how it is." She ate the last bit. "We won't be waking up focused on one another like we do now. When you tell me an appointment canceled and we have fun figuring ways to fill it—probably won't be happening. Flexibility, free time—as much as you're able to get as a pastor—and that one-another focus we have . . . It won't be gone, but it won't be anywhere near what it is now. I was already lamenting the ways our relationship would change." She looked at him. "But then I realized—we still have now."

Lance nodded. "Like today," he said. "Some free time, flexibility to be spontaneous and fly to New York, and what we're doing right now, that one-another vibe."

"So I dipped into my attorney savings, booked two airfares and a room overnight, and got tickets to a play for this evening."

Lance smiled. "I've never been to a Broadway play."

"I remembered," Treva said.

He cast a glance at the images flashing on screens around them. "I know things will change," he said, "and I can deal with less free time and flexibility. But we're just gonna have to be more creative with the one-another focus. I'm not giving that up. You're part of me." He kissed her. "I do have a question, though."

"What?"

"With all this time and flexibility we've got, why are we spending it out here?"

She chuckled a little. "Because I wanted that pizza."

He eyed the box in her hand. "You done?"

She showed him the empty remains.

He stood and tossed the box into a recycling bin. "I have another question," he said, lifting her by hand.

"What's that?" She started walking with him.

"What if we're so one-another focused we miss the play?"

"As long as we don't miss dinner." She waited with him at a crowded crosswalk. "I've got a taste for lobster bisque soup."

"You're serious? That's on your mind right now?"

"It's this father-son tag team." They walked again as the light changed. "Got me managing different cravings."

"Little man can't be flexing already," Lance said. "He might have to be happy with room service."

"Then his dad better pray lobster bisque on the room service menu."

CHAPTER 43

Faith sipped freshly brewed coffee at the kitchen table as she reread the paragraph she'd just typed.

Reggie glanced up from his own laptop across from her. "You'll be up all night, drinking that."

"I need to finish this paper," she said. "This summer session has been intense. And the next one starts in a few days."

"You've been crazy disciplined," he said. "Haven't even hit me up about the zoo."

Faith smiled. "You're not off the hook. We'll get back there before long." She looked at him. "How's your edit coming?"

"It's a new writer submitting with us," he said, "and it's actually well done. I'm not having to do a whole lot, which is nice." He glanced at her. "I'm still waiting for an article from you."

"You know that's not my thing."

"You're an English major," Reggie said. "Writing *is* your thing."

"I'm talking about social media. And anyway, what would I have to say? I'm still getting my life back on track."

"Wow." Reggie focused on her. "If I could transcribe the things you've told me you've learned in the past year about God and your Christian walk, I'd have ten articles."

"Talking to you is not the same as writing to strangers, saying, 'Here's what I learned from all my failures.'"

"People would rather hear that than 'Lessons learned from my perfect life'—which, by the way, doesn't exist."

"The other thing is . . ." Her eyes grazed her laptop screen. "I prayed, asking God if I should write something, and what I could write about, and I'm not hearing anything. Before, when I prayed I would get clarity and direction. I feel like I've got my answer."

"Which is?"

"That's not how God wants to use me," she said, "at least for now. And I understand. I basically disqualified myself."

"God's not saying that at all," Reggie said.

"How would you know what He's saying to me?"

"Because that's you and how you're feeling, not truth from the Word. Faith . . ." He paused, waiting for her to look at him. "We'd all be disqualified if God was looking at our record. There was a time you knew God was calling you to do things like this, and here's your opportunity. If you haven't heard anything, keep waiting. And get back to believing. You can't let your faith take a hit like this."

She sighed softly. This was why she didn't share her feelings of late about ministry. No one could understand what she knew deep in her heart—she didn't occupy the place she once did with God. "Anyway," she said, "I'm waiting for more articles that *you've* penned. You express yourself well through writing."

"It's always been easier for me to say something on paper." He hesitated. "Well, easier to get to the root of what I'm feeling. But that doesn't make it easy to say. It reveals too much." He lapsed into thought for a moment. "I wrote my old girlfriend a long letter after we broke up, but I decided not to give it to her. I didn't want her to have that much of me."

"I'm the same way," Faith said. "I journal so I can get to the root." She looked at him. "When did you know you had that connection with writing?"

"I would do well on school papers and whatnot," Reggie said. "But sophomore year of high school I did something dumb— wrote a poem telling this girl about a crush I had on her. Then I found out it was getting passed around."

"Yikes."

"The guys wouldn't let me live it down." Reggie chuckled a little. "But the girls raved, saying they wished a guy would write them something like that." He shrugged. "I guess that's when I knew."

"I would've never suspected," Faith said, "that a football-playing guy like you would have a deep-feeling, poetic side."

"Don't tell anybody."

"I love that about you, though."

He looked at her. "I'm starting to wonder what *don't* you know about me. Maybe I'm telling you too much. I'd better 'take it slow.'"

"Oh, stop. You know that's not what Tommy meant."

"Who knows what that meant," Reggie said. "That's why it bothered me. Obviously we're not getting physical. So take *what* slow? How much I share about myself? How much time we spend? If it's three days a week, is that too fast? Slow enough? It's so subjective."

"He knows about that deep-feeling side you've got," Faith said. "He doesn't want you getting caught up too soon. Pretty much the same as Mom said to me."

"I get that," Reggie said. "So we're supposed to do what? How do you measure out the right amount of feeling?"

"You really are deep," Faith said.

"Seriously, do I say, I'll give Faith *this* much and no more? I'll go *this* far in letting her know me." He threw up his hands. "How is that even possible? Either I'm in or I'm not. And I can't help it." His voice softened. "With you, I'm in."

Faith could feel her heart rate accelerate, the way it often did around Reggie lately. He had a way of revealing things that seemed at once effortless and penetrating.

"Well, we had the deep dive going as friends," Faith said, "so it would be hard to change it up now. And anyway I don't think we can help it. We're sitting here going deep about whether we should go deep."

Reggie's phone buzzed, and he glanced at it. "Speaking of Tommy," he said. "Says it's after eleven and he's headed to bed." He looked up. "His way of holding me accountable."

"You asked him to do it."

"And I appreciate it," Reggie said. "I can't be hanging out here all times of night while Lance and Treva are out of town. And I could lose track of time and talk to you for hours." He closed his laptop. "Let me get out of here. Not a good look for your sisters either."

Faith walked him to the door, butterflies stirring. "Is it wrong to be a little happy that it's time for you to go?"

Reggie took her hand, his backpack over his shoulder. "Only a little? I'm a lot happy it's time to go."

She smiled as they paused by the door. "So you like this decision?"

"Do I *like* only doing a good-bye kiss—at the door? Let's say, I think it was wise."

They hugged one another for several seconds before their lips came together.

"The thing is," Reggie said moments later, "good-byes can tend to stretch on for a good while."

His embrace was giving her goose bumps. "You never do that, though."

"I want to, though." He kissed her again. "I'll call you tomorrow."

"Wait." She moseyed back to the table, picked up an ink pen, and returned. "You wouldn't give your old girlfriend your note because you didn't want her to know how you felt." She held out the pen. "Promise me you'll always share your heart with me."

"Why do I feel like you'd find a way inside my heart regardless?"

"Promise."

He took it from her and brought her head to his chest. "That's not hard," he said. "I promise."

He kissed her one last time, and she sighed as she watched him walk out.

Lord, Mom and Tommy are both unsure about this . . . And I know I'm the reason. Whatever this is we're doing, let me not mess it up.

CHAPTER 44

*A*lonzo stared at the script spread before him, phone against his ear. "I don't know what to do," he said. "How can I turn this down after they went through all the work to revise it?"

"But you don't feel good about it," Cinda said. "You're just going to ignore that?"

He felt the weight of it in the pit of his stomach. "I was actually hoping they'd come back and say they'd decided to keep the script as is. It would've made my decision easier."

"Is it that you don't know what to do," Cinda said, "or you're afraid to do what's on your heart to do?"

Alonzo's gaze rested vaguely on his office desk. "It was a huge opportunity in itself. Now, with *Bonds of Time* doing so well at the box office, it's a perfect time to capitalize on that momentum. Everything is lined up."

"You didn't answer my question."

He sighed. "I'm terrified to do what's on my heart to do."

"Tell me what's on your heart," she said.

"I keep thinking about a conversation Lance and I had about living a surrendered life." He turned it over in his head even now.

"Just the thought of that scares me. Surrender my career to the Lord? That was fine when I didn't have much of a career and I wanted Him to bless it. But now . . . Who knows what He might do?" He sighed again. "But I know that's what He's saying—surrender. Starting with this project. Cinda, I feel like He's telling me to turn it down."

"Okay, so this is an answer to prayer, right?" Cinda said. "We prayed that you'd have clarity, and you got it."

"Yeah, but I thought that would make it easier."

"This totally reminds me of our lesson this week."

"What was the promise?" Alonzo said. "No, tell me the condition first."

"If I trust."

"Okay, wow. I guess when it comes down to it, that's my issue."

"We were all over the Bible on this one," Cinda said, "but we started with Proverbs 3:5-6."

"Hold up, let me look at it." He grabbed his iPad from the desk and found it in a Bible app. "'Trust in the Lord with all your heart and do not lean on your own understanding. In all your ways acknowledge Him, and He will make your paths straight.'" Alonzo stared at it, rereading it to himself.

"So what was that promise?" Cinda said.

He could hear the smile in her voice. "He'll make my paths straight." He looked at it again. "I see a couple more conditions in there, though."

"You've already been acknowledging Him," she said. "It's just that leaning thing."

"I wish I could see what that 'straight path' would look like."

"Then it wouldn't be trust, would it?"

"Okay, Lucinda."

"Ooh, I hate when you call me that."

"That's what you are in my life," Alonzo said. "You bring light." He sighed. "So many people are in my ear on this. Even Shane's telling me I'd be a fool not to sign onto this project." He was quiet a moment. "Man, trusting and surrendering . . . not easy at all."

"From where I sit, there's no one project that's going to make or break your career. I told you, seeing you in *Bonds of Time*—there's no question God has given you a gift. And if He's the One who gave you that gift? I'm thinking you don't have to worry about what the path'll look like."

He nodded to himself, thankful for her words. He just needed to own them.

"But I'm glad you recognize that none of this is easy," Cinda said. "You didn't get it when you were trying to get *me* to surrender. Talk about scary. Because of you, I'm thinking about things I've never thought about."

"Correction," Alonzo said. "You've thought about it your whole life. I just want you to think seriously about it. Have you been praying about what we talked about?"

"Not . . . exactly," Cinda said.

"So you can pray for clarity for me with the hard things, but not for yourself?"

Silence met him on the other end.

"And actually," Alonzo said, "I don't see why this is hard. You enjoy the work of a stylist, and I'm asking you to do what you enjoy."

"You know there's way more to it than that," Cinda said. "And to be honest? Why would I get vested in something like that when this relationship could end at any time? Then the stylist thing ends."

"I hear you," Alonzo said. "It's hard enough trusting God. But that's nothing compared to trusting me."

"That's not what I'm saying," she said. "Anything can happen. What's the longest relationship you've had?"

"Maybe seven or eight months," he said, thinking, "but I was never committed."

"Never?"

"Never."

"So am I sort of your first girlfriend?"

"I hadn't thought about it that way," he said, "but yeah. It's true for both of us."

"Still," Cinda said, "the point is the same. If we're being real, it probably won't last more than a few months. Then I'd be dealing with two disappointments."

"I dare you not to be a pessimist your entire life."

"I'm a realist."

"What about faith and trust?" he said. "What if God wants to bless you in unexpected ways? And what if you miss it because you're being such a 'realist'?"

"So once again," Cinda said, "you can see clearly when I need to trust, but when it comes to yourself, it's super hard."

Alonzo smiled a little. "Okay, we keep going around this same circle. So what about this—what if we jump in together?"

"Jump in what together?"

"Faith. Trust. Surrender." He sat forward in his chair. "I know you're about to head out, but what if we pray right now, asking God to take over, show us what He wants us to do, and give us courage to do it."

"Why are you suddenly willing to do all that?"

"It's less scary if we take the leap together."

CHAPTER 45

"How long do we have to stay to be polite?" Cinda spoke above the music, looking at Faith through the dim light of the nightclub.

"Considering we got here ten minutes ago," Faith said, "probably a little while longer, at least."

"It's actually a nice party." Reggie plucked appetizers from a tray. "As long as they keep this food flowing." He handed Faith a small plate, then got more for himself.

"But I'm just waiting for Jade to come tell me it's her party too, and she doesn't want me here." Cinda spotted Janice and her boyfriend on the dance floor. One thing was sure—she'd never seen her look happier.

"Hey, y'all made it!" Jordyn came from behind, draping an arm around Cinda and Faith.

"Happy birthday!" they both said, enfolding her in a group hug.

"This is Reggie," Faith said. "I might've mentioned him once or twice."

"Let me think," Jordyn said, shaking his hand. "Reggie . . . Reggie . . ." She smiled. "Nice to finally meet you."

"You as well," Reggie said.

"Do you celebrate like this every year?" Cinda said. "Rent a nightclub and pack it out? I'm wondering what you'll do when you hit twenty-five."

"We like to celebrate big," Jordyn said. "Thinking about the Caribbean next year, so be ready—"

A guy walked up, embraced her, and kissed her. "Happy birthday, gorgeous," he said.

"You said you were coming earlier," Jordyn said.

"I had to take care of some things," he said, "since I'm going home with you afterward. Or did the plan change?"

Jordyn smiled up at him. "You're staying for real?"

"It's your birthday," he said. "You know I have to make it special."

"Oh, let me introduce you," Jordyn said, turning to them. "Y'all, this is Kelvin. Kelvin, this is Faith and Reggie"—she paused—"and my sister, Cinda."

He shook hands with Faith and Reggie. "Cinda," he said, "I've heard a lot about you. Good to meet you."

"It's good to finally meet you too," she said.

"Kelvin, hey!" Jade walked up and gave him a big hug. Like Jordyn, she wore a cute party dress.

"Happy birthday," Kelvin said, "to the second-gorgeous Rogers twin."

Jade put a hand to her hip with a playful pout. "Why I got to be second?"

"'Cause this is my girl right here." Kelvin hugged Jordyn's waist.

"Happy birthday, Jade," Cinda said.

Jade looked at her. "Thanks." She glanced to Cinda's left at Reggie. "So you've got a new man now?"

"No, I'm still with Alonzo," she said.

Jade cut her eyes away as Janice walked up. She went straight to Kelvin.

"I need to talk to you," Janice said.

The two of them walked a ways away, and Jordyn followed, Jade on her heels.

Cinda looked at Faith and Reggie. "Well, that was fun. Think we can go now?"

Reggie had a fresh plate of appetizers. "Five minutes," he said, taking a meatball on a toothpick to his mouth.

"Wow, looks pretty serious," Faith said.

They watched as Kelvin headed for the door, with Jordyn in tears openly arguing with her mother. Moments later, Janice turned and walked away, and Jade went after her.

Cinda approached Jordyn. "Are you going to be okay?"

"She has *so* much nerve," Jordyn said, shaking her head. "She cheated on Daddy for who knows how long. And she brings her boyfriend tonight, after we told her he wasn't invited." She glared at her mother from a distance. "Yet she tells Kelvin he's not welcome at *my* party, and can't stay the night at the house?"

"You thought Janice would agree to let a guy stay with you overnight?"

"Jade does it all the time now that Dad's gone."

"So what does she have against Kelvin?"

Jordyn looked away. "He's married." She quickly added, "But they're separating, and who is Momma to judge me about *anything* I do?" She looked at her phone. "I need to catch him before he drives off."

Jordyn walked off, and Cinda went back to Faith and Reggie.

"If you're ready I can take you home," he said.

"Not yet," Cinda said. "I want to make sure Jordyn's all right."

Cinda passed Jordyn the bottle of hot fudge.

Jordyn squeezed more into her bowl of vanilla ice cream. "With Mom threatening to tell Kelvin's wife, he might never call back." She put the hot fudge on the nightstand and sprawled across Cinda's bed.

"That wouldn't be a bad thing," Cinda said, nestled against the headboard.

"You're taking her side?" She dipped her spoon into the ice cream.

"I'm saying it would be best for all involved, including you," Cinda said. "If that means I'm agreeing with Janice, so be it." She looked at her. "Jordyn. He's married."

Jordyn stared into her bowl. "You know why Mom was upset? She did some digging and found out Kelvin and his wife are going to the islands in a few days to celebrate their anniversary. I guess his wife posted on Facebook." She ate some of her ice cream. "So Mom says he's lying about the separation, and I'm wasting my time." She looked at Cinda. "It's not that he's married. It's that Mom thinks he'll stay married."

"What's Jade saying?"

"She says if that's the case I need to move on. I didn't feel like dealing with either of them tonight, especially since they both have company at the house." She sighed. "Thanks for letting me stay."

"I'm not saying anything different, though," Cinda said. "So you'll probably wind up mad at me too."

Jordyn shrugged. "The way you say things is different. Plus you're binging with me at one in the morning."

"It's a celebration binge," Cinda said. "It's past midnight, so it's official—happy birthday, girl."

"Yeah. Thanks." She eyed her. "Why are you being nice to me? I thought you'd disown me when you found out."

"Why would I do that?"

"Thinking about that Bible study," Jordyn said, "and people's views about sex. I knew you'd be shocked that I would . . . you know."

"Is that why you haven't come back?"

Jordyn stared downward. "I think so." Her phone buzzed on the bed beside her. "It's Kelvin," she said. "He wants to talk." In a flash she eased out of the room to call him.

Cinda looked at her own phone. Alonzo had texted about an hour ago, asking her to call. She clicked and let it dial.

"Hey, just getting home?" he said. "How was the party?"

"I've been home a while," Cinda said, "but I can't really talk. I've got company."

"Faith's with you?"

"No," Cinda said, her voice low. "It's Jordyn."

"One of the twins cutting into our time? Nah, I got a problem."

"You're bad."

"And you have a package," he said.

"I do?" she said. "How would I get a package this time of night."

"Go to the Faithful & True room."

Cinda could feel the butterflies as she got up and walked out of her room. She glanced at Jordyn, in a corner of the third-floor foyer, talking through tears. Cinda hoped she wouldn't mind praying together tonight.

She went down to the second level. "Okay, I'm walking in," she said, opening the door. She'd cleaned the room just today for guests who'd be checking in tomorrow.

"Read the verse in the crystal picture frame on the nightstand."

Cinda's mind went to Alonzo's visit. Once they'd discovered the theme of the Ever After room, they'd gone into each and explored. She hadn't known that Faithful & True was a name of God. This room was filled with who God is.

She picked up the frame and read it aloud. "'I am the Alpha and the Omega, the first and the last, the beginning and the end—Revelation 22:13.'"

"Earlier this evening," Alonzo said, "you said we probably won't last more than a few months, and I can't blame you. I don't have a good track record with women." He paused. "I don't expect you to have faith in our relationship or in me. But like we prayed,

I hope you have faith in what God is able to do in your life, beginning to end. Let Him be your everything, Cinda."

She sat on the edge of the bed as tears filled her eyes.

"Open the top drawer of the nightstand," Alonzo said.

She reached for it, her hand trembling slightly, and pulled it open. A small wrapped package sat inside. "Should I open it?" she said, swiping tears.

"Yes. Open it."

She unwrapped it and paused when she saw a velvet box inside. She took a breath and lifted the top. "Oh, Alonzo . . ."

She gently took the gold necklace from the case and brought the pendant closer. It was in the shape of a heart, and engraved on the heart were their initials—*C & A*—and the verse *Rev. 22:13*.

"How did you do this?"

"I called Treva and Stephanie and told them what I wanted to do. They helped make it happen. Did you open the locket?"

"Oh, wait." She opened to a picture of the two of them from the LA premiere.

"Cinda," he said, "I can't make promises to you and follow through like God can. I can't be there for you like He can. But if we look to Him as the Alpha and the Omega, the first and the last, the beginning and the end—our everything—this relationship just might stand a chance."

Cinda clutched the gold chain. "I feel like . . ." Emotion moved her to pause. She tried again. "God's showing me so much of who He wants to be in my life and what He wants to do—through you." She stared at the pendant. "Alonzo Zachariah . . ."

"Why'd you say my name like that?"

"A and Z," she said. "Reminds me of this verse. Has anyone ever called you Zee?"

"No one," he said. "Most people don't know my middle name."

"I feel like . . . you're part of the everything God has for me. Calling you Zee would be a reminder of God's faithfulness."

"You're giving me a reason to like my name," he said. "I actually love that."

She put the necklace around her neck and fingered the heart pendant. "This is the most special gift I've ever received. You overwhelm me."

"You started it. You overwhelmed me that first night."

"I'd better go," she said. "But I don't want to."

"I'll call you in the morning."

Cinda went back to her room, walking in as Jordyn shouldered her overnight bag.

"You're going home?" Cinda said.

Jordyn hesitated. "I'm meeting Kelvin at a hotel."

"Jordyn, why?"

"I need closure," she said. "I need to talk to him face-to-face and hear what he has to say. I told him to tell me the truth about his situation, and he said he would."

"You know he'll only tell you what you want to hear," Cinda said. "This isn't leading anywhere good. You need to stay."

"I appreciate your concern," Jordyn said. "I do. I just . . . have to go."

Cinda watched her walk out and did the only thing she could. Pray.

CHAPTER 46

AUGUST

*T*reva walked through the garage entrance to the house with shopping bags in both hands. "Wait till you all see what I picked up."

"Let me guess." Faith looked up from her laptop. "Something blue and boyish."

"Technology," Reggie said. "You've been geeked about all the baby gadgets."

"True," Treva said. "We didn't have a fraction of this stuff when my girls were babies. I've seen a lot of it with Zoe, but I'm getting a kick out of exploring what's out there. But that's not it." She chuckled, walking over to Lance as he closed the oven door. "Hey, babe," she said, kissing him. "Smells good in here. What are you making?"

"Baked salmon, brown rice, and asparagus," he said. "It's just about ready."

"I love that you love to cook." She turned to Faith. "Did I ever tell you that's how he wooed me in the beginning?"

"When I grilled steaks after the conference that night?" he said. "I wasn't wooing you. We were hungry and needed to eat."

"Then why'd you serve it on the patio as the sun was setting?"

"Because that's where the grill is," Lance said.

"With a candle on the table."

"So we could see."

Treva moved closer to him. "Well, that's interesting, because that whole dinner vibe had me feeling tingly inside."

"Now you tell me." Lance wrapped his arms around her, her tummy a barrier between them. "If I recall, that was the night you rejected me."

"I have lapses in sanity now and again." She leaned in and kissed him.

"Mom," Joy said, coming into the kitchen. "These PDAs. Seriously."

Treva looked back at her. "Girl, how is it a public display when I'm in our private house?"

"I think it's cute," Hope said, coming in behind Joy. "Mom and Lance are goals."

Lance looked at her. "We're goals, Hope?"

"Yeah," Hope said. "I want to be in love like that one day."

"Be ready to work, love bug," Treva said. "Relationships aren't easy."

Hope frowned. "What kind of work?"

"Putting the other person before yourself, being willing to compromise and not get your way, giving up some of your individual dreams for the sake of the two of you . . ."

"Oh, I can wait then."

"Yep, you've got plenty of time." Treva swished through the tissue paper in one of the shopping bags. "I know we're about to eat, but I have to show you all this." She pulled out a St. Louis Cardinals onesie and baby baseball cap. "Is this not the cutest?"

Lance grinned. "That's pretty cute. My little man, ready for the game."

"Ooh, let me see," Faith said, coming out of her seat. "Aww, having a little brother gets more and more real."

"And look," Treva said, reaching into a different bag, "I fell in love with this blue-and-green plush blanket. It'll look really good with the bedding we chose—which reminds me, we've got to figure out when we're moving Hope into Joy's room and how we're combining their furniture, and once we get her moved, we can start working on baby boy's room, because I've been looking on Pinterest for ideas for his wall. There's this hand lettering—"

"Babe," Lance said, "can we pick this back up after dinner? Because I think we have a little time before all that needs to be done."

"It seems like we have a lot of time." Treva washed her hands, got Zoe's baby food, and started spooning it into sections of a bowl. "But look how much this boy is growing—we're at twenty-four weeks. I feel like I'm getting bigger by the day. I want to get it all done sooner rather than later."

"I'll be all over it," Lance said. "I'll do the hand lettering myself if I have to."

"We don't have to necessarily go that far."

Lance smiled as he took the salmon from the oven. "Reggie, you want to pray?"

They gathered in a circle.

"Lord, thank You for who You are and all the ways you bless us," Reggie said. "Thank You for the love You've given Lance and Treva, which gives us an example to look to. We pray You watch over the baby and Treva and bless them with excellent health. We thank You for this food and pray it nourishes our bodies. In Jesus' name."

"Amen" sounded at the same time as the doorbell.

"I can get that," Reggie said.

Treva sat with Zoe and attached her bib. "Ready for your dinner, sweet pea?"

Zoe smiled up at her, grabbing at the spoon.

The noise level in the kitchen dropped to zero, and Treva looked up as all eyes faced behind her. She turned.

"Jesse?" Treva said.

He cleared his throat. "It's, uh, good to see everybody."

He went to Lance and hugged him, then Joy and Hope.

"Mrs. Alexander, please, don't get up," he said as Treva moved to give him Zoe. He hugged Treva, then lifted Zoe from her arms.

"Wow," he said, "I hardly recognize you. Look at my princess, growing so big." He kissed her cheek and squeezed her.

Treva glanced at Faith, whose focus was on the table.

"Jesse," Treva said, "I don't recall you mentioning that you were coming to St. Louis. I thought you'd be gearing up for fall semester in Chicago, now that your internship ended."

"You're right," Jesse said. "I hadn't mentioned coming. I wasn't sure I'd be able to work things out, so I wanted to wait."

"How long are you in town?"

"That's what I came to tell you all," he said. "I found out last week that I've been accepted as a transfer student into the master's engineering program at Wash U. I'll be staying in St. Louis."

CHAPTER 47

Faith pushed back in her chair and got up, taking Reggie's hand on her way to the front door. She closed it hard behind her.

"I cannot *believe* him." She walked at a fast clip, down the walkway and onto the front sidewalk. "Who does he think he is, showing up out of the blue like that?" She stopped suddenly, looking at Reggie. "And he transferred to the same school? We'll be in the same city? No warning. He's just *here*?" She kicked back up again down the sidewalk.

"Faith, calm down." Reggie pulled her to a stop. "That's his daughter in there. He hasn't seen her all summer, and you know he misses her. I'm not surprised he'd want to find a way to be part of her life."

"It's the way he goes about things," Faith said. "He should've mentioned it before now. And did he tell Brandy? Or will she be back with another rant?"

Reggie looked at her. "You're going to have to put aside what you have against him, for the sake of Zoe. Now that he's in town, you'll have to work out an arrangement so he can spend time with her. You have to talk to him."

Faith stared into the distance. "I know. And I'm glad he's in her life. I just really wish he didn't have to be in mine."

~

Faith watched as Zoe played in Jesse's arms, poking her fingers into his mouth. "So where will you be staying?"

He shifted on the sofa in the lower level, focused still on Zoe. "I found a duplex with a room for rent. Not far from here actually."

"How far is not far?"

"Sort of, two blocks away."

"You're telling me you're in walking distance?"

"I wanted to be close to campus, and close to Zoe."

Faith's stomach churned. "You didn't think to mention any of this in advance?"

"You never answered any of my text messages, Faith. I figured you wouldn't respond to that either."

"You could have told my mom."

"True," he said. "But like I said, I wanted to see if it would all come together." He played patty-cake with her hands now. "I've done a lot of thinking this summer. A lot of things became clear, and one was that I needed to prioritize time with my daughter."

Faith nodded slightly. "We'll both be in school, so we can coordinate schedules and figure out what works for you to spend time with her. We can be flexible too. I'm totally supportive of your involvement in her life."

"Faith," he said, looking at her, "I was hoping you would accept my apology."

She frowned a little. "Why are you even going there? Let's just deal with Zoe."

"Because you can hardly stand the sight of me. We need to clear the air."

"Actually, we don't," Faith said. "As long as we take care of Zoe's needs, we're good."

He focused on the baby. "I see I'm not the only one with changes this summer. You and Reggie are together now?"

"We are," Faith said.

Jesse nodded. "I just hope you hear me, that I truly am sorry for what happened at Zoe's dedication. I tried to talk to you that day and in the weeks that followed, but I understood why you refused." He paused. "I feel like we've had moments this year where we almost come together—and somehow it's gone again."

"Yeah, well, that shouldn't come as a surprise since you were living with Brandy."

"That happened some time after you hung up on me."

"And once you were living with her, you shouldn't have been down here kissing me, pretending you were still interested."

"How was I pretending? That's how I felt."

"You know what?" Faith shook her head. "Foolish me. I said I wasn't going there, and I'm not. Literally—who cares. I hope you and Brandy have an amazing life together."

"I broke up with Brandy after the dedication," Jesse said. "That's what I was trying to tell you."

Faith looked at him. "So that's what, the ninth breakup for you two? I don't care, Jesse. Your personal life is your business."

"I thought you might not talk to me at all, so . . ." He rubbed Zoe's back. "I'm good right now. I know I made the right choice. I'm looking forward to this school year with my daughter. And you and I have a shared purpose, and a shared love." He looked at her. "I can work with that."

~

"Jesse sure knows how to keep folk guessing, doesn't he?" Stephanie kicked her feet up in the sitting room with a sigh. "Feels good to sit and rest for a minute. Love having guests for the weekend, but ooh, the mornings keep you hopping." She looked at Faith. "I'm proud of him, though, making a change for his daughter."

"I couldn't sleep last night, thinking about all this," Faith said. "It's a major life shift, having Jesse right around the corner."

"What aspect of it kept you awake?" Cinda said.

"He's a wild card," Faith said. "You never know what he'll do, what he'll say."

"Something keeps him coming back," Cinda said, "not just to Zoe, but to you. He wanted you to know how sorry he was."

"If it doesn't concern Zoe, I don't take seriously anything he says." Faith drank from a bottle of water. "But at the same time, his words knock around in my head. I can't get rid of them. He's like a bad virus."

"Just keep in mind, this is all temporary," Stephanie said. "Both of you graduate at the end of this school year and could end up on opposite sides of the country."

"Do you know how long it seems between now and May?" Faith said. "I'm already dreading fall semester, with him popping up at will."

"I'm still trying to understand," Cinda said. "You couldn't sleep last night. You're dreading the semester. Why give him so much focus?"

"That's the thing," Faith said, "I don't want to. I hate that he has that effect on me."

Stephanie looked over at Cinda. "Remember last time we talked about Jesse, and I said you had to be there to witness it? Now you have a seat."

"He's a distraction, is all," Faith said. "And who has time for distractions?"

"Cinda does." Stephanie looked at Faith. "I was calling her the other day, wondering where she was. She was in the middle of one of the bedrooms daydreaming, fingering that necklace."

Cinda pursed her lips. "Faith, you know that's not true."

"It's not?" Stephanie said.

"I was deciding if I wanted to clean the room right then or wait till after lunch," Cinda said. "And I had on headphones and couldn't hear you."

"Still," Faith said, "I bet you'll be doing a lot of daydreaming while Alonzo's overseas. He'll be here Tuesday, right?"

"Just for a day," Cinda said, "on his way to London."

"What's this movie about?" Faith said.

"It's a big action film, which is really different for him," Cinda said. "It's physically demanding, so he's had to do a lot of working out and training."

"That's exciting," Faith said. "Wait till I tell Reggie. He'll love that."

"We've been talking about Jesse," Stephanie said, "but how are things with you and Mr. Porter?"

"Nice. Easy. Drama free." Faith paused. "But I have to watch myself around him. We'll be chilling one minute, maybe even fussing about something stupid—and the next minute things are sizzling, and we're like, okay, time to part."

"I love watching him around you," Cinda said. "Little things, like the way he makes sure you have what you need before he tends to himself."

"I give him a hard time," Faith said, "but he really is a sweetheart."

The front door opened and closed, and they heard footsteps approaching.

"Hey, Reggie," Stephanie and Cinda said, smiling.

Reggie looked at the three of them. "Why is this weird?" He focused on Faith. "Wasn't I supposed to come pick you up right now?"

Faith got up, walked over to him, and gave him a hug.

"What's this for?" Reggie said.

"For being you," Faith said, still embracing him. "Just for being you."

CHAPTER 48

*A*lonzo's phone buzzed as he headed to the airport in the back of a black Town Car. "Hey, Bev," he said.

"Just got word," she said. "Permission came through to film the big climax near the Houses of Parliament in London. It's the first time permission's been granted at this particular location because security is so high, so the crew is over-the-top excited."

"That's incredible," Alonzo said. "Plan B wasn't nearly as exciting, but we thought we had to make it work."

"Lots of caveats, though," Beverly said. "For example, the crew can only film there between midnight and five in the morning. Anyway, they had to alter the rest of the production schedule to accommodate the changes. This meant your itinerary had to change. You're about to board a flight straight to London."

Alonzo stared out the window a moment. His heart had been set on seeing Cinda in only a few hours. "All right," he said. "I get it can't be helped."

"You already had a demanding production schedule," Beverly said, "but with some of the filming now in the middle of the night and other parts during the day, get ready—it'll be grueling." She paused, covering the phone slightly. "Tell them I'm connecting Alonzo right now."

"Connecting me to what?" he said.

"A conference call detailing key changes," Beverly said, "because you'll hit the ground running."

The car pulled to the terminal as Beverly got him on the call. He listened to several voices, trying to get up to speed as he stepped out of the car and walked through a private entrance. An airline worker escorted him, along with another who had his bags.

"We need to move quickly," his escort told him. "Your flight is boarding shortly."

Alonzo nodded, watching as his bags got checked even as he tried not to miss important points on the call. Beverly had been right. This was information he needed to know from the moment his plane landed.

At security, he set his phone in a bin and let it travel through the screener along with his carry-on, picking it up on the other side. A cart drove him down two private hallways, which opened to a public area of the terminal right near his gate. He adjusted his hat and kept his face low, still glued to the conversation, as a few heads turned.

The more he listened, the more excitement he felt. He'd never been part of a production this big. For it to come at this time was a blessing, given the fallout of the past month. He'd turned down the project that had been revised for him, and word was the producers and director weren't happy about it. His chances of working with them in the future—all tops in the field—were slim to none. And for all Alonzo knew, they were spreading the word to others not to seek him out for future projects. He'd done a lot of second-guessing, always coming back to Cinda's reminder—*If I trust.*

But heading to London, hearing excitement about production plans—the timing couldn't have been better. He was eager for the grueling schedule. He'd be physically spent, but it was a chance to show he was committed to his craft, with respect to projects that resonated with him.

He boarded the plane, settling into first class. Minutes later his name was mentioned on the call.

"I'm here," Alonzo said, "about to take off."

"You're taking dedication to a new level," the production assistant said. "Are you really up for all this stunt work?"

Alonzo took some cranberry juice from the flight attendant. "About 90 percent of it," he said. "If I don't kill myself halfway through."

"You've done the hard part with all the daily training," the assistant said. "And I know you've practiced key fighting sequences. But we shot some new choreography for one sequence that we want you to take a look at. It's sick—elements of martial arts and street fighting. We sent it a few minutes ago so you can view it on the flight."

Alonzo could feel his adrenaline pumping. He checked his e-mail and downloaded the video as the plane began to taxi. "Got it," he said. He already knew he'd study it dozens of times.

The same flight attendant eyed him, given that she'd notified passengers twice to end their calls. He let the team know he had to go, switched his phone to airplane mode, and downed his juice as he began watching the video. As the plane climbed above the clouds, it hit him—he hadn't let Cinda know he wasn't coming.

CHAPTER 49

SEPTEMBER

*H*e'd only been overseas for two and a half weeks, but it felt like months.

Cinda checked the time—close to midnight on Friday— mentally noting the time in London—almost six Saturday morning. Alonzo's schedule was so erratic there was no way to know if he was coming or going. No way to know when he'd have a chance to call or even text. She'd thought the distance between St. Louis and LA had been huge. But they'd been in constant contact then, talking first thing in the morning, before bed, and often in between. Now she might hear his voice every couple of days, if that.

She pulled towels out of the dryer and started folding. They had Friday night guests in two rooms, another checking in tomorrow. Stephanie would be down bright and early to get breakfast going. Cinda liked working nights now—laundry, odd cleaning tasks—anything to keep her mind off of the two men with whom she associated late nights and conversation—Randall and Alonzo.

But it wasn't just conversation she missed. She missed being with Alonzo, looking into his face, searching his eyes. Cinda pushed a stack of towels to the side and started another. She'd stood in the baggage claim area two weeks ago, eager to see those eyes, not knowing why he wasn't on the flight until later, when the wifi glitch on his plane had been fixed. Through an e-mail he explained why he was on his way to London and couldn't see her. Tears clouded her eyes. She'd understood, but realized more than ever—he'd nestled deep in her heart.

Her heart reacted even now as her phone vibrated in her jeans pocket. She took it out, hoping, and looked at it. Jordyn?

R u up? I'm outside.

Cinda went to the front door and opened it. "Oh my goodness, what's wrong?"

Eyes reddened, face streaked with tears, Jordyn walked in, barely looking at her.

Cinda took her hand and led her up to her room, closing the door behind them. "Jordyn, what happened?"

Jordyn sat on the edge of the bed. "Kelvin came over tonight. All week I'd been looking forward to seeing him, but . . ." Tears slid down her face. "He said his wife found out about us and he was cutting things off." She held herself. "He said don't call, don't text, act like he doesn't exist. He was so cold. Like I didn't mean anything to him."

Cinda got a box of tissues and gave her a couple, then sat next to her.

"Then Momma and Jade started in with 'I told you so,' and I had to get out of there."

"Jordyn, I honestly don't know what to say." Cinda faced her. "Well, actually I do. But I'm sure you don't want to hear it."

"The night can't get any worse," Jordyn said. "Just say it."

"I'm heartbroken for his wife." Cinda saw Jordyn cut her eyes. "I have to tell you the truth, and that was my first thought, for his wife. Weren't you heartbroken for all that Randall must have felt when you found out about your mom and her boyfriend?"

Jordyn cast her eyes downward.

"As far as Kelvin, my only concern is that he might not mean it," Cinda said. "He might call you again once the dust settles. You have to be the one to cut it off, in your own heart."

"I guess the timing is perfect, since Momma's trying to get us to move with her to Chicago."

"I didn't know she was moving," Cinda said. "But now that I think about it, why wouldn't she? Her job is there."

"And her boyfriend," Jordyn said. "Anyway I thought I'd told you. She put the house on the market last week. Jade and I have been debating what to do. If we stay, we'll have to get an apartment or something." She paused. "I have to admit Kelvin was a big reason I wanted to stay, till tonight."

Cinda's phone dinged with a notification.

"Go ahead and check it," Jordyn said. "Only one person texting you this time of night." She blew her nose and got up, moving into the bathroom.

Cinda looked at the message.

C, getting in after a long night. 5 hrs sleep then back at it. Pls pray. Beyond exhausted. Miss u.

She prayed immediately for good rest for Alonzo, and strength, then typed back—

Praying for you always, Z. So proud of you. You got this! And God's got you. Miss u too.

She stared at it. So much more she could say. She sent it as it was.

"I've never seen you setting up for one of your makeup videos." Cinda hung out with Jordyn a week later in the twins' third-floor studio. "It's even more involved than the setup in the family room."

"Yeah, those are simple." Jordyn surveyed different makeup brushes, put a select few on the vanity table, and the rest in a drawer. "On the sofa talking into the camera. With these, I need more lights, mirrors, plus, of course, all the product."

"So whatever happened to that deal with the makeup company?"

"I told them I needed more time, with losing Dad and every-thing," Jordyn said. "But I was planning to turn it down, since Jade couldn't be part of it. Then I realized—what sense does that make? In the long run, the deal benefits us both. And stepping out on my own might be a good thing. You helped me see that, actually."

"How was that?"

"Jade and I do everything together, from work to social. But getting to know you these past few months, it's opened up a new outlook for me." She paused, two eyeshadow palettes in hand. "I don't know, it's hard to explain. I feel like, it's okay to step outside of Jade's shadow and be my own person."

"I'm excited for you," Cinda said, "and not only for this deal. I think you'll discover so much more that's in you."

"How sweet is this?" Jade said, walking in. "The two of you bonding over Jordyn's new venture."

"I don't consider it *my* venture," Jordyn said. "It's under the umbrella of our brand."

"But apparently I'm the one holding the umbrella," Jade said, "since you have to get out from under my shadow."

Cinda looked at Jade. "But you have to see what a great oppor-tunity this is, for both of you. Right?"

Jade gave a humorless laugh. "You asked me that, as if it's any of your business. I'm surprised you're even here. I thought you'd be home crying your eyes out."

Cinda frowned a little. "Why?"

"You haven't seen the latest about Alonzo? It's all over social media."

Cinda's heart stopped. "Did something happen?" She'd tried not to think the worst, that something could go wrong with one of those stunts.

"I'll show you," Jade said, pulling it up on her phone.

She passed the phone to Cinda, and there it was—a picture of Alonzo embracing a woman, and kissing her.

"In case you're wondering," Jade said, "that's Savannah Silver. She and Alonzo got a lot of buzz a year and a half ago when they were dating."

"So why is this big news?" Cinda said. "It was probably taken back then."

"You can't see the landmarks in the background?" Jade said. "They're in London. She's got a role in this movie he's filming. Spending weeks together in a foreign country—I'm not surprised they're renewing their romance."

Cinda looked more closely at the photo. What spoke louder than the landmarks were the jeans and shirt she'd picked out when they went shopping.

Jade took her phone, navigated to another page, and started reading. "Sources confirm that this exclusive photo was not taken during the actual filming. Apparently the flame was rekindled during off-hours."

"Cinda, don't jump to conclusions," Jordyn said. "You know how the blogs are. They're always looking for something to sensationalize."

"A picture is worth a thousand words," Jade said. "I said from the beginning that the novelty would wear off quickly for Alonzo." She tucked her phone in her pocket. "If you thought you had something special with him, you were naive."

"I'm gonna go," Cinda said, grabbing her purse.

"I'll go with you," Jordyn said. "I can do this later."

"No," Cinda said. "I need to be alone."

She walked the short distance to the B and B, Googling *Alonzo Coles and Savannah Silver*. Jade was right. The picture of the two of them kissing was everywhere. Cinda saw her own name mentioned as well—as one of the many with whom Alonzo had lately been associated.

She stopped just before entering the B and B, seeing an Instagram post by Savannah herself. Same picture, with the caption *I see this is going viral. Everybody's asking, so I'll confirm—oh, yes, Alonzo Coles is a great kisser.*

Cinda took deep breaths as tears slid down her cheeks. She walked inside and up the stairs. The phone rang when she got to her bedroom.

She stared at Alonzo's name on the screen.

A few seconds passed before she could answer, but she couldn't speak.

"Cinda?" he said.

"I'm here," she said.

"I'm in a car almost to our location," he said. "Someone just showed me a picture that's going around. Cinda, it's nothing. We were—"

"Who showed you? Is Savannah with you?"

"No, but—I guess you saw it. You sound upset. Cinda, listen—"

"So Savannah is someone you used to date?"

"That's true," Alonzo said.

"You slept with her?"

"In the past, yes. But—"

"And you didn't think to mention that you'd be spending two months in London with your old girlfriend?

"Cinda, she was never my girlfriend."

"Whatever you want to call it, Alonzo. You didn't think to mention that?" She stood in the middle of her floor. "I've been praying for you and worried about you, and the whole time—"

"Cinda, I'm trying to tell you it was nothing," Alonzo said. "We were rehearsing a scene and kind of joking around."

"The way you were holding her and kissing her looked nothing like a joke to me, nor anyone else apparently."

"I wish I could go into it," he said, "but I'm at the location, and I literally have no time."

"Of course you don't," Cinda said. "You've hardly had time to talk more than a few minutes the entire time you've been there. And I understood, because you were on this grueling schedule. But somehow you've got time to rekindle—"

"Cin, I'm so sorry. They're waiting for me. I'll call—"

"Don't." Cinda swiped tears. "I can't do this, Alonzo. I just can't."

CHAPTER 50

"$\mathcal{M}$rs. Alexander, Lance—I wondered if I could talk to you two for a minute."

Treva turned to Jesse from her spot on the front row of the church. Seemed like one person after another had come to talk after service, and she really needed to stretch her legs.

"You think you can come to the house?" Lance said. "Treva needs to get home and put her feet up."

"A few minutes won't matter," she said. Talking to Jesse here was better than at the house. Things were interesting enough simply on pickups or drop-offs of Zoe.

Jesse took a seat, facing them. "Something you said in the sermon today really spoke to me, Lance, about mentoring and discipleship." He paused. "I wondered if you would mentor me."

Treva and Lance glanced at one another. They'd been noticing how God had been bringing different guys into Lance's life, like Alonzo. Lance had mentored teens for years, but an older generation was coming along.

"I know you're really busy," Jesse added. "I can't imagine what it must take to run a church. Plus you've got a wife, family, baby on the way. I understand if you can't do it."

"What makes you want to do this?" Lance said.

"I've never had a man in my life to teach me anything," Jesse said. "About life anyway. And you were real from the first time I met you."

Lance leaned forward. "Let me be more specific. This wouldn't be ordinary mentoring. We'd be focusing on living God's way, being a man after His heart. That's something you want to do?"

"Coming to church these past three weeks," Jesse said, "I think about things you've said, and I have all these questions." He glanced at Treva. "Mrs. Alexander knows my mom raised me to live God's way." He shrugged slightly. "Maybe I'm finally seeing it's time."

Treva heard a baby's cry and turned, wondering if it was Zoe. But looked like Faith had already left.

"Mrs. Alexander," Jesse continued, "you were the go-between with me and Faith this summer, and I know you know all the stuff." His eyes were earnest. "I just want you to know I'm not trying to add to the drama. I won't be coming to the house or anything, only as it relates to Zoe. I'd meet with Lance wherever else. That is, if he's willing."

"You know I wouldn't say no, Jesse," Lance said. "I'd be honored to do it. You're my dude."

Lance stood up and gripped Jesse's hand. Jesse stood, moving from a handgrip to a hug.

"It means a lot that you'd say that," Jesse said. "I'm sure you don't like a lot of what I've done. But you show nothing but love."

"Treva."

She turned to see Cinda and Jordyn approaching. "Jordyn wanted to say hi," Cinda said.

"Hey, Jordyn." Treva grabbed her hand and pulled her in for a hug. "I saw you from a distance, but I can't get around as quickly these days. I'm so glad you came."

Jordyn smiled a little. "Me too," she said. "My dad loved this church. I'm starting to see why."

"Are you joining us tomorrow night?" Treva said.

"Um . . ." Jordyn glanced at Cinda, who was nodding yes. "I don't know. I might," she said.

"Okay, good people," Lance said, "I need to get my wife home so she can rest. Ready, babe?" He leaned down and put an arm around her, helping her up.

Treva came to her feet and immediately slumped back down, almost missing the chair.

"Oh, goodness," Cinda said. "Are you all right?"

Treva held her head. "I don't know what happened. I felt dizzy all of a sudden, and my feet almost feel numb."

Lance sat down, taking a look. "They're really swollen," he said. "I'm taking you to the ER."

"Emergency?" Treva said. "I don't think we need to panic. Let me get home and rest and see if I feel better."

"It's Sunday," Lance said, "and the doctor's office is closed. That's why we're going to emergency." He gave her a look. "And we *are* going. Jesse, will you help Treva on her other side so we can get her to the car?"

"Absolutely," Jesse said, moving into place.

"What can we do?" Cinda said.

Lance looked back at her. "Pray."

Treva could hardly move, even with help, with her feet so swollen. Slowly they made their way up the aisle, the church practically empty now, and to the parking lot. Almost to the SUV she felt it—nausea. Rising, rising. And suddenly she was a little panicked herself, especially when she vomited at the car door.

On Monday night Treva lay propped on her left side on the living room sofa as the women arrived, almost all at the same time.

"Sorry we had to change the location, y'all," she said.

"You're apologizing?" Stephanie took a seat on the other sofa. "I'm wondering why you didn't cancel altogether."

"I'm not in great pain or anything," Treva said. "Just uncomfortable with the swelling."

"You check your blood pressure today?" Cyd had called last evening to check on her.

Treva nodded. "Blood pressure's good, only slightly elevated. And urine and blood work were good. We were relieved they didn't say it was preeclampsia."

"What's that?" Cinda said.

"A condition in pregnancy where there's a high amount of protein in the urine and an onset of high blood pressure. If it's not treated it can lead to life-threatening complications for the baby and the mother."

"Oh, wow," Cinda said. "Definitely relieved it's not that."

"Well," Treva said, "we need to keep praying because I'm not out of the woods yet. My age alone puts me at high risk, and my other symptoms are causing concern. I'm at thirty weeks, so they're monitoring me closely."

"We're counting down for real at this point," Allison said. "Praying daily for you and this baby boy. I cannot wait till he's here."

"That's where my nerves are getting the best of me." Treva held her belly, feeling him move even now. "I'm more in love with this boy by the day. The thought of anything happening to him . . ." She lifted her notes from the floor beside her. "And you won't believe the lesson for today. I hadn't planned this."

"What is it?" Faith said.

Treva looked at them. "If I Dwell."

"Ooh," Allison said. "Protection. We're in Psalm 91?"

"Yes, ma'am," Treva said. "That's where we're starting." She looked at Jordyn, who was watching Cinda turn to it. "Hey, Jordyn, I have a Bible for you. I actually got it after the last time you were with us, when you mentioned you didn't have one."

"Oh, yeah," Faith said. "It's here on the shelf." She got up and gave it to Jordyn.

"I didn't know what you might want," Treva said. "Bibles are so personal. But hopefully it'll be okay to start with."

Jordyn ran her hand across the cover and flipped through some pages. "This is beautiful. Thank you."

"You want to read Psalm 91:1 for us?" Treva said.

Cinda helped Jordyn find it.

Jordyn read the verse aloud. "'He who dwells in the shelter of the Most High will abide in the shadow of the Almighty.'"

"That's what I'm talking about," Stephanie said. "Do y'all *see* why it's called Promises B and B? Who is like the Most High God? Just let me stay in His shadow! I'm about to get up and start praising before we even get into it."

Cyd was eyeing her sister. "All right now. I'm ready to praise Him just seeing where you are right now and how He's kept you. He is *such* an awesome God."

"Wow, sounds like a real story there," Allison said.

"Girl, we'd be here all night if I got started," Stephanie said. "Just to give you a hint—last summer I was at that Living Word women's conference drunk and vomiting in the hotel bathroom, had left my husband, and couldn't have told you the last time I'd prayed or gone to church."

"Seriously?" Jordyn said. "I can't picture that."

"Oh, she's serious," Cyd said. "I saw it—and smelled it—myself."

"You don't have to get graphic," Stephanie said.

Cyd chuckled a little, looking at Jordyn. "It just goes to show that no matter how low we find ourselves, the Lord is there to lift us up. His grace is amazing."

"This is so good," Treva said, "and we'll get into the entire psalm, because I can't wait to talk about how His angels take charge of us. But I want us to think about how good God is. In His mercy, He'll protect us even when we don't want to be protected.

He'll close doors, expose our secrets—Stephanie didn't hardly want Cyd to find out she was drinking; but it led to her attending the conference sessions. He'll even remove people from our lives."

"Talk about stories," Allison said. "Don't get me started on the men I cried my eyes out over, upset because we broke up. And now I praise God He got rid of them."

Stephanie nodded. "I got those stories too, honey."

"So think about it," Treva said. "If He'll protect us when we don't want to be protected, imagine what He'll do if we dwell."

"What does that mean, though?" Jordyn said. "I'm thinking the place you live . . . But not sure what that has to do with God."

"Great question," Treva said. "We're also going to look at John chapter 15, where Jesus says something similar—to *abide* in Him. When we receive Jesus as Lord and Savior, He's *in* us and with us. That's always. But the more of *us* that we put away, the more we're filled with Him. So He does kind of become the place where we live. As we grow, His will becomes our will, His heart becomes our heart."

Jordyn was nodding to herself, focused on her Bible.

"And this promise," Stephanie said. "'Will abide in the shadow of the Almighty.' Of the *Almighty*. Plus all the angels guarding us too?" She sighed. "I'm way too familiar with what it's like *not* to dwell like I should." She looked up. "Help me, Lord, not to dwell in those other places again."

"If I'm honest," Treva said, "I love this psalm, but I wish it were a *guarantee* that nothing would happen that I didn't want to happen. You know? I wish I could claim this promise and know that nothing will happen to my baby boy or me in this pregnancy. But sometimes He has a different purpose. I'm a witness, especially after Hezekiah died. And we still grieve over Randall."

"It's a hard truth," Cyd said. "Sometimes He'll take us *through*." She focused on Treva. "But you better stand on the promise of protection in this psalm, girl. The bottom line—we know what

God is able to do. And we're absolutely praying and standing on God's ability to protect you and this baby—and bring a big ol' healthy boy into this world."

Treva exhaled softly as she closed her eyes for a moment. *Lord, please let it be so.*

CHAPTER 51

*F*aith pulled Cinda aside after everyone but Jordyn had left. "Girl, Alonzo called you twice tonight and you ignored it—and yes, I saw it. I was sitting right beside you."

"I was supposed to answer during Bible study?" Cinda said.

"You're been ignoring his calls for days," Faith said. "Might've been nice to leave the room and answer it."

She looked away. "I was serious when I told him not to call."

Faith blank-stared her. "You are so overreacting. He said he was rehearsing and joking around."

"Really?" Cinda said. "Who jokes around like that?"

"Cinda, he's an actor. He was doing his job."

"Maybe he's been acting with respect to a lot of things," Cinda said. "And that was only one kiss the camera caught. Who knows what else he's been over there doing."

"Now you're letting your imagination get the best of you."

"And okay, fine," Cinda said. "He was doing his job. But given his job, it's always going to be something. He's got too much spotlight. And women who post what a great kisser he is."

"But you knew all of that already."

"I didn't know how deeply I would feel for him," Cinda said. "I didn't even know it was possible to feel like this. But if this is where it leads . . ." She shook her head. "I've been hurt too many times. I can't control whether someone dies. This I can control."

The doorbell sounded, and Faith moved to answer it. "That must be my baby girl."

She opened the door and laughed outright. "What a sight. A baby in a stroller next to a Doberman. Are you serious? You're walking both of them at the same time?"

"Why not?" Jesse said. "They're friends."

"Right."

"You want to see?" Jesse said. "If I can bring Lancelot inside."

Faith looked behind her. "Cinda, Jordyn, are you afraid of dogs?"

Cinda shook her head. Jordyn looked up from her spot by the sofa, talking to Treva. "No, I'm cool."

Faith opened the door for the crew to come in. "Lancelot, I haven't seen you in so long, sweet boy." She bent down and rubbed behind his ears. The big dog ate it up.

"Jesse, you've met Cinda and Jordyn, right?" Faith said.

"At church briefly," he said, shaking their hands.

"Okay, let me see what you're talking about," Faith said.

Jesse got Zoe out of her stroller and held her. "Okay, so you know how Zoe is pulling herself to a stand now. Watch this."

He put her by the edge of the sofa, and everyone watched as Zoe pulled up to a standing position, her legs wobbling as she giggled, proud of herself.

Jesse unhooked Lancelot's leash, and the dog headed for Zoe.

"I'm not sure about this," Treva said. "Won't he knock her down? Not to mention the dozen other things he could do to her."

"Keep watching," Jesse said.

Lancelot stopped in front of Zoe and moved to a sitting position, where he was still taller than she. Zoe hugged the sides of his head and rocked back and forth, babbling something in his face, laughing. He licked her, and she babbled some more.

"Is this for real?" Faith said.

"You wouldn't believe how long they go on like that," Jesse said. "Lancelot thinks he's her protector. Had the nerve to look at me crazy when I picked her up in the middle of one of their play sessions."

Faith walked over and sat next to Zoe. "So you know my buddy Lancelot, huh? Isn't he sweet?"

Faith rubbed the dog's back as Zoe kept babbling and Jesse joined in, sitting on the floor next to them.

"I've got to get a video of this," Treva said. She reached for her phone and started recording. "This is too precious."

Zoe grabbed Jesse's head now and belly-laughed as he made exaggerated faces at her.

"What is your daddy doing, Zoe?" Faith said. "Isn't he silly?"

The doorbell rang again.

"Can you get that, Cinda?" Treva said.

Seconds later, Reggie appeared.

"Hey," he said, surveying the scene.

"Hey," Faith said, jumping up. She walked over to him. "How was the social event at work?"

"It was good." Reggie looked at her. "How about your evening?"

"Bible study was really good," Faith said.

He nodded.

"I better head out," Jesse said. He picked up Zoe, hugging her good-bye, then put her down and hooked Lancelot's leash. "You're bringing her over before your class on Wednesday, right?"

"Yes," Faith said. "Around eight thirty."

"All right, cool. Have a good night, everybody."

"We're heading out too," Cinda said.

She and Jordyn said their good-byes, and Faith scooped up Zoe, walking with Reggie to the lower level.

"Why are you acting funny?" she said.

Reggie took a seat on the sofa. "I'm not acting funny."

"You're not acting like yourself either."

"I just got here," Reggie said. "How am I supposed to act?"

"Okay." Faith sat next to him, letting Zoe crawl on a play set nearby. "It just seems like you act a little different when Jesse's here."

"I act different, or you act different?"

"All I'm doing is trying to make the best of this arrangement," Faith said. "You're the one who said I needed to do that."

"Lately you seem a little distant when he's around." Reggie looked at her. "If he's here, I know you won't be hugging me when I walk in."

"That's not true."

"It's true," he said. "By the way, that was a nice family moment I walked in on."

"Ah, now the reason for the attitude comes out."

"I don't have an attitude."

Faith turned more toward him. "What do you want me to do, Reggie? I don't want you to feel uncomfortable when he's here."

"I want us to act like we normally do," he said. "I don't want to feel like the third wheel." He paused. "Are you still in love with him?"

"Why would you ask me that?"

"It wasn't long ago that you said you were. I'm wondering."

"No," Faith said. "I'm not in love with him."

"So the feeling disappeared?"

Faith redirected Zoe. "Can we please talk about something other than Jesse?"

Reggie leaned back with a sigh, then looked over at her. "Hey," he said, clasping her hand. "I apologize."

"For what?"

"When I saw you and Jesse on the floor with Zoe it hit me, how you used to tell me it was hard to get over him." He looked away a moment. "And my mind started going. It wasn't right to put that on you. You shouldn't feel like you can't give Zoe a moment to play with her mom and her dad."

"I apologize too," she said. "I probably do act a little different when he's here. It's a weird dynamic, and I'm still getting used to it. But I don't want anything to change between the two of us."

He lapsed into silence for a while. Then, "That icy day in February, when I drove your car home and we made brunch and talked for hours."

She frowned at him. "What?"

"Remember you asked about the first time I was attracted to you?" he said. "That was it."

"Way back then?"

"I stuffed it, but yeah." He looked at her. "I knew you were special."

She jumped up to get Zoe, who was trying to scurry away, and brought her to her lap.

"Hey," Reggie said, "you've got a big birthday coming up in November."

"Twenty-one," Faith said.

"What's the plan?"

"I don't know." She let Zoe stand at her feet. "I need to think about it. Probably something small with family and a few friends. And I want to do something special with just the two of us."

He stared into her eyes. "I really want to kiss you, and we're not at the door."

She felt the pull herself. "I think it'll be a really long good-bye."

CHAPTER 52

*A*lonzo woke with a start, shocked when he glanced at the clock. His body recovering still from the rigors of filming, he'd dozed off and apparently slept hard for seven hours.

He jumped up, looking for his phone, then saw it on the bed where he'd left it, waiting to hear word. He picked it up and scrolled notifications, stopping at the text from Stephanie. It was short—**Ready to update you. Call me.** She'd sent it six hours ago.

Alonzo dialed, realizing on the third ring that it was four in the morning in St. Louis. He was about to hang up when she answered with a groggy hello.

"I'm sorry," Alonzo said. "I just woke up and didn't think about the time difference."

"No worries," Stephanie said. "Here's the deal. It took the whole village to get that girl on the plane, but she's on her way."

Alonzo closed his eyes, exhaling silently. "I didn't think it would happen." And he was thankful she'd taken his suggestion weeks before and gotten a passport. "Please, tell everyone thank you. Wait, so she'll be here in a few short hours."

"Alonzo, don't mess this up. We're rooting for you."

"I hear you," he said. "Thanks, Steph."

He slid to the side of the bed and bowed his head. *Lord, I have to make that a prayer. Thank You for putting Cinda on that plane. Help me not to mess this up. I need words. I need . . . everything, Lord. This is all new to me, but You know how I feel about her. Now that she's on her way, show me what to do.*

He showered and dressed and answered business e-mails and text messages, and was about to return his manager's call when it came to him. He knew what to do. Only—he didn't know if he had time to do it.

Alonzo stood outside the secured area of Charles de Gaulle airport, searching faces of arriving passengers. He was about to wonder if Cinda had changed her mind and missed her connecting flight in New York, when he saw her. Ball cap and jeans. Looking more beautiful than ever.

A few feet away she spotted him in the crowd and held his gaze, then continued on to the baggage carousel.

He caught up to her. "Wow, no hello?"

She stared away from him. "I shouldn't have come." Her eyes flashed at him now. "And you really do think the world revolves around you, don't you? You can just snap your fingers and I'm here."

"You wouldn't answer my calls."

"Obviously. I didn't want to talk to you."

"I see you brought your shotgun."

Her eyes cut away, and Alonzo noticed—she was wearing the locket he'd given her.

"So what convinced you to come?" he said.

"Lance talked to me."

"What'd he say?"

"Things."

"Okay."

"Why are you smiling at me?"

"I can't be glad to see you?"

"No."

"*Full* warrior princess mode. With your cute self."

The carousel started up and bags began rotating around.

"I was surprised to see Paris on my ticket," she said. "Why are you here? More filming?"

"We ended production three days ago," he said. "I flew here yesterday, to meet you."

"Why not meet in London?"

"For you, I wanted Paris."

"And because you're so spoiled, you were confident I would come."

"No, I wasn't." Alonzo looked at her. "But I prayed you would. Even if you're blasting me, I wanted to hear your voice, see your face."

"Excuse me." A young woman had walked up. "My friend and I have been debating for the last five minutes," she said. "Aren't you Alonzo Coles?"

He tugged at his cap with a slight smile. "My disguise didn't work?"

"I knew it," the woman said, her eyes wider. "My friend said you were in London right now, not Paris, and even so, you wouldn't just be standing here in baggage claim." She took out her phone. "Can we take a selfie?"

He glanced at Cinda, who was focused on revolving luggage.

"Sure," Alonzo said.

The woman saw her friend coming and waved her away. "Don't even try to get in the picture, since this ain't him."

The second woman laughed as she crowded into the picture nonetheless.

They both hugged him. "Nice to meet you," they said, checking the picture as they walked away.

Cinda moved toward the carousel, seeing her suitcase. Alonzo grabbed it, and they took an elevator to the parking garage where a car was waiting. She stared from the backseat window as they drove past the sights, pulling up to a brownstone half an hour later.

"Where are we?" she said.

"The apartment where you're staying."

"Where are you staying?"

"Same building," he said, "in an apartment upstairs from you. The studio owns a handful of these."

Through a secured entrance they took a narrow elevator to the second floor, and he showed her inside. Cinda walked into the living room, drawn to the patio doors.

"We're right by the Eiffel Tower," she said. "This view is stunning."

He opened the double doors and they walked out onto the spacious patio, taking in the sights and sounds of the city.

"I'm sure you're starving," he said.

Cinda nodded, her hands on the wrought iron railing. "But I can wait. It's beautiful out here."

He leaned against the railing, looking at her. "Can we talk?"

She kept her gaze outward.

"I know you're upset about that kiss."

She glanced at him. "I couldn't understand how a kiss like that could be part of joking around. It looked pretty . . . passionate."

"We were rehearsing an outdoor scene, part of the movie's climax," he said. "And in the movie, my character and hers are lovers."

"How fitting."

"So in the scene," he said, "there's this kiss just before an explosion, when all the action starts. The point of the rehearsal was to nail down fight choreography. So I went through the motions of the part between her and me, and skipped the kiss."

She turned more toward him with a slight glance.

"The crew started giving me a hard time, saying, 'Oh, now that he's in love, he doesn't want to make out on screen.' A little later the director said to rehearse like it's the real thing, so of course the crew had to cheer when we got to the kiss—which was supposed to be passionate—and someone obviously took the picture."

Cinda looked at him. "Why didn't you say that at first?"

"I told you it was nothing, then kept calling to explain. You know the rest." He glanced down at pedestrians on the sidewalk. "At first I couldn't believe you were that upset. But I looked at what was out there, how people were playing it like another love triangle, and then I saw Savannah's post." He sighed.

"Seeing all that stuff . . ." Her eyes focused on the Eiffel Tower. "I started thinking about all the women in your life and how ridiculous it was that you'd be with me. And I knew whatever infatuation you had with me would wear off. And there was no point dragging it out because I had already . . ." She shook her head slightly.

"Already what?"

She sighed. "Already gone deeper than I thought I would."

"Meaning what?"

"Thinking about you with someone else," she said. "It hurt. And it shouldn't hurt because it's inevitable. Of course you'll move on. Better to cut it off now than—"

"You're thinking that after I flew you to Paris?"

She looked at him. "A flight to Paris is pocket change to you. What am I gonna say, oh, he flew me to Paris so this means forever? I'm not *that* naive." She paused. "But I was also upset because I kept thinking as I looked at that picture . . ." She looked away.

"Kept thinking what?"

She wouldn't look at him, but he saw her swipe a tear. "I kept thinking *He's never held me like that, or kissed me.*"

"Are you serious?" He turned her toward him. "Cinda, you're on a pedestal in my mind. I didn't want to do anything to make you think this was physical. You're so much more to me than that."

"Okay, great, I get that," Cinda said. "Does that mean you'll never hold me?"

"Now I'm confused. A second ago you were cutting this off."

She glared at him.

"What?" he said. "I need to know where you stand, because you're right. The infatuation did wear off." He took her hand and pulled her to himself, wrapping his arms around her waist. "And it *was* inevitable . . . that I would fall in love with you. But if I'm wasting my time and you're about to kick me to the curb . . ."

She looked into his eyes. "What are you saying?"

He could feel the beat of his own heart. He'd never uttered these words. "I'm saying I love you, Cinda."

She kept her gaze locked as tears spilled from her eyes. He brought her closer and held her as her arms embraced his back.

"So Lance was right," she said softly.

"What did he say?"

"He said I was shutting you out because of past hurts and missing what God had for me." She paused. "He said, 'Alonzo loves you.'"

He looked at her. "I never told him that. But I guess in so many words, I did."

"I didn't think it was really true," Cinda said. "But deep down I hoped . . . I hoped we might be feeling the same way." She took a breath. "I love you too, Zee."

He leaned his face closer to hers, and she closed her eyes as their lips touched softly for the first time, and again, and again.

He paused, looking at her.

"What?" she said.

"I still can't take my eyes off of you."

He kissed her again, more deeply, and more aware that he'd never felt anything close to this. His arms tightened a little more around her. She wanted to be held, and he wanted nothing more than to hold her. And never let go.

CHAPTER 53

*C*inda thought her heart might explode. She'd felt it from the moment she saw Alonzo at the airport. All her protests about coming—and she'd been serious—had dissipated when she saw his face. But she'd hardly been able to look at him. Everything inside of her was reacting, and she'd been trying to stay firm. Trying not to let her emotions get carried away. Trying to protect herself from ultimate hurt.

But telling her he loved her, holding her like this, kissing her—Alonzo had her heart on overload. She couldn't hold back if she wanted to.

"The wind is picking up," he said, taking off his jacket. He draped it around her shoulders.

His arm around her, they faced the railing, looking out at the Eiffel Towel.

Cinda sighed softly. "I was mean, not taking your calls. I'm sorry."

"I know how much you've been hurt," he said. "You lost both of your parents just this year. It's natural to go into protective mode." He looked at her. "But I need you to make me a promise."

"What's that?"

"That you'll stop reading these gossip blogs and whatnot," he said. "Most of those people have never met me. You know me better than anybody at this point. You have to trust me."

She nodded. "It was just hard, with you so far away and not talking like normal."

"And you talk about me being spoiled."

She leaned her head into him. "I guess I was. It's your fault. You're the one who spoiled me."

"It was hard on me too," he said. "Some days I wanted to call but I'd be so tired, my body aching, I'd just fall asleep."

She looked at him. "So how'd everything go? I wasn't taking your calls, but I never stopped praying for you."

He stared at her a moment. "It was incredible, really. So many times I thought I had nothing left, and God would just show up. I knew it was God, giving me strength out of nowhere, helping me persevere, even protecting me. I fell off this high beam, and—"

"What?" Cinda said. "You weren't hurt?"

"My ribs were a little bruised," he said, "but it could've been a lot worse. And even in that, God helped me get back and do what I needed to do." He kissed her lightly. "Thank you for praying." He smiled at her. "There was another answered prayer too."

"What?"

"Remember I was a little worried what would happen to my career after turning down that project?"

"A little?"

"I signed a major production deal last week," he said, "where I'll be able to produce my own projects in film and television."

Cinda smiled. "So you can tell the stories you want to tell."

"In the way I want to tell them." He looked at his watch suddenly. "We'd better get moving."

"To where?"

"It's almost five, so we'll get dinner, then we have an appointment at seven."

She eyed him. "What kind of appointment?"

"An appointment." He kissed her cheek. "Get dressed, and I'll be back to get you in thirty minutes." He headed for the door.

"What should I wear?" she said, moving into the apartment.

"One of the dresses Allison gave you to pack."

"How do you know about that?"

The door closed behind him without an answer.

Cinda strolled the Champs-Elysées with Alonzo, gaping store to store at the fashions on one of the most famous avenues in the world. "How much farther?" she said, a soft wind lifting her curls from her shoulders.

"I told you we should take a taxi." He had his arm around her shoulder. "I knew you'd be tired. You've been going since last night."

"I'm good actually." She wore comfortable ankle booties. "And I need to walk after all that food. I'm just dying to know where we're going." Her eyes swept the outdoor cafés. "I'm thinking something very Parisian. You arranged a cooking class with a top chef—which would be very cool, by the way. I saw something in the apartment about it."

"And I would do that *after* we've eaten?"

"You didn't think it through."

"Okay."

"Ooh, oh my gosh." She veered to a store window, pulling him along. "This is you," she said, pointing. "You need this merlot sweater."

"You passed up all those boutiques for women and zeroed in on a men's store?"

"I can see you in this." She looked over at him. "I hadn't said anything yet about your black sweater."

"You've got on a black dress."

"With a cobalt suede belt." She tugged his hand. "Do you have time to try it on?"

"Nope." He pulled her back to the path. "We've got a schedule to keep." He checked the map on his phone. "Based on what they told me, it should be down this next side street."

They turned and walked a few feet more, arriving at a nondescript building sandwiched between a café and what looked like an apartment dwelling.

"You sure this is it?" she said.

He checked the address. "That's what it says."

He rang the doorbell, and seconds later they heard heels on the other side. A woman answered, dressed in a black pencil skirt and white blouse, hair pulled sharply into a bun.

"Alonzo Coles, quite a delight to meet you." She shook his hand with both of hers, her accent thick. "I am Vivienne Girard."

"Very nice to meet you, Vivienne," Alonzo said, moving inside with Cinda. "Thank you for accommodating us on such short notice. This is Cinda Ellis."

"*C'est bon*," Vivienne said, "such a pleasure." She shook Cinda's hand the same way.

"Likewise," Cinda said, smiling. She glanced around, trying to determine what sort of place this was. They'd stepped into a front entryway sparsely decorated, but double doors had to open to more.

"So," Vivienne said, "welcome to the showroom of one of Paris's top designers."

Cinda turned wide eyes to Alonzo. "Top designer is way better than top chef." She looked back at the woman. "Is this a private tour? We can actually see the showroom?" She was giddy already.

The woman smiled with her eyes. "We have arranged absolutely for you to see the collections." She opened the double doors. "Come. I will show you."

Cinda and Alonzo walked through, then down a hallway and around a corner. She looked at him. "I hope you don't turn this into a shopping venture for me," she whispered, "because I don't need anything. You're the one who's got—"

She froze as the woman opened the door.

Gorgeous wedding gowns were on display all around.

Cinda walked further inside. "What is this?" she said, and turned—

Alonzo had bent to a knee, a box in his hand—with a brilliant diamond inside.

Cinda thought she might faint as she stared into his eyes, unable to speak. She glanced around, noticing Vivienne had disappeared.

"I can't describe the way I feel about you," he said. "You captivated me from the moment I saw you, but I couldn't have known how much you would invade my heart. You're in my thoughts, you're in my prayers, you're in my plans, you're in every vision of my future. I want to spend the rest of my life with you. Cinda, will you marry me?"

Her heart beat out of her chest as she nodded, tears clouding her eyes. "Yes."

He placed the ring on her finger and stood, sighing as he enfolded her in a hug.

"I thought you would say it's too soon," he said.

She met his brown eyes. "I would marry you today if I could."

He kissed her, a different kiss this time. Tender yet passionate, their hearts poured out, sealing the moment.

"You started this kissing thing." He nibbled her ear. "Now I don't want to stop."

"I don't want you to."

Their lips came together again, lingering, until they heard Vivienne's heels outside the room.

She walked in, clasping her hands together as she looked at Cinda's ring. "I'm the first to say it," she said, smiling. "Congratulations!"

"Thank you." Cinda beamed, her arm around Alonzo's waist.

Vivienne gestured toward the collection. "The idea is that you browse, get a feel for styles you prefer, and then we work on your custom gown."

"You're kidding." She turned to Alonzo. "I can't believe you had this all planned out—trip to Paris, propose in bridal showroom, order a custom gown . . ."

"Actually, no," he said. "I chose Paris because I love the city, but I didn't know I'd propose until early this afternoon. Didn't have a ring or a plan to come to this showroom."

"You're serious?"

He nodded. "I prayed about what to do, and this is what came to mind." He took her into his arms. "I guess God heard our prayer about jumping in together. I wouldn't have thought surrender could look like this."

⁓

Cinda leaned against Alonzo on a bench by the River Seine, soaking up their last night in Paris. "My life is about to be really different, isn't it?"

"Depends on which aspect you're talking about." He paused. "Well, yeah, it'll be really different."

"Yours will too, though." She pulled her jacket closer as a gust of wind blew. "No more bachelor pad. Have you thought about that?"

"I have," he said. "I'll actually have a wife moving into the house, and into the *bedroom*"—he waggled his eyebrows, and she nudged him—"and you'd better not bring a single cleaning supply."

"Of course I will," she said. "I can't leave things to a 'professional service.' I'd rather do it myself."

"My house was super clean when you visited, wasn't it?"

She wrinkled her face a little. "Umm . . . I mean you know, it was good."

He chuckled. "Well, you'd better get comfortable living substandard then, because you are not bringing the extra-ness to the house. You'll be too busy."

"Doing what?"

"Being a stylist."

"Are you back to that?"

"Never left it," he said. "Only now you can't say, 'This could all end in a few months.' You can do what you love. I mean, look at this." He sat up a little, opening his jacket to the merlot sweater she'd made him go back and get. "You're styling me on vacation."

"But there are dozens of other reasons why it wouldn't work."

He looked at her. "You will fight tooth and nail to stay in your protected space. What are you afraid of?"

She stared at a tourist boat moving slowly down the river. "This is the only thing I've ever really wanted to do, that I was sure I'd never be able to do." She took a breath. "If I set my mind to do it and fail . . ."

"How much buzz was there about what I wore to the LA premiere?"

"That was one event," Cinda said. "Plus, if I say I'm a stylist, people will ask about my background and experience. I have nothing. I didn't even go to college."

"It's never too late to go to school," Alonzo said, "and I'm totally supportive if that's the route you want to go. But I don't think you need years of school and whatever else to do this. God has given you a door. You just need to walk through it."

"It's not that easy," Cinda said.

"It's absolutely that easy. I'm letting my stylist go."

"You can't do that."

"I have to," he said, "because I'm convinced." He moved a couple of curls from her face, looked into her eyes, and kissed her. "I only want my fiancée and soon-to-be wife to dress me." He kissed her again. "If she won't do it, I guess I'll have to dress myself. And that would be like me cleaning a room instead of you."

She stared into his eyes. "That's the first time you said that— my fiancée. I like the sound of it."

"I like 'my wife' better," he said. "Can we start planning the wedding? Tonight?"

"Ha. I don't even want to think about what it takes to plan a Hollywood wedding," she said. "All the guests, glitzy venue."

"Who's having a Hollywood wedding?"

"What are you thinking then?"

"I don't know," he said. "But private comes to mind. And small. And soon. And private."

Cinda chuckled. "What do you think about St. Louis? Maybe plan something for spring?"

"I like St. Louis for a lot of reasons," he said. "And winter comes before spring, so I like that better."

"You sure you want to keep cutting back your bachelor days, Mr. Coles?"

"Might as well." He kissed her. "In my mind they're already gone."

CHAPTER 54

"Sweet pea, you're moving way too fast for Grandma."

Treva got a kick out of Zoe making a sport of crawling quickly away from her. Good thing her space was confined, in baby boy's room with the door closed. Treva wasn't on bed rest at the moment, but with swollen feet, a slight headache, and a thirty-five-week belly, no way could she chase that little girl.

She opened another dresser drawer and laid a stack of clothing inside, all various shades of blue. The women at church had thrown her a surprise shower the week before, and had played up the blue. She smiled even now as she put away a pair of blue pajamas.

"Da-da-da-da." Zoe drooled as she played with a big bouncy ball, saying her favorite string of words.

Treva smiled at her. "Are you calling for your daddy, little girl?"

She'd wondered what this arrangement would be like, having Jesse so near. But thankfully things had been smooth. And watching him bond with Zoe had been priceless.

She let her eyes roam the room with a satisfied sigh. Walls

painted midnight blue. A favorite verse hand-lettered on the wall. Most of the baby furniture in place. The room was almost ready, and she was more than ready to see her little man. She smiled now at his kick, rubbing her stomach. "I hear you, pumpkin," she said. "Nobody will be more ready than you."

"Okay, sweet pea," she said, walking over to Zoe. "Next stop—laundry room. And where is your Aunt Joy?"

Joy was the one supposedly babysitting this evening while Faith studied on campus. Joy had asked if Treva could fill in "real quick" while she ran to Smoothie King with a friend. That had to have been an hour ago.

Treva bent to pick up Zoe—and almost toppled over with dizziness. She wobbled back to the dresser, leaning over it, suddenly seeing spots. *Okay, this is not good.* Lance had told her to keep her phone near in case of emergency, and she had it now, on the dresser. She speed-dialed, thankful he wasn't far, at the corner Starbuck's meeting with Jesse.

"Babe, I don't know what's going on," she said, slumped over the dresser. "I'm dizzy again, my head is starting to pound, and I can hardly see."

"I'm on my way," he said. "Stay on the phone with me. Joy's with you, right?"

"No." Treva took a breath, holding the side of her head. "She went somewhere with a friend."

"You're by yourself with Zoe?" Lance said. "We already said you're not in a condition to—" He sighed. "Okay. Help us, Lord," he murmured.

She breathed in and out quickly, trying to manage the pain, keeping an eye on Zoe as best she could. The one item missing in the room was the one she needed—a place to sit. The rocking chair wouldn't be delivered till next week.

"I'm in the car," Lance said. "Where are you in the—"

Treva cried out as a stab of pain went through the right side of her stomach. She lowered herself to the floor, holding her stomach as Zoe crawled over to her.

"Hey, pretty girl," Treva whispered, rubbing Zoe's back. She tried to smile as tears slid down her face. She had a high tolerance for pain, but it wasn't just the pain affecting her. It was wondering whether something was wrong with her or the baby.

"Babe, I said are you okay?"

"I'm . . ." Another pain hit, causing her to double over. She gritted her teeth. ". . . okay."

Zoe began to cry, as if sensing something was wrong. She stretched her arms for Treva to pick her up.

"It's okay, sweetheart," Treva said, hugging her from where she sat.

The baby cried louder, and Treva closed her eyes, praying through pain that seemed to move from her stomach to her back.

"Treva, where are you?"

Lance's voice boomed through the phone and in the distance, downstairs.

"The baby's room," she said.

She could hear him scrambling up the stairs. The door swung open and Lance rushed to her side.

"I've got Zoe."

Treva looked and saw Jesse picking up the baby.

"Babe," Lance said, "wrap your arms around my neck."

He put his arms around her and lifted her to her feet as she held on. She leaned her weight on him, barely able to walk or see straight as he moved with her out of the room. Somehow his strength compensated, even as they took the stairs.

"This isn't normal." She clutched his arm as she paused halfway down, her head aching and dizzy. "Something is wrong."

"I know," he said. "We need to know exactly what's going on." He took another step with her. "Babe, we're almost there, almost to the end of this."

"What if it's really serious?" She labored with every step. "What if the baby's in distress?"

"They'll tell us," he said. "One thing at a time. You don't need to stress yourself out with speculation on top of everything else."

"I just want him to be safe." She paused again, swiping tears. "I don't know what I'd do without this little boy. Our little boy."

He kissed her. "I don't know what I'd do without either of you."

CHAPTER 55

aith moved off of the hospital elevator, looking for her mother's room. She'd left the library the moment she'd gotten Lance's text. But she had no idea what had happened.

She eyed room numbers as she made her way down the hall, finally spotting it. Through the window of the closed door she could see her mom and Lance talking to the doctor—the same doctor who'd delivered Zoe. And her mom looked upset.

Faith exhaled, taking a step back. Whatever it was, it didn't look good. Was her mom's health at risk? The baby's? She thought a moment, then headed for the waiting area she'd passed. She'd check back in a few minutes, and meanwhile, she'd pray. She'd hardly ever seen her mom in tears, which put her on the verge of tears as well.

"Faith," a voice called.

She stopped and turned. Jesse stood in a vending area off the main hallway, with Zoe asleep in a stroller. "What are you two doing here? I thought Zoe was home with Joy."

"Joy went somewhere with a friend," he said, pulling a bag of pretzels from the machine, "and was supposed to come right back.

Meanwhile, your mom had a dizzy spell and severe pains, so I took Zoe."

"Oh, no, what are they saying?" Faith moved closer in. "I tried to see Mom just now, but the doctor was in there."

"They saw something in her vitals that made them want to keep her overnight," he said. "I don't know much beyond that. I kept Zoe here because she was helping your mom stay calm."

Faith looked at him. "How did you get involved in all this anyway?"

"I was with Lance when your mom called."

"Why were you with Lance?"

Jesse paused a moment. "We've been getting together," he said. "A discipleship thing."

Faith looked puzzled. "What made you do that?"

He shrugged. "I want to learn," he said. "Thought it was time to get serious about life and faith and all that."

"That's what I thought you were ready to do back in January," Faith said, "when Zoe was born."

"That's what sparked it," he said, "at least in my heart. But it's been a process, that's for sure. I prayed with Lance a couple weeks ago, giving my life to Jesus."

She stared at him, shaking her head a little.

"Why are you looking like that?" he said.

"All that time I was praying and hoping for changes in your life —these kinds of changes—and you wait till . . ." She swallowed the rest. It was too much. Her mom. This.

"Wait till what?" Jesse moved closer to her. "Till you're in a relationship? You're not married, Faith. It's not too late for the two of us." He looked into her eyes. "Do you ever miss what we had? Yes, there was drama, but we had a friendship. We enjoyed being around each other." He paused. "Faith, we loved each other. At least, that's what we said."

She met his gaze as his words turned over in her head. This

was everything she'd wanted just a few months ago—Jesse pursuing Jesus, and her.

"I love you still, Faith," he said. "I didn't come to St. Louis for Zoe only. I came for you too. I'm asking you straight out—do you still love me?"

Faith's heart beat out of rhythm. She remembered vividly what they once had, what she once felt. "I do, but—"

"Then give us a chance to have a future, to be a family." He moved closer still. "Faith, tell me it's not too late for us."

He stared into her eyes, and everything inside went haywire. Before she could think, their lips came together, and Faith knew she needed to—

"No, it's not too late."

Faith's heart lurched at the sound of another voice. She turned quickly. "Reggie, I—"

He held up a hand. "I don't need to hear another word."

Reggie headed down the hallway, and Faith followed.

"Stop and let me talk to you," she said. "It's not what it looked like."

"Not what it looked like?" He paused a moment, turning to her. "I didn't hear you say you still love him—after you told me you didn't?"

"You asked if I was *in* love with Jesse," Faith said. "There's a difference."

"Now you're playing games," Reggie said. "I get it. Your heart was tied to Jesse for a long time, then I came along, filled the gap while he was away. Now he's back." He stepped away. "You don't have to worry about me standing in your way. Go for it. Be with the love of your life." He headed for the elevator and pushed the button.

"Reggie, don't go," Faith said. "I asked you to meet me here, so obviously I wasn't planning anything behind your back. This is all a misunderstanding."

He came toward her. "I can only go by what I heard with my

own ears, and what I saw with my own eyes—you kissing Jesse. I mean this when I say it—I wish the three of you well. I'm out."

He walked into the elevator and disappeared as the doors closed.

~

So much had changed in the space of a few days.

Faith walked into the kitchen Friday morning as her Aunt Jillian and Grandma Patsy cooked breakfast.

Jillian hugged her when she saw her. "How are you, sweetheart? I'm worried about you."

Faith shrugged. "You shouldn't be worried about me, with everything that's going on with Mom."

"They've stabilized things, thank God," Jillian said. "But I don't think I've ever seen you so sad, not even last year when you were dealing with so much. You still haven't heard from Reggie?"

"He won't return my calls or texts," she said. "We used to go back and forth all day. And I saw him practically every day. Now, nothing."

Patsy stirred eggs on top of the stove. "I kept hearing about this Reggie, then I get here, and everything has exploded. I haven't even met him." She sprinkled pepper. "But it's been nice getting to know Jesse a little more. He sure loves that baby girl."

Jillian nodded. "Carolyn's been thanking God every week for the changes she sees in him."

"Wait, who's Carolyn?" Patsy said.

"Jesse's mother," Jillian said. "Remember, she's in my Bible study group? That's how Faith and Jesse met."

"That's right," Patsy said, nodding. "So interesting that after all this time, Jesse's at a point where he's ready for a serious relationship with you, Faith. What are your thoughts about that?"

"Honestly, Grandma, I don't even want to think about it." Faith knew she'd have to deal with it eventually, within herself. Right now she could only think of how she'd hurt her best friend. If the tables had been turned and she'd seen Reggie kissing his old girlfriend . . .

Jillian looked at Faith. "What's Treva saying about all this?"

"I haven't told her what's going on," Faith said. "She's got enough to deal with."

"That's certainly true," Patsy said. "I'm glad they've kept her in the hospital with constant monitoring, no matter how much she wants to be home."

"I'm glad too," Jillian said. "And she definitely felt better knowing we were here to take care of things."

Faith nodded. "That look on her face when you two walked into her hospital room yesterday. I think I've seen her in tears more in the past week than my entire life."

"It's quite a time for her and Lance," Jillian said. "He was up and out of here before six this morning, on his way back to the hospital."

Patsy plated the eggs, adding turkey sausage and toast. "Where are Joy and Hope?" she said. "Isn't it almost time for school? They need to come eat."

The doorbell rang, stirring slight butterflies in Faith. Maybe Reggie decided to drop by before work. But she didn't want to get her hopes up.

"Can you get that, Aunt Jillian?" she said.

Jillian walked toward the door.

"Good morning," Joy said, as she and Hope breezed into the kitchen together.

"Good morning, girls," Patsy said. "I've got breakfast all ready for you."

"I don't eat that much food in the morning," Joy said. "I'm fine till lunch."

"Joy," Patsy said, "I'm quite sure your mother has told you that you need the protein and other nutrients that come from eating a good breakfast."

"What? Jilli-Jill in the house?"

"Tommy-Tom!"

Faith glanced back as the best friends from college hugged one another.

"I didn't know you were in town," Tommy said, walking in.

"Mom and I decided to come when we got the news about Treva," Jillian said. "We wanted to be here for her, help out however we can."

"So this is your mom?" he said, coming to the kitchen. Tommy hugged Patsy as Hope and Joy moved to the table with their plates. "Mrs. Campbell, I'm Tommy Porter," he said, stepping back now. "Your daughter and I were like this in college." He twisted his fingers. "I've heard so much about you. So good to meet you after all these years."

"I'm a little embarrassed by the stories you no doubt heard," Patsy said, giving Jillian an eye, "but so lovely to meet you. I absolutely remember Jillian mentioning you."

"How's Allison?" Jillian said. "And married life? You weren't too stuck in your ways, were you?"

"Allison's great," he said. "Married life is a for-real adjustment, and yes, I was firmly stuck in my ways, thank you very much. You know me too well." He chuckled.

"Can I get you some coffee?" Jillian said. "Unfortunately, Lance is already gone."

"No, I'm good," Tommy said. "I was actually stopping by to see Faith."

Faith looked at him as he walked over to her.

"Can we go into the living room?" Tommy said.

Faith nodded, anxious. This had to be about Reggie.

"Reggie asked me to give this to you," Tommy said. "I don't know why, but I guess you know the significance." He handed her the ballpoint pen she'd given Reggie.

Faith wanted to weep as she took it. "Could you tell him to talk to me?" she said.

Tommy looked away a moment. "Faith, I have to be real with you. You know how I felt about this from the beginning, that Reggie would end up hurt. That's where he is." He shrugged slightly. "I have to look out for my little brother. Right now, I think he's better off without the communication." He hugged her when he saw her tears. "I'm praying for both of you," he said. "Truth is, I think the two of you had something very special."

Tommy went back to the kitchen, chatting with Jillian and Patsy.

Faith stared at the pen, well aware of what it meant. Reggie wanted her to stop calling and texting. She no longer had a place in his heart.

CHAPTER 56

NOVEMBER

*A*lonzo and Cinda walked into the B and B early Saturday evening as Stephanie put out fresh-baked cookies for guests in an alcove of the entryway.

"Ooh, my favorite," Cinda said. "Chocolate chip."

"Well, welcome back," Stephanie said, smiling. "I assume y'all made up since you tacked on a week to your trip."

Cinda put an arm around Alonzo's waist. "We did," she said. "And thank you for ignoring everything I said about Alonzo and all the reasons I gave for not going."

He eyed her. "You had bad things to say about me?"

She gave a sheepish look. "Only, you know, minor stuff."

"Nobody was listening to Cinda anyway," Stephanie said. "We just had to get her out of her own way." She looked at Alonzo. "I'm surprised to see you, though. I didn't know you were coming to St. Louis."

"Really?" he said. "I booked a room online."

"It must not have gone through," Stephanie said. "I didn't get anything, and we're booked tonight. We'll have to see if you can—"

"Wait, I know," Alonzo said. "I booked it with my middle name. Zachariah."

Stephanie frowned a little. "But it said, Mr. and Mrs.—" She gasped as she looked at them, wide-eyed. "I know you two did *not*."

Cinda brought her hand from behind his back and flashed the ring, complete with a wedding band.

"What?" Stephanie grabbed her hand. "Oh, it's gorgeous—oh, wait." Stephanie took her phone from her pocket. "Lindell, come down. Right now. You won't believe this."

Stephanie blank-stared them. "I am so speechless right now. How? Where? What in the world?"

Cinda was beaming. "First he proposed in the showroom of one of the top bridal gown designers in Paris, then we sat down and started designing a custom gown—"

"You're kidding." Stephanie looked at Alonzo. "Dude, all that back and forth we had, and you never mentioned you were going to *propose*?"

Alonzo smiled as he shrugged. "I didn't know."

Lindell came down the stairs. "Hey, welcome back," he said.

"Babe, check it out," Stephanie took Cinda's hand and showed him.

"You guys got engaged?" Lindell smiled. "I can't say I'm surprised. Congrats." He hugged both of them.

"Um, no," Stephanie said. "Not just engaged. *Married*."

"Oh, for real?" Lindell took another look at them. "Okay, now I'm surprised."

"Cinda's telling the story," Stephanie said. "He proposed, okay go on."

"Then," Cinda said, "on our last night in Paris, we talked wedding plans and settled on this winter in St. Louis." Her eyes floated to Alonzo. "*Then* he called in the middle of the night and said, 'What if we fly someplace where we can get married *now?*'"

"So, Alonzo," Stephanie said, "what is your deal? Seriously. You just fly by the seat of your pants?"

"It's this woman right here." He draped an arm around Cinda. "She's got me doing things I've never done."

Cinda looked at him. "Like get married."

He kissed her. "How about fall in love, fly a woman overseas, buy a ring, propose—"

"Okay, love birds, can we get back to the story?" Stephanie said. "Where did you fly to?"

"Antigua," he said. "Didn't have to wait and didn't need birth certificates."

"He asked if I'd be upset about giving up my custom wedding gown." Cinda gave Stephanie a look. "Really?" She smiled. "That moment when it was official, and I was Mrs. Alonzo Coles . . ." She turned her gaze to him. "And the honeymoon was amazing."

He drew her close and kissed her. "Incredible."

"All righty then," Stephanie said. "Now that we're bordering on TMI . . ."

"But I'm a little sad," Cinda said, "because this means I'll be leaving the B and B, and St. Louis. I don't know what I'll do without all of you."

Stephanie sighed. "Don't get me teary-eyed. You have worked your way deep in my heart."

"So you feel me then," Alonzo said.

Stephanie smiled. "I *definitely* feel you. I love this girl." She hugged her. "How soon will you be gone then? Shoot, why couldn't y'all drag out the engagement?"

"Uh, trust me," Alonzo said, pulling Cinda close, "this was the better route."

Stephanie gave him a look. "TMI."

Cinda smiled. "Alonzo has to head back Monday, and I wanted a few days to wrap things up here, say good-byes." She sighed. "I don't want to miss the birth of Treva and Lance's baby, though." She looked at Alonzo. "We'll have to come back for that. We need to go tell them our news too."

"So you haven't talked to any of them?" Stephanie said.

"No," Cinda said. "We were pretty secluded, and came straight here from the airport."

"Treva had some complications, so she's on bed rest again," Stephanie said, "but this time they're keeping her at the hospital."

"For how long?" Cinda said.

"Until the baby's born."

"Oh, wow," Cinda said. "How's Faith doing, taking care of things at home?"

"Treva's mom and sister are here," Stephanie said, "so they're holding things down. But Faith's not in the best mood. She and Reggie broke up. I'll let her fill you in."

"Whoa," Cinda said. "I need to call her."

"Sounds like a lot's been happening the past two weeks," Alonzo said.

"Yeah, man," Lindell said. "It's been a little tense with the guys too."

Alonzo looked at him. "I don't know what's going on, but you think it's too late to get the guys together this evening?"

Alonzo knew things were bad from the time they negotiated where to gather. Lance's house was out, because Reggie didn't want to see Faith. Tommy and Reggie's place then seemed the perfect choice—until Lance revealed he had Jesse with him. Finally Cedric issued an invitation, both to his house and to the guys to squash whatever issues they had.

Alonzo glanced around Cedric's family room now. They'd all shown up on neutral territory, but nothing had yet been squashed.

Alonzo looked at Lance. "How's Treva doing?"

"Today was a good day," Lance said. "Her blood pressure is higher than normal, but lower than last week. Still no real signs of preeclampsia, so we thank God for that. She's got the swelling, and the pain comes and goes." He looked tired. "But I was happy to hear they're planning to induce next week."

"That's good news," Cedric said. "You'll be somebody's daddy soon. Can you believe it?"

"In some ways I'm still in shock from that first moment Treva said she might be pregnant," Lance said. "I can't wait till the baby's actually here and I can hold him."

"We've got some big life things happening," Lindell said. "Lance about to become a father, Alonzo eloping."

"I'm still shocked by that too," Lance said, smiling. He looked at Alonzo. "Man, you weren't messing around."

"I got some sage advice once," Alonzo said. "That if I find myself in the right relationship, I need to hold on tight and not let go."

Reggie looked over at Alonzo, but so did Jesse.

"I hadn't had a chance to tell you thanks," Alonzo said, focused on Lance still, "for helping to get her on that plane. I don't know how you knew," he said, chuckling.

"Knew what?" Cedric said.

Lance leaned forward. "I told Cinda that Alonzo loved her." He looked at Alonzo. "And you're wondering how I knew? Man, please. I probably knew before you did."

Cedric laughed. "Sometimes we're the last to see what's happening in our own hearts."

"You were for sure," Lindell said, looking at Cedric. "I knew Cyd had you when you started showing up for Bible study at her house. Had you ever even opened a Bible before that?"

"Nope," Cedric said emphatically, to laughter in the room. "She wrecked life as I knew it."

"Exactly," Alonzo said. "I can definitely say the same."

Jesse nodded. "Same here. That's a great way to put it."

"Are you for real, man?"

Heads turned at Reggie's comment.

Reggie had his focus on Jesse. "Or maybe you're referring to the fact that you wrecked life for Faith as she knew it."

Tommy leaned toward Reggie. "Don't go there, Reg."

"I know I didn't treat Faith the way I should have," Jesse said, "and I've apologized. But you're in your feelings, man. That's between me and Faith."

"When was it ever between you and Faith?" Reggie moved forward in his seat. "When your girlfriend crashed the baby dedication and got in her face—was that between you and Faith?" He paused. "Maybe when you saw that Faith had moved on from you and was seeing me, then you had to make it all about you and Faith."

"You really think it's appropriate to talk about this right now?" Jesse said.

"You're suddenly concerned with what's appropriate?"

"Listen," Lance said, "I was with Jesse when I got the call about us getting together, and I knew bringing him with me would be an issue."

Tommy shifted in his seat, clearly frustrated.

"And yeah," Lance said, "I could've drawn a dividing line and said Jesse stays on the other side. But this is why I brought him." He took his time, his posture relaxed. "Jesse is one of our newest members at Living Hope. He's been meeting with me personally for discipleship. Like every one of us in this room, he's done things he's not proud of. And like every one of us, he's repented and received mercy and grace." He looked into their faces. "So the question is, how are we going to treat him? Clearly I understand the personal issues involved. It's in my house. But, brothers, are we gonna rise above all this or not?"

"Let me say this," Tommy said. "I had no problem with Jesse, until he basically disrespected my brother. How you gonna step to a woman you know is in a relationship—with a brother in your church, no less—and try to break it up?"

"But everybody knows it's more complicated than that," Jesse said. "Faith and I have a history. We have a daughter."

"This is how I see it," Cedric said. "This whole thing is messy. And let's be real—it would've been convenient if Jesse hadn't joined our church. Right? If Jesse was sitting at home on Sunday, we'd be just fine." His eyes connected with each of them. "But God drew Jesse to *our* church. And he ain't faking if he's meeting regularly with Lance. I'm thinking all that's a praise. Amen? So convenient or not, we need to recognize this is God's doing and have a right attitude." He looked at Jesse. "I'm going to be real with you as well. This is all new for you. But being part of a body of believers means something. Bottom line, we love and respect one another. I hope you think about that, even pray about what that looks like."

"I'm new to all this myself," Alonzo said, "and this is rocking me, seeing godly brothers deal straight up with a situation." He looked across the room. "Jesse, this is my first time meeting you. But what strikes me is this . . . You knew what went down. You knew there'd be tension tonight. You could've told Lance you were going home. I'm sincerely wondering . . . Why did you come?"

It took Jesse a moment to respond. "Earlier this year I visited Zoe a couple of times and saw you guys together at Lance's. I never had a father in my life, and I only have a much younger brother. Real talk—I kind of envied what you had." He paused another moment. "Being at the church I've seen more of that." He glanced around the room. "I knew it didn't make sense to come tonight, but something in me wanted to see it up close."

The room was quiet, as no one seemed to know how to respond.

Jesse continued, looking at Reggie. "I disrespected you. I'll own that. I saw how much you meant to Faith, and I wanted that top spot in her life again." He shook his head. "So I'm wanting this brotherhood but at the same time I'm not being the brother I should be. I wouldn't blame you for not accepting it, but I apologize, man."

Reggie nodded soberly. Tommy walked over to Jesse, extending his hand. Jesse stood, taking it, and they pulled one another to a slight hug.

"This means we can move to the real fellowship and break out the cards," Tommy said. He looked at Jesse. "Tell me you know how to play Bid Whist, or Spades at least."

Jesse smiled. "Both."

"My man," Tommy said, slapping hands with him again.

As the guys got up to rearrange the room, Reggie made his way to Alonzo.

"I hadn't had a chance to personally congratulate you," Reggie said. "Super dope, eloping like that."

Alonzo smiled. "Yeah, I can't downplay it," he said, "it was pretty dope." He looked at Reggie. "Almost didn't happen, though, because Cinda was bent on protecting herself and wouldn't talk to me."

Reggie gave him a look. "Not the same. You two weren't dealing with one of you having feelings for someone else."

"You don't know where Faith is unless you talk to her," Alonzo said.

Reggie stared into the distance.

"Now is when you decide, bro." Alonzo looked at him. "Either you hold tight or you hand her over to Jesse."

CHAPTER 57

"It's starting," Cinda said. "All the *is-Alonzo-Coles-really-married* chatter." She poured him a glass of juice in the kitchen and looked back at her phone. "Jordyn just sent three links."

Alonzo gave her the eye. "Which you're not going to read, right?"

"Why not?" she said. "It's about us." She clicked the first link, and her mouth fell open. "They've got a picture of us on the beach, and some government official saying we bought a marriage license."

"Girl, please tell me they don't have you on the world wide web in a swimsuit." Stephanie pulled a breakfast casserole from the oven.

"They *do*," Cinda said. "At least the shot is far away. But this was supposed to be a private beach. *Rude*." She clicked the next one. "Someone's predicting how long it'll last. 'Alonzo Coles isn't known for long-term relationships. I'm skeptical he tied the knot. If so, I give it two years, tops.'"

Alonzo rested his chin in his hand, looking at her.

"Okay, fine," Cinda said. "I don't need to read the ones about us either." Her brow lifted. "Or I could join in. I opened that Insta-gram account and haven't used it. I should post pics of us every day."

Stephanie howled. "You'd have a million followers, and they'd be hating on you, for real. 'That's *my* man crush.'"

Alonzo sipped his juice, shaking his head at both of them.

Cinda walked into his arms. "I'm glad you're not a crush. You're just my man." She kissed him.

He put his juice down and wrapped his arms around her. "You're a little feisty this morning." He kissed her again. "I hate that I'm about to leave."

"I'm about to make both of y'all leave my kitchen," Stephanie said. "This ain't the beach on Antigua."

Alonzo chuckled. "But I still can't believe she's my *wife*." He sneaked another quick kiss. "You know what? Now that the chatter's out there, let's make it Instagram official." He scrolled through pictures on his phone. "How about this one?" he said, showing Cinda.

Cinda smiled. "Right after we were pronounced husband and wife."

"I didn't know you had pics," Stephanie said, coming to see. "Aww, gorgeous. On the beach as the sun set. And Cinda, your curls are popping. Who did your hair?"

"*I* did my hair," she said, smiling. "Washed and twisted for the plane ride to Antigua, then took it down and styled it." She took a bow.

"Get it, girl," Stephanie said.

Cinda looked over Alonzo's shoulder as he uploaded the picture with a simple caption—*My beautiful wife and me.*

~

"It's so funny being around you two." Cinda crossed her legs in one of the chairs around the hospital bed Monday night. "By the way, who's the oldest?"

"I'm two years older," Treva said, her breath somewhat labored. "And Jillian needs to stop."

"All I did was take out my Bible, notebook, and pen," Jillian said.

"While saying you've been waiting for this moment for eight years," Treva added. "Total exaggeration."

"Really?" Jillian said. "This isn't the first time I've seen you lead a study in eight years?" She looked at the women gathered. "She'd give me one reason after another as to why it wasn't her gift."

"What sense did it make for me to lead?" Treva said. "You knew way more Bible than I did."

"For the first couple years," Jillian said. "But you got to a point where you were studying more than I was and still didn't want to do it." She looked at the women. "It takes her forever to see what God has put in her, then another forever to act on it."

"I'm the same way," Cinda said. "At least, that's what Alonzo says. But I think it's because for so long my mother discouraged me, telling me all the things I couldn't do."

"That was me." Treva's mother sat on the other side of the bed. "I belittled Treva, telling her what she was fit to do and not do, based on my own whims."

Cinda listened, surprised Patsy would speak so openly about it.

"To this day," Patsy said, "I pray for God to uproot the junk I sowed into her mind."

"I should start praying that," Cinda said, jotting a note to herself.

"And when it comes to seeing what God has placed in you," Patsy said, "pay attention to the things people affirm in you, people who love you."

"In other words," Treva said, "don't do what I did. I ignored

Jillian and my husband, Hezekiah, for years when they tried to tell me what they saw in me."

Jillian nodded. "And God said all right, now I got Lance and Cyd."

Cyd smiled. "He's relentless like that. He planned good works for us before time began, and He intends for us to do them."

"It's crazy how true that is." Stephanie nodded from her spot beside Jillian. "For two or three years I thought God had forgotten about me. And He showed up when I least expected it—really when I'd about given up—and I saw how He'd been putting pieces in place all along. Being relentless."

"That's right in line with this lesson, Steph," Treva said. "Oh, announcement time—we only have one more lesson after this one, but looks like baby boy is delaying it. I'm thirty-seven weeks and they're planning to induce on Friday. Somebody say, 'Hallelujah.'"

"Hallelujah!" the women said.

"What's the problem, though?" Jillian said. "Baby boy arrives Friday, you'll go home Sunday, good to go with the study on Monday."

"Girl, bye," Treva said, chuckling.

"I'm bummed," Cinda said, "because whenever the last one is, I'll be gone."

"I'll send you my outline and notes," Treva said. "But you might have to bug me because I'm sure I'll be distracted with this little one." She rubbed her tummy.

"I'll bug Faith to send it." Cinda glanced over at her, but Faith seemed to be in a different place. "I've got all the lessons in a binder with notes."

"Ooh, you should've shared that binder idea," Stephanie said. "Don't you want to make me a duplicate"—she grinned at her —"whenever you get a spare moment from being Mrs. Coles?"

"I've got lots of spare moments," Cinda said. "You know he left today. First time we've been apart in more than two weeks."

"And let's be clear," Stephanie said. "They are well on their way to being as sickening as Treva and Lance."

Cinda blushed. "Sorry, I didn't know I'd like kissing so much."

The women fell out with laughter.

"Ladies," Patsy said, motioning for quiet, "we're in a hospital."

Jordyn's mouth was open beside her. "Girl, I know you're not saying Alonzo is your first kiss."

"Yes!" Cinda said, sure she was still blushing.

"My sister from another planet," Jordyn said. "Just. Wow."

Treva was smiling. "I love it, Cinda. And you sort of led us to this week's lesson too, which is—drum roll—If I Wait."

"Ohh, wow," Allison said.

Cinda looked at her. She was another who'd been pretty quiet thus far.

"I was looking at my journal the other day," Allison said. "I had written all these 'wait' verses two years ago as I prayed for God to send my soul mate." Her eyes filled. "And I'm struggling because I thought Tommy was the one, but it's just not what I expected."

Cinda waited for someone to respond, but everyone seemed taken aback.

"Here's one of the verses I wrote," Allison said. "Isaiah 64:4 —'For from days of old they have not heard or perceived by ear, nor has the eye seen a God besides You, who acts in behalf of the one who waits for Him.'" She looked up. "That says to me that after all the waiting, when He acts, it'll be wondrous. Because it's God. It'll be *blessed*." She looked aside with a sigh. "But Tommy and I have one conflict after another. I mean, come on, we're barely six months married. It shouldn't be like this."

"Do you think it's a matter of expectations?" Cyd said. "I was single till forty and did *a lot* of waiting. I had all kinds of ideas about what my marriage would look like, what my husband would be like, how much bliss would surround us." She made a face at that. "But I found out pretty quickly it was all a fantasy. It's a lot of work."

"I feel like my independence is being squelched," Allison said. "I'm used to traveling when I want, around the world. I shouldn't have to run all my plans by Tommy. He didn't expect that when we were dating, but now he's changing up the game. And that's just one example." She sighed. "And on top of everything, communication isn't good. He's just hard to talk to."

"Allison," Jillian said, "Stephanie and I started a weekly marriage prayer call after the conference last year, along with another woman. We've seen God do some amazing things. We'd love for you to join us." She paused. "I truly believe God will move in your situation. I don't know what's going on with Tommy, but I always thought communication was one of his strong points."

"You and Tommy were close what, more than twenty years ago?" Allison said. "And his communication in a marriage isn't going to be the same as with a friend."

"Very true," Jillian said.

"But that prayer call may be just what I need," Allison said. "This week has been particularly tough." She stared down at her Bible. "I thought I had issues with being single. I've got even more now."

"Allison, thank you for being honest about where you are," Treva said. "I said in the beginning that I wanted you all to react however the lesson hit you, so I really appreciate that." She paused, grimacing a little as she reached a hand behind herself to rub her lower back. "And you raise an important point. It's hard enough to wait for God, but what happens if we've done the waiting, but we feel God hasn't done His part? So let's look at the verse Allison read—Isaiah 64:4. What's the promise?"

Jordyn looked at her Bible. "God will act in behalf of the one who waits for Him." She looked up. "But it doesn't say how He'll act or what He'll do."

Treva smiled at her. "See, Jordyn? A few weeks ago you didn't know much about the Bible. Now you're learning to observe what it says and doesn't say."

Cinda bumped her leg to encourage her. Jordyn had felt lately as if she were at a crossroads, wanting to follow God but wrestling with so much else.

"Our minds tend to read a whole lot into that verse, right?" Treva blew out a breath. "Sorry, these pains are coming."

"Let me get the nurse," Patsy said.

"I'm okay," Treva said, blowing another breath. "It's not severe." She looked back at her notes. "We read a lot into it because we know what God is *able* to do. *And* we also read into that verse how *we* want Him to act."

"Definitely," Stephanie said. "I love to tell God what I think He should do on my behalf."

"*And yet,*" Treva said, "the promise is still amazing. When God acts, however He chooses to act, it's *huge.*" She looked at Allison. "Also, isn't the promise ongoing? You're thinking the waiting was over when you got married. But we're always waiting. As issues arise in your marriage, you'll be praying and waiting for God to act. And, Allison, I'm a witness—most of the acting God did in my first marriage was in my own heart."

Allison nodded. "I know this lesson is for me. I need to meditate on this for a good while."

"Let's look at other promises related to waiting," Treva said.

"I have a question," Faith said. "What if God wants to act, but you keep messing things up?" She glanced briefly at the faces around the bed. "Growing up I prayed for God to show me His plans for me. I had a heart for ministry and was waiting to see what He wanted me to do with my life. Then I took a wrong path and got pregnant." Her eyes held a sadness. "And I used to pray for God to send a guy who loved Him, serious about his faith. And I waited. And I knew Jesse wasn't that guy, but got involved with him anyway. *Then*"—she stemmed the tears with a finger beneath her eyelid—"He sent Reggie into my life, and I messed that up. I mess *everything* up."

Cyd leaned forward. "You said, 'What if God wants to act, but you keep messing things up?'" She looked at Faith. "That's all we are as humans—messy. God's hands aren't tied because we mess things up. He's God, and it's the mess that brings Him glory—because He transforms us in the mess." She paused as Faith got up to get a tissue. "God knew exactly what would happen in your life, Faith. He has a plan to use you and all you've been through and all you'll go through."

Cinda watched as Faith gave a bare nod—and she sent up a prayer on Faith's behalf, for her to believe just that.

CHAPTER 58

*T*hursday morning Treva gripped the sides of the hospital bed in labor and delivery, suffering the pain of contractions on top of abdominal pain that had resurfaced. A medical team surrounded her, poised to whisk her to an emergency C-section if the baby wasn't delivered in the next few minutes.

"Babe, I'm believing this baby is coming right here and now." Lance had an arm around her as she sat propped up. He'd been a tower of strength, but the concern shown in his eyes. "We're almost there. It's almost over."

Tears slid down Treva's cheeks. Everything had happened so fast. She'd awakened before dawn vomiting, head throbbing as if in a vise, blood pressure through the roof, and high levels of protein in her urine. For the first time, they'd diagnosed it— severe preeclampsia. They'd induced her immediately, since both she and the baby were at risk.

She could hardly focus with the pain and the numbness from the swelling. But when Lance squeezed her and said, "Push," she knew the doctor must've said the same.

She leaned forward with a loud grunt, pushing with all her might. *Please, Lord, please deliver this baby. Please let this be over.*

Her head fell back on the pillow, exhaustion and stress mingled with searing pain. She could see the doctors whispering, one of them walking out. Were they about to wheel her to surgery?

At this point she almost didn't care which route they took. Whatever was safest, and quickest. They'd given her a shot for the pain, which only meant the pain must be *really* bad, since she could still feel it. And then there was the fire coursing through her veins—an IV drip of magnesium to prevent seizures. She'd never encountered anything this excruciating in her life.

"Okay, baby," Lance was saying, getting her ready again. "Command her strength, Lord," he murmured. "I know You've got them in Your strong right hand." He squeezed her. "Push, babe. *Push.*"

Treva leaned forward with another long grunt, squeezing Lance's hand. *Help me, Lord. Please help me do this.*

"We can see him," the doctor said, joy in her voice. "Come on, little guy."

Treva kept pushing as members of the team closed in.

Lance's eyes lit up. "Did you hear that, babe? We're about to meet our boy. He's coming."

She pushed forward more, envisioning the baby's face, his little body in her arms—and heard a cry of victory from the team.

"Is he . . . Is he here?" Treva tried to see, but bodies blocked her way.

A second later it was confirmed by his own cry.

"Lance," she whispered, "that's the most beautiful sound in the world."

He leaned into her and kissed her, then closed his eyes. "Thank You, Lord. Thank You."

∽

"Zoe's got no love for her uncle at all." Faith chuckled as Zoe held onto her leg, protesting the newest baby in her lap. "Zoe, be nice to your Uncle Wes. You two have to have each other's back."

"Zoe, come here." Joy got up to get the little girl.

"I haven't wrapped my mind around it yet," Lance said. "I have a son who's named after me."

"That's the only name that was in my heart." Treva spoke from the hospital bed. "Lance Wesley Alexander, Jr."

"He is absolutely beautiful," Patsy said, standing over them. "Look at that little body, curled up as if he's still in the womb." She looked at Treva. "I don't think I've prayed more in my life than I have for you and this baby."

"That means so much to me," Treva said. "It's overwhelming, seeing the generations represented in this room and all the prayer power." She looked at Hezekiah's mom, Darlene, who'd flown in the night before. "And it means so much to have you here."

"Well, where else was I gonna be?" Darlene took her turn with the baby, lifting him gently from Faith and sitting in one of the chairs. "Call me crazy, but I feel like this boy is as much my grandchild as Faith, Hope, and Joy."

Lance smiled. "He better be. That makes him a blessed little man."

Darlene smiled at the baby. "And I almost missed your arrival, coming into the world early like that."

Jillian reached for Treva's hand. "I have never been more thankful and proud to call you my big sister." She had tears in her eyes. "You've been through so much. And I see such strength and grace in you." She took a breath. "I just want you to know how much I love you."

"Don't you think I've cried enough?" Treva said, holding tight to her hand. "If it weren't for you, I might not have realized I was pregnant till who knows when. And it was important to know, given the risks. God has used you in my life in more ways than I can count." She swiped her face. "And when are you going to tell Cecil to move the family to St. Louis?"

"Absolutely not," Patsy said. "You can't take *all* my grandbabies from me."

"Speaking of grandbabies," Darlene said, "the oldest baby is about to turn twenty-one."

Faith looked up with a slight smile. "Four days later, and Wes and I would have shared a birthday."

"I feel bad," Treva said. "We haven't planned anything."

"For obvious reasons," Faith said. "I'm good. It's really not that big a deal."

"It actually *is* a big deal," Hope said. "You'll be an official adult."

"Whatever that means," Faith said.

"I agree, Hope," Treva said. "It's a big deal, and I'm thankful I'll be home to celebrate."

"Say that again," Lance said, "that part about you being home. I'll be thankful for that too."

~

Treva awoke in the morning, trying to get her bearings. Her second day home with the baby, she wasn't yet used to the new routine. She'd been up twice in the night to feed and change him, and had a hard time getting back to sleep. Now she was finding it hard to breathe.

She turned and saw Lance still asleep beside her, then got up to peek at the baby in the bassinet—and her legs felt weird beneath her. Looking down, she saw that one was swollen, which was strange. When she was pregnant, the swelling had been in her hands and feet. She took conscious breaths, staring at little Wes curled up in his baby blue pajamas, sleeping peacefully.

She made her way to the bathroom, holding her head, an ache persisting still. Near the sink she felt herself wobble, and held on as things got fuzzy. *What is happening?*

350

Suddenly a pain struck and she cried out as she hit her knees. "Treva?"

She tried to get back to her feet, but the pain was coming in waves. She crumpled to the floor, trying to talk, hearing herself cry in anguish.

"Baby, what's going on?" Lance was on the floor beside her. "You're in pain again?" He lifted her head. "We have to get you back to the hospital."

"I can't . . . walk." Her body writhed in pain as she labored to breathe. "This is . . . different." She cried out again, her legs curling under her, trying to find a posture that would bring relief. "My head feels like it's about to explode," she said. "My body feels like . . . it's shutting down."

"What?" Lance dashed out of the room.

She could hear him talking to 911, explaining what was happening as he came back in.

"Babe, they'll be here in seven minutes," he said, laying the phone on the floor as he joined her once again.

"Lance, listen," she said. "I have to . . . say this."

Anguish etched his face. "I'm listening, baby."

"I love you . . ." She clutched his hand. ". . . so much. And I'm so thankful . . ." She bit her lip and bent over as another wave hit. ". . . I could give you a son, even if . . . I don't make it . . ."

"No." Tears streamed Lance's face. "I'm not listening to that, babe. The ambulance is almost here, and the doctors will take care of you. You'll be fine." He looked upward. "Lord, we need You. Please. We need You."

Her head fell back, eyes rolling to a close, and she could feel her body shaking uncontrollably.

"God, no. *No.*" Lance held on to her. "Don't You do this to me again. Don't you take my wife from me." He leaned closer. "Baby, say something. Anything. Come on, talk to me. Lord, You are *able* to bring her out of this. *Please*, bring her out." He kissed her cheek. "I love you, baby. Hold on. *Hold on.*"

CHAPTER 59

"They're saying it's postpartum preeclampsia."

Faith listened as Lance gave the report to family and friends gathered in the hospital waiting room.

"I thought the risk had passed once she had the baby," Jillian said.

"So did I," Lance said. "The doctor said it's a rare condition, but Treva's age put her at increased risk." A weary sadness covered his face. "So . . . She's had two seizures. They're doing all they can, but they're saying it's touch and go."

"Oh, God, no." Jillian's hand covered her mouth.

"What does that mean?" Hope said. "Mommy might die?"

Grandma Darlene drew her close. "This is only the doctor's report," she said. "God is still on the throne."

Faith cried silent tears as she held Zoe.

"Is she unconscious?" Stephanie said.

"She hasn't been awake since we got here," Lance said.

Patsy held baby Wes in her arms. "I thought the risk had passed as well," she said. "I was thanking God for answering so many prayers throughout this pregnancy. And here we are back at the hospital, with my daughter's life hanging in the balance."

"And we're going to *keep* praying," Cyd said. "Like Darlene said, God is still on the throne. And we know He's with Treva."

Lance nodded slightly. "I'm going back in there," he said. "Visitation is limited, but I'll let you all know when that changes."

He paused by Patsy, taking Wes into his arms. He kissed him, tears falling onto the baby's cheeks. "I'll take him with me for a while," he said.

Patsy gave him the diaper bag, and father and son walked out.

No one seemed to know what to say.

Faith couldn't stay there. She didn't want to keep hearing what happened as the next person arrived and lamented about her mom's prognosis. She just wanted to get somewhere and pray. She turned to leave—and saw Reggie near the doorway.

And melted in tears.

He walked over to her, taking her into his arms. Faith looked as someone took Zoe from her. Her Aunt Jillian.

"I'm so sorry," Reggie said. "I came as soon as I heard."

Faith had wondered if he would. He hadn't yet been by to see the baby, and she knew why.

"You want to walk?" he said.

She wiped her eyes, nodding.

They left the waiting room and headed down a long hallway, the first few feet in silence. She wondered who would be first to speak.

"I heard what Lance told everybody," Reggie said. "I won't stop praying until she's fully recovered."

"I'm trying to focus on God and have faith, but it's so hard," she said. "Losing my dad three years ago, now seeing Mom go through this . . . It's just hard."

"I know," Reggie said. "I'm praying for you too."

Silence overtook them again. Faith knew it was her turn this time. She took a breath and looked at him. "I wrote something the other day. I was debating whether to send it to you." She looked away. "I didn't know if you would read it."

"What is it?" he said.

"An article for the Living Word site. I felt like God was moving me, for the first time in a long while."

He looked at her. "Why wouldn't you send it? I've been trying to get you to write one."

She took a few seconds to reply. "It's about love."

He hesitated. "That's a big topic. As in, God's love for us? What?"

"I was praying to understand my feelings, so I did a word study," she said. "About the three kinds of love."

"Do I have to wait and read it, or can I get the Cliffs Notes?"

"Well," Faith said, focusing forward, "there's *eros*—desire, passion—based on attraction and romantic feeling. Then there's *phileo*—like a deep friendship." She glanced over at him as they walked. "And of course, *agape*, the very nature of God. Not based on feeling. Selfless. Sacrificial. Unconditional. The kind of love we're called to have toward one another." She paused. "But I'm sure you've heard all that before."

Reggie gave a nod.

"So after describing those," Faith said, "I talk about how God's best for us is *agape*, but sex outside of marriage can cause *eros* to overtake us, with all the distortion and confusion that come with it. *Eros* isn't even in the Bible."

Faith moved into an empty seating area and collected her thoughts before she continued. "I realized this was what I had with Jesse, an *eros* kind of love. Sleeping with him stirred these feelings that were distorted and confused—because it didn't spring from a God kind of love."

Reggie looked at her, waiting.

"With you . . ." She brought her eyes to him. "There's definitely *eros*—attraction and desire. But there's *phileo*—deep friendship. And there's *agape*—the love of God is all through you."

"I'm guessing you left that last part out of the article."

"These are the endnotes, from me to you," Faith said, "now that

I can tell you how sorry I am for hurting you. But the whole thing forced me to examine and understand where I am—not based on feelings but based on what's true."

"So what's true, Faith? Where are you?"

"The truth is that I have *real* love with you." She exhaled. "The truth is that I'm in love with you."

He stared into her eyes a moment, then pulled a folded piece of paper from his jacket pocket. "I was debating this week too, whether to give you this."

Her eyes filled. "But you gave me back the pen."

"I wanted you out of my heart," he said, "but your pesky self wouldn't leave."

"Well, are you giving it to me or not?"

He put it in her hand. "You can read it later, but I'll sum it up in two points." He paused, his gaze penetrating. "I love you, Faith. And I don't want to let you go."

She held his gaze as she put her arms around him, her lips to his, and kissed him. "I missed you so much," she said, tasting her tears.

His arms enclosed her. "I think I missed you more." He kissed her again. "And hey," he said, looking into her eyes, "Happy birthday."

"You remembered?"

"You know I did." He reached inside his jacket and produced a plain white envelope.

She gave him a curious look, then opened it and pulled out the contents. A book of tickets to the St. Louis Children's Zoo with a Post-it note on top—*Future dates*, it read.

"In case you're wondering if my love is real," he said.

She hugged him again, her head on his shoulder. "I love you, Reg," she said, emotion filling her voice.

"I hate what you're going through today," he said, "but I'm here. I'm not going anywhere."

"I'm scared about my mom."

"I know." He hugged her tighter. "Let's pray for her together."

CHAPTER 60

That evening Alonzo walked with Cinda into a waiting room teeming with people.

Stephanie waved a hand and headed toward them. "Hey, what are you two doing here?" she said, hugging them.

"We had to come," Alonzo said. "Soon as we got word, we booked a flight."

"What's the latest?" Cinda said. "How is Treva?"

"She's still not awake," Stephanie said. "And they're saying even if she comes out of it, she may not have full cognition." She squeezed Cinda's hand. "I know you're praying."

"How's Lance?" Alonzo said.

Stephanie moved closer to them. "Not good." Her voice was near whisper. "He's trying to be the strong pastor with all our church family here. But you can see it in his eyes," she said. "He went home a little while ago to get some things to stay overnight."

"Ohh," Cinda said, looking beyond Stephanie, "I was just going to ask about the baby."

Faith walked up holding him, Reggie at her side.

The four of them hugged, and Cinda reached for the little one.

"It's so good to meet you, little Wes," Cinda said, nestling him in her arms. "You're as adorable as I knew you'd be."

As Faith and Cinda talked, Alonzo moved closer to Reggie.

"I see you, bro," Alonzo said, glancing at Faith. "That's what's up."

"Thanks for the kick," Reggie said.

Alonzo nodded. "I'm sure you'll return the favor as needed."

"I just realized something," Reggie said. "When you come around now, you don't get all the extra attention from church folk. That's dope. You're just one of the family."

"That's how it feels for me too," Alonzo said.

"Hey, you two." Jordyn walked up, hugging them. "I got your text that you were coming." She focused on Cinda. "Can you stop by the house later? It's Momma's request."

Cinda looked at her. "Why does that sound really odd? Anyway, given the circumstances, it might be hard to get over there."

"I know," Jordyn said. "But try to make time."

Alonzo glanced over at Lance as he walked in, looking surprised by the number of people. He walked over to him and embraced him.

"It means a lot that you'd fly in," Lance said.

Alonzo looked at him. "I don't even know what to say. We've been praying since we heard. I can't imagine how you're feeling."

"It's been rough," Lance said. "Really rough. But man, I was rocked when I went home just now. Had the most amazing time of worship."

"Seriously?" Alonzo said. "What happened? If you don't mind my asking."

Lance hesitated. "You know . . . I think I'll share it with everybody." He glanced around. "Looks like only church fam in here."

He moved throughout the room, signaling with his hands. "Can I get everyone's attention?" he said, repeating it a couple of times until the chatter died down.

"First, thank you for being here and thank you for all the love and the prayers. I can't tell you how much it means." Lance stood toward the center of the room. "Let's come in a little closer, so we don't disturb other people in the hospital."

Alonzo put his arm around Cinda as everyone tightened up.

"I want to share something personal with you all," Lance said. "Many of you were around when Kendra died. You know I grieved. You saw I was sad. What you didn't know was that I was angry with God. I mean, the pastor's not supposed to be angry with God, right?" He took his time, looking into faces as he spoke. "I had prayed and prayed for the Lord to heal her—I felt He gave me faith to believe for her healing—and she was gone a year after our wedding."

The room was silent, all eyes on Lance.

"Treva is the only one I've ever shared that with. Now she's in crisis—almost a year after *our* wedding." He shook his head, seeming to grasp the parallel just now. "And I've been praying and praying—but there's this part of me that was saying, 'You can't go all in this time.' Because I knew—if I go all in and believe, and God takes my wife, it would crush me."

Alonzo nodded, feeling Lance's words.

"I went home a little while ago," Lance continued, "and saw this in our bedroom." He opened a bag and took out a notebook. "Treva's been doing a pilot study on the promises of God, and she's been working on the final lesson. It was open to this page," he said, turning, "with this title—If I Believe."

"Wow," Cinda murmured, along with others in the room.

"Treva's got notes on several verses in this lesson." Lance turned a couple of pages. "But her notes on this one got me— Mark 9:23—'All things are possible to him who believes.'"

"Glory to God," someone said.

"We're about to have church right here," another said.

Lance looked at the notes. "First Treva asks, 'What's the promise?'"

Cinda nodded, familiar with the format.

"All things are possible," came from different voices in the room.

"And we see the condition—to him who believes." Lance gave a sigh. "This is where it gets interesting, right? Because it doesn't say all things are guaranteed. God's not a genie waiting to make our every dream come true. He does according to *His* will and *His* purpose, and we won't always understand it. We serve a sovereign God."

Heads nodded with a smattering of "Amen."

"Let me read what Treva shares next," Lance said. "She says 'I have a lot of trouble believing. I've been disappointed, discouraged, grief-stricken, and heartbroken more times than I can count. As I write, I'm on bed rest in the hospital with severe pain that comes and goes, reminded daily of the high risk to my baby's health and my own.'"

Lance paused and took a moment before continuing.

"'But as I meditate on this promise, I'm also reminded that in Christ I'm a believer. That's a gift, given to me by God. Think about that. God is the One who gives us power to fulfill the condition—believing—and He's the One who fulfills the promise. It's all God! So by the grace of God, this is what I resolve— and what I want you to resolve . . .'" Lance looked up. "Should I go on?"

"Yes," rang out among them.

"Stop playing, Pastor," one woman said. "You better come on."

"I'm just checking," Lance said with a slight smile. "All right, this is what it says . . ." He read aloud from Treva's notes.

- **I will believe** that God is God, and there is no one like Him, who declares the end from the beginning, who plans and brings to pass all that He has purposed (Isaiah 46:9-11).
- **I will believe** that our God is the King of glory, the

Lord strong and mighty, the Lord mighty in battle (Psalm 24:8), and that He's the One who fights for me.

- **I will believe** that God is able to do far more abundantly beyond all I ask or think, according to the power that works within me (Ephesians 3:20).
- **I will believe** that God is for me, that nothing can separate me from the love of Christ, and that I overwhelmingly conquer through Christ who loves me (Romans 8:37).

Hands of praise lifted in the air. Some of the group moved to their knees. Lance continued to read.

- **I will believe** that God causes all things to work together for good because I love Him and I'm called according to His purpose (Romans 8:28).
- **I will believe** that trials in my life are producing endurance, and I can consider it joy, because it means I'll be perfect and complete, lacking in nothing (James 1:2-4).
- **I will believe** that the Lord is with me always (Matthew 28:20), and that if He is with me, I need not fear (Isaiah 41:10).
- **I will believe** that nothing is too difficult for God (Jeremiah 32:27).
- **I will believe—yes, I will believe** that with God, all things are possible.

Lance looked up. "She ends with this—'I need not fear how things might turn out if I believe. I can believe and know that however they turn out, it's filtered through the loving hands of God.'"

He let his eyes roam the room. "So I made a decision back at the house," he said. "I refuse to fear. *I will believe* everything that's listed here. And I'm praying with everything in me that God will fully heal my wife. *All* things are possible with God. Amen? Do we believe that, church?"

"Amen" and "Glory" rang out as tears streamed down faces and hands remained lifted.

A voice began singing softly. "Blessed assurance, Jesus is mine . . ."

Alonzo recognized the woman as a member of the praise and worship team.

Others chimed in, "O what a foretaste of glory divine . . ."

Lance had his hands raised now, letting the tears flow as he worshiped.

Everyone sang softly when they got to the chorus: "This is my story, this is my song, praising my Savior all the day long . . ."

Cinda turned toward Alonzo, her shoulders heaving as she wept in his chest. He rubbed her back, steeped in emotion himself.

The room moved to an extended time of prayer next, and when it ended Cinda turned to Alonzo. "I feel like I do have to go," she said, "to see Janice."

Alonzo walked with Cinda up the pathway to the front door. "Did you know the house had sold?" He glanced at the sign in the yard.

"Yeah, about two weeks ago." She looked toward the street. "I thought Jordyn was right behind us. It's hard enough being around Janice and Jade *with* Jordyn."

She rang the doorbell, and a moment later Jade stood before them.

"The newlyweds." Jade's tone couldn't have been flatter. "I haven't had a chance to say congrats."

"Thanks," Cinda said.

"How are you, Jade?" Alonzo said.

"I'm good." Jade led the way to the family room, which was populated with boxes. "Can I get you anything?" She focused on Alonzo.

Alonzo turned to Cinda.

"No, thanks," Cinda said. "Can you tell Janice we're here?"

Jade disappeared upstairs.

Alonzo took Cinda's hand and brought her close. "I've never seen you so tense."

"I never know what to do or say around them," she said, whispering. "They're not warm and fuzzy people, at least not with me. I gave up trying."

"But you said you felt like you needed to come."

"After hearing Treva's words," she said, "plus the songs and the prayers . . . I don't know. I felt moved." She glanced around. "But after two seconds of seeing Jade—" She looked up as footsteps descended the stairs.

"I appreciate your coming," Janice said. Jade was right behind her.

Alonzo walked toward her. "Nice to see you again, Mrs. Rogers." He shook her hand.

"Alonzo, welcome to our home—and please excuse the mess."

"No problem," he said.

"Hi, Janice," Cinda said. "Jordyn said you wanted to see me?"

"I did," she said. "Please, have a seat." She took the sofa opposite them. "I know your time is short, and it's my understanding you're here due to an emergency. So I'll get right to it. It has to do with Randall's will."

Jordyn came in as she said it, taking a seat by Jade.

"I don't understand," Cinda said. "I told the administrator I wouldn't contest the will."

"I have to admit I was surprised by that," Janice said. "You had every right under the law as his daughter."

"Why would I go after part of his estate after two months of knowing him?" Cinda shook her head. "It didn't feel right."

Janice nodded. "Well, a few days ago we started going through Randall's office in preparation for the move. We found something he'd been working on, a revised will that included you as an heir."

It took Cinda a moment to respond. "I'm not sure what to say. But why are you telling me this?"

"When I saw it, my first thought was that he'd been revising the will because of me." She glanced at her daughters. "About two weeks before he died, I'd told Randall I planned to leave. I thought he was disinheriting me."

Cinda focused on Janice, waiting for more.

"This particular draft was dated a week before he died," Janice said. "I don't know why he included me still. Maybe he planned to change it once the separation was official. But something about that . . ." She blew out a soft breath. "Then seeing that he'd added you—honestly, I wasn't surprised. Randall was meticulous with his affairs and . . . generous with his love."

"I still don't understand why you're telling me, though," Cinda said. "You said it was only a draft. You could've kept it to yourself."

"Jordyn urged me to tell you," Janice said, glancing at her daughter, "and after some thought, putting myself in your mother's shoes—"

"In my mother's shoes?"

Janice was quiet a moment. "If I knew I was dying and my girls had no one except the father they didn't know, my heart's desire would be for him to embrace them and take care of them." She looked at Cinda. "That's why your mother finally told you about Randall. I couldn't put myself in her shoes before. Too focused on her relationship with Randall. But Randall's taking you in and wanting to provide for you . . ." She nodded slightly. "It's exactly what your mother hoped for. It's what any mother would hope for. And frankly, it's what a father should do."

"So what are you saying?" Cinda said.

"I've given the revised draft to the administrator," Janice said, "and I won't stand in the way of Randall's wishes being carried out." She paused. "He was your father, Cinda. I'm saying you should allow him to provide for you."

"But I don't need his money," Cinda said. "I don't want to take anything away from Jordyn and Jade—"

"Cinda," Jordyn said, "when I saw Dad's revisions, I put myself in *your* shoes. I thought about how I would feel, knowing my father *wanted* to care for me. That would mean the world to me." Her voice faltered a little. "Let's be real, you're married to Alonzo and probably don't need the money. But it's about so much more than that. You'd be sharing in Dad's legacy, in things like the copyrights of his books. Just think—when *Bonds of Time* wins all the movie awards"—she smiled through glistening eyes—"we can stand proud together. As sisters. Holding up the legacy."

Alonzo looked at his wife, who was moved with emotion as well, and took her hand.

"I do hear what you're saying," Cinda said. "And it means a lot, hearing how you and Janice feel. But I want to hear what Jade thinks." She looked at her. "If this would cause you to hate me even more . . ."

Jade stared downward for several seconds. "As much as I loved my dad, it's always been painful to think of our biological father rejecting us. It's like a permanent wound that won't go away." She looked up. "And Dad's death was painful. And finding out my own mother was cheating on him . . ." She didn't look at Janice. "Life has basically been crap for a while." She focused on Cinda. "You were salt in the wound. I doubt we'll ever be like you and Jordyn, but on this issue—bottom line, it's what Dad wanted. And like Jordyn said, if I were in your shoes and my dad opened his arms to me like that, I'd run right into them."

Janice got up and moved out of the room, leaving them in silence. Alonzo put an arm around Cinda.

"You okay?" he whispered.

She nodded, staring downward.

Seconds later Janice returned and handed Cinda a Bible. "It was on Randall's desk. Filled with lots of notes. I think you should have it."

Cinda fingered through it, pausing to wipe a tear. "I, um . . . Thank you, Janice, but I think Jordyn and Jade should keep it." She got up and walked it to Jade. "I felt like life was crap for a long while too. This helped me see something different."

Jade eyed Cinda as she took the Bible, nodding slightly.

Cinda turned to Janice. "I don't know when I'll see you again, but . . ." She hugged her. "Thank you."

"I don't deserve any thanks." Janice stepped back, looking at her. "But you deserve an apology. I haven't been kind to you, and I hope you can forgive me. I appreciate the person you are, and the friend you've been to Jordyn."

Cinda swiped tears. "Of course I forgive you."

Her phone buzzed, and she pulled it from her pocket, then looked at Alonzo. "It's Faith. Treva woke up. We should get back to the hospital."

CHAPTER 61

DECEMBER

*T*reva moved about the kitchen, cleaning amid the normal Friday evening bustle, wearing baby Wes in a sling against her chest.

"Mom, they're here," Hope said, looking out the front window. She came into the kitchen and gave Treva a hug.

"Okay, have fun, sweetheart," Treva said. "Mrs. Murphy said they'll bring you back before church Sunday. Be polite. Make sure you clean up after yourself, and—"

"Mom, seriously." Hope headed for the door. "You've said this for like, twenty years."

"And you're only thirteen," Treva said, though she had to chuckle. She'd said the same to Joy moments ago when she left. "Love you, baby girl."

"Love you too, Mom," Hope said, the door closing behind her.

Treva continued wiping the counter—and felt a bear hug from behind.

She smiled. "That better be my husband."

Lance kissed her cheek. "What are you doing? I told you I had kitchen cleanup duty."

She turned. "I know, but you got that call," Treva said. "I know how it is when you have church matters to tend to. This is no big deal."

"I don't want you to overdo it," Lance said. "It's not even been a month, and you went through a lot. Plus you're up with Wes during the night. You need to rest as much as you can."

Wes stretched his little body this way and that, hands balled to a fist, eyes closed fast, then settled back in.

Treva stroked the hair atop his head. "I just can't with this little boy. Every movement is so precious. I'm a grandma feeling like a first-time mom."

"I could watch you two all day." Lance kissed the baby's cheek. "My miracles."

The lower level door opened, and Reggie emerged with Zoe in his arms.

He came toward them, looking tentative. "I wondered if I could talk to you two before Faith and I go out, while she's upstairs getting ready."

Lance glanced at Treva. "Sure," he said. "You want to sit down?"

They sat at the kitchen table, Zoe in Reggie's lap playing with a stuffed animal.

Reggie took a moment to begin. "So, you both know how I feel about Faith." He paused. "Or maybe you don't exactly, but . . ." He looked at Treva. "I'm in love with your daughter."

Treva smiled a little. "I did kind of know that, Reg."

"I've done a lot of praying," he said, "and I know we're both young, relatively speaking—she just turned twenty-one, I'll be twenty-four soon." He cleared his throat. "And I kept thinking maybe I should wait. Not to be sure—I'm very sure—but because somehow that would make it look right. But then I said, look right to whom? Because I felt God leading me a different way."

"And which way is that?" Lance said.

"Well," Reggie said, "I'm coming to you two as her mom and stepdad, as our pastor"—he looked at Lance—"and as two people who mean a lot to me personally . . ." He blew out a breath. "Wondering if you would give me your blessing to . . . to propose to Faith." He added quickly, "I know you might be thinking, how will he take care of her? Faith's still in school, I work for a ministry. So I don't make a lot of money, and we'd have Zoe to care for as well." He dodged the baby's fingers as she stood in his lap now, poking his face. "But I was moved by your words that Lance read to us, Treva. I do believe all things are possible, and that God will somehow provide for us. That is, if you give your blessing."

"Reggie," Treva said, "I have no reservations whatsoever. I'd be honored to have you as my son. I've prayed a long time about the man I hoped God would send to her. You exceed my prayers." She reached across and squeezed his hand, then looked over at Lance.

"You're a unique young man, Reg," Lance said. "If anyone has a heart for marriage, for self-sacrifice, for loving a wife the way the Lord calls us to, it's you. As for your ages . . ." He lifted his hands. "What can I say? You have a lot to learn? We all do, especially when it comes to marriage. But spiritually, you're more mature than a lot of married folk. Keep seeking the Lord, Reg, and following as He leads. You absolutely have my blessing."

Reggie exhaled, emotion visible in his eyes. "You don't know how much this means. Thank you, both of you."

The doorbell rang, and Lance got up to get it. Jesse walked in, and Zoe squiggled down from Reggie's lap.

"Dadadada," she said, her little legs wobbling toward him.

"Hey, little princess." Jesse bent down and scooped her up. "Ready to spend the weekend with Daddy?"

Reggie got up and gave him a handshake. "How's it going, man?" he said.

"Can't complain," Jesse said. "How about yourself?"

"Real good," Reggie said.

"I've got all her things right here," Faith said, bounding down the stairs with an overnight bag. "This is the first time you've done a whole weekend." She looked at Jesse. "You sure about this?"

"Am I sure?" Jesse lifted Zoe high, filling the house with her squeals. "Lancelot and I got this."

Faith laughed. "All right," she said. "Give Mommy a kiss, baby girl." Faith gave Zoe a squeeze and kissed her.

Zoe stretched her arms toward Reggie next, and he gave her a hug.

Treva watched as Faith put an arm around Reggie's waist, walking Zoe and Jesse to the door.

Lance leaned close to her. "Now that the young people are just about gone, I can put the next phase of my plan into action."

Treva looked at him. "What are you talking about?"

"Wes's bag is packed," he said. "I just need you to pack yours."

Lance opened the door to their suite at the Promises Bed & Breakfast, and Treva stopped short in the doorway.

"I can't believe you set this all up," she said.

"It's our anniversary weekend." He leaned above the baby in her arms and kissed her. "And you're the love of my life."

She walked into a room filled with roses and scented candles, smiling at the bassinet near the bed. She'd have to thank Stephanie, who was no doubt his helping hand.

Lance took the baby, who'd fallen asleep on the drive over, kissed his cheek, and laid him in the bassinet. He took Treva's coat next and hung it in the closet.

She took a look around. "I haven't been up here since the open house," she said. "Is there a reason you booked this particular room?"

"I asked Stephanie to break down the theme of each room," he said, "and it was hard to choose. I was leaning toward Faithful &

True because that's all I've been thinking lately, after the Lord brought you through that ordeal." He checked the room out himself. "And I loved Ever After, because as we celebrate one year it's crazy to think there's so much more in store." He turned. "But the minute I heard what was behind Love Always—I knew."

Treva looked at him. "What?"

"Picture love surrounding the promises of God," Lance said. "He makes promises to us out of His love for us. And He fulfills them for the same reason. Love. Through and through. Always."

"I see that in here," Treva said, nodding. She picked up an engraved frame and read it. "'But the greatest of these is love—1 Corinthians 13:13.'" She put it down and picked up another. "'Let all that you do be done in love—1 Corinthians 16:14.'"

She turned toward him. "You still haven't said why you chose it."

He put his arms around her. "I want to love you always." He looked deep into her eyes. "I want love to surround what I do for you, what I think about you, how I talk to you and care for you. Everywhere you turn, through and through."

Treva's heart beat out of rhythm. It always did when he held her. "I already see your love everywhere I turn. I hear it when you speak. I feel it in your touch." She kissed him. "Every day and night at the hospital. Every prayer you prayed. Every one of your tears. I was surrounded. Babe, you do love me, always."

"Not like I want to." Lance looked at her, his eyes filling. "I almost lost you. And I prayed for the chance to love you more and more." He kissed her, the passion igniting her soul.

"I need more words." Treva kissed him again as their tears intermingled on her face. "*I love you* isn't enough."

"Love is always enough, baby." His gaze met hers. "That's my prayer and my promise to you—love. Always."

CHAPTER 62

*C*inda worked a scrub brush along the stone-tiled wall of the master bathroom, her stomach in knots. When would they get to it?

Her eyes flitted over to her phone by the sink, as if that would speed things up. She'd tuned into the livestream of the Golden Globes nominations, and so far it seemed they'd announced every category but the one she'd gotten out of bed to hear.

"Best Performance by an Actor in a Motion Picture—"

Her stomach lurched.

". . . Musical or Comedy."

She sighed, dipping the brush into the sudsy water and putting it to the wall. Christmas. That's what she'd focus on. A little less than two weeks away. She and Alonzo would celebrate together, while his mom headed back to Chicago to spend the holidays with her mom. They'd done most of the decorating already, including the tree, but Cinda had more to do yet. And she wanted to try her hand at baking some of Alonzo's favorites—his mom said she'd teach her. And while they were at it, Cinda hoped they could do a test run of an entire Christmas dinner. She'd never been one to cook a lot—

"Best Performance by an Actor in a Motion Picture—Drama . . ."

She dropped the brush in the bucket and moved to her phone, watching as one actor after another was announced. Her eyes closed for the fifth.

" . . . and Alonzo Coles, *Bonds of Time*."

"Zee!" Cinda ran into the bedroom, glanced at the clock—5:41 a.m.—and dropped down beside him, shaking him awake. "You got it! You got the nomination."

Alonzo came up on an elbow, staring vaguely.

"Did you hear me?" Cinda leaned down and kissed him. "Congratulations. You're a Best Actor nominee."

"I didn't think it would happen," he said.

"And I would've been shocked if it didn't," Cinda said. "You know I've been praying. Next up—Screen Actors Guild. And ultimately, an Oscar nomination."

He sat up. "I don't know about all that, but this one nomination is a lot when I think about Randall. I wish he were here to experience this."

"I know," Cinda said. "I can only imagine—" She heard her phone ringing in the bathroom. "I bet it's Faith." She went to get it. "Were you watching? Can you believe it?"

Faith was squealing. "Five nominations for *Bonds of Time*!"

"Wait, what?" Cinda said. "I got so excited about Alonzo's I didn't hear the rest." She moved back into the bedroom. "The movie got five nominations total."

"What?" Alonzo got out of bed. "What else?"

Cinda repeated as Faith laid it out—"Best Screenplay, Best Original Score, Best Director, and Best Motion Picture—Drama."

"Is that amazing or what?" Faith said. "All right, gotta get back to studying for this final. Tell Alonzo congrats!"

Cinda hung up, the news hitting her. "Wow, Daddy," she whispered. Tears filled her eyes.

Alonzo took her into his arms. "It's overwhelming. It really is."

His phone was ringing now.

"You'd better get that," Cinda said. "Probably Bev and your publicist trying to reach you at the same time."

"I'll call back." He looked into her eyes. *"Bonds of Time* is part of your legacy now. I can't wait to see you represent Randall proudly." He kissed her.

"And I can't wait to represent as your wife, Mr. Best Actor Nominee." She kissed him again.

"And as my stylist."

"After awards season."

He took a step back. "Did you really just say that? After finally admitting that God wanted you to step out and do this?"

"But I already knew we'd need to wait," Cinda said. "And the nomination makes it official. Awards season is *the* season for stylists. And if things happen as I'm believing they will, you'll need a special look for at least fifteen different events. You need someone with experience, like Bianca."

"I guess it's too bad, then, since I've already thanked Bianca for her work on my behalf and told her my wife would be assuming the position."

"But she'd be happy to come back on board for this."

He got a crystal picture frame from atop the lingerie chest. "Who had this hand-lettered and framed?" He leaned in when she didn't answer.

"I might've."

"Because?"

She sighed. "I was moved by Treva's resolutions."

"And you specifically said, 'We should keep them before us, for those times we're tempted to doubt and *not* believe." He pointed at one of them. "Do you believe all things are possible with God—or don't you?"

His phone started ringing again.

"You'd better get that," she said.

His finger was skimming the list. "Maybe *some* things are too difficult for Him. 'Because Lord, I know You can do this on an *ordinary* day, but when expectations and pressure are high, I'm not sure You can handle that.'"

Cinda narrowed her eyes at him. "Is this where I remind you —'Don't wake me up to watch, Cin'—because you didn't think a nomination was possible? And I know you're already thinking you won't win."

His downward glance was concession enough.

"The thing is," he said, "we should've both learned a lesson, because there was a time you didn't think *us* was possible." He tossed the frame to the bed and brought her close. "Yet here I am holding you, Mrs. Coles." His lips grazed hers. "And kissing you."

The kiss lingered—through text notifications and another call —and left Cinda as breathless as the first time.

She sighed into his chest. "I'm tired of doubt being my default setting. What if I actually believed what that one resolution says— that whatever God has planned and purposed for my life, He'll bring it to pass?"

He tipped her chin up. "You're my warrior princess. Time to go to war on doubt—and believe."

Just the thought brought butterflies. She looked into his eyes. "What if we pray and jump in together?"

"Let's do it." He sealed it with a kiss. "I can't wait to see where God takes us."

READING GROUP GUIDE

1. Cinda wasn't one to get her hopes up. By default she was given to pessimism. At one point, when she said she was simply a "realist," Alonzo challenged her, saying, "What about faith and trust? What if God wants to bless you in unexpected ways? And what if you miss it because you're being such a 'realist'?" Do you struggle with being pessimistic? Is it hard for you to believe that God wants to bless you in unexpected ways?

2. Treva had been enjoying her life as-is and had to admit to God that she didn't want Him to be in control of her season. Can you think of a time when you were enjoying life and resented the changes God brought about? How did you handle that? Did you "come" to Him?

3. Faith knew that God had forgiven her for going astray, but she felt she'd somehow forfeited the plans He'd had for her and that she was now on God's "Plan B" track. Have you ever felt that way? Do you believe that in Christ, God's good and perfect gifts extend to you, no matter what's in the past?

4. Alonzo had attained the very thing he'd prayed for—growing success in Hollywood—yet felt empty because he'd taken his eyes off of Jesus. Think of a time when the things of this world drew you away from Jesus. How did you feel?

5. Jordyn was surprised to hear that there were Christians who actually endeavored to honor God by waiting until marriage to have sex. In your circle of friends, are there singles who have a heart to wait? If you're single, what's your heart posture when it comes to sex and waiting?

6. Jillian said this about Treva: "It takes her forever to see what God has put in her, then another forever to act upon it." Is it hard for you too see what God has put in you? When people affirm what He's put in you, do you receive it? When God moves you to take a step of faith, how hard (or easy) is it for you to believe and move?

7. In the book, these lessons from the Bible study were touched upon—If I Come, If I Call, If I Trust, If I Dwell, If I Wait, and If I Believe. Which one(s) resonated with you most? Why?

8. Take a look once more at the **I will believe** resolutions that Treva laid out. Do you believe these truths from Scripture? Where in your life can you actively apply these truths right now?

ABOUT THE AUTHOR

KIM CASH TATE is the author of several books, including *Cling* (2017) and *Though I Stumble* (2016). A former practicing attorney, she is also a Bible teacher. She's been married to her husband Bill for more than two decades, and they live in St. Louis with their two young adult children.

Connect with Kim:

YouTube.com/kimcashtate
Instagram.com/kimcashtate
Facebook.com/kimcashtate
Twitter.com/kimcashtate

www.kimcashtate.com

25976656R00227

Printed in Great Britain
by Amazon